THE REALMS
OF GOD

TOR BOOKS BY MICHAEL LIVINGSTON

The Shards of Heaven
The Gates of Hell
The Realms of God

THE
REALMS
OF
GOD

MICHAEL LIVINGSTON

A TOM DOHERTY ASSOCIATES BOOK **TOR** NEW YORK

THE REALMS OF GOD

Copyright © 2017 by Michael Livingston

Map p. 14 by Rhys Davies

A Tor Book
Published by Tom Doherty Associates
175 Fifth Avenue
New York, NY 10010

www.tor-forge.com

Tor® is a registered trademark of Macmillan Publishing Group, LLC.

The Library of Congress Cataloging-in-Publication Data is available upon request.

ISBN 978-0-7653-8035-7 (hardcover)
ISBN 978-1-4668-7333-9 (ebook)

Our books may be purchased in bulk for promotional, educational, or business use. Please contact your local bookseller or the Macmillan Corporate and Premium Sales Department at 1-800-221-7945, extension 5442, or by email at MacmillanSpecialMarkets@macmillan.com.

First Edition: November 2017

Printed in the United States of America

0 9 8 7 6 5 4 3 2 1

For Samuel and Elanor,
who are every reason

Acknowledgments

There are the usual suspects to thank: Kayla and the kids, my parents, and of course Catherine Bollinger, who is an extraordinary beta reader and a fine gardener. My family and my friends were always there when I needed them—thanks, Kelly!—and I'm enormously pleased to work with some truly talented people at Tor. I owe you all so much.

I need to give thanks, too, to the men and women around the world who have done so much not only to preserve the remains of the past but also to understand them. Ancient sites like Petra and the Temple Mount in Jerusalem, ancient writings like those of Celsus or Josephus—all of the many disparate parts of our human cultural heritage from which I have cast this story—are available only because people give their time, money, and energy to keep them so.

Last, to all the readers and reviewers who loved *The Shards of Heaven* and *The Gates of Hell,* your positive encouragement and enthusiasm has been fundamental to making this third volume happen. My thanks to all of you.

Contents

PART III: THE GATE OF HEAVEN

PREFACE

The Shards of Heaven series, of which this is the third volume, is a historical fantasy. As such, its story is intended to fit within the bounds of known history wherever possible. What happens within these pages is inspired by real events happening in real places to real people. In Jerusalem, the tiled floors in a hidden chamber below the Temple are real. In Petra, the High Place of Sacrifice, the carvings in the Small Siq, and even the obelisks are real, as is the special tomb that is today known as the Tomb of the Roman Soldier. The revolt of Herod's slave Simon was real. Abdes Pantera was a real Roman archer. And Miriam . . . well, let history judge.

The reader wishing a basic understanding of the facts of history as they pertain to the characters herein should consult the glossary at the end of this book.

Town of Sabra

Road to Sabra

Tombs

Temple of al-Uzza

Second
Stair

Two Obelisks

Tomb of the Ark

High Place
of Sacrifice

Mount
of Moses

Tombs

Stairway

Tomb of Aretas IV

Tombs

Theater

Tombs

Siq

The City of
PETRA

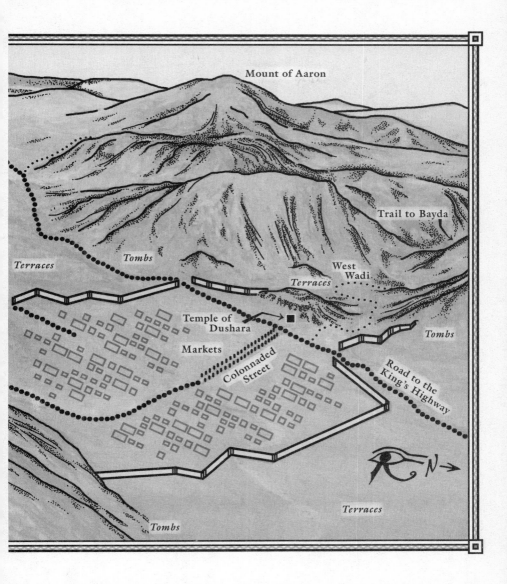

Mount of Aaron

Trail to Bayda

Terraces

Tombs

West
Wadi

Terraces

Temple of
Dushara

Markets

Tombs

Colonnaded
Street

Road to the
King's Highway

N

Terraces

Tombs

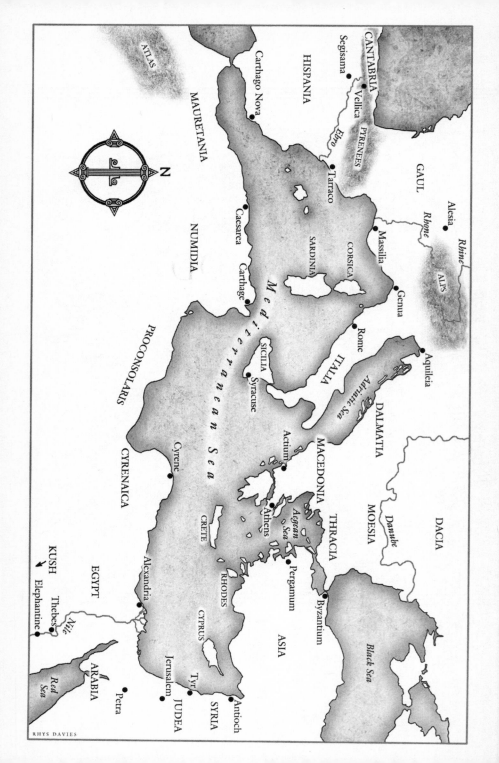

ATLAS

CANTABRIA

Segisama

HISPANIA

Carthago Nova

Vellica

PYRENEES

Ebro

GAUL

Alesia

Rhone

Rhine

Tarraco

ALPS

MAURETANIA

Caesarea

SARDINIA

CORSICA

Massilia

Genua

NUMIDIA

Carthage

M e d i t e r r a n e a n   S e a

SICILIA

Rome

ITALIA

Syracuse

Actium

Adriatic Sea

Aquileia

DALMATIA

MACEDONIA

MOESIA

PROCONSOLARIS

Cyrene

CYRENAICA

CRETE

Athens

Aegean Sea

THRACIA

Danube

DACIA

Pergamum

Byzantium

Black Sea

KUSH

Elephantine

Thebes

Nile

EGYPT

Alexandria

RHODES

CYPRUS

ASIA

Red Sea

ARABIA

Petra

Jerusalem

Tyr

JUDEA

SYRIA

Antioch

Z

RHYS DAVIES

THE REALMS
OF GOD

Men create gods after their own image—not only with regard to their form, but with regard to their mode of life.

—Aristotle

PROLOGUE

The Colossus of Rhodes

RHODES, 5 BCE

Thrasyllus leaned against the broken foot of a bronze giant and stared out at the harbor of Rhodes. The harsh calls of seabirds swirled around him, and the sky was wide and a darkening blue as the sun drifted toward the west. Beneath it the water was full of sails—fishermen, traders, mercenaries, and more—all moving, all bending this way or that upon the salt-thick breeze of the sea. Closer, along the water's edge near the gates of the city, a boy in rags was begging the dockworkers for something to eat. They appeared to be laughing at him.

Though Thrasyllus was looking away, he felt Lapis move her head to look up at him from where she was sitting on the steps near his feet. "My love?"

They had arrived more than an hour ago, carried by the tall masts of a transport ship that they'd boarded in Athens. Before that it had been a long voyage from Mauretania—across nearly the full length of the Mediterranean Sea—and Thrasyllus was more tired than he remembered being in many years. He was certain she felt the same, though she didn't question him when he suggested they climb up here to stand beside the ruins of the ancient statue. She never questioned him, not since he'd saved her life in Alexandria all those years ago, not since they'd fallen in love: the once-prostitute and her former client. A match, he thought, that ought to have been written in the stars.

It wasn't, though. He'd read them every morning and night while he'd tended her back to health—and afterward, too, when they learned day by day and month by month how to live past their past. Never had the signs spoken of it.

He was forty years old now. Old enough to know that love, as it happened, didn't work like that.

Why he'd suggested that they wander up onto this hillside, to the wide stone platform upon which the shattered fragments of the Colossus remained, Thrasyllus wasn't really certain. But he *did* know why his wife had followed him, why she sat quietly upon the steps below him while he stood lost in thought. Lapis loved him. And though Thrasyllus had seen many wonders in this world across his four decades, he'd found that the power of her love was far more wonderful than anything he'd ever known.

Indeed, her love made the ruins of the bronze monument that dwarfed them both seem somehow smaller and less significant, no matter how mighty it had once been. The Colossus had once towered over this city, after all, and Thrasyllus could only imagine what a magnificent sight it must have been. What had its metal eyes seen before it collapsed, he wondered? What great men had looked up at its height, at the seabirds that turned in circles around it like a squawking wreath? What riches had passed before the glinting light of its brows? What navies had it watched draw forth to war?

He himself had never been to Rhodes, so all he'd known of the bronze giant had been from spare descriptions in books or awed accounts on travelers' tongues. Many of them spoke of how the Colossus had once stood over the harbor, and somehow Thrasyllus had gleaned from such descriptions that it had stood astride the waters, one foot upon either shore of the harbor's open mouth. The truth, he could now see, was that while it had looked over the busy harbor it had done so from the hillside above the old city. His mistaken assumptions made him ponder what false impressions other people had of Alexandria, where he'd lived so long before: how did they describe the Great Lighthouse that watched over *its* harbor, or the great tomb of Alexander the Great in the city center? And how did they speak of the Great Library, where he'd grown up in the tutelage of some of the finest scholars in the world?

He'd not been to Alexandria in twenty years, not since he'd fled the city with the beautiful girl, Lapis, who'd become his wife. Thinking of it now, he wished that he could return there. No matter the perils that they'd faced in Alexandria, anything would be better than going to meet Tiberius.

"My love?" Lapis repeated.

Thrasyllus turned to look down at her, felt his heart thrill at the sight of her. The planets didn't align to speak of it, he thought with a smile, but such feelings were without doubt. "We need to go, don't we?"

Her green eyes warmed with a kind of regret. "I think so," she said. "The day is late. You probably shouldn't keep him waiting."

Thrasyllus nodded in agreement, but still he looked back to the sky and the birds.

The summons of the son of Caesar could hardly be denied, but that didn't mean that he was anxious to answer it. There had been too many stories about Tiberius of late. The adopted son of Augustus had long had a reputation for being a sullen and emotional man, but it was said he'd grown even darker in spirit since politics had forced him to divorce Vipsania five years earlier and marry Julia, the only blood child of Augustus. The new marriage had cemented the position of Tiberius as Caesar's presumed heir, but it had brought him little joy. Julia was widely reported to take lovers upon the most passing whim, and the delicate dance of Roman politics clearly didn't fit well with his sensibilities. Only months ago, Tiberius had abruptly retired from Rome, going into what many were calling a self-imposed exile in his secluded villa on Rhodes.

There were quiet whispers, though, that the decision of Tiberius was something more than mere disgust at his wife's promiscuity or his annoyance at Rome's intrigues. He was seeking something, it was said. Information. And he was questioning astrologers in order to find it. What it was he sought, no one seemed to know, but the astrologers were being summoned to Tiberius' villa outside this city—and many were not returning.

Thrasyllus watched a bird pause, fold its wings, and dive like a falling spear into the waters of the harbor. He sighed.

"You're right," he finally whispered. "We should start up."

He held out his hand and helped her to her feet. Tiberius' villa was not far.

Gathering up their things, they once more beheld the happy harbor. Then hand in hand, with wandering steps and slow, through Rhodes they took their solitary way.

•   •   •

A slave met them on the steps of the portico outside the villa of Tiberius. He was a short man with wide shoulders and a flat, brooding face who only grunted when Thrasyllus announced his name and his summons. Then the slave turned and led them, with no formality and hardly a look back, into the expansive home.

The villa was hardly as opulent as some of those he'd heard of in Rome—it certainly paled in comparison to the royal palaces in Alexandria that he'd occasionally had opportunity to visit alongside Didymus, the head of the Great Library and personal tutor to the children of Cleopatra in those faraway days. But from the marble tiles and mosaics on its floors to the stern statuary and delicately tended plants that dotted its clean halls the villa nevertheless spoke of its owner's vast reserves of wealth. It was, Thrasyllus observed, very different from the world he and Lapis had joined in Mauretania. There, even in their royal halls, King Juba and Queen Selene had worked hard to keep such extravagance to a minimum. The money, Juba was fond of saying, was better spent on those things that helped the city at large: aqueducts, drainage systems, and better roads for the travel of merchants.

What Thrasyllus felt here was quite the opposite. It was the need to impress and overwhelm. It was disgusting in its way, but it was also the reason Lapis had so vigorously insisted that she come along. She'd never seen anything like this world, and he would do and give anything to see her happy. That's what love was.

Taking a turn, the slave led them out into a large open atrium. The garden there was carefully manicured around a fountain at its center. The waters burbled as they passed by, the slave winding them back toward the rear of the building.

There were some of the usual sounds of a household at work around them. Pots being cleaned in the kitchen. The feet of servants shuffling from one room to the next. Livestock being brought to the barn. And, growing louder the farther they walked toward the back of the villa, the sound of threshing.

No, Thrasyllus decided. Not threshing. It wasn't the sound of feet stomping on grain, separating the fruit from the chaff. The blows were heavier, harder, a sound he couldn't place but which sent a foreboding tremor over his skin.

He looked over to Lapis, but she was gazing in smiling wonder at the statue of a Roman god that stood amid the plants. Thrasyllus looked, too, and he saw that it was Mercury, the wing-footed messenger who flew between the realms of gods and men. In his hand was his caduceus, the staff of his author-ity, entwined by two coiling serpents.

Thrasyllus felt his heart skip a beat. He'd seen a staff much like it, twenty years earlier, in the ancient temple of Carthage. That had been the Trident of Poseidon, one of the Shards of Heaven. It controlled water. Juba had used it with the other Shards in his possession, and with their power he'd opened a gate to some deep hell and brought demons into the world.

Thrasyllus fought down the surge of memory. Even now not a week could pass without him waking in cold sweat at the thought of that night. Juba had lost the Trident to the demons, along with another Shard that controlled fire. They'd escaped only with the Shards of Air and Life: the Palladium of Troy and the Aegis of Zeus. They'd escaped and locked them away, never to be seen and never to be used again.

And here the memory returned in the hands of Mercury, herald of the gods, the one who passed between worlds.

It was a sign, and Thrasyllus had only just begun to contem-plate it when the slave they were following led them through an arched passageway flanked by guards, then out of the atrium and into an open portico where Tiberius, the adopted son of Augustus Caesar, was lounging on a bench overlooking the darkening sea, watching the beating of a naked man.

The man being beaten had liver-spotted skin and white hair, and he was clearly older than Tiberius, who himself had only a few lines of gray running like silver threads through his still thick hair. The old man was naked, his leathery limbs out-stretched like those of a starfish, affixed by ropes to the pillars at the portico's edge. A thick leather gag had been wrapped around his mouth to mute his cries, and another slave was pa-tiently striking his back with an even thicker leather strap. The old man was facing Tiberius, his eyes wide in muted and ex-hausted horror, the bruises and welts hatched across his chest

marking the procession of his suffering. Another man was sitting at the other end of Tiberius' bench, and he let out a chuckle
as the next blow came down.

Thrasyllus froze and felt Lapis do the same beside him. The
slave that had led them through the villa walked on to where
Tiberius was outstretched upon cushions. As the man who
might be Caesar lifted a red apple to his mouth and took a bite,
the slave leaned over and whispered something in his ear.

Tiberius nodded and chewed. The slave stood aside and
looked up to beckon them forward.

Thrasyllus exchanged a nervous glance with Lapis. The look
of wonder in her eyes had been replaced with outright fear. He
smiled as best he could, as if he could reassure her despite his
own fright, and he unobtrusively signaled for her to stay where
she was. Though she appeared to be petrified, she managed to
nod.

"Lord Tiberius," Thrasyllus said, taking three steps forward
before bowing low. "I was grateful for your summons but can
see I've come at an inopportune time. Perhaps if I returned—"

"No, stay," Tiberius said over his shoulder. He took another
bite of his apple and chewed as a fresh blow thudded into the
man straining before him. Caesar's son swallowed, rubbed his
wrist across his mouth. "You're a hard man to find, Thrasyllus
of Mendes."

"I did not intend to be so."

"I think you did. By all rights you ought to have been in
Alexandria, working at the Great Library. But you've not been
there in quite some time, it seems."

"Yes, my lord. I am in the employ of the king and queen of
Mauretania."

Thrasyllus saw that the shoulders of Tiberius shook a little
at the word, but whatever it was that shocked or angered him,
he was quickly in control of himself again. "A shame," he said,

"to have someone of your skills hiding away in that dusty corner of the empire."

"My lord, I—"

"Since . . . what has it been? Twenty years since Carthage?"

Thrasyllus was sure that he could feel Lapis tensing behind him—she'd known his nightmares, known his terrors—and a bead of cold formed along his own brow despite the warm air. He opened his mouth, knowing that he needed to reply, yet certain he had no words to say.

"But you're here now," Tiberius continued. "And I've been looking forward to this meeting. Very much."

Another blow came down, and Thrasyllus felt his stomach lurch at the look of pain on the older man's face. "Surely I should come back—"

"I said to stay, astrologer. And stay you shall." Thrasyllus heard movement behind him, realized that some of the villa's guards were moving closer to be sure that the will of their master was carried out. "Besides," Tiberius continued, "this concerns you, too."

Tiberius waved his hand and the beating stopped. In the silence, Thrasyllus heard Lapis sob. He wanted to rush to her, to seize her in his arms and somehow run away with her, shielding her from whatever horror he'd walked into, but he didn't dare move. He didn't dare imagine what would happen to them if they tried to run.

"I don't know this man." Thrasyllus heard his own voice tremble and crack even as he tried to feign confidence.

"No, I suspect you do not." Tiberius threw his half-eaten apple out into a bush. Then the son of Caesar stood and half turned so that he could look between the astrologer and the bound and beaten man. "Thrasyllus of Mendes, court astrologer to King Juba and Queen Selene of Mauretania, may I introduce Syllaeus of Petra, the chief advisor to the late king of the Nabataeans. I say 'late' because Syllaeus here poisoned him, did you not?"

The bound old man shook his head in anguished denial, the gag preventing him from speaking.

The other man with Tiberius, still sitting, leaned into the bench so that he could look over it at Thrasyllus. He had a thick beard of dark hair sprinkled with gray and the look of a man from the east. "He always says this," the man said, smiling.

Tiberius shrugged. "So he does," he agreed. "Thrasyllus of Mendes, this is Antipater, the son and sole heir to the throne of Herod the Great. He's taking Syllaeus here to Rome."

Though the astrologer's mind was a blur of questions and facts—Herod was king of the Jews, he knew—he was still coherent enough to bow. "My lord," he said.

"An astrologer," Antipater said to Tiberius. "I rarely find them of use."

"Not a believer?" Tiberius asked.

"I believe in getting what I deserve," Antipater said, his eyes glinting.

"And you will, my greedy friend. Everyone will get what they deserve."

Behind them, Syllaeus bucked at his ropes. Antipater chuckled again, and he and Tiberius turned toward the bound man.

"Well, almost everyone," Tiberius continued. "I think you *are* innocent of the charges, Syllaeus. The old man probably died of his age. Or, even more likely, he was poisoned by his newly raised highness, King Aretas."

"The poisoning of kings seems to be going around these days," Antipater added, clearly amused.

The son of Caesar nodded. "And I imagine Aretas is framing you for the deed just to rid himself of competition from such an astute and loyal member of his predecessor's court." Tiberius suddenly turned to Thrasyllus as if he'd spoken. "Oh, yes. He was a good man for Petra, our friend here. A loyal Nabataean. You know, it was Syllaeus who guided our legions out of Egypt and out into the deserts of Arabia. My father paid him well on the assurance that he would show us the paths to the land of spices, would allow us to bypass the taxes of Petra . . . but he was a loyal Nabataean in the end. Led the legionnaires to their deaths. And somehow got out alive himself. With his coin, too! And even made it back to Nabataea, back to Petra, a hero and a humble servant. Quite extraordinary, I think." He turned back to the bound man, then walked over to tap him gently on the cheek, as if the old man were a child. "It's important to me that you know that what's happening now has nothing to do with that, though. Because in an odd sense I'm proud of you. That bit of deceit might have been against Rome, but it was cleverly done. Truly. But in vengeance I'm certain they'll throw you from the Tarpeian Rock just the same. Guilty or not, this poisoning is just an excuse to see if you can fly."

Thrasyllus cleared his suddenly parched throat. "Lord Tiberius, I have no knowledge of any of this. If this man has said differently—"

"Nothing of the kind," Tiberius said, once more cutting him off. He was smiling, almost kindly, as he turned back to the astrologer, yet there was a brooding darkness in his eyes. "Though he did hold a certain bit of information that concerns you. Information about something I've been seeking."

Something he was seeking? Thrasyllus concentrated on not shaking as the rumors of astrologers gone missing after meeting with Tiberius swirled in his mind. "I would be pleased to help, my lord, if I knew how."

"I'm pleased to hear it, Thrasyllus of Mendes. I am certain my friends feel the same."

Footsteps hushed on the stone behind him, and Lapis cried out for a moment before the sound was clamped off. Thrasyllus turned and saw that the guards at the passageway hadn't moved, but three other figures in plain white togas had silently floated up upon them. One of them—the female—was holding Lapis from behind. A long-fingered hand, as pale and bloodless as if it had been carved of the purest alabaster, was clamped over her mouth. In the instant that Thrasyllus met the panicked gaze of his wife, before he could shout through his terror, her eyes rolled back white. Lapis fell limp into slender arms that started lowering her to the ground.

The two male figures swept onward, moving toward Thrasyllus with smooth and soundless steps.

At a glance Thrasyllus knew them, though he'd seen them only for mere minutes all those years earlier in Carthage. For twenty years, in the terrors that awoke him drenched in sweat, he'd seen their unnaturally perfect bodies. He'd seen their hauntingly beautiful faces. He'd seen their dead, black eyes.

Demons. The very three that the Shards had possessed Juba to raise up from the depths of the underworld.

Thrasyllus fell to his knees and in quaking fear retched the pit of his stomach onto the stone floor.

The two male demons gracefully slid around the mess. In their wake, the inhuman creatures left the air chilled, like a moving frost. They floated on to stand behind Antipater, who turned to see them. "And speaking of poisons," the heir of Herod said to one of them, "Antiphilus, my old friend, were you able to procure what we need? I was told it's best to get it here rather than in Rome."

"Yes, my lord," the demon replied. His voice was a song. The astrologer remembered that, too. "Bathyllus will carry it," he went on to say, nodding toward the other demon beside him.

"And the letters?" Antipater asked.

"Acme will write them in Rome," Antiphilus said.

A wash of cold came across Thrasyllus once again, and then

the third demon was floating past him to stand beside the son of Caesar. When she stopped moving the edge of her draped dress swung for a moment before it abruptly fell into place as if weighed down by an unseen hand. "I will make them at your mother's house," she said to Tiberius. "Empress Livia has the finest parchments. Everything I need for the task."

"Good," Antipater said, looking back to Syllaeus.

Tiberius, too, was nodding, though his eyes were even darker now.

Thrasyllus could hear his wife's steady breathing, and he wanted to get up and run to her, to protect her, but to his shame he couldn't move. He could only stare as the three demons turned as one to look back at him with unblinking obsidian eyes. The one they'd called Bathyllus smiled, and his sculpted teeth were the color of bleached bones.

How they were here, how they'd found him, Thrasyllus didn't know. What it had to do with Antipater and poisons and letters, he couldn't possibly imagine.

But he knew what they wanted. It was the only thing he could possibly give them.

The Shards.

The demons wanted the Shards.

PART I

THE STONES OF MEMORY

1

The Rose-Red City

PETRA, 5 BCE

Squinting his eyes to watch the approaching Romans, Lucius Vorenus wearily settled himself down onto a rose-red rock outcropping. Behind him, its afternoon shadow leaving him in cool shade as it stretched out toward the acropolis of Petra, arose one of the rocky mountains that hemmed in and protected the ancient city of stone. In his first year here he'd climbed those greater heights, but he'd thankfully found that this lower vantage point, while still a scramble to reach along its cliff-framed ledge, was far easier to achieve. And the position was more than adequate: it was sheltered from the sun by the surrounding rocks, with clear views of both the main road north and the more secret path through the narrow chasm to the east. The perch had in time become as familiar to him as the aches and pains of a long life hard lived: he couldn't count how many times he'd labored up here in the twenty years since he and his old friend Titus Pullo had come to Petra to hide themselves, the little orphaned girl they'd raised as their own, and the Ark of the Covenant.

The mercantile caravan he was watching seemed to be crawling down the northern hillsides into the valley, its approach slowed by the winding of the road through the terraced farms and vineyards that seemed so out of place amid these arid mountains. The greenery was nothing compared to the gardens and fountains within the city's walls, of course, but Vorenus well remembered his shock when he himself had first seen Petra and found it an oasis in bloom.

No natural oasis, though. Petra, more than any place he'd ever seen, was a testament to human ingenuity. The rock walls that hemmed it in and protected it were cut through with channels that pulled the rains when they came off the rocks and down through larger and larger conduits into the hundreds of cisterns that dotted the growing city. The rainy season was short, but the Nabataeans of Petra made it last year round. It fed their crops, filled their cups, and made a city in the desert.

The Romans were also being slowed by the rudimentary nature of the Nabataean road, and Vorenus allowed himself a smile. The Roman merchants, he was certain, would be cursing the lack of a properly wrought surface for the wheels of their carts and wagons. That was the Roman way, of course: build the road to reach the destination. He'd done it himself, back in the days when he was a legionnaire. Back when he thought of himself as Roman, too.

Vorenus spat on the ground between his desert boots and watched for a moment as the moisture quickly sank into the parched dust that had gathered on the flat surface between stones. Though beneath his flowing linen robes he still kept his old gladius strapped to his side, there was little about him that felt Roman anymore. The men in the coming caravan weren't countrymen to him. They didn't speak with voices of home. They were foreigners. And like every other group of foreigners who approached the walls of this secretive city, Vorenus viewed them as a threat.

Squinting into the distance again, he tried to count wagons, gauge armaments, and guess at the number of the guards as they crept closer.

In his earlier years at Petra, Vorenus had worried at the threat such men could be to him personally—he did, after all, still have a price on his head, courtesy of Augustus Caesar himself—but as his stay in Petra lengthened to decades he had come to worry only for the threat that foreigners might represent to the Ark, the powerful Shard of Heaven that he and Pullo—and now young Miriam—had sworn to protect.

His own life, Vorenus figured, was long since lived on borrowed time.

Growing up in Rome, he had never expected to live to see much of his adulthood at all. He was born to be a fighter. His life would be the sword and the blood and the golden eagle standard of the legion beneath which he would surely die.

But he had survived. Fighting the barbaric Nervii in Gaul under the direction of Julius Caesar, he had lived when so many died. At Actium, under Mark Antony, death had somehow missed him—though down the mauled skin of his right arm Vorenus still carried heavy scars of that fight. In Alexandria, when Augustus Caesar had ordered his execution, he'd lived. So, too, had he survived ambush on the Alexandrian canal and the Kushite attack on the island of Elephantine.

Now, at the age of seventy-three, Vorenus knew that no matter what luck had bought him to this point, death would not forget him forever. No man was immortal, and there was no doubt for Vorenus that he had fewer days ahead than he had behind him. He'd had a good life.

So these latest approaching Romans were only a worry insofar as they were a threat to the Shard.

Vorenus turned to his right, looking across the southern reach of Petra to a narrow canyon that slashed southwest into the mountains, just beyond the city walls. There were beautiful tombs in that wadi, carved deep into the rock. The windows and doors cut into their facades stared back at him from the distance, black squares that reminded him too often of the open eyes and mouths of the dead.

A fitting image for tombs, he supposed, but hardly a comforting one.

Among them, not quite visible from this position, was the rock-cut tomb that he and Pullo had bought for the family they didn't have. It had been originally designed for a wealthy family who had decided to bury their dead elsewhere: its face was framed by four half columns that seemed to melt out of the stony canyon wall, and between them were three large niches where statues of the deceased might stand watch over their mortal remains. The previous owners had left it unfinished—there were no statues when he and Pullo had bought it, and the walled courtyard that was meant to be built in front of it as a gathering place for the family was nothing but a paved square beside the path up the wadi into the mountains. They'd finished the courtyard immediately, of course, seeing it as another line of protection for the Ark since the Nabataeans treated such spaces as deeply private areas. Only then did they commission the two statues that had filled the niches to left and right. They were of Miriam's parents—the secret pharaoh Caesarion and the Jewish girl Hannah, who had been the keeper of the Ark before they died in Egypt. The couple had been buried where they'd fallen, in the quiet ruins of a forgotten temple on Elephantine island. But they lived on, Vorenus often thought, in the precious girl that Vorenus himself had cut free of her dying mother. That Miriam had no memory of the faces of her parents made the statues important to him. It was cold stone, but he liked to think that the faces still had life when he and Pullo would sit with her in the quiet courtyard and tell her of the people they'd been.

The third niche in the facade of the tomb was still empty, as if awaiting the face of the next person to be buried within. That was how the Nabataeans did things, and he and Pullo did their best to make their tomb seem the same as any other in the valleys. It wasn't, of course. No one was buried there, and Vorenus couldn't imagine anyone ever would be. The large stone sarcophagus that they'd placed inside held not a body but the precious Ark that had fallen into their keeping when Hannah and Caesarion had died defending it. And when he, Pullo, or Miriam was seen close to the tomb—and it was rare that one of them was not nearby—they were not meeting in prayers for the dead but in a watch for the living.

He let his gaze fall to the temples and tombs that were gathered around the feet of the acropolis below him. The Nabataean priests were busy there, bringing offerings of songs and flesh to their pantheon of gods. Tallest among the buildings was the temple dedicated to Dushara, the lord of the mountains. Though adorned with tall columns at its front, from Vorenus' view it seemed a massive block of stone, painted a white that shone in the sun, as if it had been set down amid the city like a gift from the heavens.

The temple was, Vorenus had learned, meant to mimic the many stone blocks that the Nabataeans had carved to honor their deities: the blocks represented the mountains where the earth and heavens met, where men could reach up toward the divine. Once he knew what they were, Vorenus seemed to see the blocks—god-blocks, they were often called—almost everywhere he looked in Petra, but none were more prominent than the temple at the heart of the city.

Before he died, Caesarion had come to believe that the Shard within the Ark had first come to this place, that it was here that the Jews had found it and built it, forgotten though that history now was. That was why Caesarion had wanted the Ark brought here, brought home. What the child of Julius Caesar and Cleopatra planned for it once here—how he hoped to find it a permanent home in this place—Vorenus did not know.

But I got it here, he thought. I did my best.

When they'd set out for Petra in the company of the Nabataean Syllaeus—their little company always just one step ahead of the Roman armies—getting the Ark to this ancient city had seemed like it would be accomplishment enough.

Now, as Vorenus turned his tired eyes once again to the caravan that was nearing the gates, he felt more than ever that no place would ever be truly safe. Nothing was outside the reach of Rome.

Vorenus sighed and stood, stretching his legs into vigor after having sat still for too long. Knowing the mission was without hope of victory didn't mean he would stop fighting for it. That had never been his way.

An agitation of movement down in the colonnade just inside the city gates caught the corner of his eyes, and Vorenus once more found himself squinting to make something out among the antlike people busily hurrying from one marketplace to another. Petra was built on trade, and during the day the markets and the public spaces between them were a constant hum of activity—an organized chaos that would grow even more frantic with word that a new caravan was arriving. The merchants always worked hard to front their stalls well when new traders came to the city.

But this agitation was different. It felt wrong, almost like a panic.

Vorenus peered at the open gates of the city, and almost at once he saw what it was.

Cursing his old eyes, he stumbled back from the edge of the ledge and hurried for the thin scrap of a trail that would bring him down from his perch and into the bustle below.

What he'd seen was unmistakable. The glint of gold flashed

wildly when it passed out of the shadows of the city walls and into the full light of the sun. How he'd not seen it before, he didn't know, but it was there now, as clear as the spots that freckled the backs of his weary hands as they steadied his scramble along the face of the cliff.

What he had seen was an eagle. An eagle of gold, perched on a staff draped in red, carried by a man riding ahead of the arriving mass of men.

It meant that it wasn't just a caravan that was coming to the secret city of Petra today. A legion was with it, too.

2

The Fall of a Scholar

Didymus Chalcenterus awoke at his desk, his cheek resting on a stack of papyrus that was—thankfully, surprisingly—free of his scribbles of ink. He was hardly a vain man, but he was vaguely aware that it wasn't the finest idea to have the chief librarian of the Great Library of Alexandria walking about with strange jottings of ink staining his face.

Didymus yawned and lifted his head from its chance pillow. His neck was tight—it usually was when he awkwardly fell asleep while writing—and so he habitually torqued it from one shoulder to another. He was pleased when the bones shifted in response with a gratifying crack.

He didn't need to gauge the wax on the little candle that burned at the corner of his desk to know that it was still the middle of the night. In the decades that he'd been the chief librarian he'd fallen asleep in his office far more often than he'd ever made it home. He knew the feel of the predawn darkness. He knew it in the tomblike silence of a building that in hours would hum with hushed whispers and soft footsteps as his fellow scholars came to work amid the wondrous collection of books under his control.

With a sigh, Didymus pushed back his stool and stood. As he stretched his arms, his body waking at last, he resumed focus on the book he had been working on: a commentary on some of Pindar's surviving poetry. Growing up in Greece he'd been fascinated by much of the ancient poet's work, and he'd always wanted to write a book about them. That he'd never done so was a reflection of his sense that his meager skills as a writer were hardly adequate to the task of approaching such genius, but of late he'd begun to feel that humility was a luxury best afforded to younger men. He was fifty-eight years old this year, and while that hardly made him an old man it did give him a sense he should write the book sooner rather than later.

Looking down at the papers strewn on his desk he saw the last poem he'd been examining. It was one of Pindar's victory odes:

> *Momentary creatures. What is a man?*
> *What is he not? Man is a dream of shadows.*
> *But when the splendor of Zeus is come down,*
> *A shining light's upon him, and blessed are his days.*

Didymus smiled. When he'd first heard those words as a young boy, he'd thought them an exultant testament of the wonders that could come from faith in the gods. Man, he thought Pindar was saying, is nothing without the blessing of Zeus, but such a blessing could provide an eternity of glory. Later, after he'd learned of the Shards of Heaven, after he thought he knew the secret truth of the world—that Zeus had never been, that in fact the one God, the only God who'd ever been, was dead—Didymus had seen Pindar's words as sorrowful: no matter a man's triumphs and joys, his pleasures and possibilities, he would amount to nothing but shadows and dust. Man was a creature of the moment, a flash upon a world that was gone as quickly as he'd come.

Now? Didymus tapped the page thoughtfully.

Now he thought neither way of reading it was quite right. Pindar's words were neither wholly joyous nor completely sorrowful. They were the truth, of course: a man's life was a temporary thing, and all but a few would go unmarked upon the earth. But even those who would be remembered beyond their friends and family would not survive with their name.

Didymus turned from his desk to face the window behind him. One of the shutters was partially open to the night air, and through it he could see the grounds of the Museum stretching away from the Great Library, the paths and gardens lit by the stars. Beyond them were the wide streets of Alexandria, where Roman guards on patrol moved in silent groups through the darkness between the flickering fires atop street posts. There was little other movement in the city so early, though as the librarian watched he saw a few hooded figures—priests, likely— drift out of the dark and up the lamp-lit steps of the Sema, where rested the body of Alexander the Great, preserved in a crystal tomb.

Yes, he thought. Even Alexander the Great, who had accomplished more in his lifetime than any man before him, died in the end. It wasn't sorrowful to admit that truth. To admit to the fleeting chances of lives was simply to acknowledge the true nature of human existence. It needn't mean despair. Indeed, the longer Didymus had read Pindar, the more he was certain that the old poet had intended that all along: the impermanence of life was the source of its joys. The poet imagined joy as the blessing of Zeus, but that was really just a metaphor of the enduring strength of the human spirit. To be truly human was to recognize how transient life was, and in so doing to be the more grateful for whatever time you were given. A sun that shone without clouds, without night, would never be appreciated at the dawn.

"We need shadows," Didymus said, giving voice to his thoughts. "We need the shadow, if only to recognize the light."

"I agree."

Didymus jumped at the sound of another voice behind him, and he spun to see that a man was stepping forward into the light of the feeble candle on his desk. The man did not seem to be armed, and he had a kind of regretful smile upon his face. The man was younger than himself, Didymus could see, and he was wearing a dark tunic fit for travel. He wasn't one of the librarians, and no one else was supposed to be in the Library so late. The doors ought to have been locked.

"How did you—?"

"Good Apion dutifully locked the doors, if that's what you're wondering. But I know my way in. I didn't forget."

Didymus blinked, uncertain if he should shout for the guards out on the streets. How did this man know his assistant would have been the last man to leave? And what did he mean he hadn't forgot?

"You don't remember me, I think," the man said. "It's fine. I didn't expect you to. But I did know you, and you knew me. That's the only reason they let me come in here alone."

"They?"

The man nodded, and something like fear passed over his face. "Please, do not cry out. Do not try to flee or fight. Please."

Didymus blinked, half wondering if he still slept, if this was some strange dream. He didn't know the man, though now that he stared at him he could catch glimpses of a younger face he might recognize beneath the masks of time. "I'm sorry," he said. "I'm not sure I remember you. Who are you? And what do you want?"

The man sighed tiredly and gestured to the only chair in

front of the scholar's desk that wasn't cluttered with books and scrolls. "May I sit?"

Didymus swallowed hard as he worked over the distance to the nearest guards he'd seen. How long would they take to reach him?

Minutes, he decided. Far too many minutes. And with a drop of three stories outside the window, he wasn't about to jump and run.

Instead, he motioned toward the one seat as calmly as he could manage, then sat back down in his own. For a moment he thought of covering up his work, but the idea was almost laughable. Whatever the intruder wanted, it was surely not an old man's musings on Pindar.

The man looked around the office as he settled himself in the chair. "You know, I once imagined I'd make this room my own one day. Wasn't to be. So much has come and gone."

At once, Didymus knew him: the boy who'd come to them so young, who'd risen so far, but who'd left the Library when he'd instead chosen Apion to be the next in line to succeed him as head of the Great Library. "Thrasyllus?"

Thrasyllus nodded once more. "It's been a long time."

"Gods," Didymus whispered. "How long has it been? Twenty years?"

"Or more," Thrasyllus agreed. "I'm sorry I stormed away back then. I was . . . young. Impetuous. Stubborn. You made the right choice. My anger only proved your wisdom."

Didymus tried to imagine the younger man in the older one. The young man had been an astrologer, a branch of learning that Didymus had always thought unworthy of the boy's clear intellect. Apion had seemed to be the more sensible choice, his scholarship more traditional. But while Apion had done well— and would ably carry on the work of the Great Library many years after Didymus was dead and buried—the truth was that he was not as driven as young Thrasyllus had been, and more than once Didymus had wondered if he'd made the right choice. The Thrasyllus that he'd known had been a deeply dedicated man, passionate about his work. He'd been a good and loyal helper, and only much later did Didymus come to understand how much being passed over had surely wounded him. And all because he could not look beyond his prejudice against the young man's field of study.

"I, too, was stubborn," Didymus managed to say. "I'm not sure I would choose the same if given the choice again."

Thrasyllus appeared to smile, but there remained a troubled sorrow that darkened his eyes. "What was it Heraclitus wrote? 'No man ever steps in the same river twice, for it is not the same river and he is not the same man.'"

"So he did," Didymus agreed. "And, as Pericles once said, 'Time is the wisest counselor of all.'"

"I always liked Pericles."

"I remember."

"It's good to see you again."

"And you, too. Where have you been all these years?"

"I had to leave. Things happened, things I could neither undo nor forget. In the end I went west, to Mauretania. A new land. A fresh start. I found employ with King Juba and Queen Cleopatra Selene."

Didymus could not have hidden the lightness in his heart at the sound of her name if he had tried. "I remember her so fondly. How is she?" His face brightened. "Do you have a message from her?"

"She is very well," Thrasyllus said. "She has often spoken of you, Didymus, though I'm sorry to say that she did not send me with a message for you." The astrologer's eyes went to a wooden tray at the corner of the desk. "Is that still where you keep the letters going out and coming in? Where Apion now checks for such things?"

Didymus followed the man's gaze and sighed—both from the disappointment that Selene had sent no message and from the memory of a much younger Thrasyllus coming and retrieving his letters so many years ago. "It is. And I'm sorry that she sent nothing. I would have liked to hear from her."

For a moment Thrasyllus continued to stare at the tray, as if he was lost in thought. Then, abruptly, he looked up. "In truth," he said, "I don't come to you on her behalf at all. I have a . . . well, another employer now."

Didymus had to force down a sudden urge to scream out for the guards. "I see," he said, trying to remain calm. "So why have you come, Thrasyllus? Why were you sent? It was surely not to trade old wisdoms, no matter how fine they are. Surely not at this hour, at any rate."

"Ever astute," Thrasyllus said. "My employer needs something. Information."

"There is much of that in our holdings."

"Not of the kind we need."

"We?"

"What my employer wants is what I want. At least for now."

"I see," Didymus said. For a moment he was reminded of another time that someone had found him at night, seeking information. But that had been an assassin seeking the Book of Thoth, the sacred book that held the secrets of all things. The book was legend and myth, but discovering that had been the first step on a journey that would carry Didymus and his friends to learn about the Shards of Heaven and all the very real powers those artifacts possessed.

Thrasyllus reached into the folds of his clothing and retrieved a small scrap of papyrus. He slid it faceup across the desk between them. "Do you recognize this?"

Didymus looked and saw that a single symbol had been drawn upon it: a six-pointed star over-scribed with a circle. It was a simple design, but Didymus knew enough to recognize it at once. He swallowed hard and felt a sudden chill wash over him. "What of it?"

The astrologer's eyes narrowed. "Do you recognize it?"

The air was bitingly cold. Didymus fought to keep from shivering. "Thrasyllus, I . . . whatever you've heard, I don't—"

"Do you recognize it?"

So very cold. "I don't—"

Didymus was ready to lie, to fight any effort Thrasyllus might make to pull the truth from him, when a voice came from the open window that was behind him, cutting off any attempt he might have made at speech. "He knows," it said.

Didymus jolted in his seat even as the cold peaked, flung through him like a wash of ice through his veins. He pushed his hands into the arms of his chair to keep them from shaking, and he closed his eyes to try to calm his startled heart.

A second later, when he opened them, Didymus saw that he and Thrasyllus were no longer alone in the room. From behind him floated the source of the voice, a figure whose black tunic and hooded cloak were nearly motionless as he moved around the desk in perfect silence to stand behind the astrologer. For a moment Didymus felt the urge to jump from his seat and leap away through the open window, but it would be certain death to do so. No man could survive such a fall.

And no man could make such a climb.

As if in reply, the stranger raised hands whose ivory-pale skin seemed a dull glow in contrast to his black clothing. The hood of the cloak was pushed back with long fingers, revealing the most beautifully perfect face the librarian had ever seen. The man looked like a white marble statue come to life: not a great bearded deity like Zeus, but the slender, beardless, almost androgynous figure of Dionysius, the god whose embodiment even now surely stood his stony watch over his temple across the city.

Only this was no statue, and it was no god. The stranger stared at him with white-less black eyes that knew no love and no laughter. And when Didymus looked into those unblinking orbs he sensed a yawning abyss looking back. The librarian who had come to be called "Bronze-guts" felt his stomach twist and lurch.

"The feeling lessens over time," Thrasyllus said.

Didymus fought the urge to throw up, to scream, to curl himself up into a childish ball. He squeezed his eyes shut against it all, refusing to look further into those eyes, his scholar's mind stepping through facts to make sense of the world.

A demon. It could be nothing else.

And the only thing it could want would be the Shards, the fragments of God's power, weapons to be used in a conflict waged far beyond the mortals of this world.

"Speak," the demon-thing said, and its voice was winter's breath stirring a field of snow—soft, but deadly cold.

Didymus clenched his teeth together, stilled his tongue against the roof of his mouth.

"Speak," it commanded, and this time its voice was the wind through icy rocks—hard and unrelenting. It was, Didymus knew in his heart of hearts, the voice of death.

"Please," Thrasyllus whispered. "Please, I know what he can do. He'll kill you. He'll kill me. He'll kill my Lapis. And he'll kill Selene, Didymus."

In an instant, Didymus remembered again the night that the assassin came for the fabled Book of Thoth, the night that his old friend Lucius Vorenus had learned how he'd once betrayed

Caesarion and nearly caused the child's death. He'd made a promise that night, a promise that had spared him the tip of Vorenus' sword. He'd told him the one thing that in that moment he knew to be true: Didymus would die for Selene. He would do anything to keep her safe.

"Please," Thrasyllus urged. "He'll kill her and Juba both."

Didymus let out a long breath and opened his eyes. "It's the Seal of Solomon," he said.

The demon cocked its head. "Where is it?"

"You'll never get it. It would take an army."

"Where?" Thrasyllus asked, leaning forward.

Didymus held the astrologer's gaze for a moment. "It's in Jerusalem. It's hidden in the great temple of the Jews."

"We already know," Thrasyllus whispered. He licked his lips for a moment. "But do you know where?"

"He does," the demon hushed. "Bring him. Then burn the books."

"My lord!" The astrologer's eyes went wide in shock, as if he was stunned by the order and his own response. He looked around the room as if casting about for something. "But . . . there may be books of use to finding this Seal. If it is truly hidden, we may need keys."

Thrasyllus looked to Didymus with wild desperation, and at last the scholar nodded. "It is true. I'll find the books and bring them. Leave this place unharmed and I'll go with you. But if you destroy even a single jot in this Library I swear to you that I will never help you and you will never, ever reach what you desire."

The demon's blank eyes stared at him, and Didymus did his best to stare back while fighting the revulsion in the pit of his stomach. Finally, the corner of the creature's mouth curled up in what might have passed for a smile. "That, librarian, is a truth I do believe. Gather what is needed and come."

The demon turned and soundlessly moved to the door. Its pale fingers wrapped around the handle and pulled it open. Thrasyllus, clearly relieved, stood.

Didymus let out a long breath. He couldn't let them reach the Seal, but he couldn't let them harm those he loved. And while going with them wasn't a solution, it at least saved the books. And it bought time.

The demon's back was, for a heartbeat, turned as it began to float through the doorway. And in that moment, Thrasyllus silently and smoothly reached into the folds of his own garments. If Didymus had been looking anywhere else, he would not have seen it, but he'd been looking at the man, and he saw it clear as the dawning day: Thrasyllus reached into his clothes with a stabbing dart of his hand and retrieved a letter. Then, as he spun around to follow the unnatural being out into the Library, he dropped it in the tray on the librarian's desk.

The letter made the slightest of sounds, and the creature turned back to look in their direction, but Didymus was already standing, carelessly shuffling the pages of his commentary on Pindar in covering sounds. "The books I need are on the second level," he said to Thrasyllus, trying to remain calm.

The astrologer smiled in genuine relief and gratitude, then he gestured for him to follow the demon.

Passing around the side of his desk, Didymus didn't dare look again at the tray, though every part of his ever-curious mind begged him to do it.

Not that there was more for him to learn. In the flash of time that it took for the letter to fall from the astrologer's fingers into the tray, Didymus had already seen what was written upon it.

It was a sealed letter, and it was addressed to Apion.

Ανοίξτε μου, it read on the outside.

Open me.

3

WATER FROM THE ROCK

PETRA, 5 BCE

As evening approached, Miriam took her stance on a farming terrace in the west wadi, between two long rows of grapevines that webbed together like living walls. The last of the blooms were fading off the vines, but the fragrance of pollen was still heavy in the cool, shadowed air of the narrow canyon around her. At her back the little waters from the spring of Moses bounced and twisted their meandering way through the rocks, churning heedlessly downhill to where the narrow wadi cart path and the little stream's mostly dry riverbed both ended at a cliff's edge. The waters fell away then, sparkling in a cooling mist, down into deeper and deeper pools as they descended toward the dry desert farther to the west.

All of this she knew, for she'd known no other home.

And all of it she let drift away from her mind as she took in her breath and steadily drew the bowstring back to her cheek.

Miriam was a child no older than ten when she had first picked up a bow and tried to use it. Her uncle Vorenus—though even then she'd known he wasn't really her uncle—had frowned, but he'd done nothing to stop the scarred giant Pullo from enfolding his wide hands over her own as he showed her how to grip the weapon so she could properly lock her wrists as she pressed into the pull. He didn't know much about the bow, he said, but he knew that.

Even in a place like Petra, where women could own property in their own names, shooting a bow was hardly the work of a lady. So in the nearly ten years since she'd begun practicing she'd received no small share of odd looks from the Nabataeans as she had trundled off with her bow and arrows to find some place to teach herself how to use the weapon.

This place had quickly become her favorite.

Down at the other end of the vines was a sack of dried husks, leaned up against the ever-present red rocks as if it were sleeping.

Miriam patiently took aim, ignoring the strand of her own dark brown hair that danced across her vision. She stared at the target, eyeing the extended point until it was fixed upon it. Then, letting out her breath, she loosed the string.

The bow snapped forward, the string snatched the shaft, and the arrow shot forward, straight and steady. In a heartbeat it had buried itself in the sack with a coughing thud.

Miriam lowered the bow and shook her head as she walked between the vines. Even at a distance she could see that it had impacted several inches away from the last one, which was a finger length above the one before that. Her shots were hitting the target, certainly, but no matter how much she practiced they were still irregularly grouped.

When she reached the sack she stared at it for a moment. It was exactly as she'd thought, and it was frustrating.

Miriam snatched the arrow out of the sack, turned on her heels, and began marching back to her measured spot at the other end of the rows.

She was halfway there when, looking up, she saw the Roman.

Many people came to Petra, of course, from many nations of the world. Nabataea was a kingdom built on the trading car-

avans whose goods were brought from one side of the mountains to the other.

But it was no Roman merchant she saw. It was a Roman soldier, squatting at the edge of the terrace above, his own bow
strapped across his back. He was a young man, she could see,
probably only a few years older than herself. He was handsome,
and it took all the willpower she had not to flip her bow up and
try to shoot him through.

Rome was danger. Rome wanted the Ark.

"Your elbow is rotating," the soldier said.

Pretending she'd just noticed him, Miriam raised her hand
over her brow as if to further her sight. As she did so, she let
her fingers brush past her breast, reassuring herself that her
mother's necklace—with its symbol of the Shard—was hidden.
"My what?"

"Your elbow," he said. He smiled and placed his hand on the
edge of the terrace's stone retaining wall in order to vault himself down to her level. Still a row away from her, he darted his
head from side to side as he tried to talk through the vines between them. "It's rotating. You can't let it do that. You'll never
get good groupings that way."

While he was distracted with trying to find a way through the
vines, Miriam quickly glanced around her. There was no one else
in the wadi. No new smoke in the air. She tried to listen for
screams, but all she could hear was the falling water in the canyon.

Roman soldiers passed through Petra on occasion, but Pullo
and Vorenus usually knew in advance. Knowing ahead of time
gave them the opportunity to have two of their triumvirate watching the tomb where the Ark lay hidden. How had they not known
Roman soldiers were coming? And were they here for the Ark?

Smiling shyly as she approached her shooting point, she
asked him when he arrived.

"Only just," the young man said, poking his head between vines a few yards away. He began to contort his body through the gap he'd found. "Arrived with the legion."

Legion. Miriam's stomach knotted in sudden panic, and she instinctively gripped the bow in her hand harder. "Trading?"

With a grunt, the young man pulled himself through and stood before her. His grin, she could now see, was lopsided. "Oh no, my lady," he said. "Just delivering a message, I think. At least that's all I know of it."

Miriam wrinkled her face in what she hoped would look like innocent confusion. "A legion for a message? Is that really necessary?"

The Roman shook his head and looked up toward a sky that was drifting toward evening. She'd been wrong about his age, she decided. He might even be younger than she was. "Depends on who is sending the message," he said. His gaze fell back down to meet hers, and it looked like he might blush. "Anyway, you're rotating your elbow."

"I don't know what that means," she said.

The legionnaire held out his arm with his bow in his grip. "See how my elbow is to the side? That's how you want it. Your elbow is rotating to point more toward the ground."

Miriam lifted her own bow and tried to mirror the position. It was definitely different than she'd done it. She frowned.

"I know," he said. "It might feel strange at first, but you'll get better groupings. Believe me, that's how you want it." He set his bow down and walked over to her. "May I show you?"

Miriam nodded, and he stepped around to stand behind her. Then he laid his right hand on hers and pushed her arm down, lowering the bow to her side while keeping her elbow pointed out. Next, he directed her to lift it back up again.

"Perfect," he said, his breath close to her neck. "Hold the bow correctly at your side and then just lift it up into position.

You've been rotating your elbow down when you've pulled the bow up. Don't ever do that." He abruptly let go of her and stepped away again. "The muscles will get stronger, and soon it'll feel natural. It even helps you to lift and draw at the same time, which means faster shots, too." He pulled an arrow from his own gathering and held it out to her. "Here. Try it."

Miriam took the offering and lowered the bow. Nocking the arrow to the string, she took a deep breath to clear her head and then lifted and drew the bow, being careful not to rotate her elbow. She lined up the shot and loosed it an instant later.

The arrow tore through the sack, almost directly on top of the hole from the last shot.

The Roman clapped his hands. "Perfect! Soon you'll be better than I am."

Miriam carefully lowered the bow again. "I can only hope. Thank you."

He shrugged his shoulders. "Archers have to stick together. I had to learn the same things once, when I was first given my bow, too. It's interesting, though, that I've never seen a girl shooting the bow. Do all Nabataean girls do this? I've heard you have more rights than you would where I come from. Do they make you fight, as well?"

Miriam felt herself instinctively bristle at the notion that she was Nabataean—her father, Caesarion, was a pharaoh of Egypt and by all rights ought to have ruled Rome—but she swallowed such prideful thoughts. She was no princess. The necklace that her mother had passed on to her, the talisman that was all she had left of her identity, meant that she was a keeper of the Ark. And that, as Pullo and Vorenus had told her, meant that Rome was her enemy. "No," she said. "I just like shooting the bow. I like knowing I can hold my own if I ever need to do so."

The soldier looked at her approvingly. "I like that. It's a good thing." He glanced up again at the sky, which was noticeably

darker than it had been. "I should probably go. I was just told
to be sure this area was secure."

Miriam nodded down to where the cart path through the
terraced vineyards in the narrow, steep-sided wadi ended at the
cliff. "This as far as anyone goes," she said.

The young man pointed beyond the plunging drop-off, to
where a thin sliver of trail, just wide enough for a man, continued
along the edge of the mountainside. "And where does that go?"

"Around the mountain. It eventually gets to Bayda, but no
one comes to the city up that way. They take the main road."

"Good to know," he said. "Well, good luck with your practice." He turned and started walking toward the cart path.

"What about your arrow?" Miriam called after him.

He stopped and turned, his lopsided smile broad. "It's not
mine. It belongs to Rome. You can keep it. And if you need
more while we're here, just come to the camp and find me,
Abdes Pantera. Believe me, we have plenty."

Miriam wanted to reject his kindness, as the notion of being grateful to a Roman for anything made her ill. But knowing
that it would save her the expense of buying at least one more
shaft, she managed to smile. "Thank you," she said.

He waved, and then he was treading up the path toward
Petra.

Alone again, Miriam clutched for a moment at the talisman
around her neck and allowed herself several deep breaths as she
collected her thoughts. A Roman legion had come, bearing a
message. That meant they would surely be gathering with the
Nabataean king, probably with the high priest in the temple of
Dushara. Pullo had been watching the Ark, so Vorenus would
probably have gone to the temple to hear what was happening
and determine what it might mean for them.

So that's where she would go, she decided. To the temple,
to find Vorenus. He'd know what they should do.

Shaking her head free of the image of Pantera's lopsided grin, she ran to the sack and retrieved his arrow, adding it to her own.

Then she turned and ran up the path as fast as she could manage.

And as she did so, she was careful to hold her bow just as the Roman had showed her: elbow out, ready to lift and pull.

. . .

Petra was the only city Miriam had ever known, but she still knew enough to marvel at its existence. The city that spread out before her as she left the west wadi was built on a relatively flat plain, virtually ringed by high, rugged mountains. The main road ran north and south through the city: south to the town of Sabra, which was closer to the lower deserts and the western caravan roads that led to the ports on the Red Sea; and north to the ancient King's Highway, which ran east of the mountains from those same ports all the way to the prosperous city of Damascus. Beyond those two roads, the only other way into the city of Petra was a narrow path through a chasm called the Siq, which cut like a knife through the heart of the mountains east of the city. Where the mountains failed in their natural defenses north and south, the Nabataeans had built stone walls between them, but there was no need for a wall across the Siq: few knew of its existence, and in places it was so narrow that two men—or one, if he was the size of her Pullo—could defend it. The path through the Siq became a colonnaded thoroughfare through the city, passing east–west to form a crossroads with the main north–south road. Passing that, it became a track leading down into the west wadi, with its farming terraces built around a little stream that some said sprang from the rock when Moses struck it with his staff.

Miriam knew that the staff he'd held had been the Trident of Poseidon, the Shard that controlled water. So at least that part of the legend of her mother's people made sense.

Exiting the wadi, she saw the milling crowds gathered around the square in front of the temple of Dushara, which dominated the center of the city of Petra as surely as the surrounding mountains dominated the whole of the city itself. There was symbolism in this, as there was in so many things: Dushara was the god of the mountains.

Roman legionnaires were scattered among the people, but despite their presence the crowds seemed calm. Pantera, it seemed, had been telling the truth. The Romans had come to deliver a message, not to attack the city, and therefore surely not to pursue the Ark. Its presence here, she was certain, was still a secret.

Since Aretas had taken over as king, Vorenus had been acting as a kind of foreign advisor to the royal council. It allowed him to be where he could see what was happening and hear what was being said. King Aretas had offered him official status for his services, but Vorenus had declined, citing his age. Miriam knew the truth: he refused to be in a position where he'd be unable to rush toward the tomb where the Ark lay hidden. So Vorenus had remained on the periphery of the royal council—which meant that Miriam was likely going to find him among the bustling crowds.

She dove into the roiling mass of people, doing her best to seek one of the higher platforms near the western edge of the square. It seemed as if the whole town had shown up, and Miriam quickly despaired of finding Vorenus among them. Passing faces that she knew, she nodded and smiled at them, but she didn't slow down to talk until a familiar hand reached out to her from the bustling crowd of people vying to see what was happening. It was, Miriam saw as she turned, Dorothea, the old woman who sold flowers in the market.

"Child," Dorothea said, looking at the bow that Miriam was carrying, "whatever were you doing?"

Miriam smiled, feigning innocence. "Checking the vines down in the wadi for weeds."

"Weeds, is it?" Dorothea winked conspiratorially. "Monstrous ones, apparently. I suspect they'll be afraid to grow for many weeks, though."

Miriam shifted her grip on the bow. For a moment she thought about telling the old woman about the Roman archer—for some reason she suddenly had the urge to tell somebody about him—but she knew she shouldn't dare tell Dorothea. If there was one thing everyone knew about the flower peddler it was that she traded in rumor more often than she traded her flowers. Dorothea had a keen ear and a ready tongue for gossip. She was surely the last person to tell about Abdes Pantera. "Well," Miriam said, "I certainly tried."

"I hope you did well," Dorothea said. She stretched her back painfully. "The gods know I need the wine." She looked around at the tightly packed square and let out a long breath. "But for now I think my bed will do."

Still clutching Miriam's arm, the old woman tiredly took a few steps toward the more empty streets away from the crowd.

"Where's your walking stick?" The flower peddler didn't really need one—she'd walked here to the square without one, after all—but she seemed to enjoy the attention of having one.

Dorothea frowned. "Was so excited to hear the news of the legion I left it in my stall. I'll get it in the morning. Do you think you could help me along toward the road, dear?"

"I was trying to find my uncle, Vorenus." Pullo and Vorenus insisted that she call them uncles when people were around. The fact was that while neither man was her father, they'd been the only parents she'd ever known, and they'd done their best to raise her as well as two weathered warriors could manage. She'd never say it to them, but she thought of them as her two fathers, and she loved them as only a daughter could.

Dorothea's face brightened. "Then we'll go that way to-gether, child. I saw him walking toward the Siq."

Miriam nodded and took the old woman's arm to support her as she walked. It would take her longer to walk with Doro-thea, but she didn't really mind. While many of the boys and girls her age didn't like the flower seller—perhaps due to her meddling inquiries about their lives—Miriam found her to be kind and gentle. Even Dorothea's rather unsubtle nudging that Miriam should give consideration to the romantic intentions of her grandson were well-meaning in their way—though Miriam had no interest at all in the boy.

"Exciting to have the Romans here," Dorothea said as she walked.

Miriam once more thought of the Roman archer Abdes Pantera, and she looked around for a moment in the strange hope that she would see him. "I guess so," she said.

"Of course it is! They're powerful and rich and well traveled."

And a threat to the Ark, Miriam wanted to add. Instead she just nodded.

"They'll have stories, I'm sure. Maybe buy some flowers." The old woman's fingers squeezed on her arm. "Maybe find you a pleasant Roman boy."

Before she could think to stop herself, Miriam loudly and suddenly denied any interest in such a thing. Even as the words of denial burst forth, she was realizing her protest was too loud, too soon.

Dorothea immediately beamed. "Oh? No interest at all?"

Miriam's heart sank, and she was certain she was blushing. But as she opened her mouth to try a more convincing denial, she saw a familiar gray-haired man making his way alone through the edge of the gathered throng, headed west toward the col-onnaded street that led to the Siq. "There's my uncle," she said. "He's surely worried about me."

Dorothea frowned, looking back and forth between them, then sighed with a smile. "You should probably go, then. But I'll hear more about the Roman on your mind!"

"I don't know what you're talking about," Miriam said in her calmest manner. "But I'm sure you'll know anything there is to know."

"I always do, child. Off with you now."

Miriam smiled, patted the old woman's arm once more, then hurried off.

"Uncle Vorenus," she said when she finally caught up to him.

Vorenus turned to look over at her, his stride slowing ever so slightly as she kept pace beside him. "Good to see you, little one," he said.

Miriam smiled at the epithet, though as she neared twenty years of age she was hardly a little girl anymore. "You, too."

"Out practicing?"

Miriam thought about whether to tell him about the Roman archer, but she decided it was of little importance right now. "I was," she finally said. "Down in the wadi."

Vorenus nodded sagely and turned up the wide paved road between columns adorned with oil lamps that were beginning to glow as the setting sun painted the sky in swaths of deep red and orange.

They walked in relative silence, side by side, until they were passing the first of the markets on their right. Shopkeepers were gathering their wares and closing their stalls, and there were far fewer people upon the road. Miriam looked around to be sure no one was close enough to listen before she spoke. "Do we need to worry about anything?" she asked.

"I don't think so. Not unless they begin tearing through the tombs for fun." His tone made it clear that while Vorenus did not think it likely, he could easily imagine his former countrymen doing just that, impious as it was.

"But it's a legion."

"It is," Vorenus agreed. "Come down from Jerusalem."

"They came to deliver a message?"

The old man turned toward her with a raised eyebrow, but if he thought her observation truly odd he said nothing. Instead he just nodded. "True enough. It seems that Augustus Caesar has finally recognized Aretas as the rightful king of Nabataea."

"Recognized him?"

She saw Vorenus frown as he thought about how to answer her. "It means he agrees that Aretas should be the king."

Now it was Miriam's turn to frown. "But he *is* the king. He's been king for four years, ever since Obodas died."

Vorenus smiled now. "All true. But Caesar thinks most of the world belongs to him. He doesn't imagine there should be a king in Nabataea without his consent. So Aretas declaring himself king without his permission has been a thorn in their relationship." His voice, though already guarded, became even softer. "It doesn't help, of course, that Obodas was probably poisoned by Aretas."

"I thought Syllaeus poisoned him?"

Vorenus shrugged. "He may have administered it, but you can be sure that Aretas was behind the plot. He certainly gained much by it. And it's also rather convenient that Aretas was so quickly able to discern Syllaeus' involvement in the murder and then hand him over to the Romans for judgment."

They walked in silence for a time, Miriam lost in thoughts of court intrigues. As they neared the end of the colonnade, they turned south down a side street, headed toward their little home. When they'd walked even farther, she finally spoke again. "Do you suppose Syllaeus is dead?"

"If not yet, he will be soon," Vorenus replied. "We owe him much for helping bring us here from Egypt all those years ago, but I cannot say I liked the man. I don't think Petra will miss him."

Miriam nodded, and once more she saw in her mind's eye the lopsided grin of Abdes Pantera. "So Caesar agrees that Aretas can be king? That's it? The Romans will leave now?"

"Not quite," Vorenus said.

The street moved over a steep rise just before they reached their home, and as they crested that hill Miriam took in her breath and stopped short. The valley south of the city walls was dotted with a thousand tents and campfires, filling the space between the walls and the terraces there.

"The legion will be staying awhile," Vorenus said, his voice hinting at worry. "Herod is threatening to attack the city from Jerusalem, and the legion is here to keep the peace."

For a second Miriam felt a strange rush of excitement at the thought of seeing Pantera again—he could surely teach her more about the bow, she told herself—but in an instant it was washed away by the stark, dangerous reality that she was certain Vorenus already recognized: the Roman encampment was between the city and the southern valley of tombs.

A legion now stood between the keepers of the Ark and the empty tomb where it quietly lay.

4

The Boat from Rome

Didymus stood at the stern of the ship, watching as dawn broke across the walls of Alexandria behind them. Fishing boats were moving in and out of the ports of the wide harbor, and early seabirds were already squabbling across the brightening sky. Looking closely, he could just see the cupola of the Great Library rising over the jumbled buildings of the city, and the gilded statue of a man that stood atop it, holding an opened scroll toward the heavens. As the first rays of the sun struck it, the statue shined like a beacon of golden fire.

He'd spent so much of his life in that building, beneath its magnificent statue, that he'd never truly appreciated what it meant, the possibility symbolized in the lifting of that scroll, the yearning for divine inspiration.

Sad to realize it only now, when he was certain he was seeing the statue, and the magnificent city of Alexandria, for the last time.

The ship that carried him away was a simple Roman freight ship, little different from perhaps a dozen other single-masted ships that he could see riding the winds out to sea. A thick-bellied craft, it sat both tall and heavy in the water, no doubt leaving it more stable in the open waves. The rising part of its wooden sides was painted deep blue, and the carved shape of a yellow swan was perched upon the stern beside him, settled perfectly between the long twin tillers that steered its path. It was a comfortable but unremarkable ship, and Didymus was certain that the simplicity was a deliberate ruse—though it carried no freight, their vessel carried a most remarkable cargo of men and demons.

The scholar had seen them all, seen them with his own eyes, yet still he had a hard time believing what he saw.

It had been hard enough just to comprehend the demon that had come to the Library in the company of Thrasyllus. The astrologer was right when he said that the stomach-twisting bone cold that he'd felt at first would diminish over time, but that fact was of little comfort beside the horrible recognition that such a thing might walk the earth.

And indeed it did walk. Didymus had been uncertain of it when the demon was in his office: it moved through the room with the indescribable grace of the most perfect dancer, as if it floated across the floor rather than walked upon it. But as they'd moved through the deserted halls to gather up the books he desired, Didymus had seen how its legs moved in the semblance of walking, and when they'd set themselves upon the streets he'd seen the demon leave a single footprint as they crossed a track of dirt where workmen had been repairing the pavement of a walkway.

Didymus had felt great comfort in that footprint. He had etched it like a stone in his memory. The footprint meant that the demon, though not meant for this world, could perhaps be harmed by it.

The philosopher Epicurus, the scholar knew, had once said that although men could defend against most of the ills of the world, "against death, we men live in a city without walls." It was true enough, but until he'd seen that footprint he'd wondered if the demon had walls against death itself.

The footprint was hope that the demon could be killed.

He'd thought much on the matter, plotting as best a life-long scholar could manage while they'd walked through the dark streets, but such plans were dashed when they'd finally reached the boat at the port. There was another demon waiting for them there, a manlike thing that was every bit as unnaturally perfect and cold eyed as the first. And worse, there were two other men aboard as passengers. One was a dark-haired man in his forties with flints of gray in his full beard. Didymus did not recognize him, though his accent was of the east. The other man, with whom the first seemed to be in constant conversation, was Tiberius, the heir of Rome.

Whatever hope Didymus had felt in that footprint had fallen away as surely as the wake of the ship that now traced their voyage away from the port. The scholar had little chance of defeating one demon, much less two, and the presence of Tiberius left no doubt that there were even greater forces at work. He would try to play along, try to buy himself time to find a way forward that wouldn't give them what they desired, but he could not imagine how it could be done.

As the scholar stared out at the retreating city, he felt Thrasyllus come up to stand beside him at the rail. "Am I bothering you?" the astrologer asked.

"No. Just watching it go."

Thrasyllus let out a long breath. "This is the second time I've left this city thinking I'd never see it again," he said.

Didymus looked over at the younger man, whose shoulders seemed to be weighed by heavy regrets. For a moment he started to open his mouth to ask him about the letter to Apion, but then he saw out of the corner of his eye the pale figure of one of the demons watching them. "It is a beautiful city," he said.

"It is. I have missed it terribly."

There was so much that Didymus wanted to ask him—where

the demons had come from, why he was helping them—but he wasn't sure if it was safe. "I'll miss it, too, I think."

For a long time they were silent. Thrasyllus, Didymus could see, had dropped his gaze to where the waves were breaking against the hull of the ship. He appeared to be lost in thought. "I'm sorry," the younger man finally said, his voice quieter than it had been before. "I'm sorry that I had to bring you into this. I didn't want to. I just had no choice."

We always have choices, Didymus thought to himself. It was a lesson he'd not known when he, too, was a much younger man—when by helping the future Augustus Caesar he'd almost caused the death of Caesarion, one of the greatest men he'd ever known—and he knew that it was a lesson that could not be taught. It had to be learned.

"Tiberius has someone I love," the astrologer continued. "I just didn't have a choice."

"I understand," Didymus whispered.

Heavy footsteps approaching on the deck caused them both to turn away from the receding city. Tiberius was there, his eyes shadowed despite the morning light. Behind him the two demons stood, their own eyes black and impassive as stone. The white linen of the sail was snapped taut in the wind, pulling them faster and faster toward the chaos of the ocean. Looming above them was the towering height of the Great Lighthouse, the fiery light at its summit trailing a steady drift of smoke that carried ahead of them out to sea.

"So this is the librarian," Tiberius said.

"My lord," Didymus said, bowing slightly.

Tiberius grunted. "Coming for you meant a delay. But Thrasyllus insisted that we could never get what we want without you."

"I will do what I can to help, my lord," Didymus said, using the tone that he reserved for those most unfortunate occasions when he had to talk to royalty or politicians. A pathetic but very helpful voice. As he had once instructed Apion, it was the balance that was key.

"For both your sakes, I hope so," Tiberius said. Then he nodded in the direction of the other passenger aboard, the full-bearded man who Didymus did not know, standing alone at the prow of the ship. "Read your books, prepare with your studies, but Antipater can know nothing of it, do you understand?"

Antipater. Didymus noted the name, already running through the scrolls of his mind for what he knew of him. It was not much. He was the firstborn son of Herod the Great, who had ruled Judaea for nearly seventy years. Antipater and his mother Doris had been exiled for many years when his father had taken on a new wife, but he'd eventually been recalled to the court after Herod had executed that wife and much of her Hasmonean family. Herod was a powerful but dangerously unstable man, yet Antipater had managed to survive his father's erratic paranoia and even become his sole heir after Herod had ordered the execution of two of his other sons only a few years earlier. Why the heir of Judaea was with the heir of Rome in the company of two demons who sought the Seal of Solomon, Didymus had no idea.

"Of course," Thrasyllus said. "We will be careful."

Tiberius grunted again, then turned to the two demons, who watched them all with unblinking eyes. "Bathyllus and Antiphilus will see to it that you are," he said.

Both demons gave the slightest of nods, but when Tiberius strode off toward Antipater at the front of the ship, only the one they called Antiphilus glided silently behind him. The few sailors manning the ship, Didymus could see, gave both men a wide berth, and at least one visibly shuddered. None of them, the scholar imagined, would live to see the large payday they'd surely been promised for this passage. Unlike him, they had limited usefulness to whatever Tiberius had planned.

The thought gave him little comfort.

Beneath him, the ship began to buck against heavier waves as they passed the harbor wall. He turned back to the stern, back to the shrinking Alexandria, and grabbed hold of the railing. Beside him he saw Thrasyllus do the same.

"We're in this together," Thrasyllus said quietly.

"It seems so," Didymus agreed. The statue atop the Great Library, that man yearning toward the heavens, was just a glint above the city of Alexandria now. The scholar let out a long sigh. "Jerusalem?"

Thrasyllus nodded. "I think so."

"If Tiberius thinks that Antipater can help him get into the Temple, he will be sorely disappointed. He's first in line to rule Judaea after his father, but his father was an Idumaean," Didymus said.

"An Idumaean?"

"It's an old kingdom, south of Judaea, leading up into the mountains. Some books say that it was once centered in Petra." Didymus saw that Thrasyllus started for a moment at the mention of the ancient city. "You know of Petra?"

"Not much," the astrologer said, recovering himself to smile. "Just that it's built into the mountains themselves."

"So it's said," Didymus agreed. "Some also say that the great mountain above it is the rock from which a Judaean king once threw ten thousand Idumaeans to their deaths, though I think this probably isn't so."

"You don't think that place is Petra or that the king did that?"

The librarian frowned a little. "Both, I suppose, though it is certain that the Judaeans and the Idumaeans have never been too fond of each other. A lot of the Idumaeans have converted to Judaism, for instance, but they're still like foreigners in that land. They're a people apart. And the fact that Herod managed to become king of Judaea is more about politics than anything else. He was appointed by Caesar, which certainly doesn't help to make him more popular with the people. They hate Romans."

"I thought Herod ordered the construction of their Great Temple," Thrasyllus said. "We heard of it even as far away as Mauretania. My king and queen had trouble finding a few particular masons because they were already hired away for the project."

Didymus shrugged. "Since you left the Library I've invited more and more Jewish scholars to come and share their knowledge with us, to add their writings to our collections." Thinking of how he might never again see his shelves of books brought up a sudden well of sorrow in the librarian's heart, and he had to shake it away. "Well, they tell me that Herod's Temple is indeed magnificent. One of the great wonders, they say. And it contains their most holy artifacts, housed upon what is surely their most holy of sites. But they know Herod didn't build it out of faith. He might have built it to bring some of the people to his side, but the truer tale is that he surely built it for his own glory. Believe me, the priests who control the temple wouldn't permit King Herod himself to go searching through it for the Seal of Solomon—much less Herod's son. And the idea of letting Tiberius and us in there . . . it's impossible."

The two men looked back over to where Tiberius and Antipater were talking at the front of the boat. "I don't think that's what Tiberius intends for Antipater to do," Thrasyllus said.

"What then?"

The astrologer swallowed hard. "He's helping Antipater to kill his father," he whispered. "Poisons. The deed might already

be done by one of Antipater's lovers. But if it isn't, they're bringing more to try again. And they have forged letters blaming it
all on any rival claimants to the throne."

Didymus blinked. "You know this?"

Thrasyllus nodded. "I've heard enough to put together the
clues. It makes sense."

For a moment the librarian stared out at the chaos of the
sea, playing the scene out in his mind. If Antipater murdered
his father, riots would surely erupt in the streets. Roman legions
could march to restore order, and Tiberius could take the chance
to seize the Temple in the name of protecting it. Thousands
would die, but Antipater would have his throne, and the son of
Caesar would get what he wanted. "All so that Tiberius can get
the Seal of Solomon," Didymus said, thinking it through. The
Seal was a signet ring, according to legend, which had been
given by God to Solomon, the wisest of all men and king of
the Jews in ancient days. It was said that with it the king could
command both angels and demons. What Tiberius thought he
could do with it . . .

"Yes and no," Thrasyllus said. "He wants the ring, but he
knows it isn't really the Seal of Solomon."

Didymus turned, his eyebrow raised. "It's not?"

Thrasyllus was staring off into the distance again, but he
wasn't looking at Alexandria. Didymus could see that he was
looking at something much farther away, a memory that he
could not let go. "It's a Shard of Heaven, Didymus. It's the last
of them."

Didymus felt his heart sink. Thrasyllus knew. Tiberius knew.

"They already have the Shards of Water and Fire," Thrasyllus whispered. "There's a third demon, and she will have Life
and Air soon. They have plans to get Earth, too, though I don't
know where it is. What the Seal controls, I don't know, but the
demons think it's the last of them."

Didymus glanced back, saw that the demon was far enough away not to hear a whisper. "I know what it does," he said.

"You do?"

Didymus nodded slowly, knowing that he could never let Tiberius really find it, and knowing that he had to hope he could trust Thrasyllus to do the same. Far behind them, a cloud passed over the sun, and the thin light that had still been glinting from atop the Great Library went out. "The Seal controls Aether," he whispered. "It connects and binds everything. It is the very essence of God."

"But I thought God is dead," Thrasyllus said.

"I thought so, too, once." Didymus looked up past the Great Lighthouse at the wide dome of the sky and the last of the disappearing stars. "But I was wrong. God's not really dead, I don't think. He's just waiting."

"Waiting for what?"

"For us," Didymus said. "God is waiting for us."

5

A Mother's Love

Cleopatra Selene watched with amusement as her husband, sitting on the throne beside hers, endeavored to listen to the latest reports on the reconstruction of the old market in the city. The overseer providing the update was a thorough and organized man, and Juba was trying very hard to give him his full attention despite the fact that their five-year-old son was sitting in his lap and pulling on the curls of his father's beard.

"I see," Juba intoned when the man paused. "I, uh . . . please, go on, ow!"

Selene turned to the perplexed overseer with her most benevolent smile. "Our dear king wishes to say that your work sounds most impressive," she said. "Thank you for your report, and please see to it that construction remains on schedule. We want to interrupt the trade routes as little as possible."

"Of course, my lady," the man said, bowing low.

"Selene," Juba started to say, "the wall, ow!"

"Ah, yes. Also, we have had reports that some of your work has disturbed the foundation of one of the temples in the area. The goddess Tanit, wasn't it?"

Juba had plucked his son over onto his back and was tickling the boy mercilessly. "It was," he said, as little Ptolemy's peals of glee reverberated around the hall. Even the old herald at the door couldn't help but smile in amusement.

"See to it that any disturbance is rectified and the temple re-stored," Selene said.

"I will, your majesties," the man said. He bowed to them both and retreated.

Once he was gone, Juba at last released the squealing boy, who jumped down the dais and crossed the hall squealing with delight as his father chased him with bounding but slow steps, always just out of reach behind him. The boy darted and turned, weaving through pillars, before crossing the hall and running up the dais again. Selene opened her arms to him and caught him as he leaped up into her embrace.

Juba groaned, playfully heaving his breaths as he mounted the steps in mock pain. "I'm too old," he said. "The boy runs me to ground."

"My old man," Selene said, smiling and winking as Juba reached the top and leaned over to kiss her.

Ptolemy rolled his eyes and squirmed in her grip, which only made his father kiss him, too.

"Who is next?" Juba bellowed over his shoulder.

"A librarian from Alexandria," the herald said from the door.

Juba straightened up, his eyes confused but worried. "Thra-syllus, you mean?"

"No, my lord," the herald replied. "But he says he bears a sealed letter from him. The man's name is Apion. He says he has only come to deliver this letter to you. He does not know what it contains, but he says that he was instructed to deliver it most urgently."

Selene felt a knot in her stomach, but she smiled as if nothing could possibly be wrong—both for Ptolemy's sake, and theirs. "Then send him in," she called out. "Let's see this letter of his."

. . .

The midmorning sun was streaming its warmth down upon the stone balcony as Selene and Juba stood along the railing, looking out over the bustling city that they'd built into one of the richest ports of the Mediterranean. It was a glorious achievement, and on any other day she would be gazing down upon Caesarea with both pride in what they had done and hopes of what they still might do.

But not now. Now, all she could think about was the letter from Thrasyllus in Juba's hands and what it meant for them. What it meant for everyone.

"Read it again," she said, her voice barely above a whisper.

"I don't know what more you hope to hear."

"Just read it again. Please."

Her husband nodded tiredly, and for a moment he seemed far older than his forty-three years. " 'The demons of Carthage are with Tiberius. Lapis is a prisoner in Rhodes, and I am forced to help them recover the Shards they do not have. I fought them, but they learned what they needed to know. A demon is sent to take them from you, to bring them to Jerusalem. You must not let this happen. I cannot write more.' "

"A demon," Selene whispered. She remembered the night in Carthage. She remembered their faces, their pitiless, dead eyes. "A demon coming here."

Juba nodded as he lowered the letter and joined her in looking out over the city.

Selene's mind was a rush of confusion and questions, shot through with a sharp fear. "Are they safe?" she managed to ask.

"Locked away," her husband replied.

"You're sure?" There was no need to ask, but she felt compelled to do it anyway.

"I'm sure. I checked this morning. As I always do."

"It could come at any time," Selene said, disturbed at the way her voice shook.

"It will come at night."

It made sense that any attempt to seize the Shards in their vault would come in the dark, when it was easier to move between shadows, but Juba had said it with a surety. "You know this?"

"In Carthage," he whispered, "when the gate . . . when I held them all, I didn't know what I was doing, Selene. I didn't know."

One of his hands had let go of the letter and was gripping the rail as if to steady himself against the memory. Selene reached over and put her own hand upon his, though she didn't know which of them she meant to comfort. "I know, my love."

"It's my fault this is happening," he said. "I should never have sought out the Trident. I should never have been a part of any of this. I started it."

"We share the guilt," she said, squeezing his hand.

"I just want to be rid of them." With his other hand he lifted up the letter in front of him and crumpled it in frustration and quiet rage.

Selene let go of his hand on the rail and reached up to gently take the letter from his balled fist. She could feel the tremble in his bones as he relaxed the muscles and let go. He leaned into the railing and sighed. He looked as if he might weep in his despair.

Juba had been the rock upon which she had remade her life. He was a good man and a great king. He was a wonderful father and a loving, devoted husband. To see him defeated by his guilt was almost more than she could bear.

In a flash the memory came to her of the night in Alexandria that she and her now-dead brothers had been called to the room of their mother, Cleopatra. The armies of Rome had encircled the city, and night brought deeper shadows to a world that was already dark with foreboding. Selene remembered how her mother held her dead father in her arms, her bedclothes bestrewn with the smears of his blood. Mark Antony's face was slack, his eyes sunken by the despair that had led him to fall upon his own sword. Her mother had smiled at them in that moment. She had praised him and begged her children to join her in following him to the afterlife. Looking back, she could see how so much had hinged upon that moment, that choice. Selene had betrayed her mother by refusing her. And instead she had run away, run off to seek the vengeance that would fuel her life until the day her vengeance died in Carthage.

Selene smoothed the letter in her hands. In so many ways that horrible night in Alexandria that her father died, that horrifying choice she was forced to make, had determined everything to come. Juba had already found the Trident in Numidia, but until that night little else was known about the whereabouts of the Shards. Within a day of her father's death, she had met Juba at the tomb of Alexander the Great, and there he had found the Aegis of Zeus. Years later in Rome, still seeking her vengeance, she'd stolen the Palladium of Troy, and together she and Juba had taken the Lance of Olyndicus from Corocotta in Cantabria. And she and Juba had stood on this very balcony, twenty years ago, and made the fateful decision to take all of them together—four of the fabled Shards of Heaven—to Carthage, to try to unlock their full power with the help of Thrasyllus. All of it for vengeance. For their parents who'd died because of Rome, for what Juba had been made to do with the Trident, for her rape at the hands of Tiberius . . . and when Juba had tried to harness the powers of the Shards they had somehow possessed him, used him, and he'd opened a gate to the underworld, to Hell itself.

She didn't blame him, but looking over at his tired shoulders

she knew that he blamed himself. Whatever had happened to
him when he held the four Shards in his arms, it had scarred
him to his very soul. He would never forgive himself. Not
while the Shards were still a threat. Not while demons walked
the earth.

"We share the guilt," she said again, her voice stronger in
its conviction. In her mind she saw how the three demons arose
in their terrible glory, before the sacrifice of her friend Isidora
shut the gate and gave her the chance to escape with Juba and
Thrasyllus. The demons that held Lapis, which were even now
working through Tiberius, were only here because of *both* her
and Juba, because of their blind pursuit of vengeance no matter
how deserving they believed it to have been. The demons had
the Trident and the Lance—the Shards of Water and of Fire—
only because of their failures. What they could accomplish
with such powerful artifacts and such a powerful ally as Tiberius, she did not want to imagine. What they could accomplish if they possessed even more, if they had the ability
to once more open the gate to Hell, she did not even want to
contemplate.

"But it's done," she said. It was true, and it was the only way
forward. All else was despair, her father falling on his sword,
her mother drawing forth the asp. "Regrets help nothing."

"It's my fault," Juba repeated. He looked down at his hands.
"I couldn't control it."

Selene carefully refolded the letter and slipped it into the hidden pocket of her dress. "We cannot change what's done yes-
terday," she said. "What are we to do today?"

"What can we do?"

"You say the Shards are safe for now, and that the demon
will come only at night."

Juba nodded, slowly. "When I had the Shards, I felt the darkness behind them. I don't understand what it is, but it made

me open the gate. It came from the shadows. I think that means
they're stronger at night."

It wasn't much, but it was something. "We have to assume
the worst, that the demon will come tonight." What could it
do? What was it capable of? Selene shook the questions away
and looked up at the sun, rising toward noon. "So we have the
day."

"I should double the guards," Juba said.

Selene nodded. It was a commanding act, but if the demon
came—*when* the demon came—would doubling the guards
only double the deaths at their door? And if they stopped it this
night, what would come of the next? Or the next after that?
Thrasyllus said that Tiberius was with the demons now. What
would happen if he could bring Roman armies to field? How
many lives would be lost before the end finally came? "It's not
enough," she said. "It buys us time. Little else."

"We should get Ptolemy out of the palace," he said, nodding
as if in agreement with her. "Take him some place safe."

"Aren't you listening?" Selene grabbed his arms and turned
him to face her. "It's not enough, Juba. No place will be safe
if they gather the Shards. There will be nowhere to run, nowhere to hide. They will reopen the gate. Not on accident as
we did. They'll mean to do it, and they'll bring more and more
through it. It's the end, Juba. The end for us, the end for Ptolemy." The thought of her beautiful child almost broke something in her, but she shook the pain away by waving a hand out
toward the busy city below. "It's the end for all of this, all of it,
if we let them get the Shards. We can't let that happen."

Selene's voice was fervent with determination, but all she saw
in his eyes was the despair, the familiar memory of her parents
choosing to die rather than fight. Tears were filling his eyes.
"Isn't time enough?" he asked.

She knew it then. He wasn't ready to fight. He wasn't prepared to do what needed to be done. But it had to be done. She was as sure of it as she'd been about the choice to run from that room of death in Alexandria. Only this choice wasn't about vengeance. It wasn't about herself. It was about survival—not for her, but for her beloved Ptolemy, and for Juba, whom she adored more than life itself even if he couldn't take this final journey with her. It was, in the end, about love.

She hoped he would see that in time.

Selene stepped back from him, still holding his hands in hers. She smiled, though the tears were beginning to roll upon her face. She gripped his hands when she saw the confusion and pain upon his own. "Listen," she said. "There's so much I want to say, but there's far more that needs to be done. And we don't have much time."

"Time for what?"

Selene brought a finger up to his mouth, then drew herself up to replace it with her lips. They kissed, and she felt his love run through her and give her strength. She prayed that her love would do the same for him. It would have to be enough.

She pulled away from his lips and let herself fall against his chest. After a moment his arms enwrapped her in a familiar embrace, and she closed her eyes. For a minute she lost herself there, letting his breath rise and fall against her, etching this memory into her soul.

"I'm going to leave," she finally said. It seared a hole through her heart to say it, and she wondered how she would possibly say goodbye to Ptolemy.

Selene felt his arms tense. "Leave?"

She opened her eyes and pulled just far enough away to meet his eyes—but not so far that she left his arms. "Today. Within hours. I'll find some place safe for Ptolemy, somewhere away from the palace. And you'll book me passage on the next boat to Rome."

Juba blinked. "Rome?"

Selene nodded even as she worked it through in her mind. "We'll make it known that I've gone. That I went in haste. You'll order the guards away if anyone comes for the vault. No one needs to die."

"I don't understand. You just said we can't let the demon get the Shards."

"No, my love. We can't."

"But if we leave the vault—" His voice cut off as at last he realized what she meant to do. "You intend to take them with you, don't you? And you want the demon to know you've gone. You mean to run. To Rome."

"I'll take them with me," she said.

"I'm coming with you to Rome, Selene. I helped start this, I'll help end it."

Selene shook her head. "I know you would, my love. But you can't. You're the king of Mauretania. You cannot leave your kingdom."

"And you're the queen," he said, his eyes pleading.

She smiled at his bravery, at his willingness to try again despite all that the Shards had taken from him. He was a good man, a great man. The world needed more leaders like him. "I'm a queen, yes. But we both know the place of queens in this world. I could leave, you could take another, it wouldn't matter."

Juba's eyes widened in shock, and he began to protest.

"To us it would matter," Selene said quickly. She kissed him, then let him hold her in his arms once more. She thought of how her mother had fought to be respected in a world of men, and she thought of her own struggles to become the queen that she was. A good queen, she told herself. She'd been that. And it hadn't been for nothing. But it was still true: Juba was more important as a king than she was as a queen. Perhaps the world would not always be that way, but it was the way the world was for now. She couldn't leave their kingdom in chaos . . . or their son without a father.

She pulled herself back from him again. "You know it's true," she said. "You know there's no other way."

Her husband's body still seemed tense with defiance, but she could see in his damp eyes his resignation, his realization that there was no other choice. "So you'll take the Shards to Rome," he finally said.

She squeezed his hands in reassurance, hoping she would one day recall the feel of his skin against hers. "Rome is only a stop on the way."

"Then where?"

"To where they least expect it," Selene said. "To Rhodes, Juba. I'll save Lapis. And then, by the gods, I'll take them to Jerusalem."

"Jerusalem? That's what Tiberius wants. Thrasyllus said—"

"They want the Shards. And I'm not bringing them there to give them up." She took a deep breath. "I'm bringing them to fight."

6

The Mount of Aaron

PETRA, 5 BCE

In the first days after the legion had come to Petra, Miriam had made many excuses not to take her turn watching the tomb of the Ark. She had volunteered to cook and clean, she had volunteered to be the one to get water from the town cisterns every day, and she had even volunteered to wash clothes, a chore she hated. Pullo had said nothing, though Vorenus had finally raised an eyebrow at her when she suggested that she probably ought to spend the next day scrubbing the chimney of the little two-room house they shared.

It was difficult for her to admit to herself, but the Romans unnerved her. She'd lived her whole life thinking of them as enemies, thinking them the biggest threat to the Ark, the reason that she would never meet her parents. And now they were here, camped close beside the tomb hiding the Shard for which her parents had died.

Worse, Miriam could not stop thinking about the one Roman she'd met: Abdes Pantera, who'd shown her how better to shoot with her bow, and given her an arrow besides.

Some moments she chided herself for not shooting him when she had the chance. No one would have known, after all. Other moments she hated herself for thinking such thoughts.

One way or another, though, she'd thought often of the

lopsided smile on his face. And the more she'd thought of it, the more she wanted to see him again, and the more she felt foolish for being so afraid to go near the Roman camp. Pantera was not a bad man, she was certain. Neither were Pullo and Vorenus, who'd been great legionnaires in their day.

So late one day, after all her chores were done, with Pullo and Vorenus away at the tomb keeping watch on the Ark, Miriam picked up her waterskin, her bow, and her arrows—including the one Pantera had given her—and set off for the southern gate of the city and the Roman encampment that lay beyond it.

Pullo and Vorenus had explained to her more than once that the walls of Petra were not nearly as massive as those in the great cities of the world. There simply was no need for enormous man-made fortifications when those of nature were so profoundly adequate: the foreboding mountains that surrounded the city, and the stretching wastelands of deserts that surrounded the mountains in turn, were more than enough to deter a true invader army. So Petra's walls needed only to be able to repel the smaller bands of raiders who lived off the prey they could scavenge along the edges of the city's immediate control.

Still, the walls were impressive enough to Miriam, who'd known no other city. They were as tall as two homes, and half as thick, with higher towers at their gates and angles. Many of the biggest buildings in the city, like the massive temple of Dushara, were painted white, but the walls were left as natural stone. Somehow this made them even more daunting to Miriam's mind: at times they looked almost as if they'd grown up from the earth, or extended out from the feet of the high mountains above.

The gates of the city were open, as they usually were during the day, and no one stopped the nineteen-year-old girl as she passed through the unbarred path and into the Roman camp just beyond.

Miriam was struck at once by the smells of the place: the cooking fires smoking unfamiliar foods, the chalky dust floating like a haze between the tents, the horses fouling noisy corrals, and, above all, the heavy smells of the men. The legion had only been encamped for a week, but already the air was thick with their sweat and leather. The camp was a noisy place, too, a constant churn of movement as men marched or labored or rested with a rhythm that reminded her of music.

Romans, Vorenus had once told her, were nothing if they were not organized, and Miriam quickly saw the truth of it as she made her way between the tents. The camp was laid out in careful grids, broken down by the roles of the legionnaires. It did not take her long to find the place of the archers, where bow staves stood in racks beside bowyers, and men counted out sheaves from barrels of arrows.

Pullo and Vorenus had worked hard to teach her every language they knew, and Miriam chose Latin rather than common Greek to ask a few of the relaxing bowmen about the whereabouts of Abdes Pantera. The first two didn't know him, but a third sitting beside his tent with a plate of food did. The man squinted his eyes at her when she asked about the archer, then stabbed a chunk of pork with his knife. Lifting it up, he used the skewered meat to point toward the mountains south and west. "He likes to wander," he said. "He's gone to whatever is up there, I think."

Miriam followed his vague gesture and in a moment recognized the mountain that he was referring to: a steep-sided peak of ragged rocks and cliffs, it stood sentinel on the horizon, between the high basin of the city and the stretching deserts far below. From a perch at its high summit came the tiniest shimmer of white stone.

Miriam glanced up at the morning sun, calculated the distance of the climb in her mind, and then cinched up the quiver of arrows at her back. She nodded gratefully to the archer and thanked him in the most formal Latin she knew. His eyes widened a bit, but his mouth cracked into an earnest smile missing several teeth. "You are most welcome, my lady," he said.

The Roman camp was set beside the caravan road to Sabra, and Miriam hurried over to join it, knowing the path well as she followed it south, glad that she'd brought the water as the sun rose into the deep blue of a cloudless sky. The road skirted the farming terraces along the base of the mountains, not far from one of the many dry channels that crossed the basin floor like veins upon a leaf. Though parched now, the channels would run with a fierce roar when the seasonal rains came into the mountains.

The city depended on those rains, as every Nabataean knew. When the sky opened up, nature's water courses would roar down toward Petra only to be fed into an elaborate system of channels and dams. Even the mountain walls around them were made to serve the people: they were carved out not just with the tombs for the dead, but with cisterns for the living. The system halted the destructive impact of the floods, but more importantly it preserved the life-giving waters for the dry months of the year. This far from the city, though, the streams would still run wild, and from an early age Miriam had been taught by Pullo and Vorenus never to walk in a dry channel, even when there was no cloud in the sky: rain falling in mountains beyond her sight could still flow and funnel into a flash flood on the basin floor.

Two hours after she started down the road, Miriam crossed a deep ravine where three dry channels came together, and then, tacking to her right, she left the more traveled caravan road and started up the steep and rocky track toward the summit of the Mount of Aaron.

It was a warm day but not a hot one, and Miriam's legs were accustomed to hiking through the red rocks above Petra. Though outside of the town, this mountainside was little different from those. Her legs burned from the strenuous climb, but she made good headway, the small rock cairns that she passed reassuring her of her path as she followed the thin ribbon of a trail as it wound higher and higher among the cliffs above the receding basin.

An hour later, after a hard push up a final set of steep switchbacks, Miriam at last crested the edge of a little plateau upon which were scattered the weathered ruins of forgotten structures. At the plateau's far end arose the rocky height of the final summit itself, which was crowned by a squat, flat-roofed shrine painted white. A wind had begun to roll over the top of the mountain here, muting the world to an eerie howl as it swept through the battered ruins around her, and Miriam gazed at them as she passed by, her mind absently wondering about their makers and their purposes as she recaught her breath.

Now at last she saw the Roman archer: his hair flowing in the steady wind, he was standing beside the shrine, and he was looking half away from her, as if someone had called his name. He was raising his hand to his head, shielding his eyes from either the high sun or the dust carried upon the wind. His bow was still strapped to his back.

Miriam thought about calling out to him, but with the wind she doubted he would hear. So she shrugged her load with her shoulders and continued on, wondering why the weight at her back seemed lessened.

Only in that moment, with her mouth caught between a smile and a frown, did she finally see that Abdes Pantera was not alone. She stopped walking and stood in the decayed ruins below the summit, frozen in terror.

The track Miriam was following wound around the craggy hill of the summit to a sharp cleft, through which stairs had been carved that would lead up to the top and the ancient shrine. There was another man there, and even at a distance she could see that he was no Roman: he wore the desert garb of an outlaw, and in the moment before she lost sight of him she saw that he had a short blade in his hand.

Bandits. Thieves. Murderers.

She knew enough to know they never traveled alone, and her eyes darted through the ruins around her as her heart pounded in her chest. Seeing nothing, she scanned the rocks around the summit as quickly as she could.

At last she saw the second man. He wasn't coming up the old stairway with his companion. Instead, he was climbing the rocky side of the summit, right in front of her, right behind Pantera.

Miriam wanted to scream out, but the wind pressed against her like a stern hand, somehow seeming even louder than it had been. There was no way that her small voice could be heard, much less understood. She'd found the young Roman archer, but for a frightened moment she was certain she'd only found him to watch him die. She thought about running, about trying to slip away lest the bandits see her and come for her, too.

But then she remembered her bow. And she knew she could never run. Pullo and Vorenus never ran. And her parents never had, either.

Without thought, one hand was making a fist around the grip of her bow while the other was reaching back for an arrow. Her eyes didn't leave the man climbing up behind Pantera. Her fingers nocked the arrow to the string, and her feet took position, one foot before the other. Her breathing stopped, she measured the wind, and just as the bandit came up over the edge she loosed.

The shaft lanced through the air, its song quickly lost to the wind, but it sailed down and to the right of her target—just as her shots had done in the wadi—and snapped on the rocks beside the bandit as he lifted himself onto the summit. Miriam cursed, reaching for another arrow, but the bandit was already onto his feet and rushing at Pantera, a knife glinting in his hand.

The Roman flinched, turned, and even at a distance Miriam saw his eyes go wide when he saw the bandit. He reacted quickly, spinning away from the lunge that was aimed at his ribs. The knife met air, and Pantera staggered away on the rocks. He managed to pull his bow from his back, and he used the wooden length as a kind of staff to keep the bandit at bay.

Miriam had another arrow in her fingers, and she nocked it to the taut string.

Pantera deflected a strike with the wood.

She took a deep breath.

He deflected another blow, but he was losing his balance.

She let the air out of her lungs.

He was falling, down to the ground, out of her view.

Don't rotate your elbow, she told herself. *Don't.*

The bandit was rising up as Pantera went down, and in that moment the wind abruptly died upon the mountaintop. Her arm as steady as if she were shooting at a sack of corn, Miriam loosed the arrow and watched it slice through the air, straight and true, to impact in the perfect center of the bandit's back.

In the sudden stillness she heard it punch into his body with a sickening crunch. She heard him scream. He fell forward out of sight, and she heard the sound of a struggle before a cry was choked out.

Please, she thought. Please.

For long heartbeats there was nothing, then from the summit

she heard the angry cry of another voice, hard footsteps on stone, and the clear sound of a bowshot.

Miriam ran. Not away, not in the direction of safety, but in the direction of the fight.

Dodging between the crumbling lines of foundation stones, she already had an arrow to the string when she reached the base of the cleft and began leaping up the ancient carved steps toward the summit, ignoring her burning lungs as she took them two at a time.

The rock stairs made a final switchback, and then she was bursting out onto the open high ground.

"You!" Pantera gasped out.

Miriam looked to her right and saw the young archer standing next to the shrine, his bowstring drawn, the glint of an arrow pointed straight for her heart. He lowered the bow and leaned tiredly up against the white bricks beside him. Miriam relaxed her own bowstring as she hurried over toward him. "Are you all right?"

He smiled, and it was lopsided. Then he nodded down to the man facedown in the rocky dirt not far away. The arrow that he'd given her was sticking out of his back like an obscene thorn. "Thanks to you. Nice shot."

Seeing the dead man made her exhilaration start to wash away, and she felt her stomach twist and her breath catch. She looked away, back in the direction from which she'd come, and she saw the second bandit, not far from the stairs. He, too, had an arrow in his back. "I got one, too," Pantera said from behind her. "Though I wouldn't have had the chance if you hadn't been here. Do you think there are more?"

Miriam shook her head, her lungs contracting in sharp, short bursts. Her face felt numb.

She felt the Roman's hand on her shoulder, turning her away from the bodies. "Hey," he said, "let's sit down over here."

Miriam's legs felt weak, and it felt like the mountain beneath her was moving with the wind, though there was nothing but the softest touch of a breeze on the summit now. She staggered, but she moved, and the archer led her to the other side of the shrine on the summit. There was a ledge of rock there, and he gently took her bow out of her hands and sat her down upon the stone.

"Lean forward," he said. "Put your head down if you can."

Panting, Miriam did as he said, and he sat down beside her with one hand on her back. The world swam around her, and more than once she felt she would lose her stomach on the shifting ground before her, but she focused on the touch of the young man, let it hold her in place like an anchor.

After a minute or two, her breathing began to slow, and the mountain beneath her feet seemed once more a mountain: steady and unmoving.

"It's a beautiful view up here," the archer said.

Miriam took a deep breath into her lungs, blinking, and felt his hand move away. She lifted her head slowly and looked out over the steep-walled basin far below. Petra sparkled like a jewel in the distance. The Roman tents were dots against its walls. "It is," she managed to say.

"You must come here a lot."

She took another deep breath, feeling stronger. "Not often," she said. "It's a sacred place."

"Oh," the archer said. "I'm sorry. Maybe I shouldn't be here, then."

Miriam shrugged. "Depends on your gods."

"This is dedicated to one?"

Miriam looked over and saw that he was gesturing to the little square building beside them. It was a simple structure, unremarkable aside from its location, just four painted walls and a single wooden doorway. "Someone is buried there, actually. It's a tomb. The mountain is named for him."

"Must have been quite a great king."

"Not a king at all," Miriam said, finally allowing herself to smile. "He was a prophet, and he led my ancestors out of Egypt. His name was Aaron."

"You're Jewish?"

His voice sounded surprised, and Miriam looked up at him with surprise of her own, not expecting that a Roman would know anything about the Jews. "My mother was," she said. "And I know the stories."

"My mother was, too," Pantera said.

"I didn't know there were any Jews in the Roman armies."

"The Romans will take just about anyone who will serve," the archer said, laughing a little to himself. He nodded down toward the encampment far below. "You'll find many gods down there, but we're all one in the legion."

"You're from Rome?"

"Not at all. I was born in Sidon, but my father is a trader. He knows which way the winds are blowing. And they blow for Rome. That's the future. Some of my father's friends even say that Augustus Caesar is the Messiah who will unite the world, but that doesn't make sense to me. Unless Caesar is secretly a Jew."

The young man winked at her in amusement, and Miriam allowed him a smile. The idea that the Roman emperor was Jewish was indeed truly preposterous. He had taken an iron-fisted control over Jerusalem, pressuring both King Herod and the Jewish high priests to bow to his will. As he did with King Aretas in Petra, Augustus seemed to believe that no man should rule without his consent, as if he were truly the son of the god that Rome had declared his adopted father to be. In fact, his uncompromising pro-Roman policies throughout Judaea, and the legions that he had put in place to enforce them, had done more than anything else to reinvigorate Jewish dreams of a Messiah who would, above all else, deliver them from Roman rule. Though she knew too much of the truth to partake in the ritual observances of the small community of Jews in Petra, she was still close enough to them to have heard of the past glories of Israel and its present plight: so many people, it seemed, were waiting for someone to come and destroy Rome, to bring God's kingdom on earth.

That it hadn't happened didn't seem to affect their faith that it would, and Miriam knew that she could not speak to them of the real truth, the real reason no Messiah had come and none ever would: God was dead, and one of the few pieces of Him that remained sat in the empty tomb that she and Pullo and Vorenus would guard for the rest of their lives.

"No," she said, "I don't think Caesar is the Messiah."

"I don't think there really will be one," Pantera said, his voice suddenly serious. "I think we're supposed to save ourselves, make our own way in the world. And Rome . . . well, if you serve in the legion long enough then they'll let you be a full citizen." The archer grinned mischievously. "Don't tell anyone, but I lied about my age to enlist as soon as I could."

Miriam nodded, as if this made all the sense in the world. Then, without really knowing why she was doing it, she held out her hand. "I'm Miriam," she said.

The archer smiled and leaned his bow against his side in order to take the offered hand. "Abdes Pantera," he said as she clasped it. Then his cheeks blushed. "But I guess I'd told you that before, didn't I?"

Miriam nodded, releasing his grip. Her gaze drifted down and caught sight of his weapon, which was chipped and cracked from where it had stopped the bandit's knife. "Your bow," she whispered.

"Hmmm?" Pantera took a moment to look away from her, then he lifted the bow so they could more closely examine the damage. "Oh. Well, I don't think it was made for that," he said.

Miriam allowed herself a light laugh. "No, it wasn't."

The Roman sighed and stood, offering his hand to help her to her feet. "I guess this means only one thing," he said, his lopsided grin returned. "If we run into any more trouble, you'll have to be the one to take care of it. Are you okay to walk now?"

"I think so," she said, "but I'm not sure I want to see them again."

"Me neither," he said, though from the calm steadiness of his voice she was sure that these were not the first dead men that the archer had seen. "But I need to just check the bodies really quick. Stay here."

He left, and Miriam stood beneath the sun, beside the tomb of Aaron, staring down at the city.

Pantera came back only a few minutes later. He was still grinning. "All set," he said. "Let's walk down together. We can send some other men to clean the mess. And if anyone asks, do you want to tell them I rescued you?"

Miriam smiled in earnest. "Not a chance," she said. "I'll see to it that everyone in your camp knows how Abdes Pantera of Sidon was saved by a girl."

The young man sighed in mock pain.

It was Miriam's turn to grin mischievously. "Give me some more arrows, though, and I might be persuaded to tell them that I only made my second shot because you taught me not to rotate my elbow."

"Deal," he said, looking proud.

Miriam nodded, shook his hand, and then took a few steps before she realized that he was looking at the shrine still. His eyes were closed and his lips were moving silently.

After a moment, he opened them. His eyes looked like they might be wet. "Aaron," he said, "the brother of Moses. Do you think it's true? Do you think he really passed through here? That it all really happened?"

"I know it did." Miriam looked down to Petra, down toward the distant place where the Ark of the Covenant rested in the silent dark. "Our people call this the Valley of Moses," she said.

Pantera stared after her. "The Valley of Moses," he repeated. "From the Exodus. The home in the wilderness."

Miriam only nodded. Then she raised her arm and pointed to the prominent mountain against which Petra was built, the one that loomed up over the tomb of the Ark. There were two great stone obelisks upon it, lifting skyward like horns. "And that," she said, her voice quiet, "that is his mountain."

7

The King and the Demon

In the silence of an empty court, Juba sat on his throne. The curtains behind him were all pulled back, and the welcoming breeze of a moonless black night flickered the tongues of the two lit braziers that sat to either side of the raised dais. The little light they managed cast dancing shadows across the open space before him, the negative images of the twinned seats of the king and queen.

No, Juba thought. Not twins. Not anymore. Not while one sat as empty and lifeless as the room's swept floor of tiled stone.

Selene leaving was the right thing to do. It was the only thing they could do. He was sure of that.

And yet this night felt like death. It felt like a hole had been cut through to his heart, as if it had been stripped out of him. He'd cried when they'd made the decision. He'd cried when she'd held little Ptolemy in her arms and told the squirming boy that she had to go away for a while. He'd cried again when they'd packed up the Shards they had and she'd turned to go.

And he had cried every hour since.

The chest in which they had kept the Palladium of Troy and the Aegis of Zeus all these years sat in the middle of the chamber before him. Its lid was open, laying bare an empty space that felt like a mirror of his own body. All that was left was a terrible void where he'd once been full and sure.

How had it come to this?

He'd been sixteen when he'd found the Trident of Poseidon. The old priest who'd kept it—Syphax had been his name, Juba remembered—was the first man he'd ever killed. He didn't do the killing back then, but he'd ordered it just the same. Ordered it to preserve the secret, to hold the power, to better prepare for vengeance against Rome.

How many had died on that journey? There was Syphax, and then the man who'd carried out that killing, Laenas, had died on his behalf in Alexandria. Juba himself had killed his own loyal slave Quintus, the first time he'd used the Trident of Poseidon to take a life. And there were so many others whose names he didn't know, but whose souls weighed on him in dreams turned to nightmares. The old craftsman who'd helped to repair the Trident. The innocent men on the trireme at sea, when he'd first truly engaged the enormous power of the Shard. Then the hundreds who died at Actium by that same divine strength. The men beneath Alexandria when he'd tried to find the Ark. The men he'd slaughtered when, for a moment, he'd had possession of that artifact's enormous might. Caesarion had been among those, he knew: the half-brother of Selene, massacred by his hand. And the nameless, faceless Cantabri he'd destroyed in a heartbeat when he'd taken their lives in escaping from Vellica.

All dead. A number beyond counting.

And nothing compared to what he'd brought into this world in Carthage.

He rarely allowed himself to think on that night—the terror was too real—but now, as he sat alone in the throne room of Numidia, he forced himself to remember it all.

Rome had taken so much from him—his father, his homeland—yet back then Juba was finally beginning to let his thirst for vengeance go.

Then he'd learned what Tiberius had done to Selene while Juba was a captive in Vellica. The idea of it made Juba want to spit even now, even so far away from the act.

Tiberius had raped her. Juba knew there was no medicine to take away the memory of that horror, but he'd thought that vengeance might be a salve for the wound upon her soul. He couldn't take away the pain of what she'd experienced, but he could give her a chance for revenge. He could return to her the power that Tiberius had taken away.

And yes, Juba admitted to himself, he'd done it in his own rage.

He remembered placing the four Shards at his feet in the night-dark temple of Ba'al Hammon in Carthage, near the pit where the worshippers of that god had once burned their own children alive. The Trident of Poseidon, the Lance of Olyndicus, the Palladium of Troy, and the Aegis of Zeus. He remembered putting on the Aegis, feeling the warmth of that armor upon his chest, and then he remembered drawing the Shards to himself, one by one, summoning their enormous powers.

Darkness overwhelmed so much of his memory then. Not a blankness of not remembering, but a shadow that was a will not his own. It had taken hold of him as he'd held the Shards. It had drawn him on, directed him, and he'd pulled forth from that shadow a power that stood triumphant upon his heart long before he knew what he had done.

He'd opened a gate to Hell.

Three demons had entered the world. And if not for the sacrifice of Isidora—one more death upon the ledger of his life— far more would have come through.

The darkness had controlled him, but he knew he'd had a

choice. He'd always had another path before him, and he'd not taken it. All along.

And so all of it, from the day he'd found the Trident to this night alone—all of it—was his fault.

The softest hush in the shadows stirred him from his memories, and Juba raised his head. He let out a long breath into the darkness. "I've sent everyone else away," he said into the darkness. "We are alone."

The demon drifted into view from the far corner of the room ahead of him, slipping silently out of the darkness to stand, half in the black and half in the feeble light of the lamps. It was the woman, or at least the one who seemed made in a woman's image. She wore pale, ghostly cloth over her alabaster skin. It shimmered gently. Her hair was the color of golden thread, falling in slivers of shadow over her delicate brow. Her eyes were dark pools that swallowed everything—the light, and, for a moment, his soul.

She was perfect, even more beautiful than he remembered.

"I remember you," she said.

Her voice was a whispered song, and it brushed over Juba like a feather upon his skin. "And I know you," he said.

Her face was a balance of symmetry, her smile showed precise lines of teeth. "You brought me here," she said. "You opened the way."

Juba swallowed hard. "I didn't really know what I was doing. I wouldn't have done it if—"

"Oh, I don't think you mean that," she said, cutting him off with what seemed a whispered rebuke. "I think you knew. You wanted it. In your heart. Vengeance." Her face lifted, as if she was scenting the still air. "For a woman, was it?"

"I'm done with that. It's over."

"I'm certain she was lovely. A pity she's not here."

Juba stood, and he made careful steps down from his throne

to stand behind the empty chest. "Selene is gone," he said, and not for the first time tonight he wondered if he would ever see her again.

"So she's run away," the demon said. She pursed her lips, then ran her tongue across them. "I'd heard as much, but I needed to see if it was true."

"You'll not find her. And the Shards are gone, too." Juba kicked over the chest, letting it fall open toward her. "You'll never find them, either."

The demon glided forward, her hips a rhythmic sway. Her eyes rocked from his to the empty chest and back. They were unreadable and blank, like the eyes of the sharks that he'd seen fishermen pull from the bay. "I didn't just come for them. I came for you, too, Father."

"Don't call me that."

"You brought me into this world." Her head lowered as her gaze moved down over his body, then she looked up and smiled. It was a look of unbridled lust. Even his wife had never looked at him that way. "I've learned so much since then. I work for Empress Livia now, did you know that? One of her maidens. She calls me Acme."

"I'm not your father. I opened the gate. But I didn't want to. I—"

She slid up to him, smooth as silk drawn across glass. "I feel like I owe you something," she said. "You brought us. You want us. You want me."

The smell of her filled his head. It was the scent of roses after a rain. "You're a demon," he managed to say.

Her head shifted to one side. "A harsh word for something greater than you."

"Greater?"

"You're made in our image, Juba of Numidia. You and your kind. You're copies."

"Copies?"

"Oh, yes," she said. "But imperfect ones. Images seen through a broken mirror." She looked him up and down once more. "But you'll see that I'm not flawed."

"You're perfect, Acme."

She was closer, her face rising up toward his. "Yes. Perfect. In every way."

"Perfect," he repeated, knowing it was true.

"Yes," she breathed.

"But you're not Selene."

The blade in his hand was not a long one. He had not dared to imagine he could hide even a small dagger. At best, he thought, he could hide a short knife. So he'd sharpened it. Then he'd carefully gripped it in his fist, awaiting his chance. Now that it was here, he didn't hesitate. While the demon had been looking into his eyes, he'd spun the blade into readiness. Then he'd punched it forward, burying it in her gut.

The demon screamed, a high-pitched and piercing shriek, and her hand shot up, slapping him away from her.

As if he'd been flung by several men, Juba flew backward through the air. He crashed against the steps of the raised dais, grunting with the impact. The knife skittered away into the dark.

The demon hissed, and her fingers felt up the wound at her belly. Juba, his head spinning as his hands and feet scrambled for purchase on the stone, saw that the lamplight wetly reflected off her fingers when she drew them away. He saw, too, that the nails upon her pale fingers were long. And they sharpened to a point, like a hand of tiny daggers, or the talons of some deft beast.

But she can bleed, he thought. And if she can bleed, she can die.

Until this moment, he'd actually doubted that it could be so. Perhaps Selene had a chance after all.

The demon stared for a moment at the dampness upon her sharp-nailed fingers, then she stretched out her neck and smiled at him across the shadows. "You're a fool," she spat. "More clever than I suspected, but still a fool."

Her hand lowered to her side, and she crouched as if preparing to pounce. If she felt pain, she showed no sign of it.

Juba's feet finally landed solidly on the stone beneath him, and he kicked himself up the steps toward the thrones as she lunged forward with a scream. Her fingers scratched across the stone just inches from his feet, grating in the dark.

Juba lashed out with his left foot, kicking her across the face. Her head turned with the blow, but she came onward, hissing as she sprang up to land upon him just as he reached the top of the dais.

The demon's clawed fingers lunged for his throat. Juba caught one with his right hand but only managed to deflect the other: he screamed out as her nails ran furrows across his skin before sticking and plunging into the flesh of his left shoulder.

Her pale face was above his, her bone-white teeth bared as her lips peeled back in an ever-widening maw. She hissed again, and where before he'd found the scents of roses her breath now smelled of dead and rotting things.

Juba's free hand fumbled upward to try and grab her hand and pull it away, but the nails pressed harder into him, twisting. His left arm went limp and fell back. "It could have been different," she sneered. "It didn't need to end like this. You could have helped me."

"Never," Juba gasped. Each breath brought new jolts of pain from where her nails had dug into him. "Never again."

"The girl has gone to Rome. The city is talking of it. Where is she taking the Shards? Tell me."

"No," he panted. "Never."

She ground against the bones of his shoulder, and the agony became a white flash of fire that struck away his breath and forced him to close his eyes as his heartbeats tolled the time of his suffering.

At last the demon stopped probing and Juba coughed in contorted pain. "Please," he managed, "I can't—"

"You can, and you will, or I will begin to tear apart your softer pieces." Her tone was idly threatening, as if she was in no hurry at all. "And if that still fails to persuade you, there's always the boy. Ptolemy is it?"

Juba's eyes widened. "You don't know—"

"Where he is?" For a moment her black eyes registered something that might have been pity. "You fool. I know exactly where he is. Tell me where she's taken the Shards."

"You wouldn't—"

One of her fingers twitched. "Tell me."

Juba focused his resolve, then he painfully lashed upward with his knee, trying to get her off, fighting for a chance to survive, but she spun away from the thrust. Spinning on her grip in his skin, her feet scampered across the stone like the legs of a crab until she loomed over the top of him.

Juba screamed, high and raw and ragged, and in that moment the door of the throne room finally opened.

The demon looked up, shrieked in anger, then twisted and shoved herself away from him. One of her hands took one last swipe at his face, ripping jagged lines across his cheek, but the wound was not deep.

Arrows sang out in the chamber, whistling over him to clatter and break upon the empty thrones. He heard the demon hiss once again, and then he rolled over and looked up to see her shadow disappearing over the edge of the balcony beyond the open window.

The footsteps of his guards were rushing forward. "My lord!" one called out.

"I ordered you away," Juba said. He started to pull himself to his knees.

"There were screams, my king. You're wounded."

Juba waved him off. "Just pursue her," he ordered. "Don't try to fight her. Just see that she gets aboard a ship. See that she leaves Mauretania."

The guard hesitated. "My lord, you don't want us to—"

"No," Juba said. There was enough blood on his hands. "Don't try to fight her. Go. Now."

He heard the men snap to salute, then he heard their feet rushing away.

When they were gone, Juba knelt in the darkened hall between the empty thrones of Mauretania. Alone, he would await the dawn. Alone, he would weep for what he'd done, and for what he'd failed to do. And alone he would await the safe return of the son he'd had with the one true love of his life.

She had a chance. He knew that now. She had a chance, and the demon would pursue her, away from her husband and her child, just like Selene wanted. It was all that they could do, and he had to hope that it would be enough.

The blood dripping from his shoulder and face made a pool about his knees, but Juba did not notice it.

He only knew that he was alone.

Alone. Always and perhaps forever.

Alone.

8

The Road to Jerusalem

No one had welcomed them when they arrived in Judaea. This seemed hardly unusual to Thrasyllus, but he'd never been anyone worthy of such honors. He was only a mere scholar. Through all his reading he'd never heard of celebrations over the arrival of a scholar—not even one who was the head of the Great Library itself, as Didymus was. Their more politically powerful companions aboard the ship from Alexandria, however, were bothered by the lack of a greeting waiting for them in the new port that Herod had built.

Antipater in particular was clearly very distressed. Herod had apparently sent his son a message in Rome, warmly summoning him back home to Judaea, and though Antipater had every intention of poisoning his father, he was still greatly bothered by what he considered a lack of respect. He was the heir of Judaea, he kept repeating as they began the carriage ride inland to Jerusalem. Did he not deserve pomp upon his return from Rome?

Antipater's dour mood turned to palpable fear when, late in the afternoon, they reached the outer villages around Jerusalem. Cresting a hill to first look upon they ancient city, he found his welcoming party at last: a contingent of Herod's guards, who directed them to a small home off the road.

Standing at the door was an old woman with a look of un-
ease on her face that sharply contrasted with the rich finery in
which she was clothed. She said nothing, only pressing a single
finger to her lips before moving inside through a door. Their
little party dismounted and followed: two princes, two scholars,
and two demons. The carriage was pulled around to the side of
the house. The Roman guards waited outside.

It was a modest home, Thrasyllus could see. He'd seen many
just like it, spread from one end of the Mediterranean to the
other. A main room, a kitchen, a sleeping chamber or two. Not
rich enough to have its own toilet or bath, but not so poor that
it didn't have a four-foot-high statue of some god or another—
Thrasyllus couldn't tell who the weathered standing figure was
supposed to represent—beside the entrance.

Inside, it was just as the astrologer had assumed. The main
room had sparse furnishings—a table and chairs, a chest, and a
reclining couch—but it was simple fare. There was no great
wealth here, and no inhabitants to be seen beyond the old
woman who stood in the middle of the open space, waiting for
them to enter. Beyond her was an open window, and through
it Thrasyllus could see a hillside and the edge of the ancient
walls of the city of Jerusalem.

As soon as the door shut behind, Antipater stepped forward.
"What is the meaning of this, Mother?"

The woman rushed forward to embrace the heir of Judaea,
who stiffly welcomed it, as if he was embarrassed to show af-
fection to her in front of Tiberius.

As they embraced, Thrasyllus ran through the shelves in his
mind, trying to think if he knew her name. He had been around
his former teacher long enough to know that Didymus, standing beside him, was doing the same. When his own shelves of
knowledge came up empty, he leaned toward the librarian to
ask, but already old Didymus was leaning over to whisper the

answer. "Doris," he said, his voice barely audible. "First wife of Herod."

"You shouldn't have come," Doris said to her son. "Did you not get my letter? I told you to stay in Rome."

"I received no such letter."

One of the demons—Antiphilus, the one that Antipater so often called a friend—floated around the side of the room, taking deep breaths of the air as if he was scenting for something. The demon they called Bathyllus stayed beside the door, near Tiberius and the two scholars.

Finally releasing her son, Doris shivered, though she gave no indication that she might wonder why the room had suddenly chilled. She turned to Tiberius and made an extravagant bow. "Lord Tiberius," she said. "I welcome you to Judaea."

"You knew of our coming," Tiberius replied.

"My spies at the port. As soon as I heard I rode out to meet you. I had to bribe the guards for this chance to meet. I fear I can do little more."

The eyes of Tiberius were even darker than usual. "What does Herod know?"

Antipater's face was flushed with confusion, as if he still hadn't put together the picture of the puzzle that was so readily apparent to everyone else in the room. His mother turned to look at him with a look like pity. "Your uncle is dead," she said.

"What? How?"

"His wife," Doris said. The old woman glanced back at Antiphilus, who'd taken a position behind her. "She poisoned him."

"Unfortunate," the demon said in reply. "That poison was intended for Herod. Her husband was to give it to him."

"Well it seems he learned that his wife was unfaithful to him. He threatened to tell Herod everything. So she killed him." She glared at Antipater, whose face had gone slack. "Couldn't keep your prick out of the wench, could you?"

Antipater opened his mouth to reply, but Tiberius cut him off. "Herod knows of Antipater's involvement?"

"The wench told all," Doris said. "But my once-husband doesn't want to execute yet another son. He doesn't want to believe her."

Tiberius pursed his lips and nodded thoughtfully.

"Am I to be arrested?" Antipater asked his mother.

"You're to be taken before Herod under guard."

"On what charge?"

"Conspiracy. For now. You are to answer questions."

"Then we may yet proceed," Tiberius said to Antiphilus.

The demon's eyes were blank as lifeless stones. But he nodded. "If the king has no certainty, he will surely not make an arrest. We can still proceed."

Antipater brightened up. "And if he thinks I've not done it—"

"He is quite certain you did," Doris interrupted. "He simply lacks evidence."

Evidence. Thrasyllus stared, thinking. If Herod had evidence of what Antipater was doing, he'd be arrested. Herod would live. And the plan of Tiberius and the demons to get into the temple and find the Seal of Solomon would be thwarted. But what evidence was there?

"We will still proceed," Tiberius said. "You'll deny all, Antipater. And you, my lady, will keep far away from the court."

"I am already banished from Herod's presence," Doris said.

"Good," Tiberius said. "And we will proceed. We brought more poison in case the first was not enough. It will suffice."

"I still don't understand why we can't use the Roman forces to help?"

"Because they are in Damascus under the command of

Varus, and he only desires to keep the peace." Tiberius looked hard at Antipater. "You and I know there will be rioting when Herod is dead, of course. Varus will do his part when that time comes. His legions will be summoned, and they will be brought to bear to restore order, beginning with the Temple itself."

"The Temple?" Doris asked.

"It's the heart of the city." The tone that Tiberius took made it clear he thought this the most plain of facts. "No, more than that. It's the heart of the faith of the city. It is Jerusalem's soul. It must be protected."

Antipater chewed on his lip, then nodded. "Of course," he said. "The Temple above all must be secured."

"Precisely." The son of Caesar beamed like a proud father. "You'll make a fine king. And Varus will do it when the order comes. But he will not want to put his men in harm's way without such a need. He doesn't want Herod dead. He won't understand how much better things will be with you upon the throne. Your father has had his time."

"My father is mad."

"I agree. It's remarkable that you've survived. He's killed how many of his sons?"

"Two," Doris said. She looked as if she might spit. "And a wife and her mother."

"Truly mad," Tiberius agreed. "But Varus is a general. Politics don't concern him. When the time comes, he will do what needs to be done, but the less he knows the better. We will proceed as planned."

"Everyone will suspect you," Doris said to her son.

Antipater grinned. "We have letters to say otherwise."

Letters! Thrasyllus suddenly took in his breath. Didymus turned in his direction, but no one else seemed to have noticed.

The astrologer's mind raced as the others plotted the death of a king. He remembered now. The demons had spoken at

Rhodes of the letters that they had forged to frame Antipater's rivals. If he could get those letters, he'd have evidence of Antipater's plans. *That* would be enough for Herod to arrest him. Surely. But even if Thrasyllus managed to get ahold of them, how could he, a foreign astrologer under constant watch, get them to the king of Judaea?

One step at a time, he thought. Didymus had taught him that when he'd first come to the Library. Any complex problem could be resolved once broken down into its component parts. One step at a time.

The letters would be in the carriage. The carriage was outside.

So that was the first step. Get out of this room.

Thrasyllus swallowed hard, took a breath, and then quietly turned toward the door behind him. The demon they called Bathyllus was there dead eyed and pale. The astrologer fought down revulsion, and instead tried to look scared and weak. It was, he thought, not hard to do.

"I need to go to the latrine," he whispered.

The head of the demon rocked to the side, as if asking a question.

Thrasyllus shifted his weight uncomfortably. "I need to relieve myself," he said. "It isn't far. And I've nowhere else to go. Nowhere to run."

The eyes of Bathyllus were blank. Not for the first time, Thrasyllus felt the sharp awareness that matters of living men and women were of no concern to the demons. Whether he lived or died or pissed himself on the floor simply didn't matter.

Thrasyllus set his fear into a kind of panic, and at last the demon nodded a single time and then stepped aside.

The astrologer let out his breath in genuine relief, then whispered his thanks as he walked past him, opened the door, and stepped outside. Didymus watched him go with a quizzical look on his face, but Thrasyllus didn't dare chance telling him of his plan.

Back out in the sunshine, Herod's guards were waiting, milling about outside. They looked up at him, saw who he was, and then returned to talking among themselves. It clearly didn't take long to dismiss him as a threat, Thrasyllus observed.

It was true, he supposed. He was no one important. He was no great man. He'd lived a life of regrets. And it was true, too, that he'd always been a coward. Maybe he still was. But even a coward could strike his blow, he thought. He'd made it out of the house. The next step was to find the letters. Then get them to Herod somehow.

The wagon was to his right, drawn up against the side of the little home. He took two steps in that direction before a small voice in his mind noted that the door had not immediately shut behind him. He stopped in his tracks, scuttling the dirt beneath his feet and holding his breath as he turned about as if looking for the latrine. As he did so, he saw that Bathyllus had followed him outside. The demon was quietly shutting the door, and it was turning its pale head in his direction.

The astrologer saw, too, that the latrine was on the opposite side of the house from the wagon, far to his left.

Gritting his teeth in frustration, knowing he had to keep up the charade, Thrasyllus spun on his heel and strode in that direction, hurrying as quickly as he could.

Chancing one last glance over his shoulder before he entered the little stone building, the astrologer saw that Bathyllus did not move from his position by the door where the others were talking. From there the demon could still measure what was happening inside, while keeping a clear eye on the door of the latrine. Thrasyllus smiled at the hideous thing, once more showing his gratitude, and then he was inside.

The latrine was typical of most that the astrologer had seen in the empire of Rome: like the baths, it was one of the few places where the entire cross-section of society might be found, passing time as equals on the privy. The building was simple in form. It had only a single, square room. A basin of water for the washing of hands was set against the back wall opposite him, sitting stale and quiet. To either side of that, lining the walls left and right, were the seats of the Roman latrine itself: a long, low bench with regular hand-breadth slots in its top and front— places for men to stand or for men and women to sit. Thrasyllus could hear the slow burble of hidden water within the bench, slowly seeping the human waste downhill to a deeper cut in the earth where it would be someone's foul job to collect it.

There was a man sitting on the bench, relaxed as he relieved himself, and he opened closed eyes when Thrasyllus entered. He nodded at him as if in welcome.

The astrologer managed a quick smile in return, but already he was looking around in increasing desperation, searching for some way to proceed yet finding none. Aside from the door the astrologer had entered, the only accesses in or out were two squat windows on the walls to his left and right: big enough to allow a cleansing breeze to pass through the otherwise fetid air, but high enough to still provide privacy for those in the latrine.

Thrasyllus hurried to the one opposite the man, being careful not to step into one of the dank privy holes as he hopped up onto the stone bench. He reached up the wall, desperately trying to reach the window, but it was several inches too high.

The other man said something in a language that the astrologer could not understand, though he was relatively certain the man was asking what on earth he was doing.

It was a question whose answer Thrasyllus didn't know. He jumped, scraping his fingers along the stone lip of the window. They came away dusty. There was no way he could grip well enough to pull himself through, even if he had the strength to get up.

"Leaving?"

Thrasyllus spun in fright at the voice, and he breathed a sigh of relief when he saw the older scholar backlit as he stood against the doorway. "Can't explain," the astrologer said. He'd never told Didymus about the letters. There simply wasn't time. "But trust me."

The head of the Great Library of Alexandria looked over to the other man in the latrine, who was looking both confused and concerned, and he gave him the slightest of nods. Then he hurried over to the wall where Thrasyllus was and put one leg up beside his. He intertwined his fingers and braced them against his knee, making a kind of step. "Up and out," the astrologer said. "Hurry."

Thrasyllus started to lift his foot into Didymus' hands and brace himself for the jump. As he did so, the older scholar looked back over to the third man in the room and said something to him in his language. The other man chuckled and nodded knowingly.

"What did you tell him?" Thrasyllus asked.

"Told him your wife beats you and you're trying to get away to pay a debt."

Thrasyllus shrugged. "I do have debts," he said. And then together they were lifting and jumping and he was up and out the window, scrambling down off the wall outside.

"I'll try to delay them," he heard Didymus say. "But be quick!"

The astrologer didn't need to be reminded. He was already moving around to the back of the latrine, peering around the corner to see if he could see anyone. Satisfied that he was out of view from the front of the little house where the others were, he scampered through the dirt as quietly as he could, darting between walls and wagons until he reached the corner of the house.

Through the open window at the back of the house he could hear them talking inside. Antipater was complaining about the failure of his aunt to poison his father. Tiberius was scheming for the future, for their latest plan to murder Herod.

The demon Antiphilus was close. Thrasyllus could feel the presence of him in the abrupt chill in the air. He'd scented the air back in the room, and for all the astrologer knew it would only take a single sniff for him to realize that Thrasyllus was outside where he wasn't supposed to be. He had no choice, though. It was a risk he would simply have to take.

Crouching low, moving slower this time, Thrasyllus crept across the building below the window, holding his breath when he heard the voice of Tiberius growing louder.

He reached the corner. Peeking around it, he saw the carriage, sitting unattended in the middle of the street that ran there. Then, glancing back, he saw the head of Tiberius just coming into view at the window. Swallowing his gasp, Thrasyllus spun around to the side of the building and sprinted for the door of the carriage.

. . .

He hurried as fast as he could, but by the time he was reaching the latrine he could hear Didymus talking to the demon. Coming around the last building, Thrasyllus could see that the two of them were out in the middle of the street. Didymus was on the ground, holding his ankle and complaining that he'd twisted it on one of the little stones there.

It wasn't much of an excuse, but it had Bathyllus delayed for the moment as the creature turned its black eyes from the door of the latrine to the man moaning at his feet.

The astrologer bolted across the open space to the back of

the latrine building. There was a short ladder there, meant for helping with the process of cleaning the privy, and Thrasyllus quickly propped it up against the wall below the window and clambered up and in.

The third man was gone, and the latrine was empty as he dropped down onto the seats. Then he jumped down, his feet hitting the tiled floor in the same moment that the shape of the demon filled the bright doorframe.

The astrologer smiled in genuine relief, nodded, and then straightened his clothing. "I had to go," he said.

Bathyllus said nothing, but moved aside when Thrasyllus approached. The astrologer tried hard not to hold his breath as he stepped back into the street and began walking back toward the little house. He felt the eyes of the demon following him intently.

Didymus was still sitting in the road, and the astrologer stooped to help him up. As he did so, he pulled the little bundle of letters from his pocket and pushed them into the librarian's stomach. Surprised, Didymus fumbled with them for only a moment before burying them away from sight.

"To the guards," Thrasyllus whispered as he pulled the older man to his feet. He nodded to where one of them was already walking over to see if he could help. He kept his voice low, but it was full of his every desperation. "To Herod."

9

THE BLOOD-RED MOON

RHODES, 5 BCE

For all that she had cried since leaving Mauretania, for all that she had despaired over leaving Juba and her beloved Ptolemy behind, Selene felt something of her sorrows melt away as she climbed up to where the Colossus of Rhodes lay fallen, half buried in the night-dark hillside upon which he'd once stood. It felt at last as if she was doing something good, as if she might make some small measure of peace with the wrongs she felt she'd committed.

Hidden from view between the great trunks of the statue's broken legs, the queen of Mauretania slipped her traveling bag into a shadowed recess where one of the bronze plates of the Colossus had been twisted open against the ground. Then, looking around to be sure she was alone, she pulled the Palladium of Troy from a small satchel at her side.

The little statue had been as tall as her forearm when she'd stolen it from the Temple of the Vestal Virgins in Rome. The top third of it was gone now—broken when Tiberius had raped her on the Roman frontier at Vellica. Now the black stone once hidden at its center was exposed, allowing her to directly access its otherworldly power to control Air.

It had been years since she'd touched the power, and she hesitated to do so now. The last time they'd tried to use the power, at Carthage, they had brought together all four of the Shards in their possession—the Palladium and its power over Air, the Aegis of Zeus and its power over Life, the Trident of Poseidon and its power over Water, and the Lance of Olyndicus and its power over Fire. They had hoped to control the combined Shards, but instead it seemed as if the power they'd unleashed had held a will of its own. Through Juba a gate to Hell had been opened, and three demons had been unleashed upon the world. Her friend Isidora had died to close that gate. Juba's life had nearly been lost, too.

Selene shivered, remembering the smells of death and burned flesh, before she managed to shake the dark thoughts away.

Gods and demons didn't matter right now, she tried to tell herself. All that mattered here was the raw power, and her ability, she hoped, to control it once again.

Selene stood, rocking her shoulders and resettling the weight of the metal breastplate that she wore beneath her loose-fitting dress. It was the armor of Alexander the Great, but far more than that, the black stone mounted at its center marked it as a Shard: the Aegis of Zeus, with the power to control and extend and preserve Life—as it had for Alexander, and as it had for her husband, too.

These were the only Shards they had left now. The Lance and the Trident had been taken by the demons at Carthage. It was only by a miracle that she'd been able to use the Palladium and the Aegis to whisk them away to safety.

A miracle.

She sighed at the thought. There were no miracles. Not really, for there were no gods left to perform them. That meant there were only the acts of people like her. Selfless or selfish. Intentional or random. Each little decision reverberating out into the lives of other people like ripples on water.

So be it. She'd made her decision.

Selene took in her breath, then let it out again, focusing her thoughts. In the stillness that followed, she raised the Palladium to the Aegis of Zeus. The Shard of Life warmed against her skin, giving her strength that rushed into her and filled her as if she'd been empty, pouring more and more as she opened herself to it and drank it in. Then, slowly, she raised her right hand to the broken top of the Palladium and pressed her flesh against the blacker-than-black stone exposed there.

She fell down into it suddenly. Like a violent, rushing stream the power carried her down into the stone that was and was not her. Slipping and sliding into the pooling darkness, she struggled to grab hold of something to arrest her descent as she fell deeper and deeper into herself. She felt one of her legs lose strength, and she was dimly aware that she sank to one knee.

For a moment she thought she heard herself scream, but it was like the distant echo of thunder behind mountains.

No, she called out. *No!*

In response she heard Juba's voice, calling out from the memories of her youth, when he'd first taught her how to control the power by giving into it, by letting it ride through her. *Let go,* he had said.

But that's how it took control of him, another voice cried out in her mind. You can't let it control you.

But to fight was to die, she shot back. Like quicksand, the harder she would fight against it, the harder it would pull her down into oblivion.

In panic, straining with the effort, her mind reached out through the surrounding dark, found her grip on the Palladium, and released it.

The air flexed around her, popping as the pent-up power let go. Selene opened her eyes, panting as she stared at the Shard fallen in the grass beside her knee. She slowed her breathing into deep, steady breaths, feeling the thrumming warmth of the Shard in the breastplate.

The Aegis was a comfort. Its steady presence supported her, giving her what she needed. She remembered that from before, when she'd used it at Vellica. When she needed calm, the Aegis gave her calm. When she needed strength, it gave her strength. It had done the same for Juba, he'd said. When he was wounded it healed him. When he could fight no further it gave him the power to go on. When he was angry . . .

Selene blinked, looked up at the stars above her.

Juba had said that when he was angry, when he had thirsted most for revenge, the Aegis had fed that, too. He'd done things he couldn't remember. He'd killed and killed and killed again. All to get what he wanted.

The Aegis might not have ever seemed a threat to her, but of course it was. Used for the wrong reasons, *any* power was a threat.

From the beginning they'd been using the Shards wrong. She could see it now. She thought she'd been letting herself fall into the power of the Shard. She'd let that power carry her into itself. She'd used it, but she'd never understood it.

The darkness into which she'd fallen when she touched the Shard was not in the stone. It came not from some Heaven or Hell. The dark power she'd tapped was inside of her. The darkness that had overtaken Juba in Carthage had been inside of him, too. His rage. His despair.

The one God had wanted to give them freedom. He'd died to do so. And in the Shards they'd been given a power that was just as free. It was a power that would be shaped by their mortal, willful desires. What to do with that power was one more decision they had to make, one more ripple. She'd been making those decisions all along, each time she'd touched a Shard, but she'd never seen it so clearly before now.

Selene took in a long, deep breath of the cooling night air. When she released it from her chest, she watched the exhalation rise like a slow cloud. It drifted, thinning, then dissipated into the great nothingness between the earth and sky.

No. Not nothingness. The sky was filled with the breath of life. Hers. Her husband's. Their son's. She breathed the air of countless souls. Her mother's breath was up there, too, a whisper in the wind of the world.

Selene smiled, imagining how her mother's breath mingled with hers, how life touched life across the spans of time and space, how her parents—so long dead—were still keeping her alive.

The darkness wasn't the only source of power. There was love, too.

Selene reached down into the grass and picked up the Palladium from where it had fallen. She stood. She held it before her and stared at its broken top. The stone there was blacker than black, forever seemed to be swallowing the light, yet even so it glinted almost as if it was wet. Almost as if light were held there, trapped and yearning to get out.

No darkness lasts forever, she thought. The sun rises. Hope survives. Love empowers.

Selene thought of her mother and father, her brothers, her husband and son. She thought of laughter and love. She thought of the sun and the light that even now was within herself, as trapped as the light in the stone.

With calm certainty, Selene closed her eyes and wrapped her free hand over the Shard. The power of the darkness was there, but instead of bending herself into that pooling black and falling into it, instead of drawing it up and out into the impossible stone in her hands, she pushed herself away, up toward a pure, streaming light that she now knew had always been there, waiting.

Touching her skin, the Shards of Heaven came alive.

The Aegis gave her strength. It gave her a surety of purpose. Through it she felt the life of her breathing. She felt, too, the memory of other lives lived. Even here, she wasn't alone.

Through the Palladium she reached out into the air around her. Before she had twisted that element, churned it into winds, but now she felt it surrounding her like a calm and silent sea, at once peaceful and brooding with possible danger. She let it flow around her, beneath her, and she began to rise.

Selene opened her eyes. No wind disturbed the grass that was falling away beneath her feet. No storm clouded a sky now lit by the moon. Slowly, she turned to face the hill beyond the Colossus. She'd find the villa of Tiberius up there. And there she'd find Lapis, a prisoner because of what she had done.

Selene was done running. It was time to set things right.

. . .

It was after midnight when the daughter of Antony and Cleopatra settled out of the night sky and into the open square atrium of Tiberius' villa. She descended in silence, like a feather draped onto cloth. Her sandaled feet touching the ground, she let go of the Shard that she had held in her hands, and she quietly slipped it into the satchel that still hung at her side.

Around and through the atrium was a large garden of carefully potted plants, their leaves delicately trimmed. The colored tiles of the floor beneath her feet were freshly swept. Not far away, in the center of the atrium, a small fountain burbled in a steady rhythm.

Nothing else could be heard. Nothing else moved.

Thrasyllus had said that Lapis was being held here. But if so, where?

In the back of the villa, surely. No doubt in some cold and forgotten corner.

Selene began to make her way through the manicured atrium, thankful that the swept floors kept her footsteps light.

There was a hallway at the back of the atrium, leading out into the rear yards, and Selene hurried into its shadows. She paced along it, stopping only to peer into opened doorways or to listen at locked doors. She passed kitchens and storerooms, but no place to hold a prisoner.

The hallway ended at an arched passageway, and beyond it Selene could see an open portico that emptied out into a moonlit slope of grass. In the distance, but growing closer, she heard the whispers of two men walking outside.

Selene pressed herself into the shadows of the archway and peered around the corner to her right.

The portico was deep in darkness, backlit by the brightness of the moon. She could see little of it to her right beyond a cushioned bench facing two columns not far away. Iron rings were fixed to the columns there, and bindings of rope hung from them.

Whatever took place here, Selene was glad not to witness it.

Out in the moonlight beyond the silent reminders of torture, she saw two imperial guards making their way across the grounds, just coming into view from the darkness between a stack of hay and a small shed.

Perhaps that was where they had her?

In the same moment that the thought occurred to her, Selene heard movement to her left, on the other end of the portico. Her heart skipped a beat, expecting to see another set of guards appearing there, but for the moment she saw no one else.

The sound had been close, though.

Selene took a quick glance back at the two guards outside in the moonlight—they were still far away, and she felt sure she couldn't be seen in the shadows—then she stepped out from the passageway and began to make her way across the portico.

She could see doors across the back of the villa on this side, and she abruptly caught the scent of human waste. Her stomach curdled, but Selene pressed forward, creeping closer to the farther door, which seemed to be the source of the smells.

It was a heavy oak door, and it was bolted with iron. Swallowing her urge to be sick, Selene pressed her ear to the wood, listening.

Labored breathing. The sound of cloth scraping on stone.

The smells, the sounds . . . for a moment Selene remembered being ten years old, shoved into a dank and despairing cell with her twin brother, awaiting their turn to be paraded through Rome as a measure of Augustus Caesar's conquest of Egypt. He'd made them wear chains of gold, fetters wrought of their dead mother's hard-won treasures.

But Alexander Helios was dead. Their kingdom was lost.

Once again, Selene found herself shaking away dark thoughts.

That was the past. It was done. She couldn't forgive Rome for what it had done, but she understood now that no measure of revenge could recover what she'd lost. What mattered now was the living.

Lapis was here because of the Shards, because of her.

She'd lost Isidora to dreams of vengeance. It was long past time to start making things right.

Selene pulled away from the door and looked behind her. The two guards were close enough for her to hear that they were chatting with one another. And she could see now that their circuit would bring them around this same corner of the villa, far too close to her. If she stayed where she was, they'd see her for certain.

She took a step back toward the passageway to hide, then heard movement from that direction, too. Footsteps were echoing up through the arched passageway.

Cursing silently, Selene spun and stared at the metal latch of

Lapis' cell. It was a heavy loop of iron that slipped over a thick wooden peg on the door. There was no lock. She'd only need to lift the latch free, then pull the bolt out from the hole in the stone wall.

Her fingers wrapped around the metal, and when she strained at lifting it she felt the Shard upon her chest feeding her new strength.

The loop came up from the wood, caught for a moment, and then with the slightest of creaks it came free.

The footsteps were very close.

Concentrating, forcing herself to move slowly, Selene now pulled at the bolt, sliding it out of the stone as fast as she dared.

She could hear now that the footsteps approaching from inside the villa were from another pair of guards. She could hear them whispering now, too.

The bolt at last slid free, and with a gentle tug the door began to swing open. A new wash of smells made her eyes water and her throat constrict as she fought the urge to gag and retch, but Selene held her breath as she spun herself through and inside. She caught sight of the two guards walking out into the portico a speeding heartbeat before she pulled the oak shut behind her.

Selene froze there, huddled against the door in the sudden blackness of the cell, trying to listen past her own suddenly panicked breathing—praying they'd heard nothing, praying they wouldn't see the undone latch. Calm, she told herself. Calm.

Behind her, Lapis moaned.

On the other side of the door, the guards were approaching.

Selene looked around as if she might find something in the black to help her. Foolishness, of course. There would be nothing in the cell but the prisoner.

Groping across damp stone, she searched for Lapis and finally found her huddled against the back wall of the little room.

Her fingers touched her leg first. It was gaunt, the skin slack. Selene felt sores and open wounds, but no fetters.

Whatever they'd been doing to her, it ended now.

Lapis moaned to be disturbed, and her limbs contracted in protective instinct.

"Shhhh," Selene hushed. "I'm not going to hurt you."

The limbs froze. "My queen?"

Not anymore, Selene thought, smiling grimly in the dark. "Yes," she whispered. "Quiet now."

She heard the sound of Lapis nodding—cloth shifting on stone—and she felt her way to the woman's thin fingers and gripped them reassuringly. Just hang on, she thought.

Outside, the footsteps approached along the portico. One of the men chuckled. She heard them hail the other guards. And then she heard one set of footsteps stop just outside the door.

He'd seen it.

Selene squeezed Lapis' hand again, then she let go of her and stood. She turned to face the door. The guards had all stopped there. She could hear their voices. One man had pulled his gladius.

Calm, serene, Cleopatra Selene reached into the satchel at her side. At her feet, Lapis had gathered herself to her knees, and she was clinging to her leg.

The door shook as hands found the open latch and began to pull.

Selene's fingers found the Palladium. Her hand enclosed the Shard. "Hold on," she said.

The full, pure power of the Shard erupted outward.

Iron split. Stone fractured. Wood splintered.

The door launched from its shattered hinges, flung out into the moonlight like a child's toy thrown from the hand of a god.

The guards were blown back with it, their bodies scattered away with a sound of screams that was replaced a moment later by an ear-splitting pop as air rushed back into the void of the little cell.

Lapis was still gripping her leg, shaking. Selene dropped the Shard back into her satchel and reached down to her. Feeling the strength of the Aegis, she lifted the woman easily to her feet and put her arm under her shoulder to help hold her upright.

"It's time to go," she said.

Selene turned and strode toward the broken mouth of the cell. The two guards who'd been standing immediately outside had been crushed by the heavy door as it flew outward. They were awkwardly heaped on the ground outside, unmoving. The other two had been kicked out into the moonlight, too. They'd been slung to the ground, where they were moaning from bruises and broken bones.

Her back straight and her head held tall, Selene stepped over the debris where the door had stood. If she could get Lapis outside, she could fly away.

Heartbeat by heartbeat, the two women made their way to freedom. They crossed the portico. They started down the steps, down toward the grass below. They passed out of the shadows and into a moonlight that seemed less bright.

"Stop!"

The voice came from their right, out from where the first pair of guards had come. Selene's head snapped in that direction, but already she was feeling the shifting weight of Lapis. The other woman had seen the danger first. Even as the fifth guard loosed his arrow across the open yard, Lapis was flinging herself forward with the last of her strength.

The shaft buried itself in the woman's chest, the air in her lungs coughing out into the moonlight as the impact drove her out of Selene's grip.

Selene watched her fall in slow motion, in shock, but then

her eyes were spinning back to the distant guard. He was already lifting another arrow to the string.

As he loosed again, as Lapis slid onto her back, Selene knelt. The second arrow sailed over her head, snapping into the stone cell behind her, but already her left hand had found the Palladium.

As it did so, her right hand pulled back and struck out, a punch into the empty air. It carried across the distance—in slow time Selene could see the air compressing wave to wave, growing in power—and it impacted against the man's chest, pounding into him like a massive and unseen hammer.

She spun at her knees and backhanded another pummeling wave toward the villa's passageway behind her. The supports of the archway snapped and gave way. Bricks and wood fell. The portico cracked. It began to give way.

"My queen," Lapis gasped.

Selene let go of the Shard. As the portico was collapsing behind her, she turned back to the woman in the grass. The arrow seemed an obscene thing, rooted in her chest. Bright red blood was seeping into the tattered remnants of her fouled shift.

No. Isidora. Now Lapis. Oh gods, no.

"Thrasyllus," the dying woman managed to say, ". . . taking him to Jerusalem."

Selene nodded as she knelt. "Just stay with me, Lapis. We'll get him together."

Lapis shook her head, weakly but firmly. "No," she said. "An Ark."

Selene's mind raced with questions, but they fell away with her tears. "Just stay with me, please."

"Petra," Lapis said, her voice urgent. "Petra."

"We'll go," Selene said, gripping her frail hand. "Together."

The woman's eyes had rolled up toward the sky. They went

wide in shock, and in the same moment the light that fell upon her face was the color of blood.

All the world, it seemed, was bathed in it.

Selene looked up, and she saw that the moon, hung far above, was glowing red, fierce and full of rage.

She felt a primal fear, an animal's fright at forces it could not understand. She thought of angry gods. She thought of war and portents of doom. But more than that she thought of Lapis and Isidora and all the others who were dead because of the Shards.

"No," she said, turning away from the blood-red moon to the dying woman before her. She tore open her own dress, fingers finding buckles and unclasping them one by one. "You're not dying tonight."

The Aegis fell away, and the red light fell upon her exposed skin as she set it upon the ground. Then she gripped the blood-slick shaft of the arrow. "I'm sorry," she said, and then she yanked it free.

Lapis gasped. The wound bubbled.

Saying a prayer of hope to gods that weren't there, Selene lifted the Aegis and set it firmly upon the woman. She buckled it as best she could. One of the Romans, she saw, was rising to his feet. He was holding his head, but he was holding his sword, too.

Selene ignored him. She reached down to lift Lapis into her arms. Her hand fell into her satchel and grasped the Shard there.

Then, with a kick toward the sky and the stars and the blood-darkened moon above, they took flight.

10

The Mount of Abraham

It had been three days since they'd met Antipater's mother on the road to Jerusalem. Three days since they'd at last arrived in the ancient city of the Jews and entered Herod's great palace.

Three days, then, since Antipater had been arrested by his father and put on immediate trial with the help of Varus, the Roman governor of Syria who—by happenstance, it seemed—had been in town to inspect the garrison there.

The arrest had been shocking in its abruptness, and the trial had been shocking in its speed. The widow of Herod's brother Pheroras had confessed her affair with Antipater and their plan to poison the king. Servants had given testimony of the illicit affair. And Pheroras' widow had even brought forth what was left of the poison. Despite being the son of Caesar, Tiberius had recused himself from the proceedings in order to reassure Herod and his men of his innocence even though he'd arrived with Antipater. Thus it was Varus who had summoned a condemned prisoner and made him drink the poison in view of the court. The man died in front of them all—thrashing, seizing, coughing up splatters of blood as his eyes rolled to white. Even so, it had seemed that Varus had been inclined to have pity on Antipater, for it was a difficult thing to condemn a prince.

It was only then that Herod had produced a small bundle of

documents. In it were forged letters, in which Antipater's rival siblings seemed to incriminate themselves in the plot to poison Herod. The letters were, the court saw, brilliant matches for the handwriting of the innocent siblings: perfect forgeries only exposed for what they were by another letter, this time in the clear hand of Antipater, in which he described the entirety of the plot to his co-conspirators.

Didymus had tried hard to feign surprise. But of course he knew who those conspirators really were. He knew *what* they were. And he knew how such evidence had come into the king's possession, because it had also been three days since he'd managed to slip that same bundle into the hands of Herod's guards, after Thrasyllus had risked his life to steal it.

Herod had wanted his son executed on the spot. Varus agreed that Antipater was guilty, but as a mere governor he announced that the fate of royalty was beyond his station to decide. Antipater's fate would be determined by Caesar himself. And so Antipater was led away, screaming and weeping, to spend his days in a deep and dark cell of the palace, while letters requesting guidance were immediately sent to Rome. Antipater's co-conspirators were less fortunate. The widow of Herod's brother was sentenced to death, as were a handful of other servants. Antipater's mother was banished from the city. And Antipater's friend Antiphilus—who was said in the letter describing the plot to have been the one who procured the poison—was sentenced to immediate execution if he was ever found.

Only then had Didymus realized that while Tiberius and Thrasyllus were both in the court, the two demons who'd kept watch over them seemed to have disappeared.

They weren't gone, though. Didymus hadn't seen them, but now and again in the days since he would feel their presence in a passing chill at the back of his neck, or in a sudden breath of unexpected cold that washed into him. He had no doubt that he and the astrologer were somehow still being watched.

Even now, as he stood upon one of the balconies of Herod's palace and stared out over the ancient city of Jerusalem, he was certain that dark, unblinking eyes were out there somewhere, staring up at him.

From the room at his back, Didymus heard the sounds of Tiberius making notes on a wax tablet. The son of Caesar had been writing a great many such notes to himself, Didymus thought, though whether it served as an unusual activity for the heir to the empire, the librarian did not know. He at least suspected that Tiberius was trying to find a new path forward for his aims. Antipater's arrest had completely destroyed his plan to take control of the Temple following the assassination of Herod. The anxious tapping of his stylus on the wooden frames of the tablets or of his fingers on the top of the desk at which he sat were, like the quiet heartbroken weeping of Thrasyllus in the night, a background of noise that Didymus had grown far too accustomed to hearing since they'd arrived in Judaea. Given his own status as a veritable prisoner of Tiberius, Didymus suspected that such sounds would have been all he'd hear regardless of their whereabouts, but they were especially difficult to avoid because the storm that had recently pounded the city had kept them all inside, confined them to close quarters with the windows shuttered.

The storm, it seemed, had followed them across the sea, arriving the day after they rode through the towered gates of Jerusalem. It was an unseasonable rain, they were told, and its sudden tumult had caused the astrologer to mutter more than once about the signs of the gods—as if the very existence of the Shards of Heaven that they sought didn't invalidate both gods and divine signs.

But today the rain had finally abated. When it did, Didymus

had immediately thrown open the shutters to take in the sunlight and the city below. No matter what else was happening,
the librarian's academic mind thrilled to at last experience
Jerusalem.

He hadn't been lying to Thrasyllus back on the boat out of
Alexandria when he'd told him of the Jewish scholars who more
and more frequently visited the Great Library. He'd often heard
them speak in wonder of Jerusalem. They called it the most holy
of sites.

Didymus also knew much about the place from the various
books about the east that he'd read over the years—not least
because the history of the Jews figured so prominently in the
history of the Shards. The Ark had been kept in this city, as had
the Trident once, and of course the Seal of Solomon was probably hidden somewhere in its Temple still. But even beyond such
facts, the City of David had been central in the history of
the Jews. Indeed, it had been central to the whole history of the
eastern end of the Mediterranean: the wars fought over its
control were numerous. When Didymus and the others had
approached Jerusalem, the scholar had seen first-hand why the
city had been witness to so much conflict: it sat at the point of
high land where the deep valleys of Hinnom and Kidron met,
a site from which its occupiers could control a wide swath of
the landscape around it. These natural protections had been
supplemented by the construction of high walls that encircled
its inhabitants and made the place seem, at least from the point
of view of the librarian, impregnable. Didymus had heard much
about the enormous building projects that had been undertaken
by King Herod, including the strengthening of those thick
walls, but when Didymus had first seen Jerusalem he had felt
that it was a place as old as time itself.

The palace of Herod was just one small part of the massive
building programs the king had undertaken during his reign.

A fortress, it was built against the tall western walls of the city, immediately adjacent to its main gate, overlooking the Hinnom Valley. From the balcony high upon its side, the librarian had a commanding view of the bustling streets of the city.

Didymus heard Tiberius sigh behind him, and he reluctantly turned around enough to see the Roman setting down his stylus. "We need a Messiah," the son of Caesar said.

Sitting in a chair across the room, Thrasyllus looked up. "A what?"

Tiberius peaked his fingers in front of him, staring across the space at the younger scholar. To Didymus the Roman seemed to be weighing something in his mind. After a few moments he pointed at one of the open books upon the desk at which he sat. "Do you recognize this?"

"A book."

"Not *a* book. *The* book," Tiberius corrected. He picked up the stylus again and used the end of it to gesture around the room. "At least as far as these people are concerned. It's their scriptures."

"I know something of it," Thrasyllus said. The astrologer exchanged a quick glance with Didymus, knowing that they'd both read of the Ark of the Covenant in its pages. "But I know nothing of a Messiah."

Tiberius turned to look at Didymus now. His eyes were even darker than they usually were, as if he'd not slept well in days. "Do you?"

Didymus saw no point in lying. "I do. A Messiah is a liberator. The word means 'anointed one,' I believe, because a Messiah is usually anointed with the holy oil of the Temple here in Jerusalem."

"So it's a Jewish king," Thrasyllus said.

"That's right," Tiberius said.

Didymus frowned for a moment, thinking. "Actually, I don't

think it has to be. Sometimes a high priest is called a Messiah. And I believe their scriptures call Cyrus, king of the Persians, a Messiah, and he was hardly a Jew."

Tiberius cocked an eyebrow. "Why Cyrus?"

Didymus turned and pointed out across Jerusalem. "Because of that," he said.

The other two men rose and joined him at the balcony, following the line of his outstretched arm to where he pointed. "The Temple," Thrasyllus said.

Didymus nodded and let his arm down as they all stared at the massive building on the higher side of the city opposite them. It was white stone, like much of the city, but it stood taller than anything in sight—its height surpassing even the high towers of Herod's palace. The Temple was surprisingly fortresslike. From the vantage point of the palace balcony Didymus had been able to make out the multiple runs of high walls that enclosed smaller and smaller spaces upon the leveled platform of the Temple Mount. He could even see the long courses of the retaining walls below it all, which helped hold in the dirt and rock they'd surely used to level the area. At the center of it all was the structure of the inner Temple itself: an imposingly tall structure of polished white stone that gleamed in the sunlight, crowned with a ring of gold. The sides of the building were smooth, but the front edifice had four marble columns framing great wooden doors. "That's not the First Temple," he said.

"Herod rebuilt it," Thrasyllus said, seemingly anxious to show his knowledge.

Didymus nodded. "He did. But what he was rebuilding wasn't even the First Temple. It was the second. At least the second."

"Explain," Tiberius said, his eyes narrowed.

"The mountain beneath the Temple is said to be where their great patriarch Abraham once nearly sacrificed his only son in order to prove his fidelity to their god."

"An evil god to ask such a thing," Tiberius said.

The librarian shrugged. "Most gods are," he said. He blinked, surprised that he'd spoken so frankly—especially when Tiberius' adopted father was already spoken of as if he were a god like Julius Caesar before him—but Tiberius didn't seem disturbed in the slightest. "Anyway, there might have been a shrine of some kind built there at that time. And later on, it was King David—"

"King of the Jews," Thrasyllus said.

"Yes, king of the Jews. King David later built a shrine there to commemorate his own coming to terms with their god, and then his son, Solomon, replaced it with what the Jews call the First Temple."

Now it was Tiberius who interrupted. "When the Seal was first hidden."

Didymus nodded, knowing how little he could hide from the Roman. Though Tiberius came and went from their quarters, the scholars very rarely left. Indeed, since Alexandria almost the only contact they had been allowed with anything other than each other had been the old tomes that Tiberius insisted they pore over looking for clues to the exact whereabouts of the Seal in the Temple. The son of Caesar took regular updates on their research, reading over their shoulders, telling them to work faster, ensuring that nothing they found was kept from him. "If we are right, then yes: Solomon had possession of the Shard and hid it beneath the First Temple."

"We *are* right. I'm certain." The gaze of Tiberius focused on the magnificent structure in the distance. "And it's still there. I can feel it."

I hope not, Didymus thought. Then, looking back out at the Temple himself, he continued. "What Solomon built stood as the heart of the Jewish people and their religion until it was destroyed by Nebuchadnezzar and the Jews were taken to Babylon as slaves. Sixty years later Cyrus and his Persian armies had captured Babylon and sent the Jewish slaves back here to Judaea. He passed a decree that they be allowed to construct what they call the Second Temple. It was that building that Herod has repaired and expanded, and it was that victory and decree that led to the Jews calling Cyrus a Messiah. He liberated them."

"But you said we need a Messiah now," Thrasyllus said to Tiberius. "I don't understand. You're Rome."

Didymus, too, turned toward Tiberius as his own thoughts finally coalesced. "Not liberation for Rome. Liberation *from* Rome. If a new Messiah arose, the people would fight against Rome. There would be chaos. And in the chaos—"

"The Temple could be taken," Thrasyllus whispered.

Tiberius nodded, looking out past them both at the building in the distance. "We can't kill Herod now, but the greater plan was a good one," he said, speaking as if they were all in assent as to the necessity of the task. "We simply need to be patient. We need to bide our time. A Messiah will set the city on fire, and in the destruction we can still use Varus and his legions to secure the Temple—just as before. It's only a matter of how to begin. Fire comes from flame. And every flame begins with a spark."

Didymus stared out at the peaceful city, shivering as he imagined the bloodshed Tiberius was willing to unleash.

"And I think I know what we need," Tiberius said, seemingly talking as much to himself as to either of the scholars. He grinned, nodding out toward the Temple in the sun. "That's our tinder and our flint. And Herod, I believe, can easily provide the iron we will strike against it."

· · ·

Later that day, Didymus and Thrasyllus were alone in their room when four of Herod's guards came for them. The armed men said nothing of where they were taking them, but the scholars knew they were powerless to do anything but comply. Without a word, the guards led them along dark passageways, down narrow stairs, and finally through a thick wooden door out into a small garden beside the palace where they'd been kept.

Tiberius was there, with a small squad of six legionnaires. He smiled when he saw the scholars approach, and he made a show of opening his arms to embrace them in welcome. "My friends," said the son of Caesar, "I am pleased you could come. I want you to witness this."

Didymus looked over at Thrasyllus as Tiberius pulled him close, but it was clear from the astrologer's expression that he was equally uncertain about what was happening. "What are we to witness, my lord?"

"You'll see," Tiberius said. He nodded to Herod's guards, who immediately began marching toward the gate. The little party of Romans followed.

Herod's palace stood at the southern end of the walled fortress that was the royal district of Jerusalem. High and thick walls separated this area from the rest of the ancient city, and when the sun drew down toward the west—as it was now—Herod's great towers drew daunting shadows over the tiled roofs and open squares of Jerusalem. The fortress itself was a kind of town within the city: beyond the palace itself, it had gardens and pools, bakeries and barracks, essentially everything Herod might need to remain safe and comfortable even if Jerusalem rebelled against him.

The gate that they passed through into the ancient city was massive and heavily guarded, and the difference between the clean and well-tended grounds within the fortress and the dirty and chaotic public streets outside it could not have been more striking. Even as the day was drawing toward evening, Jerusalem was a busy, buzzing hive of merchants and markets and travelers. The streets were filled with people who seemed to be going somewhere, and they were lined with merchants shouting to hawk their wares to them all. It was raucous and bewildering, yet Didymus found it a strangely soothing relief of life after the seclusion of the locked chamber in the palace.

His relief was short-lived. Only minutes after they entered Jerusalem's busy streets, the librarian felt a wash of cold come over him. And when he looked behind, he saw that two pale and familiar figures had melted out of the crowds to glide in their wake.

Didymus again glanced over at his fellow scholar. The astrologer had looked behind, too, and when their eyes met Thrasyllus swallowed hard in fear.

The path they followed wound from street to street, but their destination was quickly clear as the great edifice of the Temple rose before them.

Everyone called Herod's work on the Second Temple a restoration, but in truth it was far grander in its aim. In a project befitting his own enormous ego, Herod had begun by declaring nature unfit to his purposes: the flat summit of the Mount of Abraham—leveled in the days of King Solomon if not generations earlier—was simply not big enough to contain the grand scope of his vision. Massive retaining walls were built around it, and bucket by bucket slaves filled the empty spaces behind them with dirt and stone scoured from the valleys below. By the time they were done, the Temple Mount had more than doubled in size. The perimeter was lined with porticoes, and at its northwestern corner a fortress stood sentinel over the complex, housing a garrison assigned to protect its grounds. Along its southern edge, the side they were approaching, Herod had ordered the construction of a giant stoa—a wide, column-filled expanse that was enclosed from the elements and populated by merchants and meeting spaces. The fall from the point of its red-tiled roof to the valley below the retaining walls was measured in hundreds of feet.

The only thing that stood taller upon the Mount of Abraham, gleaming against the sky in the middle of it all, was the Temple itself.

And beneath that, Didymus feared, was one of the Shards of Heaven.

Their party made a turn around a line of buildings and at last found themselves making their way through the open space beside the high retaining walls that leveled the Temple Mount. Heading south along the west side of the complex, they passed under a high archway that was topped with a walkway leading to the upper levels of the Temple stoa, high above. What the purpose of the walkway was, Didymus didn't know, and he didn't have long to consider it before they had reached the southern end of the complex. Here they turned again—below the stoa now—and began climbing a set of wide steps toward the height of the Mount of Abraham and the holy Temple at its crest.

The open spaces here were crowded, but they were not as hurried as they had been down within the city. The people here were supplicants, not travelers. They came to seek guidance, to seek help, to seek blessings. Many of them, Didymus could see, were making their way to ritual bath areas in order to purify themselves before continuing onward toward the holy summit. Still others carried small animals or were pulling them up the steps on leads. Above the looming walls of the stoa, lines of smoke trailed lazily into the late afternoon sky, and even before he could smell the sweet balm of the Temple's incense Didymus could smell the charring scent of its animal sacrifices.

There were five archways into the stoa: Didymus could see three next to each other far off to his right, and Tiberius directed them through the right-hand archway of another pair before them.

Even for the librarian, who was trying to take note of all that he saw with a scholar's attention to detail, it passed by in a blur. The stoa was enormous—stretching far to their left and right, yawning up to the distant roof above them—and it was filled with the chaotic commotion of people moving around and between the pillars that made long aisles across its expanse.

Didymus, accustomed to quiet and stillness, found it stifling despite its enormity. He thought, too, how inappropriate it all seemed. It was commerce and trading and money-changing . . . all at the heights of what was meant to be a most sacred place.

Thankfully, it did not take them long to pass through the stoa and step out from the covered portico onto the wide platform of the Temple Mount itself. Didymus, who'd studied it for so long, found it at once familiar and exotic. The entirety of the mount was covered with paving stones set in careful geometry. It was only covered local stone out here where it was exposed to the sky and the weather and the feet of non-Jews such as they were—Gentiles, the Jews called them—but Didymus had read descriptions of increasingly elaborate pavings as one moved into the inner areas inside the walls of the Temple proper.

There were several circuits of walls upon the platform of the mount. The area they were crossing now, just inside of the perimeter porticoes, was the Court of the Gentiles. Within it was a roughly square area, framed by a low wall of latticework that the Jews called the "soreg": it separated the area in which Gentiles could move from what was the original area of the Temple Mount, which was only open to Jews. Within that stood the larger walls and many buildings of the innermost Temple complex, surrounding further divisions of walls—smaller and smaller areas open to a smaller and smaller elite few. Inside it all was the sacred building of the Temple itself, which stood triumphant upon the center of the summit, aligned east to west so that the main doors between its magnificent golden pillars opened upon the rising sun.

As Didymus thought of the further divisions of the sacred Temple—how within it all, like a nut within a dozen shells, was the Holy of Holies, where only the high priest could go, and beneath which the Seal of Solomon was surely hidden—the party marched toward the eastern side of the complex.

Near the southeastern corner of the soreg, Tiberius called the party to a halt. He exchanged a quick word with the Roman and Herodian guards, and the men marched forward without them, turning the corner and heading directly for the main gate of the soreg, which faced the inner gates of the Temple itself. It was as far as a non-Jew dared to go if he valued his life. As they departed, the guards left the two scholars alone with the son of Caesar and the two pale-skinned figures who were not men.

The demons floated up in their wake to stand beside Tiberius. The one that they called Antiphilus leaned close to whisper something in the Roman's ear.

Didymus yearned to get closer, to strain in an effort to hear what was being said, but even as he wished it so he was distracted by what was happening ahead of him.

The guards did not turn. They marched purposely—unerringly, in perfect military fashion—toward the soreg gate of the Holy Temple of the Jews.

Even before the armed men halted at the gate, a crowd was forming both around them and within the Temple itself. Didymus heard a few voices in the crowd—young and old, male and female—spitting curses at the men, but mostly the crowd just seemed anxiously curious. They gathered to watch, to witness whatever was about to happen.

I'm witnessing, too, Didymus thought. That's why Tiberius brought us.

The guards fanned out, and in unison they turned around to face the growing assembly of people. They had, Didymus could see, formed a kind of protective arc around the outside of the soreg gate. And within that space, only two Romans remained.

One of them was carrying something. Didymus hadn't noticed that before. Whatever the object was, it was heavy and solid, and the Roman was carrying it in a frame-supported canvas bag over his shoulders. As the men took position around them, the other Roman helped him unlimber the load. Standing directly before the gate of the Holy Temple, they busied themselves unpacking the bag at their feet.

At first, Didymus couldn't see what it was. His view was blocked, and all he knew of what was happening was the self-satisfied smirk on the face of Tiberius, who had promised to bring to the Temple a spark that the son of Caesar hoped might grow into a flame of chaos.

On the other side of the soreg, within the inner grounds of the Temple, a crowd of Jewish priests had gathered—mirroring the crowd of people outside it. As the two Romans began to lift what they had brought, those within gasped and visibly took a step back. They looked at each other in confusion, in anger. Didymus heard the sound of hammering.

Then the Romans stepped back, and the librarian saw what they had done.

The spark that Tiberius sought had not been struck with iron. The last light of the sun struck over the roofs and walls of the Temple, and what it lit upon in the shadows—what it made to shine in glorious and terrible, blasphemous horror upon the soreg gate—was gold. Even from across the increasingly crowded space of the Temple Mount, Didymus could see exactly what it was that the foreign soldiers had mounted to the gates of the Holy Temple of the Jews.

The golden eagle of Rome.

How Tiberius had set Herod to allowing it, the librarian didn't know. He imagined that he'd told the king that Antipater's actions could be read as an indication of Judaean disloyalty against Roman authority. Herod, if he wanted to keep in Caesar's favor—if the old man wanted to keep his crown, and perhaps what was left of his life—would do well to prove his submission to Roman oversight. And what better means than to place the sign of Roman power upon the very seat of Judaean power?

Or perhaps Tiberius had bribed the king.

Or maybe Herod was indeed as mad as Antipater thought he was.

It didn't matter. Not truly. All that mattered was that the golden eagle of Rome had been affixed to a gate of the Temple.

Seconds of stunned silence passed. Didymus took an instinctive step backward.

"By the gods," Thrasyllus whispered.

Two young men stepped out from the crowd. They began to scream in their language, and though Didymus did not know the words they shouted, he understood them. It was a cry of revolution. A call for the end of Rome.

The two men turned about, imploring their countrymen as they gestured to the protective arc of nervous-looking guards. One of them saw Tiberius and the scholars and pointed at them, too.

Tiberius had been grinning, but Didymus felt that expression push away like the light of the fast-fading sun. He, too, took a step backward, and Thrasyllus with him. Only the two demons stood unfazed, their heads turning as if in bemused curiosity as they witnessed the boiling human rage before them.

Finally, in a single moment, something in the crowd broke. Backed by the imploring young men, more than half of them rushed forward with an extraordinary roar of anger. The rest turned and began running at the two scholars and the Roman beside them who was, though they could not know it, the son of Caesar himself.

It was, Didymus would later recall, an orgy of blood and belief. He did not see the deaths of the guards, but he heard them, shrieking out their ends as they were torn apart, limb from limb, rendered by the bloodied hands of the streaming, screaming mob.

He and Thrasyllus turned to run but found their way blocked by a second wave of people rushing out from the stoa behind them. Despairing, Didymus had just closed his eyes to pray— he didn't know whom to—for a quick end, when he was grabbed by the arm and pulled away to his left.

The grip was cold, like frozen and impassive stone. Didymus opened his eyes to see that Antiphilus had hold of him, and the demon was pulling him toward the eastern portico of the Temple Mount, a part of the structure he would later learn was called Solomon's Porch.

A large man rose up in front of them. His eyes were bulging, his cheeks red in his mob-fueled lust for blood. He lifted a long log of wood, surely meant to feed the fires of sacrifice within the sacred precinct, and he swung for the demon's perfectly formed skull.

Antiphilus, without losing his grip on the scholar's arm, gracefully bent backward like a dancer sliding forward upon a stage. Floating beneath the killing blow, the demon's free hand shot up, fingers extended as it struck into—and then through— the bottom of the man's jaw. In a flash, the demon gripped and pulled its hand free. The big man made a sound like a scream at the edge of water, burbling in froth as his life's blood sprayed into the darkening sky and fell like a splattering rain upon the face of the man whose students had called him "Bronze-guts."

Didymus, still lurching forward in the grip of the demon, vomited upon himself even as another threat loomed up and was torn apart before him.

Minutes passed in a blur of nightmare as those who rose up before them died. Antiphilus had known of the Beautiful Gate, an eastern gate to the Temple that stood along another stair running from the Temple Mount down into the valley that separated it from the Mount of Olives. The three Romans and two demons fled by it, barely escaping the tumult that was engulfing the Temple.

They wound their way around the complex, and soon they were passing by the great steps below the stoa, retracing their path through the streets of Jerusalem. The crowds they saw now were rushing toward the Holy Temple in a frantic mob, passing around the Romans like they were fish swimming against the stream.

The five of them slowed from a run to a walk. Didymus, in stunned silence, reached up and wiped the gore from many faces off his forehead.

At last, as the hurrying city grew sparse, the little party paused. Night had fallen, and they could see in the distance that a great fire had been lit outside the stoa, at the southern edge of the Temple Mount. Around it, their faces flushed by the flickering tongues of fire, the people danced and sang and shouted and raged.

And then, as a chant of vengeance rose into the deepening night, far above the ancient city of Jerusalem, the moon was abruptly swallowed by darkness. In a flash, the broad circle of it turned to blood.

Silence enveloped the city. Standing on one side of Didymus, the astrologer Thrasyllus took in his breath. "A sign," he whispered. "War. Death upon death."

Didymus swallowed hard. He nodded.

And then a new chant began. Louder and bolder with every beat of the scholar's terrified heart.

The demons were silent. But on the other side of Didymus—as if the deaths of those torn apart behind them mattered not at all—Tiberius began to laugh.

Messiah, Didymus heard Jerusalem cry out. *Messiah.*

PART II

The Year of Four Messiahs

11

Secrets Untold

PETRA, 4 BCE

Miriam twisted her way through the narrow crack, the sandy dust lifting into small clouds around her steps. Behind her, Pantera was trying to step where she did, to hop over the bigger boulders as she did. For the third time since they'd entered the narrow canyon, she heard him miss his mark. His boot thunked noisily on one of the small rocks that littered the floor, and he cursed quietly at himself. "So you know where you're going?" he asked.

Miriam smiled to herself but didn't look back. "I do. Are you sure you're keeping your eyes on the trail?"

In his silence she imagined him blushing and trying to refocus his attention on the earth.

He liked her. She wasn't such a fool as to miss it. Ever since the day on the Mount of Aaron that she'd killed a man to save his life—a moment that still gave her nightmares a year later—the Roman archer had seemed to always be around. If he wasn't on patrol himself, he'd be wherever he thought she'd be. In time, she'd made sure that he knew where that would be. As now, she always had her bow with her. He'd continued to help her learn to use it over the months. So, like him, she carried the weapon in the Roman style, strapped to her back using a leather harness that he'd made especially for her. Some days they practiced together. Other days they simply walked and talked and laughed. He never pushed his interests in her, but never for a moment did she doubt them.

And then, a few months ago, she'd realized she genuinely liked him, too. Not just as a companion, but perhaps as something more. She'd introduced him to Pullo and Vorenus, and in time they, too, had grown to approve of the young man.

Still, it had taken until today for her to be willing to share the only place in Petra that might be more precious to her than the tomb that housed the Ark of the Covenant. She was supposed to be watching that tomb today—in another canyon entirely—but once she'd made up her mind to bring Pantera here, she couldn't wait.

Besides, there'd never been a threat to the Ark. Not once in her whole life. She kept watch out of duty and habit, but not out of fear.

Miriam's pace quickened as she lifted herself over a large rock that had fallen across the breadth of the thin defile. Her secret was close now.

She hadn't told him where they were going, only that it would be a surprise. He'd made a grand show of bowing in response. Wherever she would go, he said, he'd happily follow.

That was three stubbed toes ago.

"It's just ahead," she said.

"You sure I'll like it?"

I hope so, she thought.

But of course he would. He'd love it because she loved it.

More than that, though, she'd already seen that he had a deep interest in the monuments of Petra. Whether it was the ancient shrine atop the Mount of Aaron or the magnificent tomb for the late King Obodas that they'd passed this morning while walking through the Siq. As so many visitors did, he'd marveled at the Siq itself—the high-walled crack through the mountains served as the secret southern entrance to Petra, yet it was only two men abreast in places—but he'd marveled even more at the former king's tomb, which was truly magnificent. The structure—a carving, really—was slowly being cut out of the solid stone wall of the gorge. Like the rest of the hundreds of tombs in Petra, it was being revealed slowly from the top down, as if it had always been there, hidden in the bones of the earth, only waiting for the hands of men to melt the rock away around it. It had only been a year since King Aretas had ordered it built to honor his dead predecessor—dead, so many assumed, by his own doing—but already Miriam could see that the tomb in the Siq could be one of the most astonishing monuments when it was complete: the facade of its roof was intricately formed, with beautiful designs, was crowned with a massive and beautiful urn. Already there were rumors that the urn contained a hidden chamber, filled with untold riches, but of course Miriam thought it nonsense. The stone carvers had no such secrets in their hands. They simply ran about on their scaffolds, chipping away the rock that didn't need to be there, following the arcane scratches indicating great pillars, wide steps, fake windows, paradoxically building it up by tearing the stone down.

Pantera had thought it fascinating. Miriam was sure that he'd be watching the workers still if she hadn't pulled him away with the promise of something more special to her.

The path they were on was sometimes called the Small Siq, an even thinner gorge that set off from beside the mouth of the larger one. It was little used, hardly anything more than a gash in the mountains, running from the southern entrance of the Siq to the northern edge of Petra. There was little reason for anyone to use it these days. Indeed, one of the things Miriam loved about the path was its seclusion.

Well, that and the feeling of something ancient that she got from the forgotten, cavernlike hollow that she'd found there.

Just ahead she saw the entrance.

Smiling even wider now, Miriam turned through the crack in the canyon wall, which widened into a natural chamber that had been further carved out by hands long forgotten. Miriam stepped aside as she came to it, giving room to let Pantera see it all.

The Roman archer took in his breath as he stopped to stand and stare. "Miriam, it's . . ."

Miriam nodded. "I know."

The two of them unstrapped their bows, and she followed his example in carefully setting hers against the stone wall. Then she watched him as he scanned the little hollow. Following his gaze with her own, she tried to see it through his eyes.

He stared at the far wall, just as she had when she'd first come to this place. The light from the Small Siq illumined that wall first, so it was natural to look there while eyes adjusted to the dimness in the hidden space.

The long-ago carvers had known this, of course: they'd made their first decorations against that facing wall. A welcome, she thought.

They were niches, most of them: shelves formed by hollowing out the stone walls. Similar carvings could be found throughout the Small Siq and indeed all over Petra once you knew where to look for them. Sometimes left as simple indentations in twos or in threes, other times elaborately carved into the shapes of altars focused on a single indentation, the niches largely stood empty now, but older Nabataeans, like the ever-talkative Dorothea, would whisper of how most of the niches once had god-blocks in them, those rectangular stones meant to represent the mountains and the connection between men and their ancient gods.

While she could see such workings almost anywhere in and

around the city, no place made her feel the antiquity of Petra
more powerfully than this secluded, nearly forgotten place.

"I think it's one of the oldest carvings in Nabataea," Miriam whispered. "Maybe even older than the obelisks on the
Mount of Moses."

"Blocks again," Pantera said, his eyes passing over the carvings. "Like the obelisks. And like the big temple in town. The
stone uniting heaven and earth, like the mountains themselves."

"Moses climbed a mountain to speak with his God," Miriam said, her voice hushed in a tone of reverence. "I think that's
why they carved the obelisks there."

"You think that the mountain here, above that tomb we saw
them building, is the true Mount of Moses? I thought he was
on Mount Sinai."

"Sinai isn't far. They passed through there on their way from
Egypt. They found a home in the wilderness here."

"So here they supposedly built the Ark."

Miriam blinked. For a moment she was tempted to tell him
that the Ark was real, that it was here, that even now it sat quietly at the foot of that very mountain—on the other side of
it from the Siq and the construction of the tomb of Obodas—
but she swallowed away the impulse. She'd sworn never to tell
another soul. As if to remind herself, she raised her hand to her
chest and idly fingered the metal symbol hidden beneath her
clothes. She was a keeper of the Ark. She'd been born one.

"Supposedly," she whispered.

"And a moon." The archer pointed up into the shadows, to
one of the higher carvings. Like so many of the oldest carvings,
it showed a god-block of stone in an altar frame. But above it,
curving like horns toward heaven, was a crescent moon.

It was this carving, more than any other, that had always
seemed so special to Miriam. It seemed somehow older than

the others. More vital. More important. She'd spent hours staring at it, wondering what it meant. Was it a sign of how the people who made this place worshipped the sun, that giver of light? Was it a symbol of the encompassing sky? Or was it the moon itself that they worshipped, a light in the darkness of night?

She'd never expected the Roman to see it.

"Maybe," she said. "I look at that one a lot. It feels like home. I don't know why."

"Beautiful," Pantera breathed from beside her.

"I always thought so."

"Not the carving," he said.

Miriam turned to him, saw that he was no longer staring at the ancient signs of worship. He was staring at *her*. His eyes sparkled. His mouth was parted in something like hope and astonishment. As she turned to him—as she returned his stare with her own—he blinked and stuttered. "I mean, the carvings are, too," he said. "But I . . . well . . ."

Miriam smiled at him, and before he could say anything more she leaned forward and joined her lips with his.

.   .   .

They made love. Soft and discovering, wandering and tantalizing and pure and real.

When it was done, when the heat of their passion was spent, they lay upon the dirt floor amid their strewn clothing. Her chest rose and fell, her body more full of life than she'd ever known, and once more her eyes turned up to behold the moon upon the wall.

It was brighter now. Her eyes had adjusted so far to the shadows that she could see it now in a greater light. The god-block beneath it wasn't a simple rectangle. It had what looked like little wings protruding from the sides of its top, as if someone had placed a flat stone atop the god-block. The crescent moon was centered upon that wider surface, and Miriam wondered whether it was meant to be rising or setting beneath that horizon.

Or was it meant to be, as it was, frozen in time? Had the moon been captured, locked by the carvers into this image of balance?

Pantera stirred beside her, and Miriam, smiling, set such wonder aside to find wonder in the joy of his embrace.

Late in the afternoon, when they at last roused themselves from their love and strapped their bows once more to their backs, they were slow to leave the solitude of the Small Siq. They walked with measured steps, hand in hand. Pantera spoke of his home in Sidon, of his family and friends. Miriam was content to listen to his voice, which was soothing and calm. They kissed now and again, and her heart yearned to linger, but she knew they needed to return to the city. She had been away too long.

Their smaller path emptied out at the mouth of the larger Siq, and there they turned to their right to begin making their way down its thin course toward the city.

Pantera, sighing, pointed to the beauty of the rocks around them, and it was the true that it was beautiful. When she looked closely she could see how the rose-hued stone was actually banded with shades of color, like grains in wood. Rain had crossed these with dark streaks where it had made its way down the high walls over thousands of years, and the eroded bends and twists in the stone made it easy to imagine faces and forms in the rock.

Perhaps, she thought, they were the faces of ancient gods. Perhaps all gods began thus.

They heard the sound of the construction before the Siq abruptly opened up and left them facing the busy scaffolding where in time the tomb of King Obodas would be. Here, too, Miriam wanted to pause, but she could see by the shadows upon the ground that the day was growing long. Pullo and Vorenus would be worried if she did not soon return.

Without a word to the Roman, Miriam began to make her way down the road toward the city as it wound through the canyon running west toward the large amphitheater on the southern edge of Petra. Pantera, as she expected, kept pace beside her. Whatever his thoughts were, there was a smile upon his face.

"Child," came a voice. "I didn't expect to see you out here."

"And I didn't expect you," Miriam said, turning to see Dorothea. The old woman was sitting on a rock in the shade of the canyon wall, fanning herself with one hand. Her walking stick was set against the rock behind her, and at her feet was a basket of flowers.

Dorothea's eyes glinted mischievously first at the bow upon Miriam's back and then at the Roman archer beside her. "Practicing the bow again, are we?"

"It's good to practice," Miriam said.

"Good to hit the target," the old woman replied, cackling a laugh. "I *told* you I'd find out the Roman who caught your fancy."

From the corner of her eye, Miriam saw Pantera blush. For her part, she just rolled her eyes. "Think what you will, Dorothea, but don't be spreading whispers you don't know are true. Aren't you supposed to be back at your market stall?"

The old woman sighed. "Market is empty this afternoon, ever since word came about Herod. Thought I might see if the workers needed anything for their wives on the way home. Or lovers."

"What word of Herod?" Pantera asked.

Dorothea fixed him for a moment with her gaze, apparently disappointed that he'd not risen to meet her teasing. "The king is dead. And you, young man, are no doubt expected at your camp. All the Romans are in a frenzy about it."

When Pantera looked at Miriam, his eyes were filled with a

fear that she'd never seen before. It was the fear that whatever he faced, it might be apart from her.

"We should go," she said, and she grabbed the archer's hand to begin pulling him away.

Dorothea nodded, again smiling to herself knowingly. But they hadn't taken three steps before the old woman called after them once more. "I almost forgot, child. I think someone was looking for your uncles. A woman. She was asking in the market about a couple of Romans coming to Petra years ago. Around the time you came to the city."

To Miriam it felt like her heart had suddenly leapt into her throat and stuck there. She swallowed hard. "Oh. Probably family, I guess."

Dorothea nodded sagely. "I suspected as much. I told her about your family's tomb, of course."

Miriam's heart skipped a beat, and her gaze shot toward the great rock of the mountain that sat between them and the tomb hiding the Ark of the Covenant. "Of course," she mumbled. "Thanks."

The old woman began to hum happily to herself, and Miriam's legs began to carry her away of their own accord, onward toward the rose-red city that had become her home. Her mind raced. Her hand found the necklace around her neck, the twists of metal that was all she had left of her mother. Her fingers ran along the cold edges of the symbol of the Ark, then they wrapped around it and clutched it.

She was supposed to be there. Watching. Keeping it safe.

"Is everything okay?" Pantera asked from beside her.

"I don't know," she said. Then, as if waking to the danger, she suddenly stopped and turned to him. Releasing the necklace, her hands found his shoulders, gripping where she'd so recently laid her head. "I don't know. But this is important. I need you to run and find one of my uncles."

Though Pantera was still nervous around Pullo or Vorenus, he nodded his head vigorously.

"Good. As fast as you can. Find them. Tell them the keeper is in need."

"Keeper?"

"They'll know what it means."

"What about you?"

Miriam looked up at the Mount of Moses, up toward the great platform where the two obelisks carved from the living rock were waiting. On the other side of the mountain was the Ark. On the other side of the mountain, somebody might already be trying to take it. "I'll meet them," she said. Not caring who might see, she stretched herself up to kiss his confused face. "Now go. Run!"

12

The Mount of Moses

PETRA, 4 BCE

Though they called it by another name and had long ago forgotten its history, the Nabataeans still held the Mount of Moses sacred: there were altars to the divine upon its height, and distant generations had wrought from the living stone the bending processional path that rose up to meet them from the floor of the Siq. In some places the path was painstakingly carved out of daunting cliff walls. In still others it ran atop carefully cut stones and paving that flattened the slopes or filled in the great cracks of the mountainside. Through it all, hundreds upon hundreds of steps rose. Ever higher. Ever closer to the sky and the gods above.

Her heart pounding from more than the climb, Miriam took the ancient stone steps up the mountain two at a time. Around her the cliffs of the mountain rose and fell away, and the boulders and craggy rocks that lined the ancient path made strange shadows in the lowering light of the sun.

Not once had she truly imagined that someone could find them, that someone could find the Ark. Like Pullo and Vorenus she'd kept watch, but she'd never thought of the act as truly protective. It was something deeper for her: Pullo and Vorenus, the Ark and the emblem hanging from her neck . . . these were the only connections she'd ever had to her dead parents. Keeping watch was a duty to a memory that she'd made from the stories she'd heard of what they'd seen and done. The Ark was the only family she'd ever known.

Following the processional path as it turned and angled up a shadowy crevasse, Miriam pressed on without slowing. Her legs and lungs burned with a furious fire, but the discomfort was nothing compared to the gnawing feeling of dismay in her gut.

That the Ark could truly be in danger, that someone could have found it, found them . . . it made no sense. No one knew where they were. And who could now be looking for the Ark?

But there was no other explanation for what Dorothea was saying. Someone was in Petra. Someone knew they were here. A woman. That's what Dorothea had said. A woman was looking for them.

And here Miriam was, a mountain away from the watch she'd promised to keep.

Mind reeling with questions, stomach gripped with guilt, she labored on. Panting but flying up the rocky steps, until she finally surged out of the crevasse, heaving herself up and over the last rise to where the processional path met the strangely flat plateau of stone where the two obelisks stood, lined east to west.

It had only been a few years since Miriam had unlocked the secrets of this flat space and the two obelisks. Like so many others, she'd imagined that the points of stone, tall and thick as they were, had been somehow brought here and raised up into their places. But then one day she had climbed here from her watch at the tomb of the Ark below and in her boredom had looked closely at the stones. The obelisks, she saw, were not shaped stones piled upon one another like the pillars of the great temple in the city. They were, instead, of one piece. More than that, like the tombs carved out of the cliff walls far below, they had been hewn from the mountain itself. Whatever the shape of the Mount of Moses had once been, ancient hands had stripped away the rock heart of it here until all that remained was this smooth plateau and the two obelisks, rising into the sky like fingers pointed at the gods.

For the Nabataeans, the obelisks had little meaning now. They were like lonely sentinels, guarding the path as it continued onward: down a short, sharp slope to a little saddle, where the ceremonial buildings huddled against a small ridge of striated natural stone. Beyond them was a farther summit just north of the plateau, one that overlooked Petra itself. The Nabataeans called it the High Place, and none but the high priests and those who attended the sacrifices were welcome there. Like the obelisks, the altar of the High Place was carved out of the stone, open to the air but cut off by a wide and thick wall that ran like a fence across the ridge. The wall was meant to hide that most sacred space and protect it, but of course Miriam had long since ignored the processional archway with its locked door and simply climbed the walls to see what was on the other side.

Her path today wouldn't take her there, though. And no matter what she wondered about the past, for the moment the flatness of the ground mattered only in the fact that her legs welcomed the change in slope. Her pace did not falter.

Hurrying down past the obelisks, Miriam came to the saddle where the processional path forked. To her right, the path passed the low stone buildings where the priests would prepare themselves for the sacrifices on the High Place and then proceeded up the steep slope toward the wall enclosing that farther summit. To her left, the steps instead headed downward: a second route up the sacred mountain that rose up out of the canyon on its western side—the canyon where stood her family tomb and the hiding place of the Ark of the Covenant.

Taking a deep breath, eyes focused on her feet to prevent a misstep that would break bones or worse, Miriam began skipping steps—downward now—back into the shadows of the approaching night.

· · ·

Coming down the path toward the city, on flatter ground now, Miriam at last caught sight of the tomb that Pullo and Vorenus had purchased to hide the Ark when they came to Petra. There were other big tombs in this canyon, but the columned tomb with the statues of her parents, Caesarion and Hannah, looking down from their high niches still caught the eye. The statues were Pullo's idea, and he and Vorenus had spent weeks with the sculptor ensuring that the representations were as accurate to their memories as they could make them. The sculptor had been frustrated, Miriam was sure, but the two old Romans had paid well. And Miriam was forever grateful to them all for what they'd done. Now, when she thought of her parents, she had faces to imagine—stone or not.

The statues looked down on an enclosed courtyard where the family of the dead could gather for dinners and prayers within the privacy of its walls, a Nabataean custom of bridging the death of the tombs with the life of those left behind. As Miriam skittered to a halt on the path, she saw that the statues ahead of her looked down on something else, too.

The path beside the walled courtyard was not empty. There were two women in simple traveler's clothes there, standing and staring over the wall at the tomb in the mountainside. One of them had leaned over to the other, whispering something in her ear, then nodded and took a step forward toward the door leading into the courtyard.

With hardly a thought, Miriam slipped the bow from her back, one hand pulling free an arrow while her eyes remained fixed on the two women below.

It wasn't a long shot. Not by Miriam's trained and practiced eye.

She pulled the string, her breath slowing in perfect accord to the tensing wood in her firm grip. She focused, saw the mark in her mind, framed the shot, and loosed.

The arrow shattered on the paving stones just inches in front of the feet of the woman approaching the door.

The two strangers gasped and spun in Miriam's direction, but already she had another shaft nocked and pulled back.

"I hit where I aimed," Miriam called out.

The woman in front had one hand in a satchel at her side, but it seemed frozen there as she looked up at the girl on the path above. "I believe you," the woman said.

A whisper of wind washed dust up the path. Miriam blinked, but she didn't shift aim away from the two women. And she didn't falter. Whatever failures she had today, losing sight of these women would not be one of them—whoever they were.

"The next one is aimed at your chest," she said.

"I believe that, too," the woman in front replied.

"And I'm at her back," came a steady and familiar voice.

Miriam flashed her gaze farther down the wadi path, and she saw Pantera there, his bow drawn. Behind him, coming up the path with his familiar, determined gait, was Vorenus.

The woman who stood behind the other turned, saw the second bowman and the approaching man and seemed to grow more fearful. The other, with her hand still in her satchel, just smiled at Miriam—as if she knew something she did not.

Feeling more confident now that Vorenus and Pantera blocked any chance of escape down the canyon toward the city, Miriam began walking closer. Bow still ready, she kept her focus on the woman who was smiling. Whoever she was, Miriam decided, her confidence made her dangerous. "Who are you?" Miriam demanded.

Vorenus and Pantera were closing in behind the women, and the older man carefully pulled his old gladius from where it was hidden in his robes. The ring of sliding metal at last moved the smiling woman to turn her head back to look at the two men.

She didn't react at all to the presence of Pantera, but when she saw the older Roman, her eyes froze and widened. The arm in the satchel went stiff and then limp. Her mouth opened and closed, as if she couldn't believe what she was seeing.

"Vorenus?" she asked.

He stopped and stared, his sword hand strangely unsteady.

"Vorenus." The woman's voice was suddenly quiet, almost childlike. "Vorenus, I never thought—"

"Selene?"

He gasped at speaking the name, as if he feared to break some spell, and the sound broke something in the woman. She turned, her arm coming free from the satchel, and then she was running to him, and Miriam could see that Vorenus was starting to cry as the gladius fell from his hand and he opened his arms to embrace her.

Miriam lowered the bow, but she didn't put it away. Pantera, she saw, did the same. She walked down to stand close to the second woman, who was watching the woman Vorenus had called Selene embrace him like a long-lost father.

"Vorenus?"

It was Pullo, lumbering up the path behind them. At his voice, Selene pulled away from Vorenus to look down at the big Roman. Vorenus began to laugh as she looked at the mighty man with something like confusion on her face. He reached down to pick up his gladius and used it to point down at his old friend before he returned it to its hidden sheath. "Oh, it's him," he reassured her. "A little worse for wear, but it's him."

"Selene?" Pullo croaked. "By the gods, is it true? Selene?"

Selene laughed, too, and she ran down to bury herself in his massive chest. He rumbled a sound of joy like nothing Miriam

had ever heard from him, and he picked the woman up and happily lifted her in a gently crushing embrace.

Pantera walked around to stand beside Miriam. He was still
eyeing the second stranger, but he seemed just as wary of the
two Romans. Feeling a little guilty, Miriam wondered how hard
it had been for him to summon her "uncles."

After a moment Pullo set the strange woman down and they
walked up to join Vorenus and the others.

The two old Romans gripped each other at the shoulder,
beaming at the woman.

"This is a friend of mine," Selene said, gesturing toward the
second woman. "Her name is Lapis. She's long been in my trust."

The Romans made welcoming gestures, and Lapis appeared
to let out a long-held breath. Now that she was closer, Miriam
could see that the woman's face was thin and her eyes troubled.

Vorenus at last looked up at Miriam. He smiled, though
she could see the tears in his eyes. "It's fine," he said to her.
"Everything is fine. Her name is Selene. Now queen of Mauretania, though you wouldn't know it to look at her clothes
just now. Cleopatra Selene, daughter of Cleopatra and Mark
Antony."

Pantera started as if he'd been slapped. Miriam stared as if
she could not possibly have heard what he said correctly.
"Cleopatra?"

Vorenus nodded, and Miriam saw him look up toward the
statue of her dead father. "And so the half-sister of Caesarion."
A new emotion trembled his voice. Miriam just stared in dis-
belief as his gaze then fell back to the woman he'd just embraced. "Selene," he said, "this is Miriam. The only child of
Caesarion."

Selene took in her breath sharply. "Caesarion . . . survived?"

"A long story," Pullo said. His big hand fell on her shoulder as if he feared her collapsing. "That's him," he said, pointing with his other hand toward the statue over the wall. "The other statue is of Hannah, his wife. Miriam's mother. She was beautiful."

"We lost them when Miriam was born," Vorenus said.

Selene stared up at the statues there, and Miriam saw the pain of loss hollowing her eyes that had only moments ago been filled with joy. Her hand rose up to touch Pullo's hand on her shoulder. Her fingers looked small compared to his, yet they didn't seem weak. No matter her pains, nothing about her seemed weak to Miriam. At last Selene swallowed hard, as if she was pushing something down. And when she turned away from the statue of her half-brother it was to look at his daughter. "I guess that makes you my niece."

Miriam's back stiffened at the stranger's voice. It was all too much, and she felt like she needed to run back up the mountain or back to their house. She needed time to think.

Selene took two steps toward her, then faltered and stopped as if she was reading something in her face. "You're very good with that bow," she finally said. Her gaze turned to Pantera. "Did you help teach her?"

Pantera blushed, and only then did Miriam realize how strikingly beautiful Selene was. People said that Cleopatra had been one of the most beautiful women in the world, and Miriam could believe it looking at her daughter.

"I have tried, my lady," he stuttered. "She's naturally skilled, to be honest . . . um, my lady."

"I'm grateful," Selene said, smiling. Miriam felt a heat rising in her chest, and a strange sensation like the hairs rising on the back of her neck, but then Selene was turning back to her, and the smile she had was warm and kind. It was the smile of familial love that was forever frozen in the stones looking down on her from above. "Your father, I know, would be proud," she said. "He was the best man I've ever known. Could I talk to you about him sometime?"

Miriam choked on something—her rage, her need, her confusion—and in the end she just nodded.

Selene smiled and thankfully shifted her attention back to the Romans. "I think we have a lot to talk about," she said to them.

"So we do," Pullo said happily.

"Like how you're here," Vorenus said. "And why."

"Another long story." Selene seemed to be thinking as she glanced back at Miriam and Pantera. "You have something," she finally said to Vorenus, her tone cautious. "Someone is looking for it. I came to be sure it is safe."

Vorenus took in a deep and tired breath, and Miriam saw his eyes flash quickly to the door of the courtyard. She knew what he was looking for there: the locks and the carefully laid tripwire that would reveal if anyone had passed through the entrance. "It's safe," he said at last.

Selene and Lapis both shared what seemed a sigh of relief. "We need to be sure it remains that way," Selene replied.

"We can talk about it soon," Pullo said.

Pantera, as if he sensed that he was in the middle of something uninvited, touched Miriam lightly on the arm—a kind of goodbye, she thought—before he started to move away.

Vorenus turned at the movement, and his attention froze the younger Roman, whose face genuinely blushed as he looked uncertainly between Miriam and the man he thought was her uncle. "I won't ask what happened," Vorenus said. His voice seemed even deeper than it usually was. "But I'll tell you this: even after all these months, Pullo here still wasn't sure about trusting you. But then that look in your eyes when you came to get us says everything we could ask to hear. You did well, legionnaire. Thank you."

"Thank you, sir," Pantera managed, blushing hard.

Pullo stepped over, as if he intended to block the archer's escape. Miriam saw Pantera's eyes widen at the imposing enormity of the older man. "There's more, though," Pullo said. "Herod is dead. We just found out. And with that news came orders from Varus. Your legion is leaving, bound for Jerusalem."

Miriam saw Lapis start at the name of the city, but then Pantera was speaking. "Leaving?" His voice was pained, and when he looked over to her and their eyes met she saw the same agony in his face that she felt in her own. They'd only just been with each other, just professed their love—and now he had to leave?

"Legion leaves before the dawn," Pullo said. "Already the tents are coming down."

Pantera was looking at the ground, as if he didn't dare meet anyone's eyes. "I don't want . . . ," he started to say. "It's not . . ."

"You need to go," Vorenus said. His voice was somber. "You'll already be missed, and I know the legion, son. Don't let it come to the lash."

Pantera nodded at that, his shoulders trembling with a wave of awareness and fear. At last he looked up to Miriam. His eyes were damp. "I'm sorry," he said. "I don't want to go, but I have to. I'm just sorry."

Miriam, too, felt tears forming on her face. "I understand. It's your duty." She looked at Vorenus, feeling at once resentful of him and conscious of the emblem at her neck and the connection to her parents that it represented. "We all have our duties."

Pantera started to say something more, then seemed to think better of it. He blushed again, then his back stiffened. "Well, I should go. I'd be pleased if I saw you again. On the way out." He looked to Vorenus. "With your permission, sir."

Vorenus nodded, and Pullo stood aside for the young archer to pass. Pantera looked around at them all, trying to smile and lingering on Miriam, before he moved away.

As he left, Miriam wanted to be sick, wanted to scream, wanted something, anything to make it better.

Selene came to her side, and the queen's hand fell upon her elbow. "I'm sorry," Selene said.

Pullo was watching as Pantera disappeared into the city below. "You sure we can trust him? One word to the legion—"

"Don't worry," Vorenus said. "He'll be fine. And I'll be there."

Miriam felt close to breaking. Too much was happening. "What? Where?"

The two older men turned back to them. "Some Nabataeans are going with the legion," Vorenus said quietly. "To see that peace is kept."

"He volunteered to go with them," Pullo said.

Vorenus looked up at Selene, his face creased with thought. "I didn't know about you yet."

"It's a good thing," Selene said. Her grip tightened on Miriam's elbow.

"It won't be long," Vorenus said. "And Pullo knows everything as well as I do."

The big man smiled. "Well enough. You were ever the brains, my friend."

"And you the strength," Vorenus replied, his voice hardly more than a whisper.

"You're going because you don't really trust him?" Miriam blurted out, an accusation in her voice that she wasn't sure she intended.

"No," Vorenus said. "I was going to go when all we knew was that Pantera was going."

At last the truth of what was happening made its way through Miriam's emotions. "You . . . volunteered to go for me?"

Vorenus started to reply, then he looked up at the statues of Caesarion and Hannah. "I have seen love," he said. After a moment his gaze fell back down to Pullo. "I've *known* love. And I'll do what it takes to bring him back safe, Miriam."

"Go back to the house for now," Pullo said to her. "It's a good time to be alone for a bit. We'll take the watch here for now."

Miriam's tumult of emotions had rolled into a numbness. She looked from the faces around her to the path where the archer had gone. She wasn't sure what to think or feel or say.

"We'll all come along in a while," Vorenus said. "I just want to check things here again. But then we all need to talk, and I need to get my things. The legion leaves before the dawn. I'll see to it that the young man comes with me."

Miriam nodded, and step by step she managed to start down the path back toward the city. The sun was nearly down now, and lights were on in the windows of the houses that she was soon passing.

Her legs ached deeply from her run over the mountain. Her chest ached from a deep well of pain. Her eyes hurt from the tears that quietly rose and fell.

She didn't go straight home. Instead, she walked down to the colonnaded street and into the heart of the city. She had no destination, no certain direction, but she didn't feel like stopping and she didn't want to be alone. She stopped now and again to watch other people as they walked from one point to another.

"Child!" came a voice from behind her.

Miriam took a deep breath and quickly wiped at her cheeks and eyes to be sure they were devoid of tears before she turned around. There was no reason to give Dorothea anything more to gossip about. The old woman, she saw, was walking out from the market, hobbling on her walking stick. "It's good to see you again," she said, though in truth she was thinking how it had been Dorothea who had broken the dreamlike happiness that she'd shared with Pantera.

"I was looking for you," Dorothea said when they'd closed the distance between each other.

"Oh?"

"Wanted to apologize, child."

Miriam blinked. She wasn't sure she'd ever heard the flower-seller apologize for anything. "What for?"

"That woman who I thought was looking for you—"

"Oh, don't worry," Miriam interrupted. "We found them."

Dorothea looked confused. "Them?"

"There were two of them. You were right. They were family."

The old woman shook her head. "No. There was only one."

"Only one? Are you sure?"

Dorothea nodded. "Just one. And I'm sorry, but she must not have been looking for you. You seemed anxious about it all, and it seems there just wasn't a reason to be."

"What do you mean?"

"That's what I came to tell you, child. I just saw her again." Dorothea lifted her walking stick to point down toward the main gate of the city. "She bought a horse at the market and left not long ago, riding hard."

"Oh," Miriam said. She looked back up toward the tomb of the Ark for a moment, then scanned back to look down toward the gate. Beyond it, she knew, was the road north to Judaea. It was the road that Abdes Pantera and Lucius Vorenus would soon take.

Miriam felt a frown creasing her face. She didn't know what it all meant. She didn't know if it was even something that she needed to tell Pullo and Vorenus about. They had so much on their minds already. And the doors to the tomb hadn't been opened.

"Whatever she was looking for, she must have found it," Dorothea said.

"She must have," Miriam agreed. "Whatever it was."

13

The Holy Temple

JERUSALEM, 4 BCE

It had been only a matter of hours since the third demon had arrived in Jerusalem. Acme, as they called her, had swept into the room with a near-perfect grace. Her coming had surprised Didymus—just as it had seemed to surprise Tiberius and even the other demons—yet it was the fact that she seemed to possess some flaw that had immediately drawn his attention and focus. While he couldn't be certain what slight imperfection marred her movements, the scholar had spent as much time as he could in trying to determine what had changed about her. Whatever it was, it was the smallest of flaws, and yet it felt vital somehow. *Something* had changed. His awareness of it flitted like a moth at the edge of firelight: he sensed it, he could see it in flashes and hints, though he still knew not what it was.

She had come in a rush. That much was certain. Before the doors to their quarters had shut, he'd heard the guards she left in her wake talking about a horse nearly ridden to death. They'd looked at her with their own kind of shock, rubbing their arms as they wondered why the air in the hallways had grown so cold.

Despite her haste, however, she'd not seemed tired. For all that he'd seen of the demons, he'd never seen them tire. He'd never even seen them sleep.

She was with the other two demons now, floating ahead of

the three mortal men: Thrasyllus walked beside the librarian, and Tiberius was striding behind them. The demons seemed to form a kind of advanced guard as they made their way through the unruly streets of Jerusalem. Not that they anticipated much resistance: around their party, in turn, marched a fully armed company of Roman soldiers.

Tiberius had said nothing of their destination. He hadn't needed to do so. After talking with Acme he'd simply laughed and told the two scholars that it was time. Then he'd summoned the Roman commander to make final arrangements.

The scholars had known what for. It was the only thing the son of Caesar had let them think about or read about in the many months of their captivity in Jerusalem.

They were at last going to the Temple.

As far as he had told the scholars, and as far as they'd been able to ascertain themselves, Tiberius had no hand in Herod's death. Though he'd conspired to kill the king with Antipater—who'd been executed a mere five days before his father's death—Tiberius had been just as surprised as anyone else when Herod had become ill and died.

He was not at all surprised, however, with what followed.

Judaea, almost overnight, had erupted in madness.

Herod's will called for Caesar to divide his kingdom, and Augustus was reportedly planning to do just that, but it was a process that would take months to complete. Meanwhile, the king's daughter and his surviving sons were busy seeking to establish control of various parts of the kingdom. At the same time, the spark of revolution that Tiberius had set at the Temple Mount the previous year was now lit into burning flame. From nearly every corner of the realm, sensing in the death of the king an opportunity, men were declaring themselves Messiahs, the promised deliverers who would free Judaea from foreign control. From Idumea came whispers of an insurrection. In the town of Sepphoris, a man named Judas had gathered hundreds to his banner and seized the royal armory there. Closer, a shepherd named Athrongeus had crowned himself king of the Jews and was slaughtering Roman troops wherever he found them. And not two days had passed since one of Herod's own slaves, Simon, had declared himself a Messiah ordained by Gabriel. He'd stolen Herod's crown from the palace and headed toward Jericho seeking supporters eager to evict the Romans.

Worried about chaos in the very heart of the Roman client-kingdom, the meager number of Roman troops in Jerusalem had made a plea for reinforcements to Varus, their general, who was with his legions in distant Damascus. Word had returned that he would begin marching south in their direction, re-establishing control as he went, and a Roman contingent in Petra, strengthened with a Nabataean force, would be marching northward doing the same. As conditions had rapidly deteriorated in Jerusalem, however, the Romans there had become increasingly fearful of their own safety. They were more than ready when Tiberius—spurred by whatever news Acme had brought him—had suggested to the Roman commander that Herod's fortress would not withstand the siege that the Jews were rumored to be preparing. Far better, he suggested, was the fortified high ground of the Temple Mount.

Though it had taken him longer than he had planned, everything had fallen into place for Tiberius. If Didymus hadn't despised the man, he might have been impressed.

Ahead, the Temple loomed.

Didymus had not been on the streets since the day that they'd gone to witness the placing of Rome's golden eagle upon its soreg gate, but he could not count the hours he'd stood upon their distant palace balcony and stared at the magnificent complex. Between his experience and his observation, approaching the Temple felt familiar.

But still dangerous. Intimately and innately dangerous.

Blood would be spilled by their coming. Didymus was certain of it.

Whatever plans the citizens of Jerusalem might have been preparing, they were not ready to face the company of armed Romans as they made their way through the city. No one resisted. No one stood in their way, even as they reached the Temple Mount, climbed its wide steps, and filed through the stoa onto the wide expanse of the Court of Gentiles.

As before, the men marched toward the soreg gate, where the golden eagle had been mounted before the rioters had torn it down, smashed it, and ripped apart the Roman guards who'd affixed it there.

It would be different this time, Didymus knew. The men carried no symbol of Rome. They *were* Rome: enough men to fill a garrison, resolute in aim and armed for battle.

And they wouldn't be stopping at the soreg, that wall meant to divide the holy place of the Jews from heathen Gentiles like the Romans. It was time, Tiberius had said.

They were going inside.

People fled before the marching men, scattering in panic. Most ran for the porticoes around the perimeter of the Temple Mount. They'd run the news to the city below that Rome had seized the beating heart of Jerusalem. The reaction would be swift, Didymus knew. Thousands would die because of what Tiberius was doing this day.

A smaller number of Jews fled into the confines of the soreg, into the Temple itself. The priests were there. It was their holiest of sites. God, they surely thought, would protect them. God would strike His enemies down.

Didymus wanted to weep, wanted to be sick, wanted to cry out to them. God wouldn't turn aside the Roman blades. God wasn't listening to their prayers.

If any god was coming to the Temple Mount today, it was coming to bathe it in blood. God was Tiberius now. God was the demons. God was death.

And Didymus, to his shame, could do nothing more to stop it.

The priests inside had shut the soreg gate and barred it, but the gate was no point of fortification. It was a symbolic act, and the priests knew it. As soon as the bars were in place, they were hastening into the taller, thicker walls of the Temple.

The main body of the Romans halted, but the first line hardly hesitated. In perfect coordination they approached the low wall in pairs, one man boosting another up and over the top. The gate was unbarred. The remaining soldiers parted, and the three demons floated forward, with Tiberius leading the two scholars behind them.

No one, Didymus thought, seemed to recognize what blasphemy they were committing.

The Roman commander was a man named Sabinus, and through some unspoken agreement he separated from his men and approached Tiberius. After a brief exchange that Didymus could not hear, Sabinus gave his fellow Roman a quick nod of acknowledgment and then began to bark orders to his men to secure the complex.

As the legionnaires hurried off, Tiberius looked up at the golden walls of the Temple. Beneath his dark eyes a smile was creasing his face.

The main gate of the Temple before them was glorious, but Didymus knew that Tiberius had no intention of forcing it. All he wanted was the Seal of Solomon. It would be found—if the Shard was here at all—within the inner Holy Temple where only the priests were meant to go. Going directly through the complex would mean struggling through multiple fortified gates as they fought their way through the Court of the Women before reaching the Court of the Israelites where the Holy Temple stood.

Instead, Tiberius motioned their tiny party along the southern wall. There were more doors there, smaller entrances for the priests and other members of the Jewish elite to access the chambers lining the most holy places. Tiberius pointed to the third set of doors, which stood almost even with the high, golden front of the Holy Temple farther inside. The water gate, Didymus knew. Beyond it was the chamber where the priests prepared themselves for ritual cleansing. They'd avoid the Court of the Women altogether.

"Come, scholar," Tiberius said. "It's time."

For a moment, Didymus stood confused. Then Thrasyllus stepped forward. The astrologer's arms were shaking.

"Don't be frightened," Tiberius reassured him. "They'll see to it that you'll survive."

Didymus felt cold wash over him, like the breaking of a wave in winter. A moment later, the demon they called Bathyllus was floating up to stand beside the younger scholar. "All is well," the demon whispered in its perfect voice. "The mortal speaks truth. You're useless dead."

Didymus stared. "Thrasyllus?"

"I . . . I'm sorry," Thrasyllus whispered. "They have Lapis."

Before he could say more, the demon's hand was sliding silently up to rest against the back of his neck. Its fingers were thin, its nails sharp. Thrasyllus stood in petrified fear.

With its free hand, the demon pulled free from a pocket of its robes what looked like a heavy medallion on a thick silver chain. The medallion was a casing of twisted metal—silver, copper, and gold—and at its center, nestled within the snaking metallic vines, was a stone the size of a child's fist. The stone was jet black, somehow shining like oil even as it seemed to swallow the light around it.

It was, the scholar knew, a Shard of Heaven, mounted in what was clearly a new and easily hidden setting.

Didymus had seen its like only once: when Alexandria fell, he'd seen such a black stone upon the armor of Alexander the Great. And later that fateful day, he'd seen an even larger disk of such darkness upon the surface of the Ark of the Covenant.

And now here. Another Shard. In the hands of a demon.

When Bathyllus held the chain of the medallion out to him, Thrasyllus reached to take hold of it with shaking hands. The scholar stared at it as if it were a thing possessed.

It might be, Didymus thought.

From behind them came shouts and the clashing of metal. Didymus looked back, and he could see by the commotion that the citizens of the city had begun their attack on the stoa to the south. In almost the same moment, shouts arose from the porticoes of the Temple Mount to the east and west.

The people of Jerusalem were encircling the Temple Mount.

Thrasyllus, too, had turned at the noise, but Acme drifted up to stand on the other side of him now. Her hand arose to his cheek in a balance of gentleness and seduction. "The door," she said. Her words moved over him like a whispered song, and her perfect fingers brushed his face, turning him back toward the inner Temple and the door to the baths of purification.

Almost as if he were in a trance, his shaking quelled, the astrologer lifted the medallion between himself and the water gate door. Acme began to drift away, back toward Didymus, but her fingertips lingered for a last moment on his flesh. Thrasyllus shivered as the connection at last was broken. Then the fingers of Bathyllus squeezed in on the back of his neck, and the demon whispered something in his ear. Thrasyllus, nodding, reached forward to wrap his hand around the black stone before him.

Mortal and demon screamed as one, and a line of roiling fire lanced out from the Shard and slammed into the door before them.

Didymus yelled, too, shielding his eyes from the searing light and the shock of debris as the door erupted with a roar.

When the flash of heat was gone, Didymus blinked up and saw that the door had been reduced to splinters on shattered hinges. Nothing else remained but smoke.

An icy hand suddenly gripped his neck, and Didymus felt another presence within him. It was Acme. He felt her inside of his mind even before he saw that she was standing beside him, her black eyes alight with the promise of his mind's imaginings. Her grip on his neck was firm and sure. Her presence within him seemed to be whispering instructions into his mind, as if he were a puppet and she was gripping the strings. He felt his foot rise, unbidden by him, as his body began walking forward, following Bathyllus and the puppet of Thrasyllus into the smoking hole in the Temple.

14

The Holy of Holies

The priests burned last.

Jews had holed themselves up within the Temple when the Romans marched upon the Temple Mount. The women could go no farther than the Court of the Women, but dozens of men had gone through the thick gates into the courtyard before the golden-fronted Holy Temple itself. There the men had begun to prepare themselves to fight to prevent anyone opening the sacred doors and the secrets within.

They died first.

Didymus could do nothing but witness in horror. The men inside were armed, and they were willing to fight to the death. But there was no fight against the Shard that the demons made Thrasyllus use against them.

Beside him, Didymus listened to the demon Acme laugh—a sound high and pure and beautiful—as the dozens gathered before them, armed with blades and cudgels and Temple implements now turned to weapons. She laughed, and because she gripped his neck, gripped his mind, Didymus laughed, too. His stomach heaved as his own mind revolted, but still his laughter came, ripped out of him in an act far more intimate, far more violating, than anything she could have done to his body.

As they laughed from behind, Bathyllus focused through the

astrologer's being and unleashed from the Shard a wave of horrible liquid flame that passed across and through the men who'd gathered to stop them.

The screams rose and just as quickly fell. The throats that cried out were silenced, the lives that gave them voice turned to ash by the sheeting flame.

When it was over, all that remained was dust and smoke and the horrific sound of wailing from the women on the other side of the gate to the east in the Court of the Women that they'd avoided. Then a wind arose from the west, and the clouded dust of the destruction was swept away.

The demons were not done. Bathyllus led Thrasyllus up the steps toward the massive doors of the Holy Temple. The powers of the Shard in the astrologer's grip broke them open, and the priests on the other side were borne into flame by the light of a second sun, their prayers to God choked off into an echoing silence.

Thrasyllus, gasping for air like a fish yearning to be returned to the sea, now stood between the broken doors of the Temple, which gaped like an obscene maw. Bathyllus whispered something more, and only then did the astrologer release the Shard that the demon held before him. And Bathyllus released his grip on the astrologer's neck in return.

The demon staggered for a moment, the source of his energies seemingly spent, but then the one they called Antiphilus was there, steadying his companion, who put the Shard back in his pocket.

Thrasyllus simply fell. Exhaustion dropped him to his knees. Despair made him fall to all fours as he retched through a wailing sound that seemed to have been ripped from his very soul.

It was only then that Acme released her grip on Didymus and pulled the icy tentacles of her mind out of his own.

The weight of his own body buckled his knees, but the

librarian steadied himself enough to stagger forward up the steps and kneel beside Thrasyllus.

"Oh gods," Thrasyllus whispered. "Oh gods."

Didymus placed his hand on the younger man's back. "Breathe, my friend. Breathe."

The astrologer shook his head between heaves. "Oh gods. What I did . . . what I felt."

"You didn't do it," he said. "They did."

But even as he said the words he knew they weren't true. He'd felt that horrible and mocking laughter. He hadn't willed it, but it was his body. It was his soul.

"Now you've dirtied the tiles," Tiberius said from behind them.

The son of Caesar strode up the steps into the temple with his back straight, his hands folded behind him as if he had no cares in the world. He stepped around the two men on the ground, gingerly stepping past the mess in front of Thrasyllus.

There was a fine mist of dust in the air, and Didymus watched in horror as it settled to the ground in tiny drifts of gray and sooty black.

Ash, he realized. All that was left of the priests who'd come here to honor their God, to seek their protection, to yearn for their comfort.

All dust now. Swept aside by the steps of the living.

The Holy Temple to which they'd devoted themselves was a testament to the love they had for their God. High above them the ceiling was a gold sheet between gleaming wood beams. The columns that held it up were smooth pillars of turning white marble so pure it seemed to glow. The floor was cut stones that had been fitted together so close that Didymus doubted a knife blade could slip between them. The marble rows of blue, white, and green, intricately patterned to stars and squares, rolled out before them, flanked by a magnificent seven-branched

golden lampstand and a small acacia wood table overlaid with
gold upon which stood twelve loaves of fine bread. At the head
of the chamber was a linen curtain that descended from the ceiling. Colors swirled upon it—blues, purples, and scarlets—an
image of fires that rose into golden threads of angelic beings
rising up toward the arching heavens and an unseen God.

Behind that veil, Didymus knew, was the Holy of Holies, the
most sacred space of the Temple. It was there that the Ark ought
to have been, had it not been taken away generations earlier to
be saved from the Babylonians. It was there, no matter whether
the Ark was there or not, that the Jews who'd died this day believed their God lived and breathed.

Tiberius clapped his hands together, and the sound echoed
up through the cavernous space of the Temple, emphasizing its
emptiness. He turned to Didymus, who was still on the floor
beside a weeping Thrasyllus. "So, scholar, we come to it. This
is the reason I let you live. The Seal of Solomon. It's here in
this place."

Didymus said nothing. He looked to Thrasyllus, who was at
last calming himself enough to nod.

The demons were circling close. "You're here for a reason,"
Antiphilus said.

The astrologer managed to nod. His breathing was coming
in more regular movements.

"Well?" Tiberius asked.

Didymus took a deep breath of his own and tiredly rose to
his feet. "We shouldn't be here," he said. "This is a holy place.
It's wrong."

Tiberius spread his arms to the walls of the building and
smirked. "Do you believe in the God of this place?"

Didymus opened his mouth but didn't know what he should
say. He hadn't believed in God, but then he had. Now, after
what he'd seen today . . . what God could allow such terror?

"The Seal," Tiberius said. "It's here. Where?"

Didymus stared at the man. What could he say? What could he do?

"How many more need I kill?" Tiberius waved his hand into the air, gesturing absently to the fine particles of ash that still floated there. "I don't want all this death. But I'll kill as many as I need. I'll burn this Temple to the ground if I need. Man, woman, and child—"

At the librarian's feet, Thrasyllus shuddered. "Beneath us," he croaked. "The chamber."

Tiberius grinned. His gaze bored into Didymus. "Show me."

Didymus looked around. The chamber was indeed beneath them. The Cave of Souls, some called it. A hidden chamber cut into the solid rock beneath the exquisite tiles of the Holy of Holies, the very spot where Abraham had nearly slain his own son in honor of their God. It was there, in the hidden and secret place, that the Seal of Solomon was kept.

He didn't dare show them where it was. But did he dare not?

"Show me!" Tiberius yelled. "Now!"

Didymus flinched. "Inside," he heard himself saying. "It's inside."

Tiberius followed the scholar's gaze toward the great veil of the linen curtain. "I see," he said. And then, as if it meant nothing at all, he walked across the exquisite stone floor of the Temple and pulled aside the veil.

The son of Caesar walked into the Holy of Holies.

Thrasyllus managed to get to his knees, and Didymus helped get him to his feet. The two male demons were already passing beyond the curtain, but Acme had stayed back. She stood behind them, and her siren song pushed them forward, beautiful but deadly. They walked on, Didymus half carrying the spent man, because they didn't know what else to do.

The Holy of Holies was smaller than Didymus suspected. It was in the shape of a cube. Five paces wide, five deep, and five tall.

At its center was an oil lamp on a small gilded table. Its single flame shakily licked the disturbed air of the chamber. A low and padded stool was beside it, and Didymus could imagine how a priest might kneel there, his eyes gazing beyond the flame, hoping to see the face of the divine.

"Where?" Tiberius asked, his voice impatient. "Your books brought us to this place. Where is it?"

"There are hidden doors," Didymus whispered, remembering how they had read so many books, combed so many scrolls to discover the secret. "Behind one is a stair. Behind the others is death."

Tiberius looked to Antiphilus, and the demon nodded in agreement. "Twelve doors," it said, scanning the walls. "I see them."

The doors were indeed easy enough to see, once you knew they were there. They were tightly fitted into the walls—their outlines only barely visible—but there were shallow handholds around the room, indentions just deep enough to use as grips to open each potential entry. There were four on each side wall, and four on the back wall.

"If you don't know which one," Tiberius said to Didymus, "I will bring legionnaires in one by one to open them. A dozen is a small price to pay. And I assure you that *your* death will be long and painful indeed. I will make you watch, screaming, while I burn your Library to the ground. I will let you bleed your last upon its ashes."

"Please," Didymus pleaded. "We aren't meant—"

"Meant to have it? Indeed, *you* are not. But *I* am. Tell me where, or the first death you'll see is your friend gutted alive in this place."

Thrasyllus sagged in response, too exhausted to fight, too despairing to care.

"Let me do it," the one called Bathyllus whispered.

Antiphilus nodded, and the demons lips thinned in a wide grin.

"No," Didymus croaked. "I'll find it. Just let us go." They would find it with him or without him, he was sure. And dead they couldn't fight whatever followed. In life . . . at least there was a chance.

"When your purpose is finished, I'll let you go. You have my word, scholar." The heir of Caesar gestured around the perimeter of the room. "Now, show me."

Didymus nodded and hobbled Thrasyllus to the wall, where he leaned him to keep him upright.

"Don't," Thrasyllus managed. "You can't let them."

"It's fine. It'll be fine. Just rest. Get your strength."

Didymus took a deep breath and turned. The demons just stared—Bathyllus looking slightly disappointed—but Tiberius stepped aside as the scholar stepped into the center of the room.

"Twelve doors," Didymus said. "For the twelve tribes of Israel, descended from the twelve sons of Jacob."

Gingerly, Didymus knelt down before the table, as a priest would. He closed his eyes for a moment—in acknowledgment of the sanctity, in assurance of his memory—then opened them to begin pointing at the doors from left to right, four to a wall around the room. "In order of birth, Reuben, Simeon, Levi, Judah, Dan, Naphtali, Gad, Asher, Issachar, Zebulun, Joseph, and Benjamin. Each tribe had a region, a part of the promised land. All except the Levites. They were given the keeping of the Temple, of this most holy place."

Didymus stood and walked solemnly to the third door on his left, imagining how the Levite priests had so often done the same. "The door to the chamber was meant only to be accessed by the tribe of Levi. The third door." He ran his fingers across the wall, remembering the hidden door to the chamber of the Ark in Alexandria so long before. His fingers slipped into the shallow handle. He took a deep breath, and he started to pull.

"Did-mus," Thrasyllus gasped from the wall.

Didymus froze and turned. Thrasyllus, for all his exhaustion, was shaking his head. His eyes were wide.

"Not Greek," the scholar managed to say.

Not Greek? For a moment Didymus blinked, confused, wondering what it could mean, his arm flexing to pull the door open anyway . . . and then with a lurch of realization he knew what the younger man meant. Greek was read from left to right. So was Latin. So was almost every language he knew.

But not Hebrew. The language of the Jews was read from right to left. He wasn't about to open the third door. He was in front of the tenth.

He pulled his fingers back carefully, lest he disturb the door and whatever trap lay beyond it. He stepped backward slowly, gingerly, before he allowed himself to breathe again.

"What is it?" Tiberius asked.

"Wrong door."

"Wrong door?" Tiberius asked, incredulous.

"Hebrew reads right to left." Didymus nodded to Thrasyllus, who nodded back in clear relief. Then he walked across the chamber to the third door on the right. "An easy mistake to make."

One of the demons hissed.

"Easy mistake? And what would have happened if you'd made that easy mistake and opened it?"

Didymus shrugged, remembering how the trap beneath Alexandria had drowned everyone but himself and Juba the Numidian. "I don't know," he said. "But it would have been bad."

This time he didn't hesitate. His fingers slipped into the shallow depression, and he pulled open the door with a gentle tug.

No death awaited him. At least not yet. Beyond the door was instead a smaller chamber that led to a stair cutting back in the other direction, sinking downward beneath their feet.

When Didymus turned around he could see that the eyes of Tiberius were fierce with the fires of triumph. "Bring the scholars," he ordered. And then the son of Caesar strode back to the table, retrieved the oil lamp, and muscled past Didymus.

Light held high, Tiberius led them down into the cool shadows of the secret cave beneath the Holy Temple of the Jews.

15

THE SIXTH SHARD

JERUSALEM, 4 BCE

His arm beneath the astrologer's shoulder helping to keep the exhausted younger man upright and moving, Didymus descended into a darkness lit only by the hungry flame of the lamp in the hands of Tiberius. The stairs beneath their feet were roughly hewn, a strange counterpoint to the pristine beauty of the treasured rooms above.

It was not a long descent. A mere fifteen steps downward and they found themselves once more on level paved ground.

Fifteen steps. And yet it felt like a world apart to Didymus.

The air was increasingly cool, perhaps even crisp as they had descended, and now at the end of the steps they stood facing a chamber, a hollow space that sat directly beneath the Holy of Holies. The Cave of Souls was not large. Between half and two-thirds the area of the sanctified chamber above, it was roughly square, with an uneven ceiling following a natural band in the rock. In a few spots upon the ceiling, tool marks still betrayed how human hands had worked to enlarge the gift nature had provided atop this holy mountain.

The light of the lamp in the hands of Tiberius revealed two small shrines in the space, simple niches that appeared to be cut directly into the bedrock. Both were overarched and decorated with arcane signs and letters that Didymus could not read.

Looking from his left to his right, Didymus saw that each niche within the Cave of Souls held a block of stone, the clear object of each shrine's veneration. The first was a thin cylinder, perhaps as tall as the scholar's forearm. Upon its smoothed surface, shadowed by the lamplight, was the carving of a tree, stretching up from its roots to blossom with life just below its rounded top. The second block of stone was shorter but broader at the base: a perfect, featureless pyramid. Small cushions rested on the floor before each shrine, and Didymus imagined the priests—all of them dead now, he reminded himself in horror—kneeling on them in worship.

Didymus wondered at the stones—part of his mind already swirling with theories about how these strange objects related to the faith of the Jews—but he knew that he had no time for such rumination. Tiberius wasn't looking at the niches in the walls.

He was looking at the floor.

Though less magnificent than the patterns of colors of the exquisite cut stone of the Temple above, the floor here was still fitted tiles, white with crystalline seams that reflected the light. In two spots upon the floor elaborate inlays of carefully cut tile had been made. The closer and far smaller one was a black square, framing a pattern of red and white diamonds pinned by black triangles that enclosed a second black frame around a white square. Within that square, in turn, a black circle had been carefully inlaid into its center, superimposed by an upside-down triangle that had been crossed through by a horizontal line through its lower half. The second, much larger tile inlay was also a black square, but this time it enclosed a broad, pale-colored circle ringed by triangles pointing outward like flames. At its center was a much smaller black circle with six points protruding from its round surface.

Tiberius looked from inlay to inlay, before he walked over

to stand upon the closer, smaller one. Lifting his foot, he stomped down hard upon the strange design in its center. The sound that returned was empty and hollow. He looked back at the demons with a new determination upon his face.

The one called Antiphilus came forward, and the son of Caesar retreated off the stone. Kneeling down, the demon ran his pale fingers along the symbol, tracing it with almost tender care. "What lies beneath," he whispered.

"What lies beneath," the other two demons intoned.

Then the demon, resting one hand upon the surface, reared back with his other. He held the position for a moment, lips moving in what looked like some kind of silent prayer, before he closed the raised hand into a fist and punched down upon the tile.

The blow came down as hard as a hammer strike. Didymus felt it reverberate through his feet on the floor. And he saw it smash through the center of the inlaid tile, shattering it into slivers of stone.

Antiphilus pulled aside the broken pieces, one by one, as Tiberius brought the light over it to see what was within.

The others leaned forward, too, and Didymus found himself wanting to join them. Whatever horrors he had seen this day, whatever sin it was to have penetrated the Temple and now broken this sacred stone, as a scholar he still yearned to know what treasure was within.

From his side, he felt Thrasyllus pulling away from his support to lean against the wall of the cave. The younger man was still weak, but there was a defiant light of life in his eyes. And there was, too, an understanding. "I'm fine," he said. "Go on."

Didymus nodded, and then moved over to join the others. The last piece of the stone was coming away in the demon's hands, revealing a small stone depression holding several items wrapped in linens. Antiphilus reached down to pull the wrappings away from the top one. Inside, he revealed, was a flat, dark gray stone, crudely inscribed with words in the same alphabet that was above the shrines in the chamber. Hebrew, surely, but an old form of it, different from the kind of script Didymus had seen used in texts at the Great Library.

One of the two tablets of the Ten Commandments, Didymus assumed. Whatever the priests displayed in the Temple above would surely not have been the original. It would have been a copy of the ancient artifact, with clearer words, gilded lettering upon a polished surface. It would have been made to look sacred and holy, a divinely crafted thing—not a rough-edged rock chiseled by the hand of an old man.

Why the tablets would be here and not with the Ark—wherever that was—Didymus didn't know.

Antiphilus felt around the hole, but found nothing but the second tablet and some other artifacts that Didymus didn't know and that the demon seemed not to judge of any value.

The demon looked up at the one they called Acme. "So it is as you say," he said. His voice was a quiet hiss in the Cave of Souls. "We were right. The Shard is indeed in Petra."

Petra!

Didymus fought hard to control his reaction even as his mind reeled. Thrasyllus had said that the demons already had the Shards of Water and Fire, and that they'd have Air and Life soon enough. But the Shard of Earth, the Ark of the Covenant, was not yet in their grasp. Acme must have discovered it was in Petra, and it was that news that had so spurred them to action upon her arrival.

If the Ark was in Petra that would mean Caesarion was there. And good Vorenus, too, if he yet lived. He'd heard nothing of them since the attacks on Elephantine Island so many years ago.

I must warn them, he thought.

But how?

Antiphilus rose up and floated to the second inlay in the floor. Once more he knelt, and once more he gently traced its design. "What lies beneath," he whispered.

"What lies beneath," the two others repeated.

Again the demon's fist rose up and then slammed into the floor at the center of the ancient inlay, destroying it in a single, vicious blow.

Tiberius lifted his light and all but the astrologer looked to see.

It was a smaller depression than the first, which seemed strange to Didymus given the overall size of the inlays. The broken pieces of tile had fallen on a layer of once-rich linens that Antiphilus pulled out of the hole and set aside. Beneath that, resting on a second, deeper bed of linens, were two small glass vials half full of a clear oil the color of honey. And between them was a tiny, latched chest of dark wood with old hinges and a metal inlay of the same symbol of a circle with six points upon it.

The demon's long, pale fingers reached down and gripped the box with a nearly loving care. The other two demons seemed to lean even closer, their full focus on the little container that was raised up from the hole into the flickering light of the Cave of Souls.

Didymus sensed a movement in the air behind him, like an exhalation of a thousand breaths upon his skin, and it felt like maybe there was a new coldness in the chamber.

No one looked away from Antiphilus and what he held. Tiberius was leaning so close over him that Didymus absently wondered if he would fall over.

The demon's grip shifted, freeing one hand so that his fingertips could catch hold of the latch and lift it.

It definitely *was* getting colder. Not the chill of the demons, but a drop in temperature as if a storm were brewing over the

Temple Mount outside. Antiphilus didn't notice it. None of the demons did.

The latch came free and the old hinges creaked as the lid opened.

Yes, Didymus thought, even as he focused on what the demon was revealing. He could hear the storm now. A beating rain, hard and fast. Unnaturally fast.

Inside the box was a ring displayed on a wooden housing. The metal band repeated the same symbol as the chest itself, but the librarian's eye saw it only for a moment. His attention quickly focused instead on the small, flat stone set upon it. Like the Shard of Fire, the stone was a strangely gleaming black. To Didymus it looked like a sinking pool of darkness, pierced through with a somehow even darker slit like the eye of a cat.

"The Seal of Solomon," Tiberius whispered.

"Drown with it," Thrasyllus croaked.

Didymus turned at the other man's voice, and so was the first to see the rising rush of water that was pouring down the steps into the Cave of Souls. Thrasyllus was standing beside the steps where he'd left him, still leaning against the stone wall, but his hands were before him. In his fingers he held a second medallion, the Shard of Water in a new setting.

Acme made a high screeching sound, instinctively reaching for the pocket of her robes and finding it empty. Bathyllus spun and tried to launch himself at the human, but the wave of oncoming water pushed out his feet. Tiberius, too, was scrambling, trying to keep his lamp aloft while keeping his balance.

Didymus, quicker to see the water, had braced against the initial blow. He stepped forward slowly against the tide, angling his way toward the wall and Thrasyllus instead of facing the direct onslaught of the water that had become a raging cascade down the stairs. Already the water was to his knees, visibly rising with each heartbeat.

The astrologer was gritting his teeth now, holding back a scream as his hands shook with the power that was flowing through him.

The Shard was killing him. Didymus could see it.

The power was stripping away his life, moment by moment. Whatever control he'd had over the Shard of Fire, it had been directed by Bathyllus. Facing a Shard alone now—already exhausted, with no preparation for the act—he was being destroyed from within.

The water was up to their waist, shockingly cold. For a moment Didymus thought he heard the echoing boom of a mighty thunderclap, but the sound was drowned out by the roar of the churning torrent filling the Cave of Souls.

"Let it go!" Didymus shouted. The younger man would die if he didn't. Perhaps he would die even if he did. "Thrasyllus! Let go!"

The astrologer opened his mouth and screamed, raw and inhuman, and at last his fingers shot open. Thrasyllus fell down the wall, unconscious. The Shard fell into the rising waters that pushed it across the room, the metal chain flashing in Tiberius' lamplight as it swung wide of the heavier metal housing. Didymus splashed at it with one arm, managing to touch the links of the chain for a tantalizing moment, but then it had passed him.

The astrologer was limp, and the water pulled his body from the wall. He lay on his back for a moment, floating, before the currents flipped him facedown.

"Thrasyllus!" Didymus jumped through the water now, fighting to land each step well enough to propel himself forward, inch by inch.

The main current down the stairs now caught the astrologer and sent him spinning into the chamber. Didymus dove, caught him, and turned him over. He felt the younger man's lungs rise a moment before his body convulsed, coughing out water.

The current and the weight of the other man spun Didymus around. His feet had held on something—the broken edge of the first hole, he realized—and so for a moment he stood there. The water was pounding into his back, but less viciously than it had been moments earlier. Thrasyllus was in his arms, his body stretching out in line with the current. And before him, huddled against the far wall of the Cave of Souls, were the three demons and Tiberius, who still held his lamp high.

Acme was holding the Shard of Water, and Bathyllus had the Shard of Fire in his hands. Both of them were smiling, their bone-white teeth shining in the lamplight.

Antiphilus stood between them. He was smiling, too. In one hand he held the Seal of Solomon, the Shard of Aether. His other hand gripped the back of the neck of Tiberius. The son of Caesar was crying, but the demons showed no notice. One by one they placed their hands on the Seal. Tiberius, at a whisper from Antiphilus, reached up with a trembling hand and did the same. For a moment Didymus saw his dark eyes shoot open with horror and revulsion.

Then all four of them, in a bright flash of twisting light, seemed to fold in on themselves. There was a pop of air rushing into and out of the chamber all at once.

And they were gone.

For several heartbeats, Didymus stood in stunned silence within the sudden darkness.

Nothing could stop them now, could it? Not with such power. Not with so many Shards.

The water had ceased to rush into the Cave of Souls. It was only a trickle now, draining down out of the Temple above.

Light grew in the air behind him, casting his faint shadow

against the empty chamber. The storm was gone, he supposed. The sun was coming out.

No, he reminded himself. They didn't have all the Shards. Not yet.

So there was still hope.

He just had to get to Petra. Somehow beat them there. Somehow save the Ark.

The prospect daunted him. He had no idea how to do it. But every journey, no matter how long, began with a single step.

He'd heard that somewhere. Or read it. He couldn't remember now.

But it was true, he supposed. Start with a single step.

Thrasyllus coughed in his arms, and Didymus shook himself into movement. "Come on," he said, more to himself than the still unconscious astrologer. "Let's start with getting out of here."

16

New Powers

The horizon had the faintest hint of dawn beneath a sky still strewn with stars as Selene stood with Pullo beside one of the obelisks atop the Mount of Moses.

"There she is," the big man said. "On the wall of the High Place."

Following the line of his outstretched finger, Selene saw the shape of a young woman outlined in the predawn darkness ahead of them, standing atop what appeared to be a wall across the plateau. Miriam appeared to be staring down at the lights of Petra, settled like fireflies in the valley below, but Selene was certain that the young woman she'd just met wasn't looking at the twinkling stars of the still-sleeping city. No. Her eyes would be beyond it, to the turn of the road that extended east out of the valley, where the last lights of the departing legion were disappearing in the distance—and Vorenus and the young Roman archer with them. "The High Place?" she asked.

Pullo's arm lowered. "It's an open-air temple. A place of sacrifice to their gods. She climbs up here a lot, I think." He let out a quiet and knowing laugh. "She climbs just about everywhere in these mountains."

"She is a strong young woman," Selene said.

"She's had to be."

Selene looked up at the big man. She'd grown to be strong herself in their years apart—grown from a child to a queen— and still she felt the urge to be small with the mighty Titus Pullo. His voice was a comfort that brought back a childhood of peace that often felt like another lifetime. And his face, familiar despite the crisscrossing of weathered scars, still made her feel safe and protected. There was such strength in him, as there was in Vorenus, and yet they both had such deep warmth and love. "I could hardly imagine two better men for her to grow up with," she said.

Pullo blinked in the starlight. "We have tried. But we're just a couple of soldiers, Selene. She should have been with family."

"Family isn't always blood. You and Vorenus are family. Always have been."

"Maybe. But maybe it's something more. Blood matters. And you're the closest family she has now. The closest she's ever met. You should talk to her."

Selene wanted to do so, she desperately yearned to do so, but she also didn't know what to say. "And so . . . talk to her about what? About how Caesarion used to ruffle my hair?"

Pullo smiled. "Maybe. Sure. Tell her about how her father was a real person, not just the stories of the two old men she calls her uncles."

"She calls you 'Uncle'?"

"It was the best we could come up with. Less conspicuous than having her call us 'Father.'"

Selene allowed herself to smile. "I like that. Uncle Vorenus and Uncle Pullo."

The big man shrugged. "I've been called far worse," he said, and he turned to start back down the path toward the valley of the tomb.

"Where are you going?"

"I'm on watch tonight," he replied, lumbering down the

steps with a tired and halting gait that seemed almost obscene against her memories of the vigorous man of her youth.

"And what if she doesn't want to talk to me?"

"You'll think of something," he said over his shoulder. "You were always a clever girl."

And then he was gone, and Selene was left alone. After a few moments she realized her hand had fallen into the satchel she still had around her shoulders. Her fingers were running across the cool outer stone of the broken Palladium of Troy. She drew them back and sighed, at once wishing she was back home with Juba and also feeling certain that this moment here was exactly where she was meant to be.

Her eyes flicked back up to Miriam with sudden realization, and she began to walk in her direction. She knew what she wanted to say.

By the time Selene had followed the path up to the processional archway that split the wall across the plateau in two, Miriam had jumped down to the other side. Dawn was growing closer, and in the thin light Selene found that the door in the archway was locked. And she was, she was certain, too old and too much a queen to be climbing the stone after the younger woman.

Frowning for only a moment, she calmly moved her hand back into her satchel, and this time gripped not the Palladium, but the Shard of Air exposed by its broken top.

She expected power to rise to her command. As often as she had used the Shard, she knew its ebbs and flows as surely as she knew the freckles of age upon the backs of her hands.

Yet what arose when she touched the Shard was far more than what she expected. It was a torrent of energies, the roar of a tornado when she'd expected the shift of a breeze. It was a pulse of power that threatened to consume her all at once, like an oncoming wall of water that would seize her and drag her under its weight.

She gasped, choked, and with a force of will managed to let go of the Shard.

She'd closed her eyes against the shock of it, and when she opened her eyes she could still feel the power of the air.

Selene stood beside the wall for almost a minute, catching her breath and collecting her thoughts. She'd gripped the blacker-than-black stone in her satchel for only a heartbeat, but in that brief second the energies that had gathered around her were unlike anything she'd felt before. It was greater than Carthage, and it had coiled around her like an invisible serpent.

The power of that serpent was enough to strike out and obliterate the wall before her with only a moment's thought. But she hadn't been ready for it. And so she knew if she'd held on to it any longer that serpent would have tightened its coils and crushed her.

She hadn't been ready for it.

But if she was . . .

Selene straightened her back, adjusting her shoulders and raising her chin with the pride of the daughter of Cleopatra. She took a deep breath of the cool air. And then once more she reached into her satchel and gripped the Shard.

The power erupted once more, but in her mind she held a shield, and she set herself behind it, driving back the power step by step until she had pushed it back into the stone and held it at bay beneath her straining grip.

So much power. So much more.

If Carthage had been a place sanctified by men, this mountain was sanctified by something much greater indeed.

Still taking deep breaths to steady herself, Selene pulled forth a strand of the power that surrounded her. She let it run through her and then let it fall to coil itself in tongues of dust about her legs and feet.

And then, trembling but a little, she floated up into the air, over the wall, and down onto the temple summit above the ancient city of Petra.

. . .

Child of Egypt, queen of Mauretania, Cleopatra Selene had seen many temples in her life. In Alexandria there had been temples to dozens of deities, large and small: from the forested hill of the Paneum, where they honored the goat-man god of the wild, to the great temple precinct of Serapis, the divine protector of the city. In Rome she had seen the Temple of the Greatest Jupiter high upon the Capitoline Hill. In Caesarea Mauretania she and Juba had restored and built their own great temples to gods they didn't believe in. In Carthage, in flashes of memory she'd rather forget, they had seen the dark pit at the temple of Ba'al Hammon, where the ashes of sacrificed children fell.

The High Place of Petra was like and not like anything she'd ever seen. As with so many other sacred places, it was high upon a mountain, but while most others were enclosed, the High Place was open to the sky and the wind and the rain. In that respect, she thought, it was a lot like the obelisks she'd left behind on the other side of the wall. They were similar to the many obelisks she'd seen growing up in Alexandria, but they also had an antiquity, a feeling of natural belonging—as if they'd always been a part of the mountain, not made by human hands. And they were exposed directly to the heavens above, almost as if they pointed there.

The summit stretching out before her now had been cleared to a largely flat surface. There was a small square ritual pool not far away from where she stood, filled with clean rainwater that Selene could see shimmering darkly in the predawn light. And beyond it was a space that she assumed to be a sacred court: a rectangular area cut down a step into the mountain's exposed rock core, perfectly leveled and covered over with what looked like pale white stones. At each of its four corners, and midway along its eastern side, were five waist-high stone slabs of various sizes. And between them around the paved courtyard, with two on the west side, were six thin stone pedestals—their crowning, upturned bowls meant, Selene suspected, to be filled with oil and set alight. Between the two pedestals on the west side, just at the point where the mountain gave way to the cliffs that dropped down toward the canyons and the city far below, the natural stone rose free of the white pavings in a stepped altar, with a raised stone fire pit beside it. Miriam, she saw, was standing before those darker shapes, in the middle of the paved court.

Selene made no attempt to silence her footsteps, preferring that the girl hear her coming before she announced herself.

Sure enough, she saw Miriam turn at her approach, see her, and then look back down the valley.

Selene walked up until she stood beside the only child of her dead brother. In doing so, she saw now that the lowered court area wasn't completely paved. Right in front of the two altars, right at Miriam's feet, was a short rectangle of stone raised up a few inches from the flat surface. It was covered with carefully cut tile: a black rectangle traced its edge, encasing red and white diamonds that, in turn, enclosed a second black rectangle. At the center of that, unmistakably, was a six-pointed black star on a white stone background.

"I didn't expect to see anyone here," Miriam said. Her voice was quiet, though whether it was from the clear sanctity of the site or to still her emotions, Selene didn't know.

"I can go," Selene said. "If you want."

Miriam didn't reply, and Selene looked out to see that the younger woman was, indeed, watching where the legion had disappeared. The lights were all gone. There was nothing to see there but empty canyons.

"Do you want me to go?"

Miriam pursed her lips. "No, it's fine," she said.

"I miss my husband," Selene said. "We had to be apart. Duty. I know that. But I still wish it wasn't so."

Miriam said nothing, but Selene saw that the younger woman's face seemed to relax a little. That was a start at least.

"What was his name?" Selene asked. "The archer."

Miriam's jaw clenched for a moment, and she froze, as if she was trying to decide whether to burst out in anger at the question. At last, she only let out a long and tired breath. "Abdes Pantera," she said. "He was from Sidon."

"A strong name. I won't ask if he's a good man. He must be."

Miriam smiled at that, and she at last released her gaze from the distance and looked down at the oddly tiled stone at her feet. "He is. But I wasn't thinking about him. I don't know if that's wrong or not."

"You were thinking of Vorenus," Selene whispered.

Miriam nodded, her gaze still focused on the rocks. "He knew how I felt. He offered himself to go with the legion because of that. He's a good man. I knew that, but . . ."

Her voice cracked as it trailed off, and Selene's smile was sad. "Knowing he loves you is one thing. Seeing it is something else entirely."

"I just—I have this terrible feeling I won't see him again." Miriam was crying now, and when her head leaned toward Selene the older woman quickly leaned into it herself, allowing Miriam to rock over sideways against her. It was, Selene thought, the closest thing to a hug she was likely to get.

"It's just a show of force," Selene said, patting the younger woman on the opposite arm as their shoulders leaned into one another. "Vorenus says it's just a show of force, and I'm sure he's right. This kind of thing happens a lot. Doubtful to be any fighting. And if there is, you know Vorenus will see him safe."

"I hope so."

"I know so."

They stood for a minute leaning into each other, the faint glow of a coming dawn growing around them, until Miriam pulled away and straightened her back. "This is an altar," she said, looking up at the taller outcropping of stone before them. "They make sacrifices here."

"Of what?" Selene asked, unable to keep the image of the pit at Carthage out of her mind.

"Animals mostly, I think. I'm not actually allowed here."

"Yet here you are."

Miriam smiled a little at that. "And so are you."

Selene allowed herself a quiet chuckle, and was glad for the feeling of lightness it brought to her heart. "I can't say that I was ever one to do what I was told. Your father once said I was too smart for my own good."

Miriam's gaze was upon the brightness of the eastern horizon, and for a moment she seemed lost in thought. "You've become a queen. So I think it turned out good."

The memory of Tiberius throwing her down upon her marriage bed at Vellica flashed through her mind, and Selene had to physically shake the recalled sensations away. Miriam looked over at the sudden movement, and Selene tried to smile it away. "Not every rule is meant to be broken, but some certainly are. Caesarion knew that."

Miriam's face tightened, and she again turned her eyes to the east. "What was he like? My father, I mean. I . . . he died the night I was born."

Selene wondered whether she should reach out to embrace the young woman, to share the pain of his loss, but it seemed too much, too soon. "Your father?" She took a long, deep breath, picturing him in her mind. "You know, in one of my earliest memories of him he was practicing swordplay with Titus Pullo in one of the yards of the palace in Alexandria. It was right before the war started, I think. He was young and handsome and strong. Always was. I remember that word had come from some Roman messenger. My parents had to go to the court and make plans. Everyone in the palace was on edge and scared. And even then, young as he was, Caesarion was there for us. He was the older brother, but in truth he was like a father to me through many of those years. Pullo and Vorenus, too, I suppose. But Caesarion was always there. He always knew what needed to be done."

"Vorenus says he gave his life to save the Ark."

There was a hurt in Miriam's voice, a pain like a persistent thorn, and Selene reached out to touch the girl's arm. "He did and he didn't, Miriam." Earlier, before he'd departed to join the legion, Vorenus had told Selene about their years apart, and about the tragic night when he'd been lost. She'd seen it through the Roman's eyes, but when she'd closed her own she could see it through the eyes of her dead half-brother, too. "He wanted to save the Ark, of course. He knew how important that was for all of us, but he also knew how important it was for your mother. He loved her, and she must have been an extraordinary woman for him to feel such devotion. So he did it for her." Selene took a deep breath to control her own emotions and steady her voice. "But I can tell you that it wasn't the Ark, or your mother, or the whole world that he was thinking of in the end. It was you, Miriam. With his dying breath he was trying to save you, to give you a chance. And seeing the woman you are becoming, he did the right thing. Right to the end. He loved you then, and he loves you now."

Miriam shuddered, and then she turned, tears flowing down

her cheeks as she fell into Selene's embrace. "I miss him," she managed to say. "Both of them."

Selene pictured Caesarion. Her other brothers, Alexander Helios and Ptolemy Philadelphus. Her parents, Antony and Cleopatra. And the others who'd died to get her to this place, like Isidora. "I miss them all, too," she whispered, and she let herself weep.

Overhead, the stars were going out, one by one. At the eastern horizon, the disk of the sun had finally cracked over the edge of the earth. It was a new day.

After a minute, Miriam suddenly stirred in Selene's arms. "What's that?" she asked, straightening up.

"What's what?" Selene let go of the younger woman and turned east to where Miriam was looking. There was a great wall of rugged peaks there, a jumble of cliffs and crags and sparse trees clinging to life on the edge of oblivion. Selene saw nothing else.

But then there was a strange flash of pale blue light against one of the hillsides that stretched along the side of the road that the legion had taken, a tiny burst of color in the shadows of stones. It snapped into being, but before Selene's eyes could focus upon it, the light was gone. "I don't—"

It flashed again, the same light coming alive only to consume itself at the very moment of its birth. But this time it was closer. And a heartbeat later, it had popped again, a bubble of the same pale blue that flashed in and out of existence again. Closer still. Ever closer. Tracing a line across the hillside above Petra like a lightning bug skipping across the mountains, moving at impossible speed.

Miriam had pulled away in her curiosity, but now her body language had turned to concern. She had a bow on her back— the same she'd used to threaten Selene—and she was pulling it free. "What is it?" she asked again.

Selene didn't know. But whatever it was, it was coming. Fast. And she was almost certain she knew where it was headed.

One hand fell into her satchel. The other reached out and urgently gripped Miriam's arm. "Do you trust me?"

The younger woman looked back and forth from the popping light to the woman she'd only just met. After a moment, she nodded.

"Good." Already Selene was feeling the coiling of air around them, the staggering power that was so much stronger in this place—strong enough, she hoped, for both of them. She pulled Miriam closer even as she stepped forward and embraced her with one arm. "Then hold on to me. Whatever happens, don't let go unless I tell you to."

The power coiled, tightened, tensed. Selene closed her eyes to concentrate on it, to accept it and make herself one with it. Somewhere in the back of her mind she made a prayer.

"What are you doing?"

Selene opened her eyes. "We're going to fly," she said.

Miriam's eyes were wide, but something like a smile was at the corner of her mouth. She gripped herself to Selene's chest—saying nothing of the thick breastplate there—and she nodded, as if their taking flight was the most natural thing they could do.

And so, as the last of the stars went out in the sky above, they did.

17

The First Attack

Titus Pullo tried not to think about how he once would have bounded down the rock-hewn steps from the summit. Age did that to anyone, he supposed, as tasks once simple grew harder with the passing of years. It happens to everyone, Vorenus had told him more than once.

No doubt it was true. Vorenus was usually right about things. But that still didn't make the awareness of his own failing body any easier to accept.

His breathing wasn't labored as he reached the wadi floor and the path began to level out. He took some solace in that, at least. His lungs were still strong.

Not the rest of him, though. The pain was near to constant now, though he'd managed to hide it well enough from Miriam. Even Vorenus, close enough as they were, wasn't aware of how deep the veins of agony could course through his legs and back.

The good priests in Alexandria had done the impossible in saving his life. The explosion he'd set to help Vorenus and Caesarion escape from Juba and the Romans that morning had ripped the flesh from his back. The rocks that had fallen had crushed and broken the bones of his body. They'd saved his life. They'd given him a new chance to be something, to do something, but no one could have truly put him back together again. Some days were better than others, but no days were painless now.

The moment he'd seen Vorenus again on that canal of Alexandria, though, was the moment he'd stopped caring about all that pain. It was the moment he'd decided that if he was meant to wince through life, he'd be happy to be living out those days—however many there were—with a man that he truly loved at his side.

Which was probably why he felt more tired tonight. It wasn't the climb up and down the mountain. It was the fact that Vorenus was gone.

Pullo sighed, and he instinctively looked down the wadi, over the lights of Petra, at the dark and hulking wall of the mountains north of the city. Somewhere beyond them was a road, a cloud of kicked dust. Somewhere beyond them was another old man, not so broken as he was, but still hiding his own aches and pains, marching along with one eye on the road and one eye on Miriam's Roman archer.

He and Vorenus had talked a lot about what to do with the young man. For months they'd seen the two of them dancing about one another's feelings, and it was that dance more than anything else that had convinced them that the archer's intentions were good. After all, Vorenus had once said, Pullo had never taken so long to woo a girl in his life.

Pullo smiled at the memory.

As he did so, upon the distant mountainside, something flashed.

A light. The thin color of a clear blue sky. Like a circle unfolding itself in the dark, it twisted into being for a moment, and then all again fell into shadow.

Pullo stopped and stared.

In the same spot it flashed again, but this time in reverse: a light seemed to open in the dark, as if the cover had been pulled from a lit lamp, but in an instant the light folded back in upon itself. It consumed itself, and it was gone.

Pullo chewed on his lip, wondering what it could have been. A shepherd after an errant animal, his light seen between rocks?

It could be. But then Pullo had never in all his years seen a light twist like that. Never.

It wasn't right. It wasn't natural.

Pullo started to walk again. But faster this time.

And then the light twisted into being once more. This time it was closer. So Titus Pullo ground his teeth against the pain and started to run as fast as his crippled body would let him.

The Ark wasn't far. The path down the wadi wound between tombs and courtyards, and Pullo had walked it often enough to know exactly when it would come into view.

When it did, he saw that the blue light had arrived first. It flashed into being on the path beside the door of the walled courtyard in front of the tomb. Pullo instinctively lifted his arm to shield his eyes from the bright surge of light in the shadowed canyon. When he lowered it again he saw that the light was gone, but the space was hardly empty. There were four people standing there now. Suddenly. Impossibly.

Pullo thudded to a halt in surprise.

The mysterious strangers were looking at the tomb where the Ark was hidden, but at the sound of his lumbering footfalls one of them turned in his direction.

In the shadows Pullo could hardly make out any of their features, but he knew one of the four was a man from the sound of his voice. It had the high, whispering quality of a song, but it was unmistakably male. "This is the place? You are certain?"

"Yes," one of the others replied. This one was female, with a voice that was sweetly sibilant, like a seductive serpent's. "Inside."

"Open the door," the first replied. "Use Fire."

There was a sound of movement, and one of the four made a whimpering sound of pain and exhaustion.

Pullo reached into his robes for the gladius that was always there. At the sound of it coming free, the one who had turned in his direction cocked his head, a look of curiosity.

"Very well," said the one who seemed to be in charge. "You can kill him, Bathyllus. But be quick about it."

The figure who had been looking at him pulled away from the others and framed himself in the path as if he meant to block Pullo's advance. The man's movements were liquid smooth, slow but purposeful.

The one who had spoken had already turned back toward the door of the tomb, as if the order to kill Titus Pullo was enough to know it done. "Burn it," he said.

Pullo hadn't fought since Elephantine. Twenty years, was it? And that had been with Vorenus at his side. But he knew the feel of the weight of the gladius in his hand. He knew the steps of the dance of killing a man. He'd done it enough.

The conditions might have been different over the years, the enemies might have had different faces, but in the end the deaths were all the same. It was a simple thing to do. A blade was a blade. And a man was a man.

One only needed to start to see it done.

He looked up, ready to use *this* blade to kill *this* man, and in that moment one of the three huddled figures in the dark screamed in a horrible wail of agony—a sound that Pullo had never heard in the wars of men. And in the same instant, in the same heartbeat, a boiling jet of liquid fire erupted from them. It struck the door of the courtyard around the tomb he and Vorenus had bought. It struck, and the door and part of the wall exploded up and away in a thunderous storm of rock and molten flame.

Pullo was flung backward into the steps behind him, the air bursting from his lungs.

He hit the stone hard. The world spun. He heard an inhuman screech of glee over the ringing in his head and the tumult of destruction.

Fearing an immediate attack, Pullo kicked himself to his left and instinctively tried to scramble to his feet. But his legs didn't bend beneath him like they once did, and his feet failed to find purchase on the stone. In the end he only spun around and over onto his side, looking back down the path from which he'd been thrown.

The man facing him had hardly moved, but the others had. As Pullo stared, feeling terror for the first time that he could remember, the three figures had slid into the smoke around the gaping breach in the courtyard around the tomb of the Ark. They were gone.

Pullo planted his hands on the dusted ground and heaved himself to his feet, desperate to move, to fight, to stop them. Only then did the last figure he was facing advance.

It did not walk. It glided forward, almost as if its feet did not touch the ground, and the cloak about its body hung unnaturally still. Pullo felt a sudden chill that pierced his clothing and skin and his very bones.

Earlier that night, Selene had spoken to them of demons. She'd told them of the pit from which they'd arisen. She'd told them of their power and their hunger. She'd told them to be very, very afraid.

And Pullo was. He now knew what he faced.

The demon floated closer. Menacing. It raised its hands to reveal long fingers the color of pale marble. Pullo swallowed hard as he took his stance, trying to ignore new pains in his back and hip. Trying to steady the blade in a hand that wanted to shake from his cold fear. Wishing he had Vorenus by his side.

For how could a man defeat a demon? How could he possibly do it alone?

The demon, almost as if it sensed Pullo's doubt, hissed and swept toward him. Pullo, with no choices left, roared and lurched forward on his hobbled legs.

The demon was too fast. It shifted through the space between them with blinding speed, grinning, swimming around him in a kind of circle, toying with the bigger man as he struggled to keep his stance. When Pullo finally lunged at it, the demon slid around the blow and left him teetering off balance. Then it spun behind him, and with a calm precision raked its too-long nails across Pullo's right shoulder.

Pullo screamed and threw his weight backward, hoping to slam the demon into the ground, but already it had slipped away. Instead of striking a blow, Pullo just fell awkwardly to the ground. And before he could rise up to defend himself, the demon had floated over top of him. Its foot crushed down on Pullo's wrist, and for all the bigger man's strength he could not move it.

The demon bent at the waist. It smiled as it did so. Its teeth were a perfect row of white the color of bleached bones, and when it opened its mouth it spoke with the fetid air of death and decay. "I will taste you before you die," it sang.

It raised up—as if it was stretching its limbs before it began the process of rending his flesh—and in that instant an arrow slammed into its shoulder.

The demon hissed, an angry, wounded sound, and it stepped off of him, looking up.

A powerful wind kicked down, staggering the demon and spitting dust into Pullo's eyes.

It passed over them both, and when it did so—like goddesses

descending from the heavens—two women fell out of the sky and onto the still-standing wall of the courtyard. The light of the dawn was upon them.

Miriam was already fitting another arrow to her bow. "Get off my father," she said.

18

The Garden of Gethsemane

The storm didn't so much form over the city as it appeared there—a sudden column of roiling and swirling black cloud, flashing hot and angry. Beneath it, the deluge was just as swift—a torrent of water rushing down like a window had opened to heavens of water above.

People screamed and fled, or fell to their knees in worship. To them, it was retribution for the desecration of sacred space by the Romans upon the Temple Mount. It was the coming of a god.

Juba did none of those things. He knew the truth. No god had come to Jerusalem.

The moment he'd heard that Romans had marched upon the Temple, he was almost sure he could guess what was happening. He was already nearing the foot of its high walls when the storm had appeared above.

So while the rest of the city stopped or recoiled in terror from what was happening above the Temple, the king of Mauretania saw the terrible storm and began to sprint against the tide, speeding his way to the wide southern steps. If the Trident of Poseidon was on the Temple Mount, then Tiberius had to be there.

And maybe Selene, too.

Juba had cursed himself a thousand times since the day Selene had left, since the night the demon had attacked him. Every time he looked into a mirror and saw the scars etched across his face—or instinctively tried to lift his left arm and found it near useless—he remembered the despair he'd felt, and he was ashamed.

He had failed his love that day. He had failed her and he had paid for it in blood. The arm would never be right again. The scars upon his face might fade, and eventually he could hide most of them within his beard when it grew back—the surgeons had been forced to shave it all off to tend to the cuts—but he would forever feel the wounds and know they were there. And it was right that it was so. He had failed her, and justice demanded a payment for that failure.

So be it. He would carry that shame just as he carried the marks of his wounds.

But he had also made another decision that night. He would no longer despair. Whenever he thought of the shame, whenever he thought of his wounds, whenever he thought of what horrors might stand before Selene . . . he forced himself to remember how the she-demon who called herself Acme had bled.

He'd felt her blood on his hands. He'd seen it mixing with his own upon the tiles. She could bleed. She could die. And past the despair was the courage to fight to see it done.

Selene had found that courage before him.

He had given his orders to his stewards. He had seen to the care of his son. He had bought passage on the fastest ship he could find. He only hoped he was not too late to do his part. He had no weapon beyond a dagger and a short sword—and only one good arm to use either—but even if his part was to die distracting a demon long enough for Selene to kill it, that would be enough. It would mean he tried. It would mean he fought.

His arm was near to limp, but as he ran up the steps of the Temple Mount he was pleased to learn his legs were still strong. He took the stone courses two by two, bounding his way past those who'd fallen prostrate or were moving in the other direction.

Thunder was everywhere. Deafening him to the screams he saw on faces fleeing from the unworldly vision. The concussive forces of each pounded on his chest like a drum, as if determined to drive him back.

But he pressed on. As the sky flashed black to yellow to white to black again, he pressed on. As he struck the wall of rain and could hardly see ahead, he pressed on. Though the waters pouring down the steps threatened to take his feet out from under him, he pressed on.

And then, all at once, the rain stopped.

Juba looked up. The column of black that had churned into sudden existence above the Temple Mount was spinning itself apart from the inside, dissipating into vaporous tendrils that were stretching out as the dense cloud dissolved. The thunder had stopped, too, and with it gone there was an eerie silence upon Jerusalem.

Something flashed in the corner of his eye. Juba turned to look, and he saw four figures huddled together near the edge of the cleansing pool—figures that he was certain he'd not seen before.

Three of them were peering upward at the clouds, and his own gaze instinctively followed theirs. Then, when he looked back down again, they were gone. They'd disappeared. As if they'd never been there.

He shook his head even as his mind tried to filter what he'd seen. He'd seen them only for a moment, and he felt like he knew them, but none of them was Selene.

Turning back to the Temple Mount, he ran on, ducking into the doorway of a columned hall along its southern side. Men had been fighting here, he could tell—Romans and Jews were dead each by each upon the ground—but none were fighting in this moment. They were either cowering or gathering themselves to their feet in still-stunned awe.

Juba ignored them all. The storm had been gathered about the Temple ahead, and he ran there, weaving between the statues of men prostrate or turned in wonder.

He was halfway to the beautiful Temple itself when he saw two figures limp out from a ruinous hole in the side of its walls. One of them was Thrasyllus, and the other was a man he'd not seen in years, his arm under the astrologer's shoulder, half dragging the younger man toward a gate in the lower wall around the inner complex.

Didymus.

He was older than when Juba had last seen him—as were they all—but he was unmistakable. What he was doing here, Juba didn't know, but he was helping Thrasyllus, who'd risked his life to warn him and Selene about the demons. For now that made him an ally.

Juba angled for the gate, arriving just behind the two scholars. A company of Romans was there, arrayed in a kind of half-circle around the point of entry, guarding it. Citizens of Jerusalem, their crude weapons no match for Roman armor and blade, lay in bloodied piles around the legionnaires.

The Romans, like the lines of enemies around them, were still in shock, staring at the dissolving storm. Didymus limped past them without a look, moving through the gate and making his slow way across the paved space of the Temple Mount toward the portico on its eastern side.

At last one of the citizens was stirred from his amazement.

He saw the two scholars, recognized them as the foreigners they were, and started to raise his weapon even as he turned to shout at them.

Juba had but one working arm, but it was enough. In the instant the man drew in his breath, Juba brought the pommel of his dagger down upon his skull.

The citizen fell to the ground—silenced but alive. He'd awake with a headache, Juba was sure, but he would awake.

Didymus had turned at the motion, and his eyes widened. "Juba, I—"

"Selene," Juba said. "Where is she? Where are the Shards?"

The scholar's eyes darted across the scene before him, as if he half expected to see something there. "Gone. We must hurry to catch them."

Juba hurried to his side. Sheathing his dagger, he hoisted Thrasyllus over his still-good shoulder. Near as Juba could tell, the scholar was nearly unconscious. He moaned, but he didn't fight. "This way," Juba said, starting to turn back in the direction he'd come.

Didymus put his hand upon his arm. "No," the librarian said, pulling him east. "This way. Solomon's stairs."

Knowing no better option, Juba nodded and followed Didymus into the shadows of the eastern portico and the stairs toward the Kidron Valley far below.

• • •

As the sun shone down from a now cloudless sky above, the three men took their rest amid the vines of a garden on the other side of the narrow valley. They sat down upon the stone ledge of a terrace and leaned back, panting. Juba had carried Thrasyllus most of the way down to the base of the valley, and then he and Didymus had taken turns bearing the third man's weight this far back up the other side. They were tired, all of them, but Thrasyllus was shaken by something far more than just physical exhaustion. The rising slope of the Mount of Olives at their back, the rising wall of the desecrated Temple Mount before them, Didymus explained what he knew.

When the scholar was done, Juba stared at the distant stones of the sacred place before them. It was so much, and he felt the old despair rising. "So this ring—the Seal of Solomon—allows them to go anywhere?"

"It allows them to move through the Aether," Didymus said, nodding. "It's like an invisible fabric that binds all things. So yes, anywhere they know. Instantaneously. They could be in Rome right now."

"Or they could have the Ark. They could be in Petra."

Didymus shook his head, his hair reflecting silver in the shapes of sun and shadow in the garden. "I don't think so."

"You said the Aether could take them anywhere."

"Anywhere they *know*," Didymus corrected. "You need to know a place to go there. It's not some map you can point your finger to and be there. You need to know where you're going."

"But you said that the female demon—the one who attacked me—must have been to Petra. She knew the Ark was there."

"It's the only thing that makes sense," Didymus agreed. "She was in Petra. She saw enough to know the Ark was there."

Juba tried to ignore the memory of pain that swelled at the thought of that night. It made him want to reach up and rub at the scars of his torn shoulder. "How did she know it was there?"

Didymus frowned. "That's a good question."

"I told you," Thrasyllus said to Juba, his voice hushed in pain.

Juba reached over and squeezed the scholar's shoulder in sympathy for what he'd been through. "You did. You warned us and took a great risk to do so. Thank you."

Didymus abruptly stood up. He walked to the nearest vine

and reached up to touch one of the leaves. "So that's how," he said.

Juba rubbed at his legs. For all his tiredness, though, he managed a smile. "You're ahead of me, librarian."

Didymus turned. "Don't you see? It's Selene. She knew of Petra. She went there. And the demoness followed her."

"So she's in Petra? Even now?"

"We must assume so. It makes sense."

"And the demons on their way. We've no way to warn her."

"We can try to get there."

"They can get there instantly. They're surely there already."

Didymus shook his head, looking to Juba like a disappointed teacher. "Only to a known place, Juba."

"You just said the demon was there."

"But she can't use the Shard. None of the demons can. The Shards need life, and the demons have none. Tiberius is the one using the Seal. Yes, he's controlled by the demons now— the fool, he's become their puppet—but it's still Tiberius who is using it. I saw as much with my own eyes."

Juba understood at last. "And Tiberius hasn't been there, so he can't take them there."

"I don't believe so," Didymus said.

"Then we have time."

"Some. They can still use it to speed their path from hill to hill. As long as the strength of Tiberius holds out, anyway."

Every time the man's name was spoken, Juba wanted to spit. But for the moment he fought down his revulsion at the memory of what the Roman had done to Selene. For the moment, he was willing even to think the best of the man if it would increase the chance that they could reach Selene and the Ark before the demons did. "Do you think maybe he will resist them?"

"None can," Thrasyllus whispered.

Didymus looked at the younger scholar with pity. "It's true. He cannot resist them. Our hope is not that he is strong. Our hope is that he is weak. Using a Shard is difficult. You know this."

"It uses a man up," Juba said. In his own pity and understanding, he once more gripped Thrasyllus in shared understanding. "You'll get better, but the recovery takes time."

Thrasyllus managed a wan smile and looked off down the valley as it curved around the side of Jerusalem.

"So it does," Didymus agreed. "And Tiberius is as mortal as we are. I doubt he can take much more than either of you took. With the help of the demons he can use the Seal, but it will steadily exhaust him. He will need rest along the way. It may take them several days to reach Petra."

Juba allowed himself a smile. "So we count on his weakness. I like that. It gives us time."

"Perhaps. And following them is the only thing I know to do."

Juba nodded, but he knew that didn't necessarily resolve their problems. As he looked around at the other men he saw how tired they all were. "But how?"

Didymus opened his mouth, then shut it again. His shoulders seemed to slump. "I guess I was hoping perhaps you would have an idea on that. Transportation isn't exactly my area of expertise. Horses, maybe? We need a ride."

Thrasyllus was still looking down the valley, but he abruptly stirred and lifted himself up to a more upright position. He coughed, winced in pain, and then managed to lift a weary arm and point. "How about a rebellion?"

Juba and Didymus both turned to look. Passing out of the city, riding hard, was a storm of horses. Armed and angry men. Makeshift banners were unfurled around a man at the front of the mob, and the sunshine was flashing brightly from something upon his head.

"Is that who I think it is?" asked Didymus.

Thrasyllus nodded and started trying to get to his feet.

Juba stood and reached down to help the exhausted man to his feet. "Who is it?"

Didymus seemed to be close to laughing. "It's one of Herod's slaves, I think. His name is Simon. And unless I'm wrong—"

"You're never wrong," Thrasyllus whispered.

"Well, unless I'm wrong, he's wearing Herod's crown."

19

No Choices

As a child Miriam had wanted to rise up like a hawk against the bright blue sky. To fly, she thought, was to be free. Free of the ground. Free of the bonds of stone and sand. With jealousy she'd watched birds soaring with the wind, stretching their wings to ride it high above the deserts and mountains, striking out against the clouds in search of the great sea to the west.

She'd longed for it. She'd dreamed of it.

Yet now that she had taken flight, now that Selene—somehow, through some extraordinary power—was carrying them over the Mount of Moses, Miriam found she wanted nothing more than to reach the ground.

The strange blue light had flashed its way to the hillsides above Petra, and now its direction was clear. It had flashed where the Roman encampment had stretched itself in the open space between the city walls and the terraced farms east of the city, and then it had flashed at the foot of the wadi just east of the Mount of Moses—the canyon holding the tomb that hid the Ark.

Clinging to Selene, hanging in space as a wave of air sped them over the cliffs and down toward the tomb, Miriam saw the pale blue light flash onto the path beside the small court-yard before the tomb. In her mind, she drew a line between the places the light had flashed, remembering back to her own hikes in and around the city. The places were all in a sightline from one another. Was that the reason it had stopped outside the walls of the courtyard? If so, then there was a chance that whatever it was couldn't get in.

At last she saw them. Four people just visible in the growing light. And a fifth, Titus Pullo, was farther up the wadi.

"Demons," Selene said.

Demons.

It was an impossible thing to say. An impossible thing to be real. But Miriam didn't doubt it all. It was only as impossible as it was to fly.

Everything Pullo and Vorenus had said about the Ark, everything they'd said about the Shards of Heaven . . . all of it and more was true.

As if in confirmation, a line of roiling flame shot out from the huddled group of demons, and part of the courtyard wall exploded in fire and debris.

Selene shuddered, and the air around them shuddered, too.

Three of the figures disappeared into the smoke of the courtyard. The third floated toward Pullo, the man who, along with Vorenus, had raised her as his own. Pullo bravely raised his sword, but the demon danced around him, making him limp and hobble in circles. The big man, so solid and strong in her eyes, now seemed old and broken, his defeat inevitable.

"He needs help!" Miriam shouted over the winds that were pushing them down toward the scene. "Faster!"

"I have to control it," Selene gasped. "You don't know. It's so much."

But it was too slow. Pullo—her beloved Pullo—was going to die before they ever reached him. He was no match for the demon. Surely none of them was.

The big man lunged, missed, and Miriam saw the demon

dart into his back, slashing at his flesh. Pullo fell backward and down, and the demon was upon him.

"Oh God," Selene croaked.

As if in response to her anguish, the wind surged under their feet.

Under their feet.

Miriam was holding on to Selene, but in a flash she knew that the truth wasn't that Selene was carrying her. The air was carrying them both.

She let go.

She teetered for a moment on the churning invisible wave, but she didn't fall. So she slipped the bow from her back, an arrow from her quiver.

The demon was looming above Pullo, victorious.

Miriam pulled. Aimed. Loosed.

The arrow sailed nearly true. She aimed for its heart, but instead the shaft pounded into the demon's shoulder. It was no killing blow, but it was enough to force the creature back off the wounded Pullo.

And then the two women passed over them, and Selene began to release the wind. Like feathers they came down, dropping onto the corner of the courtyard wall that still stood. By some unspoken agreement, Selene was already turning to face inside, peering into the smoke and debris where the other three had gone. Miriam took her balance on the wall. Once more she began to take her aim.

"Get off my father," she said.

The demon was turning to hiss at her—rasping and angry— but Miriam was unafraid. Pullo had stood against it. Vorenus would have done the same. And behind her were the statues of her parents, who'd given their lives for what they loved.

She loosed another arrow.

She aimed again for the demon's heart, but this time the

creature was ready. Its arm swung—faster than thought—and the arrow clattered harmlessly away. It seemed to smile.

From beside her, Selene summoned a gale of wind that spun down from the sky and blistered through the courtyard that she could not see. Shrieks sounded out in response. And then Selene was leaping out into the air and out of sight, hurtling away on a wave of wind.

Miriam had no time to look. Already she was drawing another arrow, but the demon on the path below her was gathering itself to attack. It burst upward at her, hissing fiercely, and Miriam had no time to draw her bowstring for another shot.

Instinctively she raised her arms to fend off the blow, gritting her teeth as the thing crashed down into her. Its long-fingered hands, tipped with nails like claws, flexed toward her throat, but her raised bow caught just enough of the strikes to stop them for the space of a heartbeat.

Then her feet slipped from the tiles atop the wall, and she fell away from the attack, plunging backward into the courtyard.

Miriam's back arched. Her feet, in their last instant of contact with the wall, kicked.

For a moment she hung in space. The world slowed to a crawl as she fell. She saw the demon crouched atop the wall, swiping at the air where she'd been. And she felt her body twisting, turning in midair as it reflexively wanted to see the coming impact.

She saw Selene. In the second that she hung in the air, Miriam saw it all in a kind of slow time. From the wall, Selene had seen the others were almost across the threshold of the courtyard. They were only steps from the tomb itself, where the Ark rested in a niche reserved for the dead. She'd released a gale at their backs, and it had knocked the three figures down upon the threshold of the tomb.

Selene was flying as Miriam fell. The winds she had summoned were spiriting her across the open courtyard, throwing
her into the mouth of the tomb. It was a race to the Ark, and
Selene was determined to see that she stood between the demons and the object of their desires.

But one of them was up.

Miriam saw it with perfect clarity as she plummeted from
the courtyard wall.

Selene's wind had leveled them all, but one of the demons—
the other male—was quick to react. He'd been struck down,
but he'd just as quickly sprung into action behind a man who
was with them. He'd put an object in the man's hands. And as
Selene flew over them, he'd grasped the man by the neck with
his left hand of darkness.

Fire erupted from the object.

The torrent of flame was wild and ill aimed at first, but Miriam recognized that it was a matter of moments before it was
controlled and aimed. Selene, she saw, would die in the air.

So slow had time become as Miriam fell that the ground
came with a suddenness that she did not expect. She struck the
ground with a lung-evacuating cough, and she slid across the
paved stones, her eyes glancing back to the wall just in time to
see the demon atop it launch himself after her.

What remained was an instant. Far less than a heartbeat, it was
time enough for only one decision. The arrow she'd pulled was
still in one hand. The bow she needed was in the other. She
had time enough for a draw against the falling form of the demon attacking her or against the rising form of the demon
attacking Selene.

It was no choice at all.

Still sliding through the dust and debris that had covered
over the surface of the courtyard, Miriam kicked herself over
in a ball, trying to protect her head. When she uncoiled her

momentum, she came down upon one knee, facing the demons and Selene. Already she was drawing the string back.

There was time enough for a single shot, and all of her being pressed into the bow, just as Abdes Pantera had taught her. Press, hold, and release, he'd said.

And so she did. The bow loosed, an exhale of air.

The shaft wobbled in the air—the fletching vibrating past the bow as it loosed—but then it caught the air and flew. In a flash it struck across the right arm of the demon that was directing the power of God against Selene.

The demon shrieked as the arrow ripped across its arm—tearing through whatever passed for flesh upon it. The mortal human in the grip of his left hand wailed, too, and the line of unnatural fire he'd been aiming at Selene skipped across the courtyard. It glanced across Selene, and she screamed—human and horrible—as the fire made her release the Shard and she lost control of the air above the courtyard.

Miriam saw the woman tumbling, ablaze, and then she saw her disappear into the mouth of the tomb ahead of the demons in the courtyard.

Selene had beat them.

It was all Miriam could think.

She'd beaten them. She'd won.

Miriam turned back, smiling, just in time to see the demon come down from the wall behind her. So be it. She'd made her choice.

The demon landed on two light feet and, ever in control, the unnatural being took a single, graceful step forward and plunged its long fingers into her gut.

It was the end. She didn't need to see the blood or feel her heart stop to know it. She'd had a choice, and she'd chosen the Ark over her life.

Miriam gasped. The bow dropped from her grip.

The demon smiled, its head turning in a look of curiosity as its hand twisted in her stomach.

She felt a tug and pull deep inside of her, but her eyes never looked away from the beast before her. She would not cry. She would give it no satisfaction. Her parents didn't beg in the end, and neither would she.

She heard a roar, and she saw the shine of a blade swiping through the clearing air. The head of the demon, still smiling, broke loose and fell away from its once-perfect body.

Pullo was behind it, already reaching out to catch her.

Miriam wanted to smile, but the silent stone was quickly rising at her back. And, with it, a welcoming darkness.

20

Daughter of Pharaohs

PETRA, 4 BCE

The right side of her body rippling with flame, Selene tumbled into the shadows of the tomb like a fallen angel. Out of instinct she closed her eyes and ducked her head to her chest, trying to make herself small, and she bounced once against the stone floor, then struck again and rolled, careening into the back wall of the tomb.

For the next heartbeats, her world was nothing but a surging fire that engulfed her flesh.

It was the Lance of Olyndicus, she knew. The Shard of Fire. She'd seen herself how it set men ablaze with molten heat and left behind only the ash and char.

How she still lived if she'd been hit, she didn't know.

Had the demon missed?

Or was it the power of the Aegis that kept her breathing, kept the pain muted enough for her to think?

There was no doubt that she could feel the Shard of Life at her chest. Its presence coursed through her with every heartbeat. Sustaining. Empowering. Invigorating.

Buoyed by its presence, she opened her eyes and saw what the Lance had done.

Most of the clothes on the right side of her body had turned to cinder, but the actual blaze seemed to have been snuffed by her impact. Otherwise the rest of her clothes would be gone, too.

What was left at her side was a raw tear from her shoulder to her thigh, deep and undoubtedly mortal. Remarkably, there was no blood. The elemental heat of the Shard had cauterized her veins even as it stripped away her skin and the layers beneath it. What remained was just the wound, wide and terrible, exposing flashes of white ribs amid red-brown muscle. The smell of cooked meat hung in the air.

She wanted to throw up at the sight of it, at the sheer horror of it, but the Aegis pulsed at her chest. It made her calm. It made her think clearly.

This was always going to end in death, she reminded herself. No life lived forever. Didymus had taught her that when she was young, long before she'd seen the deaths pile up around her. What mattered was what a person did with whatever time they were given.

She'd done much wrong. She knew that.

But this, here and now, was a chance to do something right. It might be a fool's cause to fight against such power, such horror—but it was the right cause.

The room was not large. Beyond the open doorway she'd plummeted through, it extended into the mountain perhaps only twenty feet to the wall behind her back. It was squarish, and to her left and right there were deep recesses carved into the walls—places, no doubt, for entombment. They were empty.

Which meant that the Ark, the Shard of Earth, was in a third recess behind her.

Her right leg and shoulder weren't working, but fortunately she'd slid to a stop on her left side. Gasping, convulsing between her body's expectation of death and the Shard's will to live, she pushed herself up to a sitting position on the floor.

While her back rested on stone, her head leaned back into space and touched wood.

Selene thought of what her beautiful Juba had once done to try to possess it, the lives he'd taken in his anger and his thirst for revenge. And then she thought of her beautiful half-brother, Caesarion, who'd given his life to protect it in his love and his thirst for a better world.

My turn, she thought.

She'd lost her grip on the Palladium when she'd been struck, but it hadn't fallen from her satchel. She reached down with her left hand and gripped the broken statue, lifting it out.

Such a simple thing, she mused. How long had it sat in the Temple of the Vestal Virgins in Rome, untouched and unnoticed? Its power was there the whole time, hidden in its beating heart, just waiting for someone to unleash it.

The light in the tomb changed. A shadow had risen up to fill the doorway. A man, with his back against the light.

"Selene," Tiberius said.

Before she could answer, another shadow rose up behind him like a silent fog. It reached a long-fingered, almost skeletal hand up to the back of her rapist's neck.

Tiberius visibly stiffened. His hands rose up before him.

The Lance. Fire. Death.

Selene's working hand lifted the Palladium to the thrumming Aegis upon her chest. Air. Life.

Heat surged into the room from the air outside the tomb, focusing down and through the two men. But tendrils of that same air swept around them, snaking across the walls and floor and ceiling of stone, gathering into a vortex that pulled at Selene's black hair.

When the roiling flame shot across the space between them, a gale of wind uncoiled to meet it with the roar of a thousand storms.

Air and Fire impacted with a concussive blast, fanning the flames out until they were an infernal wall of slashing fire that radiated across the breadth of the tomb. Selene shut her eyes against the shock of the blinding light.

She screamed as the power coursed through her, as it fed from her. From beyond the wall of flame she heard another scream, and she knew that it was Tiberius. A small corner of her heart wanted to revel in whatever pain he felt, in whatever ways he was being torn apart, but in truth she felt sorry for him. She pitied him, for he was not strong. He did not have love.

And love, she had learned, was the greatest power of all.

Selene opened her eyes to the glare. The barrier of wind she was holding between them was bent back toward her, threatening collapse from the edges where it met the stone walls.

"No," she said. And then again, more forcefully, "No."

She lifted her head from where it rested against the wood of the Ark. She bent forward, and the wall bent, too: moving ever so slightly back again.

Caesarion had given everything.

Her right side still useless, she bent her left leg underneath her.

Slowly she pushed herself upward, her back sliding up the wall, then inch by inch up the side of the Ark.

She wanted to look at it, she wanted to turn and use it, but there was no time. And her power would be enough. Against these demons, against the whole of the world, her love would be enough.

She was standing, leaning against the Ark.

Her left leg came forward, and the right slid forward behind it. She rose away from the wood. Fresh waves of pain raged up from her torn body, but she pushed them aside. They would have their moment. But not now. This moment was hers.

She stepped forward, and the wall of air stepped forward, too.

The agony of Tiberius was a wail now. She limped another step closer, and the wall of wind moved with her. The edges where it met the stone on either side of her were straightening out.

Another step, and the fire was thinning. She could see the two figures beyond it now, shimmering through the coursing veil of flame. Tiberius. The demon.

And another demon, too. The female. She was clamoring up beside the first.

She looked scared.

Selene limped forward again, and now she saw another figure through the flames. Beyond the demons, beyond the tomb, a hulking man who could only be Titus Pullo was lumbering through the sunlight with a sword in his hand.

The demon had something in her hand. She clawed for the neck of Tiberius. When she reached it, the fire stopped. For an instant she saw that Tiberius was starting to go limp, his eyes rolling to white, his mouth agape. But then he and the two demons clinging to him folded in upon themselves and in a flash of pale light were gone.

Unhindered now, Selene's wind launched forward even as she released her grip on the Palladium. It spun out from the tomb in a frenzy of dust, kicking the mighty Pullo to his back as if he were a rag doll.

The Palladium fell into her satchel, and Selene managed to stumble forward toward the open doorway. She caught herself there against the right side of it, leaning against the stone.

Pullo was on his back. Beyond him, she could see, lay one of the demons and Miriam.

"Oh God," she whispered.

The demon's corpse was headless. The front of Miriam's shirt was shredded. Bright blood was everywhere.

From the ground, Pullo groaned. Selene leaned her right side farther into the stone where he wouldn't see.

"Pullo!"

The big man coughed. "Selene?" One of his hands was lifted to his head. The other seemed to be scrambling for the blade that had fallen from his grip. "Where are they?"

"Gone," she called out. "But I need you to get up, Pullo. I need your help."

He pushed himself upright, wincing, battered by wounds old and new.

"Hurry," she urged. "I know it hurts. But you've got to make it. Just a little longer."

He lumbered to his feet, swaying, still in a kind of shock. He started to stumble toward her, catching and recatching his balance like a drunken man. "You're hurt?"

Selene swallowed hard. "Just hurry," she said.

He was trying not to cry, she could see. "Gods, Selene . . . Miriam, I tried—"

"There's time," she said, willing away her own pain, sloughing it off and letting what was left of her feed back into the Shard upon her chest. "Just hurry."

He reached her, and his eyes were still disoriented.

Selene gripped one of his arms fiercely, willing him to look into her eyes. "Focus, Pullo. Look at me. Take me to Miriam."

Her own wounds were still in the shadows. But he could see enough of her tattered clothes to know there was a problem. "You're hurt."

She nodded toward the courtyard, sending his attention there even as she used her left arm to pull herself painfully into the crook of his right elbow. "To Miriam, Pullo. Now."

Titus Pullo was a soldier. He knew an order. He knew to obey. And so he lifted her weight, knitted his brow in concentration to keep himself upright, and together they hobbled out into the sunlight, out through the destruction, to where a young girl lay in a pool of red upon the stones.

"Set me beside her," Selene said. She couldn't tell if Miriam was still breathing. She couldn't tell if her heart was stilled. But she had hope that there was time for one last miracle.

Pullo started to lower her down, and only then did he see the right side of her body. "Oh, gods. Selene—"

She ignored him, her working left arm reaching for the clasps of the breastplate. "Help me get it off," she said.

Pullo was frozen. "Without it—"

"I die either way," she said. "Miriam might yet live. Help me. Now."

Pullo reached down. His big, strong hands shook as he fumbled with the first of the clasps she couldn't reach.

Selene reached up and touched his quaking arm. "It'll be all right, Pullo. It's my choice. Do this for me."

He was weeping openly now. But his arm had stopped shaking. And his fingers undid the first clasp, then the second.

Selene closed her eyes for a moment, pushing her will to live into the throbbing black stone, imagining her soul being drawn into it.

"Selene," Pullo said.

She opened her eyes and looked into his. For all that he'd been torn apart, his eyes were the same kind eyes she'd known as a child. She nodded. "Do it," she said.

The Aegis had fused into her charred flesh on the right side, and she ground her teeth as her skin tugged, cracked, and tore. But she did not cry out.

As the Shard pulled away she could almost feel its power

grasping at her essence like invisible fingers. She did not fight it.

And then it was off, and Pullo was putting it on Miriam.

Waves of pain were surging up at Selene from everywhere, but she felt them only like a distant rumble in the back of her mind. Her left hand had fallen back to the ground, and somehow it had found the hand of Miriam beside her. She gripped it.

"Move the Ark," she whispered.

Pullo was kneeling. He was saying something, though she couldn't hear him. He knew what he needed to do, though. He was a smart man, despite his protests. It would take time for the demons to come back, but not long. And they'd come better prepared this time. Petra wouldn't be safe. He knew that.

She thought of Juba and wondered what he would tell their son. She loved them. She would give anything to see them again. But she wasn't sad. She had done what was right. No regrets.

She thought, too, of her parents and her brothers. Of all the ones who'd gone before.

If there was anything more to come, she hoped she would see them there.

She felt herself falling away. The sky was but a point of light as the darkness rose. And she saw that Pullo was there. But it was a memory, a younger, unscarred man from a more innocent time. He was frightened, for he did not belong.

"Go back," she tried to say, and her voice breathed like a final sigh. "You're not done."

And then he was gone, but she wasn't alone. The sun was coming up. She was rising, her back to the sun as dawn broke the shadow and cast its light over green and fertile lands that stretched and stretched like a never-ending song. Children were running there, laughing as they danced below her feet, and she was certain she knew their names.

Somewhere, in a distant, dry land, she still felt the touch of Miriam's fingers in her own. And just before that last bright point of light went out, she felt them move.

Somewhere, somewhere far away behind her, she smiled.

PART III

THE GATE OF HEAVEN

21

GABRIEL'S REVELATION

Standing on a rocky slope, not far from the summit of the mountain, Juba looked out upon the darkness of Judaea. In the distance, he could see that Jericho was still burning. Herod had kept a royal treasury there, and Simon's ragtag army had been merciless in taking it and destroying anyone who opposed them.

Not that they were stealing it, of course. Not from their perspective. To them, Simon was a Messiah. He was the rightful king of the Jews, proclaimed—so they said—by the archangel Gabriel himself. The riches, like their lives, were his.

Juba had never seen anything quite like such combined passion of religious and military devotion. It was both stirring and frightening, and he wondered at the political implications of such a mentality. It was just the sort of thing he enjoyed talking to Selene about.

Selene.

Juba couldn't help but sigh longingly. By whatever gods were in this world, he missed her. The chance to see her again could not come soon enough.

He hoped that Didymus would be successful in steering the rebels south, toward Petra. They'd joined with Simon and his growing force just outside of Jerusalem, and as they'd ridden west Didymus had left Thrasyllus in the care of Juba while he worked to endear himself to the leaders. It hadn't taken long for the white-haired old librarian to prove himself a helpful source of information for the slave-turned-Messiah. It had been Didymus who suggested the assault on Jericho—riches, and a ride east when Simon had been planning a turn north.

The crunch of earth nearby signaled the approach of Thrasyllus. Three days had passed since they'd left the Temple Mount, and the astrologer's strength was increasingly improved. "I won't ask," he said.

Juba smiled. They'd known each other long enough to know that they were both missing their loves tonight. They were certain that if Selene was in Petra, Lapis was, too. "I'm sure they're fine," he said.

"I hope so." The scholar came up to stand beside Juba and joined him in staring west at the glowing fires in the distance. "But Jericho cost us a day. If Didymus can't convince them to turn south now—"

"We steal horses," Juba said. He'd already made his mind up on that point. "We'll go just before the dawn. I've helped myself from some of their supplies. We'll be hungry on the way, but we'll have water."

Thrasyllus let out a breath in obvious relief. "Hunger I can take. Just need speed."

"I agree. But we also need to get there. The roads are dangerous. The whole countryside seems at war with itself. The longer we can stay with this band, the better off we are." It was a balance, Juba knew. The sort of decision he'd been judging for years back in Mauretania.

"Let's hope Didymus can do it, then," Thrasyllus said.

"He can indeed," Didymus said from the darkness behind them.

Juba felt his heart thrill in his chest as he turned and saw Didymus making his way down from the tents gathered around a little shrine at the summit of the mountain. "We'll turn south?"

Didymus nodded in the moonlight. "We will indeed, though I can't take all credit. It was a near thing between my advice to raid south and John, who wants Simon to go back to the Temple Mount and bring God's glory there. He continues to talk about a rather desperate battle between good and evil happening upon the Mount of God."

John was one of the most vocal priests in the army. A young man with a soaring charisma, he'd caught the attention of many with his devotion to the idea of a Messiah and his soaring proclamations of the change that would come with him. Juba was naturally distrustful of him. "Another of his prophecies?" he asked.

"They're saying it is. I've found out he was born not far from here, actually. A place called Qum'ran." The scholar pointed to the darkness of hillsides south of Jericho, near the beginning of the deep flat of black that was the Dead Sea. "There somewhere, I'm given to understand. Secretive community. Very secluded. The sort of place I would like, I think."

"You said it was a near thing between you," Thrasyllus said.

"It was. But Simon was far more than a slave in the shadows during his many years in Herod's palace. He was listening. He heard the Romans and Herod alike discuss strategy, discuss plots. It's quite impressive, really. He knows he doesn't have enough men with him yet to hold the Temple against the Roman reinforcements that are apparently coming down from Syria. Despite all his talk of being a Messiah, in the end I think he knows that battles are won or lost with blades and blood. He trusts more in that than in the possibility that the heavens will open up with an army of angels to fight behind him."

Juba allowed himself to smile a little at that. It was bewildering to him how convinced these people were that God was fully capable of saving them at any time, but that He was just waiting for some future moment to do it, allowing them to suffer whatever horrors in the meantime. It was a cruel and, he thought, arbitrary vision of a deity. "Any word on that Roman army? Do we know where they are?"

The Roman reinforcements marching down into the land of the Jews were much on the mind of Simon and his men. In Jericho, they'd heard the rumor that at least one legion was marching south, intent on hunting Simon down.

"They expect scouts to come back soon. But in the meantime Simon plans to ride south himself, to take the King's Highway ahead of them and nip at the borders of Nabataea. It won't get us to Petra, but it'll get us most of the way there."

"Good," Juba said. "You did well."

"I've tried."

For several minutes the three men looked out at the stars and the land stretching west toward the flickering fires of Jericho and beyond.

Juba, for the first time in a long while, was feeling something like real hope. They were going to ride south. They'd get closer to Petra. To Selene and Lapis and the Ark. Closer to defeating Tiberius, defeating the demons.

At times it could seem so impossible, but he had to hope.

"You know," Didymus abruptly said, "the Jews say this is the mountain upon which Moses was allowed to see the land that God promised to them."

"The Moses the Jews believe led them out of Egypt and brought them the Ark?" Thrasyllus asked. He hadn't studied the Jewish histories as thoroughly as Juba and Didymus had, but he was passingly familiar with them.

"The very same," Didymus said.

"Their God didn't allow him to actually enter it?"

"Not in the stories," Didymus answered. "He'd done something God didn't like along the way. I can't recall what."

Juba shook his head, once again astonished by the odd faith of these people. He was also, truth be told, a little astonished to hear the scholar admit that he couldn't remember something.

Didymus gestured to the little shrine on the summit. "Apparently many Jews think he's buried here on the mountain."

"Why are we camped here, then?" Thrasyllus asked.

"Because our friend John is not among those who think he's here," Didymus said, smiling. "He favors another spot, and he seems to like the idea that camping here shows just how wrong the others are."

"That and it's a good vantage point," Juba said. "Hard to be surprised by anything up here."

Didymus nodded. "As you say."

"Seems every hill and valley in this country has some sacred history to it," Thrasyllus said. "It's strange."

Didymus shrugged. "Well, they've been here a long time."

For a moment Juba had a longing for a home he could only remember in fleeting glimpses. What histories were lost when Rome conquered his native Numidia? Were there sacred hills among his own people that he'd never learn?

"There are also stories, I'm told, that some of the Jews believe the Ark of the Covenant is hidden here on Mount Nebo." Didymus laughed a little to himself. "Strange how close we can be to the truth sometimes and not know it."

Juba sighed. "Any other news?" he asked.

"Only that John has proclaimed a new vision from the archangel Gabriel. They're already calling it Gabriel's Revelation."

"Anything interesting?" Thrasyllus asked.

"My Hebrew is rather rudimentary," Didymus admitted. "There's a reason I've done most of my talking with them in

Greek. But I'm fairly certain I caught one bit. John says that Gabriel has decreed that a great war is coming."

"That's nothing new," Juba said.

"True enough," Didymus admitted, "but he says that the archangel speaks of the coming of blood to Jerusalem—from the north, I think—and a great leader will come, backed by the archangel Michael, and that if he dies then three days later he will rise again, a prince of princes. Something to that effect."

"Must be reassuring for Simon," Juba said.

"Who's Michael?" Thrasyllus asked.

"Another of their great archangels, like Gabriel, the one John claims is speaking through him. Michael is second in power only to God Himself. His name, if I have my Hebrew correctly, means 'He who is like God.' John clearly thinks the end-times are upon the world."

"A war to end all wars," Juba whispered.

Didymus sighed. "I think they say that of all wars."

"I don't think this war will end well for these men," Thrasyllus said.

"Perhaps not," Didymus said, "but I'm doing what I can to teach them about the need for some basic field tactics. And Simon is a quick learner."

Juba laughed a little. "A librarian turned field commander?"

The old man smiled even as he tried to look offended. "As Plato said, 'Necessity is the mother of invention.' We need this band to get us as close to Petra as we can. And I've read my Caesar and my Hannibal. I know a few things."

"Just don't get ahead of yourself," Juba said. "What's written in books and what's done on the field can be two very different things."

Thrasyllus nodded in agreement. "It was Plato's master, Socrates, who said that 'The only true wisdom is in knowing you know nothing.' Sound advice."

THE REALMS OF GOD

"True enough," Didymus said, holding up his hands in mock defense as his long white hair bobbed in the moonlight. "And that's exactly why I in my wisdom advised them to turn to you, Juba, for the real fight."

Juba blinked in surprise. "What?"

"Oh, yes, indeed," Didymus said, clearly pleased with himself. "I told them the truth: that you're a prince descended from a line of great princes. An heir, one might say, to Hannibal himself. They were tremendously pleased to hear it."

As Juba gaped, another man came trotting down to them out of the darkness. He held a small scrap of paper that he handed to Didymus. Then, seeing Juba, he turned and made a clumsy kind of salute before retreating back toward the summit.

"Hannibal?" Juba said when the man was gone.

Didymus nodded, his eyes still scanning the note. "His name carries far," he said. He finally finished reading and looked up. "And it seems a fitting choice in light of the news. Simon's scouts report that Gratus has sent a sizable force of Romans after us. We'll be moving within the hour. Good news, as it goes, since the Romans will encourage Simon to move south with all possible speed."

It was true. Speed meant a chance to get to Petra—to get to Selene—sooner rather than later. But even so, Juba couldn't believe what the librarian had done. It seemed plain enough from the reaction of the messenger. "Gods, are they expecting me to take command?"

"Of the cavalry, yes. They've no elephants at hand, but we're also not crossing the Alps. Horses will have to do."

The idea of being in battle revolted him. It brought up memories of Actium and Vellica, of death and deeds he would regret for the rest of his life. "I'm not a leader, Didymus."

"You're more than either of us are," the scholar replied. "I only know my books, as you yourself said. And you're more than any of these men are likely to be. You're a king."

"A king is not the same thing as a commander."

"Didymus is right, though," Thrasyllus said. "And anything that helps us get south faster is a good thing."

Juba took a deep breath. They were right, though the prospect turned his stomach. "South," he said.

Didymus nodded. "They'll want us in the command tent, Juba."

As Juba looked up at the stars and sighed loudly, Thrasyllus took his arm. "For Selene and Lapis," the astrologer said. "For our loves. There's still time."

"Do the stars tell you that?" Juba asked.

"Just my heart," Thrasyllus said.

22

Death of a Messiah

Vorenus found Pantera on the northern wall of the ancient fortress of Karak. The sun was high and hot upon the deserts around them, and the dust of the approaching army had been easy to follow as it made its way south along the King's Highway.

The archer glanced back at his approach, saw who it was, and smiled. "Do we know who they are?" he asked.

Vorenus took a position alongside the younger man and joined him in staring out at the cloud rising among the horses and men. "Rebels," he said. "Organized under the direction of a man who claims to be the Messiah."

"Seems to be a lot of Messiahs these days."

Vorenus nodded. He understood only too well the desire for such a leader. One who brought victory and strength and pride. One who seemed to be favored by God Himself. He'd known Caesar, after all. The first and true Caesar, a man he would have followed to the ends of the earth, as men once had Alexander the Great.

A man, in the end, who was murdered by his own people.

The same would be the end for most Messiahs, he figured. Though this one—Simon was his name—would probably not get that far. Rome would see to that.

"The legion will march out soon," Vorenus said, relaying what he'd learned in the war council inside the fortress.

Pantera frowned a little. "But he can't touch us in here."

It was true. Karak was built on a sharply rising hill, surrounded by valleys on three sides. The ancient walls were thick and strong. They had water. They had supplies. It would take a massive army indeed, with time and engines of siege, to dislodge them. But this wasn't about the legion.

"He can't strike us, but he can strike the city below, and more besides. A lot of innocent people would die. We want to meet Simon head-on before he gets that chance."

The young Roman looked down at the buildings jumbled around the hill. His cheeks reddened slightly. "Of course."

Vorenus knew that look of shame. And he knew, too, the shortsightedness of inexperience. "All's well," he said. He clasped a strong hand on the youth's shoulder. "A lot of men will die today. Let's just keep our minds on making sure it isn't us."

"Us?"

"They made the decision that the Nabataeans would hold the fortress here as a reserve. So it seems I'm dressing up to go out."

Pantera nodded, looked up, and was clearly surprised as he at last took notice that Vorenus had shed his travel garments and was wearing the uniform of a Roman legionnaire. "You're coming with us."

Vorenus stretched his neck and pulled at the leather armor. "It's a bit tighter than it once was, but it still fits."

"You really were a legionnaire?"

"A centurion, once upon a time. A long time ago."

"You're doing this because you don't think I'm good enough." Pantera's voice betrayed his wounded pride.

"No," Vorenus corrected. "I'm doing it because I made a promise to Miriam. I intend to keep it. That's the only reason."

From within the fortress a horn blew, then another, calling the legionnaires into muster. He'd not heard it in decades, but the sound struck a familiar chord in Vorenus' heart. Much though he'd grown to fear Rome, the call to arms thrilled something deep inside of him. "Actually," he said, turning away from the wall, "I suppose that's not the only reason."

Romans were hurrying from the walls down into the courtyard of the fortress. Nabataeans were moving in the other direction. Pantera took a deep, long breath that made Vorenus wonder if the young man had ever been in a real battle before. "What other reason then?"

Vorenus looked up at the sky, cracking his neck and hoping for new strength in his old body. "Truth be told," he said, thinking of how Pullo would laugh at him for admitting it, "sometimes I think I like it."

· · ·

This was not how it was supposed to go.

The Romans had arrayed in heavy lines across the King's Highway on the edge of a rise just north of Karak. Not only did they outnumber Simon's force, but they had better arms, better training, and were better rested. It was, they were sure, the prelude to a slaughter. Superior tactics made up for many deficiencies, though. Vorenus had seen it at Actium. And now he was seeing it again.

The rebels fought with a fervent glee, a combination of bloodthirstiness and piety that was unnerving. More than that, though, they also fought with a shocking amount of organization. Vorenus had reluctantly positioned himself closer to the back of the Roman lines—farther from the fighting but better situated to keep an eye on Pantera's unit of archers—so he'd only seen the initial enemy formation in glimpses. But it had been enough to surprise him. Most ragtag forces displayed only local cohesion—one unit within the whole force might operate with practiced orchestration, but the units to either side of it might do little more than engage in barbaric chaos.

Not so Simon's little army. They'd formed proper ranks at the outset: thinning out to match the breadth of the Roman lines, if not the depth. And they'd even interlocked themselves as best they could within those lines.

More impressive still, they'd not thrown themselves into battle with the kind of wild abandon that was typical of rebels. They'd just formed ranks and waited for the Romans to make the first move.

The Romans, fully confident in their superiority, had been happy to oblige. The horns had blown. The legionnaires had stepped as one. The first volley of arrows had been sent up in a buzzing swarm.

Vorenus had seen armies turn and run at the sight of Roman precision, but the rebels had confidently held their ground. Arrows had taken some, but their thin lines were harder to hit. They'd raised what shields they had, but otherwise they'd simply waited.

Only when the first Roman ranks were within the range of slings had they moved: they'd loosed a volley of their own— sending rocks that found ready targets among the massed Romans—and then they'd taken a step backward.

The front lines of the Romans had cheered and marched on. The line of the rebels had continued to give ground.

Vorenus, near the center of the mass of men, saw what was happening as the fighting began in earnest upon the Roman right and left. The rebels hadn't been retreating. Their line was giving ground, but it was doing so from the center out: as the Romans pressed forward, the line of the rebels wasn't falling back, it was bending away. The rebel wings had held position, and they began to rip savagely into the legionnaires there, which only encouraged the Romans to close their ranks even further as they funneled, tighter and tighter, into the space ahead of them.

The dust was choking, the dead were piling up, and the worst was still to come.

Vorenus looked down his line to where the centurion in charge of his company was still ordering the press forward. Standard Roman tactics. Vorenus had done it a hundred times or more. But now a measured march to death.

"We've got to stop!" Vorenus shouted over the noise. "We've got to pull back and regroup!"

The centurion was a fresh-faced young man. Vorenus wondered if he'd ever seemed so young himself. He looked over at Vorenus with stern reproach. "Forward!" he shouted.

Vorenus, still being carried onward, cursed not having Pullo at his side. In addition to their love of each other, the big man was like a tree on the field—he could always tell Vorenus what was happening.

Without him, Vorenus resorted to jumping as best he could to see over the crowd, using the shoulders of some of the men around him to get higher. Some of the men yelled at him, others just looked confused or annoyed at his antics, but more than a few of the younger and far less experienced ones started to watch him with signs of worry on their faces.

At last he saw it: a cloud of dust moving fast around the left wing of the rebels. Vorenus saw it and knew it for what it was, for the inescapable fact of what was happening. Like Hannibal's Numidian cavalry at Cannae, the rebel horses were swinging round to lock them in like a gate on a slaughter pen.

"Cannae!" he shouted at the nearby centurion. He pointed through the melee at the dust of the driving steeds. "Turn to the rear!"

The centurion was caught between the confused tumult and his anger at this old legionnaire once more daring to give orders.

He raised his vine-wood rod of office as if he intended to strike Vorenus with it.

Ignoring him, Vorenus began shoving his way through the legionnaires around him, pushing toward Pantera's unit, which was still sending arrows toward the rebel lines—shafts that were mostly falling, he was sure, behind the enemy's thin ranks.

Men were jostling against each other now. The rebel wings were holding well enough that the Romans were being pinned closer and closer together as they pushed forward, as they marched step by step into encirclement. Few of them seemed to have figured out what was happening. But more and more would. There'd be panic then, as the trap tightened. Panic and death.

Time was running out.

"Pantera!" he shouted, trying to find the boy in the increasing chaos.

The thrum of bows sounded to his left, toward the very back of the lines, and Vorenus angled there, hoping it was the right unit.

Pushing his way through the crowds he saw the rebel horsemen coming clear of the Roman flank. He saw them begin to swing around into the Roman rear.

He saw, too, at last, Pantera's unit. The archer's commander was nowhere to be seen, and it seemed Pantera had taken control of the men. He'd turned them about to face the new threat and was already yelling at them to target the horses.

Vorenus smiled in what he supposed must be pride.

"Loose!" Pantera shouted, and the volley sailed out, strafing the riders. Several fell from their steeds, but the stream didn't slow. A dark-skinned man at their front waved a sword about his head, leading them onward with fierce determination.

Vorenus stumbled through the last line of infantrymen to reach the archers. They were already drawing and releasing another volley. But Pantera, he saw, was not shooting into the broad mass of the charge as it rounded at them. Instead, he was pressing himself smoothly into his bow, as calm as still water, taking careful aim at the dark-skinned leader.

Vorenus came up short and stared. Around and behind him, the other archers and the rest of the legionnaires were trying to retreat away from the charging line of horsemen. They were scrambling into their own men, the start of a panicked stampede that further compressed the trapped Roman lines. Only Vorenus and Pantera stood apart: the archer taking his patient aim, and the old warrior staring at his target, thinking the impossible.

Just as Pantera let go of his bowstring, Vorenus dove into him. The shaft shot forward as Vorenus tackled him to the ground, and they both saw it careen low, plunging into the chest of the leader's horse.

Pantera cursed loudly—Pullo would have liked it—but there was no time for more words. The ground shook with the charging horses, and Vorenus threw himself atop the younger man, rolling them into the smallest target and then tucking his head and shoulders over Pantera's face as the hooves came.

For long seconds the world was thunder and earthquake, and Vorenus expected to die. A horse kicked his side, almost pitching him into the way of another charger, but his armor took the blow well, and he didn't lose his grip on the boy.

Then the first wave was gone. The sound of battle returned to the world. The choking cloud began to clear. As it did, he looked up to see that the horse Pantera had shot had come down. It had buckled when it was hit, and its front legs were broken. It had crashed upon its left side, and it was huffing in agony.

Vorenus painfully lifted himself off the archer, and they helped each other up to their feet.

"Made me miss my shot," Pantera said, coughing dust.

"Saved your life," Vorenus said in a gruff voice. With one hand gripping his side—a broken rib, he figured, maybe two—he used the other to point toward the fallen horse. "And you still hit."

Behind them, the Romans were dying, but Vorenus ignored them. He wore the uniform, but they weren't his people. Pantera was safe for the moment. He'd run with him, hide and make their way back to Karak, perhaps. But first—

Wincing, Vorenus made his way through the dust to the horse. The rider was pinned beneath it, straining to get out from under its weight. Every time the horse jerked and spasmed, he gasped and groaned.

"Want to explain?" Pantera started to ask.

Vorenus held up his hand, silencing the boy. He pulled out his gladius and loomed over the rider who stopped struggling and stared back up at him. The man's left arm looked like it was broken, and his left leg, pinned beneath the horse, was surely in bad condition. He was unarmed and no threat. "Are you a Numidian?" he asked, using his best Greek.

The man stared up at him, his eyes wide as the horse twitched and cried out.

From behind him, Vorenus heard the archer's bow pull and snap. There was a harsh, terrible sound that Vorenus knew too well, and then the horse was still.

The dark-skinned man let out a sigh of relief.

"Vorenus," Pantera said. He came up beside him, pointed back toward the Karak. "More riders."

Vorenus looked up and saw that there were indeed more riders coming in hard. The Nabataeans who'd held back.

No. It was more than that. Much more than that. Behind the long line of horses ran perhaps a thousand men. And at the head of them all flew a golden eagle.

Romans. Part of another legion. Where had they come from?

He looked back toward the battle. The rebels had done well—remarkably well—but most of the Romans who were left would survive. In minutes it would be over. Simon, like most Messiahs, would die.

"Vorenus?" the dark-skinned man asked. "Lucius Vorenus?"

Vorenus looked down at him and swallowed hard. "I'll ask again," he said. "And if I don't get an answer I believe my friend has another arrow." Beside him, taking the hint, Pantera nocked an arrow and drew it back menacingly, aiming for the man's eye. "Now, are you a Numidian?"

The man nodded. "My name is Juba," he said in Latin. "I'm here with Didymus of Alexandria, and I'm looking for my wife."

. . .

Seeing that they were dressed as Roman soldiers, the second Roman force had swept around them as they'd dislodged Juba from beneath the horse. His left leg wasn't broken, but his knee had been badly twisted, and his left side, from his broken arm down to his swollen knee, was badly scraped and torn from sliding on the dry earth. Cutting the reins from the dead horse and padding from the saddle, Vorenus and Pantera fitted him with a sling.

Leaving Pantera to help stop the worst of Juba's bleeding side, Vorenus then limped back through the carnage, searching for the men they called friends.

The destruction of the rebels was total. No one had run from the field. God was with them in their faith, and so they'd fought until they were a tight ring around their leader, who called out for the wrath of God, assuring them of divine intercession to come.

And then someone—one of his own men, no one knew who—had shoved a knife in Simon's back and sent him to meet the maker he so desired.

Leaderless, the rest of the men had laid down their arms and thrown themselves on the mercy of Rome.

It would be no mercy at all. Vorenus knew how Romans worked. The men would be marched back to someplace public. Probably Jerusalem, he figured. There they'd be tried and found guilty by a Roman judge. And they'd be crucified, one by one, the suffocating horror reserved for those who denied the authority of Caesar.

He wanted to tell them to fall on their own swords, to save themselves the pain and the indignity and die with honor, but he knew that they wouldn't listen. They were believers. And though they were willing to lay down their arms now, they did it in faith that their cause would rise again.

Foolishness, Vorenus thought.

The prisoners were being rounded up when he reached that end of the field. The legionnaires were standing in a partial circle around them, shields on the ground like a wall. None of the captured men was so foolish as to try to run through the open space the soldiers had left them. That was where a few centurions waited, proudly adjusting their helmets as they awaited the arrival of the commanders and the general staff.

Other legionnaires were busy pulling bodies away from them, making a path through the dead for the arrival of their superior officers. Not far away, another group was hacking at a body— Vorenus assumed that would be Simon's—while other men searched the field, helping comrades or dispatching enemies with bloodied spears.

None of it shocked Vorenus. He'd been one of these men. But it was a waste. A horrible, senseless waste.

"What do you need?" one of the younger centurions asked when he approached.

Vorenus was exhausted, and he found himself fighting to maintain his composure in the face of so much pointless death. "Just looking for two Roman citizens, sir. They were spies, working to help infiltrate this rebellion; I was told to look for them here." Vorenus looked past the centurion at the prisoners. "Didymus?"

There was movement among the prisoners, but the centurion ignored it. He was instead staring at Vorenus. "I think I know you," he said.

Vorenus smiled through his exhaustion, still looking past him in hope of seeing his old friend. "I don't think so," he said.

"You're the one who tried to give me orders," the centurion said. "And then you ran away, didn't you?"

"Vorenus?" came a familiar voice from the crowd of prisoners. A glimpse of white hair bobbed among them.

"You *are* the one," the centurion said. He had his vine-wood rod in his hand and he raised it to strike.

Vorenus, so tired he was, acted without thinking. He caught the younger man by the wrist and held it. A second centurion beside him stumbled back in his shock, his hands fumbling toward his sword. "I *did* give you orders, you fool. I told you to turn. I told you what was happening, and if you would have listened to me a lot more of your men would still be alive today."

"Unhand—" the other centurion started to say.

Vorenus twisted the one man's wrist, using it to move him over and throw him back into his fellow officer. Then, ignoring the pain of his ribs, he pulled his gladius free with a smooth ring of metal. He held the point forward at the throat of the first of them. "I am a centurion of the Sixth Legion. I bled at the side of Caesar before you were born, and I have strict orders to retrieve these men from custody. Hand them over. *Now.*"

"That would be the *former* Sixth Legion," came a voice from behind him.

Vorenus turned. It was no one he knew, but he knew who it was. The son of Caesar had walked up behind him, two gaunt figures beside him, dressed in black cloaks despite the desert sun. But even as he thought about the heat, Vorenus felt an unnatural chill push through the air, a cold that slipped through his clothes and into his skin like a thousand tiny blades.

"The Sixth Legion that fought with Caesar was the Sixth Legion that turned traitor with Mark Antony," Tiberius said. "And the only centurion of that legion I can imagine being out here is Lucius Vorenus, a man long ago condemned to death."

"Vorenus?" one of the centurions said.

"In the flesh," Tiberius said, nodding. "So do retrieve his friends. You can take the rest of this lot back to Gratus in Jerusalem. Send them with my compliments. But these men are indeed on a very special mission. They'll be coming with me."

The centurions were scrambling to salute and comply. Vorenus just stared at Tiberius, taking measure of the man. His eyes were dark and hollow, as if he hadn't slept in days. And though his voice had the calm, natural authority of a man born to power, there was something hollow and weak about him. As if he'd lost part of himself.

When he noticed Vorenus watching him, Tiberius simply smiled in return. "You know," he said, "my father ordered your death a long time ago. It's remarkable that you survived. But here you are near Nabataea, as Syllaeus told me."

Vorenus, defiant, straightened his back in pride. It hurt to do so, but he felt better for it.

Didymus was brought up beside him, along with a second man. "Speaking of resilient," Tiberius said, "my dear Thrasyllus and Didymus. I suspected you'd make it out of the Temple alive, but I never imagined I'd see you out here." He had an unreadable look on his face, as if he was torn between being impressed by them or wanting to take pity on them. At last he smiled, as if they were all friends. "It is well, though. You helped before, and perhaps you can help again."

Thrasyllus seemed as if he wanted to say something, but he

caught himself and bowed his head with a broken sigh. Didymus was looking down, too, but not in submission. He was looking at his hands.

"I'm going to get my glory soon," Tiberius said. "You'll see." His voice quavered slightly with a kind of blind passion of faith. Vorenus imagined it was the kind of tone Simon used before the end, as the would-be Messiah had stood in defiance of the world crashing down around him.

Vorenus was listening, but he wasn't watching Tiberius. His attention was caught by what Didymus was staring at. His old friend's hands—the hands that had handled a thousand books in the Great Library of Alexandria—were smeared with blood.

"And I'm pleased about you, too, Lucius Vorenus," Tiberius said. "It's good that you escaped my father's judgment. I believe we have a much better use for you than mere death. I think you can help us."

Vorenus, at last looking back up at the son of Caesar, met the man's eye. "I'll die first."

Tiberius smiled again. It was very certainly a look of pity this time. "I don't think so," he whispered. "Show him, Acme."

One of the hooded figures was floating forward, and Vorenus could see beneath the shadows of her cloak she was a beautiful woman with skin like purest porcelain. Her hand was reaching out—an elegant, almost seductive motion.

"Vorenus!" Didymus abruptly cried out. "Don't!"

But her hand was there, and as it caressed his cheek and slid to the back of his neck, Vorenus couldn't pull away.

"It's easier not to fight," Tiberius said. "It's better this way."

The son of Caesar was turning and starting to walk away. Vorenus wanted to run, wanted to scream, but instead his legs were moving. His sword was back at his side. He was walking beside Tiberius as a couple of legionnaires brought the other men in their wake. He was dimly aware that Didymus and Thra-syllus were being dragged along. But when he looked ahead of them all, across the field of the dead, he felt a dim kind of sol-ace that Juba and Pantera were nowhere to be seen.

"Now, my friend," Tiberius was saying, "there's something I want in Petra, and you're going to help get it for me."

23

The Voice of a Friend

PETRA, 4 BCE

Pullo pushed another log into the fire. It was desperately hot in their one-room home, but he wanted it hotter still. Beneath the piles of blankets on her bed in the corner, Miriam's body was still scorching to the touch, shaking now and again as if cut through by an otherworldly fever that she could not fight.

She was alive, though. That in itself was a victory.

Pullo needed victories. The past days had been filled with far too many defeats.

He swallowed hard, using a blackened poker to situate the new wood over the glowing ashes, willing himself not to think of the other fires he'd seen. The unnatural flame of the Shard that the demons had unleashed upon Selene. And Selene herself . . .

He blinked away the emotions, trying to swallow them, trying to keep the memories and their sorrows at bay. Later—if somehow he survived—he could deal with them. Here and now, there was only the fact of Miriam's present fever, the need to make her ready to move.

Gods, he needed Vorenus—now more than ever.

A noise outside startled him, and he spun around from the fire, his gladius abruptly in his fist.

Footsteps on the road. One person. Light-footed.

Pullo crept toward the door and stood behind the hinges, his heart pounding with both hope and fear.

"Pullo," the girl named Lapis whispered from the other side.

Pullo let out his breath, nodding in his relief, but he didn't let his guard down entirely. There was too much at stake. He reached out with the point of his blade and slipped the latch. "Come in," he said.

The door pushed open, slowly, and a bright beam of daylight broke into the shuttered home. Pullo blinked, squinting, surprised that he didn't know it was daytime. But he stayed where he was while the girl made her way into the little house. He could see she had two fresh buckets swaying in her hands. Inside them, the sunlight shimmered in ripples of clear water from one of Petra's many cisterns, a balm to pull the heat from Miriam's fevered brow.

No one else came through the door. No other sounds met his ears. Nodding to himself, Pullo put his weight against the wood—wishing it was twice as thick—and pushed it shut. Only when it was latched—only when the intruding light had been shut out and they were once more enveloped by the accustomed darkness—did he lower his blade and let out the breath he'd been holding.

Lapis looked back at him and nodded in understanding and concern. Over the past days she had ignored his tears, just as he'd ignored the way her arms would shake in fear when she dipped the cloth to try to bring cold water to Miriam's fevered brow. More than once she'd told him to get some sleep, then said nothing of how he'd lie in his bed, staring with red eyes at the fire that she tended in his absence. And more than once he'd insisted that she needed rest, then said nothing as she'd lain down in Vorenus' bed, turned to the wall and trembling as he'd taken his turn patting the damp cloth.

They'd otherwise spoken little to each other. Whether she felt the same, he didn't know, but Pullo was certain that if he tried to speak of his sorrow it would consume him.

And there was, at any rate, no time for grief. The demons, he knew, could be back any moment, appearing in a bubble of pale light before the flame began. For two days now, he had expected to see them every time he turned around.

Life was fear now, and the stress of it only made his exhaustion even more profound.

He needed to get the Shards away from Petra. He knew that. The Ark. The Aegis. The Palladium. The demons knew they were here. They'd be coming for them. The Shards couldn't stay, and every hour he didn't move them was another hour he could have them moving ahead of the demon's pursuit.

But what good was running? He couldn't defeat the demons alone. It was true that he'd managed to slay one of them—he'd set its haunting remains to the torch where it had fallen, and he'd smiled as the flames shriveled its too-perfect skin before the sight of it melted into the growing fire—but the cost of doing so was truthfully almost too terrible to bear. He'd swung the blade that brought death to the creature, but the death wasn't his to claim. It was Miriam's. And now she seemed to stand at the gates of death, the Aegis of Zeus somehow holding her back from passing through to the other side. That thin thread of hope was, in turn, only still bound to this world because Selene— who'd given so much of herself to save the Ark from the clutches of the demons—had given up the Aegis to give her half-brother's daughter a chance at another tomorrow.

No. Pullo knew he had no cause to claim the kill.

All he had that was truly his—all that he seemed to have left at all now—was tears.

And worse, he hadn't even known what to do. When it was

over. When she was gone. He'd simply sat in the rising sunlight, holding the hands of the two girls who'd been as daughters to him in this life.

Lapis had come then. And after her screams, after her shock, she'd helped him. She'd gotten him moving again, had made him take first one step and then another. Together, they'd moved the Ark. Together, they'd moved Miriam. Then together they'd taken Selene to a pyre of her own in the temple of Dushara. He'd not told the priests who she really was, but he'd paid well, and he'd been sure that they'd treated her with dignity. For a minute Pullo had stood watching while the Pharaoh's daughter had gone to the torch. Lapis had cried. Heaven had swallowed the smoke. Then, as the flames were still feeding, still rising, he'd turned away and gone back to the home he'd once shared with the absent Vorenus. He'd turned back to the tasks of the living, to trying to save the life of Miriam, somehow kept from death by the power of the Aegis of Zeus.

Wordlessly, Lapis had followed him. She had nowhere else to go. And she seemed to understand that her love of Selene meant a love for the young girl whose life the queen had given her own to save—and a love for the mysterious Shards of Heaven, which she'd helped bring from the tomb at the foot of the mountain to this little home in the city.

It was hardly the best place for them, but Pullo simply didn't know where else to go. He couldn't move Miriam without killing her. The Shards couldn't remain without losing them.

Perhaps after Vorenus returned, he thought . . . perhaps together they could find a way out. They could buy the time they needed. They could find a new place to hide.

Lapis was already dabbing Miriam's brow with fresh water, so Pullo tiredly sat down in a chair beside the door and looked across the room to where the covered bulk of the Ark filled a hastily cleared space. Surrounded by the clutter of life, the Shard seemed both strangely out of place and entirely at home. The Palladium still rested in Selene's satchel, which rested against the Ark's base. He'd taken it from her broken body after she'd died.

The other Shard, the Aegis, was still strapped to Miriam's body, the breastplate once worn by Alexander the Great providing her fragile hold on life despite her terrible wounds.

Her gut had been torn open by the demon. Pullo had seen it himself in a memory that refused to be stilled no matter how much he wanted it to stop. It was, without doubt, a mortal strike. He'd seen the strongest of men die from far less.

But if not quite alive, neither was she dead, he reminded himself.

It was a victory, he reminded himself. It didn't feel like one, but it had to be.

.   .   .

Eight hours later, it was dark outside when Pullo took his turn with the buckets. The moon was a turned-up crescent in a cloudless sky above the sleeping city, and by its light the big man made his solitary way through the quiet and empty streets. There were cisterns dotted throughout the city, but one of the closest was uphill, on the slopes of the Mount of Moses—not far from the ruins of the now empty tomb where Selene had died.

Pullo climbed to it, his tired feet carrying him thoughtlessly along a route he'd memorized years before. He went to the cistern, dipped his buckets to fill them, and then straightened his back and stood. Balancing the water, he turned and looked back out over Petra.

Such was his exhaustion that he had stood there for several seconds before he realized that something had changed.

The space west of the city, between its protective walls and the rising steps of its sustaining terraces, ought to have been an empty band of black. But it wasn't. It was dotted with campfires and the illumined peaks of white tents.

The Roman legion had returned.

The buckets slid out of his grip and clattered across the stones, but Pullo was already moving. He was old. His body was broken. Yet he sped as fast as he could manage down the steps of the cistern and onto the paved streets. His feet knew the way back, and he ran with hope rising in his heart.

If the legion was back, then Vorenus should be back, too.

His old friend would know what to do. Together they could move the Shards. They could survive another day.

Pullo—smiling, ready to wrap that little man in a crushing hug—lumbered around one last corner and saw the house ahead.

All was as he'd left it. The door was still shut. The windows were still barred. But from within he could hear the muted sound of talking. He heard his old friend's voice.

"Vorenus!" Pullo shouted as he came up to the door. With a shove he had it opened, and he burst into the room.

At first he was blinded by the light of the roaring fire, which was shockingly bright after the darkness outside. He blinked, his hand shielding his eyes, and after a moment he saw that Vorenus was indeed there. He was standing at the bedside of Miriam. He had turned in Pullo's direction, but he made no move to come to him. His face, as Pullo blinked it into focus, was slack and unreadable.

Lapis was seated in the chair beside the bed, right beside Vorenus. The rag in her hands was dripping water onto the floor, and she was staring off at the wall.

"Vorenus?"

Vorenus turned slightly, and Pullo saw that there was another figure in the room, standing in the shadows behind the two of them. It was a woman clad in black, her pale skin and perfect features just visible in the darkness of her drawn-up hood. She smiled at him, and her teeth reflected back the fire.

Pullo gasped and reached for his sword. He felt his fingers wrapping themselves around the handle. He felt them tighten.

Then he felt fingers on his own neck, and a piercing cold pulsed through his body, as if tendrils of ice were snaking through his veins.

He wanted to scream out in shock. He wanted to throw himself back against whomever it was—whatever it was—behind him.

Instead he just stood, locked in place, his arm still stretched across his body, his fingers still gripping the gladius at his side.

"And this is Titus Pullo," a voice said. Out from behind him, a figure came into view. He was a Roman, clearly, and he had thick black hair, streaked with threads of gray. He walked calmly in front of Pullo, who raged against the power that somehow held him frozen, willing himself to reach out and grab the man who'd killed Selene. He succeeded only in making the slightest of sounds in his clenched throat, a kind of whimper that made the man pause in his walk and turn to look at him with both disdain and pity. "Such a strong one," he said. Then, staring at Pullo's unblinking eyes, sneering with obvious superiority, the man who Pullo was certain must be Tiberius reached over and pushed the door shut.

"You've certainly been busy," Tiberius said, looking around the room in mock appreciation. "Not the grandest of accommodations, but I'd say it was well managed indeed given your status as wanted men. I honestly had expected you all to be hiding in a cave somewhere, like that tomb where you'd been keeping the Ark."

Inside, Pullo was at war. A foreign power had infiltrated his mind, gripped it and somehow severed it from his body. It was as if he were a prisoner within himself, straining in vain against unbreakable shackles of ice. But he refused to give up. The man who'd killed Selene was here. Despite the cold, all he could see in his mind were the flames.

"I do need to thank you for gathering the Shards up for me. Earth, Air, and Life, too," Tiberius continued. He pointed at each in turn before allowing his attention to linger on Miriam's fevered form. "Such a lovely young girl. I'd say that it's a pity her life is bound to the Shard, but just as you came in to join us we were discussing what an added benefit that could be. So all is well that ends well. I do wonder whose little bastard she is, though."

Tiberius, sneering, looked from Pullo to Vorenus, then settled back on Pullo. Though the big man couldn't move, Tiberius seemed to recognize the struggle within him. "Let him speak for a moment," he said. "Just a few words."

He felt the grip on his mind loosen, and abruptly his fist clenched in his rage. He panted from a sudden exertion of the mind. "You killed Selene," he gasped, and then the icy grip tightened upon him and stilled his tongue once more.

The look of haughty disdain on the face of Tiberius vanished in sudden and hot rage. "Selene is dead because of you!" he shouted. "You fought and she died!"

He spun on his heels, seething, gesturing wildly at the Shards. "She shouldn't have even been here. She didn't need to be here. It was that fool, Juba. I know. He pushed her to come, not man enough to come himself. Nothing but a simpering *beast.*" He paused, panting, and finally turned back toward Pullo as if he had some means of responding. His eyes were shockingly dark and hollow. "No, old man. I didn't kill her. She was meant to be mine and you took her from me. You, Juba, my father . . . you *all* took her from me."

"Tiberius, it is time," came a whispered voice from behind Pullo.

The son of Caesar's jaw flexed, and his shoulders shook, but after a moment he nodded and walked back to the door. Opening it, he called out. Seconds later, Pullo heard several pairs of footsteps crunching outside.

Tiberius left the door open as he began to pace in the room, muttering to himself. One by one, three Romans entered and stood at attention beside the door. Two were centurions. The third was a rough-looking man with cruel malice in his eyes.

"Orders, sir?" one of the centurions asked.

Tiberius looked up abruptly, almost as if he had been startled. But his eyes focused quickly. "You'll take the girl in the bed and this box here," he said, pointing to the Ark. "Two carts. Don't touch anything on the box but its poles. And if you touch the armor the girl is wearing I'll feed your hands to dogs. Understood?"

The Romans nodded as one. "And the others?" the first centurion asked.

"Others?" Tiberius seemed confused, then looked around at Pullo, Vorenus, and Lapis. He shook his head as if clearing it. "Yes, of course. Kill them quietly. They're of no use now."

"With pleasure," the younger of the two centurions said. He seemed to be staring at Vorenus, and he slipped the blade from his side with genuine relish. The others did the same.

Tiberius turned away, and Pullo saw the hot light of the fire glowing red on his skin. For a moment, it almost looked like he was crying. Then he blinked at the flames and his mouth creased upward. "No. Wait."

While the three Romans froze, the son of Caesar walked closer to the fire. He picked up the metal poker and shifted the wood there. The flames kicked higher as the fuel moved. "Send the others in to take the things we need. Then we'll send a runner to the legion to attack the city." He smiled to himself as the flames grew before his eyes. "You three, meanwhile, will bind our friends here and gag them tight. You'll stay back, and burn it down behind us. Let the flames take them alive."

"Burn the house, my lord?" one of them asked.

"The house. The city. Fire and battle and blood."

24

The Shards Gathered

Far above Petra, Didymus stood beside Thrasyllus at the edge of a cliff. The crescent moon was high in an impossibly clear sky, its two horns glowing sharp upon the great dome of glittering lights that was slashed through by the glowing shape of the Milky Way. It was stunning and exhilarating, a sky that lifted the spirit of man even as it emphasized his smallness within the cosmos.

But neither man was looking at any of that. They were staring down at Petra, down where the smoke was billowing from a house in the middle of the city.

Didymus was no fool. He knew the portent of the smoke. The small company of Romans that Tiberius had extracted into his service had dragged him and Thrasyllus up here the moment they'd all arrived in Petra, but Vorenus, ever under the spell of the demon behind him, had led Tiberius and the other creature into the city itself. He'd taken them to find Pullo and those with him. He'd taken them to find the Shards.

The smoke, he feared, was an outward sign of the truth he feared in his heart. Pullo would be no match for the demons. No one could be.

"I could jump," Thrasyllus whispered.

Didymus nodded. The thought had occurred to him, too.

Just one step, the moment of flight and the fall, and it would be done. Silence. A new and eternal dark.

"I can't decide if that's courage or cowardice," the astrologer said.

Didymus couldn't look away from the smoke. He was crying, he realized, and he suddenly found himself thinking of the fall of Alexandria. He'd had a chance to go with Caesarion and the others to find the Ark, to go out on an adventure of impossibilities, but he'd instead gone back to the Great Library, back to be with his books. He'd thought at the time that his was an act of bravery, an act of defiance against the looming threat of Rome. But had he truly thought he could stop such powers? Or had he gone there to die, to burn with his books if the Romans put them to the torch? And if that was so, how was he any different from Mark Antony, who'd fallen upon his sword that night?

He took a deep breath to clear the cascade of questions from his own mind. "Why did you stay?" he asked Thrasyllus.

"Stay?"

"In Alexandria. When the Romans came. You stayed at the Library with me. Most of the others left, but you stayed. Why?"

Thrasyllus sighed. "I had no place else to go. And I guess I felt like it was my duty."

"You were a good man," Didymus said quietly. "I'm sorry if I didn't really say that before."

The astrologer smiled. "That means a lot, teacher. Thank you."

"Seems too little to say."

"It's enough." Thrasyllus finally turned away from the city to look up at the sky. "Why did you stay?"

"Me?"

"You didn't have to be there. I remember how you came back just as the Romans were marching in."

"I was just thinking about that. I remember being close to despair, and I remember thinking that they'd probably burn it all down, but I guess . . . well, I guess I came back because I had hope."

"Hope?"

"That being there meant I had some chance of doing something right."

"You did do something right," Thrasyllus said. "You met with Juba, I remember. And you saved the Library."

"But in doing so I helped set us on a course to this," Didymus said, nodding down at the fires below. Had it all been his doing? Was there something he could have changed?

Thrasyllus let out a hollow laugh in the night, and Didymus looked over to see him shaking his head with a grim smile on his face.

"What is so funny?"

"I was just thinking how important we can think ourselves to be, when in truth there is so much else in the world at work."

"That sounds a bit like the astrologer in you," Didymus said, but he smiled, too, for it was the truth. Each of them had played their part to come to this moment. Each of them had to burden the blame.

"I suppose some things are just true no matter who says them."

Didymus nodded, then nodded again more forcefully. "And you're right on both accounts," he said. He followed the gaze of Thrasyllus up toward the stunning sky. It was indeed beautiful. "And I think maybe I was wrong back then to mock your astrology, your reading of the stars. I'm sorry for that, too."

"Don't be. There are no gods to appease, no maps to bind us to our fates. We both know that now."

"But perhaps we are still bound, all of us, person to person and sky to sky. Perhaps in that truth, in that interconnection, we can see in the stars a reflection of ourselves and what we can do. Perhaps that makes you more right to look up than any of the rest of us who keep our faces down in our books."

Thrasyllus looked over at him with genuine gratitude, and he offered his hand. "It takes us all," he said. "If God is dead, we're alone in this together, right?"

Didymus took the hand and earnestly gripped it hard and well. Then he nodded back up to the stars. "So, astrologer, what do the stars tell you this night?"

Thrasyllus smiled and he looked back up. "I stopped believing long ago," he said. "I don't remember everything I once knew."

Didymus pointed up at Jupiter, at Scorpio, and piece by piece they filled in the map of the heavens. "You remember enough. What do they say?"

Thrasyllus looked down at the smoke of the city, now flicking little lights of flame, then at a sound from behind them he turned to look back toward the High Place of Sacrifice atop the Mount of Moses.

Didymus looked, too. There were upturned stone bowls atop six stone pillars around the paved rectangle that stretched out before them on the summit, and the Romans who had dragged them up here had filled them with oil and lit them. By those hungry lights they could see through the dimming dark to the source of the bustle of movement they heard. Farther to the south, the ridge was cut off by a high stone wall. There was a professional gate in the middle of it, and it had been thrown open. Men were marching through it. Two of them carried a litter, with someone prone upon it. The two remaining demons were there, too, as was Tiberius. Behind them came four more men, and atop their shoulders they held the long wooden poles of the Ark of the Covenant. Pullo and Vorenus were nowhere to be seen, and the scholar felt the pit of his stomach begin to fall once more.

But in that moment Thrasyllus reached over and gripped his shoulder. "The stars say there's hope in a leap of faith."

"A leap of faith?" For a moment Didymus thought once more of despair and the cliff. "What does that mean?"

"I guess it means there's still something more we can do," Thrasyllus said.

Didymus sighed. Faith? A leap? "It's so little to go on."

"But it's not nothing," Thrasyllus said. "And one of us will figure out what to do. I have faith in that, I guess."

. . .

How the demons knew what to do, Didymus did not know, but it was clear that they had a plan. At the foot of the ancient altar on the west side of the paved space, a rectangle of stone protruded perhaps a handsbreadth above the paved floor. It was tiled carefully, and from their vantage point at the northern edge of the summit the scholars both recognized in its making the same kind of design as they had seen in the chamber beneath the Holy of Holies in Jerusalem: the cut tiles formed a black outline of a rectangle, enclosing a pattern of alternating red and white diamonds around a second, smaller black triangle. At the center of that, in the center of the stone, the tiles were made to form a six-pointed black star on a white stone background.

"The symbol of the Jews," Thrasyllus had whispered to Didymus, who only nodded as they watched, flanked by Roman guards, feeling both fascination and increasing helplessness, as the demon who called himself Antiphilus approached the symbol and bent down to kneel over it.

In Jerusalem, the demon had broken the tiles to reveal the hidden secrets beneath—including the Seal of Solomon itself. Here, he seemed to be reading something. As he did so, he pointed first to the northwest corner of the paved court, to one of the five waist-high stone slabs around the space—the one closest to them. "Fire," he said.

The demon Acme floated there, moving sinuously, and she smiled over at the two scholars nearby. Thrasyllus trembled, but all Didymus could feel was the chill of her presence and the unmistakable sensation that he was in the presence of something purely and undeniably evil.

After she placed the Fire Shard upon the designated slab, Antiphilus once more looked down to the symbol on the ground. He pointed next to the northeast corner slab. "Air," he said.

And so it went. The broken stump of the Palladium was placed where he directed. The Seal of Solomon came next, placed on its slab midway along the eastern side. Then the Trident of Poseidon, on the southeastern slab. The Ark of the Covenant was placed on a larger slab to the southwest.

Antiphilus turned at last to the two Romans who stood a little ways in the dark with their companions, holding the litter between them. From their vantage point opposite the paved summit, the scholars still could not see who it was upon it. "Life," he said, and he pointed directly west, to the stone altar close beside him. "Place her there."

Her? Didymus strained to see who it was, hoping it might be Selene, but it was a younger girl he did not know. She was alive, but she appeared to be unconscious. There was a breastplate upon her chest that he had not seen in the flesh since Juba had worn it on the day Alexandria had fallen.

The two Romans moved up the steps of the raised altar and set the litter down where Antiphilus directed. Then they walked away to join their comrades, who were gathered on the south side of the paved area, beside the small square pool.

At last, Antiphilus stood. Acme floated up beside him, and Tiberius stepped out to join them, too. "Is everything as it should be?" the son of Caesar said.

"Air makes Fire," Antiphilus said, pointing around at the Shards on their slabs. "Fire makes Earth. Earth makes Water.

Water makes Life. And Life makes Air. Earth unmakes Air, Air unmakes Water. Water unmakes Fire. Fire unmakes Life. Life unmakes Earth. And Aether binds all in one."

Tiberius nodded at the girl on the litter. "And her?"

Antiphilus cocked his head at her, as if observing some foreign thing. "She will have her use. Put the others in position. One man to each of the rest of the artifacts." To Didymus, his voice was a poisonous song, but he could see no hesitation about acceptance in the hollow eyes of Tiberius. "Tell them not to touch them until my command."

"And then?" Tiberius asked, his voice an almost pathetic, needy whimper.

The demon turned its black, emotionless eyes toward the son of Caesar. "Then we will see *their* use," it said.

25

Up in Flames

Teetering between the craggy heights looming up to his left and the canyon plummeting down into the shadows to his right, Juba winced in both pain and fear as the donkey beneath him skittered on the thin wisp of trail. The beast, seemingly undisturbed, fumbled for a moment before it gathered its hooves beneath it. It snorted, bowed its head, then plodded forward.

Ahead, Abdes Pantera—the young Roman archer who'd nearly killed him and then saved his life—held the leather lead of the beast and was doing his best to hurry it up the angled scar that they were following across the mountainside. If he was concerned about the fact that death seemed to be only a single misstep away, the young man didn't show it. He was, if anything, in fine spirits as they made their way through the midnight darkness beneath a crescent moon.

"You've taken this route before?" Juba asked.

"No, my lord."

Juba tried to sigh, but it came out as a gasp when the donkey's weight shifted unexpectedly beneath him. He choked off the sign of agony until the shock of it wore off. He'd soaked through more bandages than he could count on the torn-up left side of his body, and he was suspecting that the current set was nearly spent, too. In that regard, it was probably a good thing that it was dark. "You don't need to call me that," he said when the wave of pain finally passed.

"You're the king of Numidia, yes?"

"We aren't in Numidia."

Pantera shrugged. "Blood is blood," he said. "Doesn't matter where you are, my lord. And it's no trouble to me. Just so long as you don't think I got you the donkey in devotion."

Juba couldn't see the young man's face, but he imagined that he was smiling. The archer seemed to be a genuinely kind man. In the brief minutes they'd all been together it was clear that Lucius Vorenus had trusted him, which for Juba spoke volumes. Selene, after all, had spoken of Vorenus in such glowing terms that Juba had at times wondered if the legionnaire had ever been real at all. If Vorenus trusted him, then Juba would trust him. And certainly he'd earned that trust and more by first hiding him when they saw Tiberius and then announcing that he'd bring Juba to Petra, to his Selene. It was an act of abandonment from his post and his duty, a betrayal of Rome and the legion that would be repaid—if it was discovered—with death.

"I still don't know why you did it," Juba said.

"Because you can hardly walk," Pantera replied, his tone making clear how obvious this fact was. And it was true: with Juba's wounded left side leaving him able to only shuffle at best, Pantera had decided to steal transportation almost immediately. Amid the chaos of the legion departing the castle at Karak, the archer had slipped in and grabbed the strongest-looking beast he could find. Juba had ridden it down the King's Highway and then through the small Petra suburb of Bayda to reach this little-used back route into the mountain city. They'd wanted to do everything they could to escape the attention of the Roman legion that was marching ahead of them. The Romans would have men posted on the main road, Pantera was certain, but none of them would know of this hidden trail.

"Not the donkey," Juba said, patting its neck gratefully. "Though stealing it *was* a crime. I'm asking about helping me at all. They'll kill you if they find out."

Pantera looked up at the stars for a moment. Then he seemed to let out a light laugh. "It's the usual story," he said.

"What's that?"

"Did it for a girl."

"A girl?"

The archer glanced back over his shoulder to grin. "Surprising?"

It was Juba's turn to chuckle. "Not what I expected, I suppose. But I'm not one to judge. That's why I'm here, too."

"The lady Selene. I only saw her for a few minutes, but she seemed like a good person."

"The best," Juba corrected.

"So you really love her?"

"She's my wife."

Pantera's steps hesitated for a moment, as if he was choosing how to respond. "I guess . . . growing up I heard that people like you don't marry for love."

Juba felt his back stiffen instinctively. "People like me?"

"Rulers," Pantera clarified.

"Oh," Juba said. "Well, that can be true. Sometimes the powerful marry for power or alliances, for riches or appearances. But I'd hardly say it's true for everyone."

"So you married Selene for love?"

The mention of her name brought fresh longing into Juba's heart, and he smiled. "Not at first. Caesar married us for his own ends. But we grew to love each other."

Pantera nodded thoughtfully, and he and the donkey trudged

on in the darkness for several minutes. Juba did his best to resituate one of his bandages as he balanced on the animal's back.

"Do you believe in love at first sight?" Pantera finally asked.

Juba chewed his lip on the thought for a moment before answering. "I suppose I do. Is that what you have waiting for you?"

Pantera's head shrank down slightly, as if the archer was embarrassed. "I think so. I mean, I met her and felt something at once. It was like a thunderbolt from the sky. But that just seems silly."

"Love is never silly," Juba said, looking upward at the moon.

"But I'm so young," Pantera said. "I've experienced so little. To say I love her . . . Do I know enough to even know what love is?"

Juba smiled. "Love isn't one thing. And it isn't the same in the beginning as it is in the middle or the end. It's a journey. The best kind of journey, in fact: one that changes you both together. So no, you don't know what love 'is'—and neither do I. We are learning what it can be. And if you know enough to wonder if you know enough to be in love . . . well, you're ready for it."

Pantera nodded once more, and his posture relaxed. "I do love her," he whispered. "Whether we're ready or not."

"Love at first sight," Juba mused. "I wouldn't change a thing about what I have with Selene, but that must be an amazing thing. I'm happy for you."

Pantera glanced back over his shoulder and smiled in gratitude.

The trail they followed clung to the steep slope rising to their left like a precarious shelf, and it had been rising slowly as they'd moved south. At the same time, Juba was noticing that the opposite wall of the deep valley was growing closer as the minutes passed. "How far?" he asked.

"To Petra? Not much further."

"Is the city at the head of the valley?"

The Roman archer's head bobbed in the light of the crescent moon. "Essentially. There's a cliff at the head of this wadi. Then a few farming terraces. The path becomes more like a road there—broad enough for a cart. Just beyond that it cuts into the bigger valley where Petra lies."

Juba nodded, though Pantera wasn't looking. If it wasn't far, then Selene wasn't far. And that gave him comfort. "So who is yours?"

"Mine?"

"The girl. The one you love. The reason you're risking everything for me."

"Ah." Pantera let out a long breath, as if he was savoring a memory. Juba knew that feeling all too well. "Her name is Miriam," the younger man said. He spoke the word like it was a precious, perfect thing. "Vorenus is one of her two uncles."

Juba smiled. "Vorenus likes me. You like his niece. So if you help me—"

"It's like I'm helping her, too."

"And getting into the good graces of her uncles."

"Something like that."

"A good plan," Juba said. "You're a good man, and I'll tell them so."

Pantera paused to look back and nod his chin in acknowledgment. "Thank you, Juba," he said. Then, before the king of Numidia could respond, he turned back around and started the donkey forward with a grunt. "It's not far now," he said.

· · ·

The walls of the deep canyon had been continuing to tighten when it abruptly bent eastward and suddenly there was, as Pantera had hinted, a large step in the wadi floor: a cliff that cut across its head from wall to wall. The heights of the mountains to either side remained high and steep, but the thin path they'd been following was no longer scraped from the side of a rocky slope, hanging over a void of darkness. Instead, it angled out to meet the top of the cliff, where it joined a wide path alongside a riverbed that had only a trickle of water running along its center. When the rains came, Juba imagined, far more powerful waters would be rushing down through the wadi, and they would make for a most spectacular sight when they launched themselves off that plummeting point.

The terraces there were thick with vegetation, and Pantera whispered how it was at one of these that he first saw Miriam, the girl he loved.

They followed the wider cart path as it meandered east, and soon the Roman archer brought Juba into the wide valley of the city itself. The city was asleep beneath the stars, and the paved, empty streets sped their pace as Pantera led them by twists and turns to the house of Miriam and her two uncles. They didn't know where Vorenus and the others had been taken, but they strongly suspected that the Romans would keep such prisoners in their camp just outside the city. So the plan, such as they had one, was simple. They would make their way in secret to Pullo, Miriam, and Selene. Together they would find a way to free their friends and then flee the mountains.

It was a good plan. And Juba felt his hopes rising with each step they took closer to the house.

Then they smelled the smoke.

Another turn, two, and they came around a corner to see that the house Pantera was leading them to was on fire. Flames weren't visible yet, but a thick smoke was billowing through cracks in the wooden shutters that covered the windows.

The door, they saw at once, was barred shut from the outside. And there were two Roman centurions standing in front of it. One of them, Juba saw, had his wife's satchel. They were facing the door, torches in hand, and the one with Selene's satchel seemed to be laughing as he reached his brand forward and set it to the wood.

Juba said nothing, but he reacted at once. He kicked his one good leg into the side of the donkey. The creature startled forward, hooves clattering on stone. Pantera, who'd had the lead, let go of it and spun out of the way. Bouncing, still kicking to spur the little beast onward, Juba struggled for a moment to find and pull the blade from his side. He was halfway to the two Romans when at last his hand gripped it and pulled it free. All he could think about was how Selene—his Selene—might be inside. How these men wanted to see her burn.

The centurions turned. They saw Juba and shouted, and the younger of the two—the one who'd set fire to the door—bolted upright and started to draw his gladius.

A whistle sang past Juba's head, his hair flicking across his face as the arrow sailed past him and ripped through the neck of the other centurion. Blood sprayed into the smoke like a misting rain.

Juba rumbled forward like a madman, teetering on his donkey with his sword pointed forward like a short lance. The donkey, smelling smoke and blood, brayed in fear and yanked its head sharply to the left. With no lead in hand, no means to turn the beast back, Juba simply launched himself off its back, aiming as best he could for the remaining centurion.

The Roman spun his arms around like a windmill, trying to land a strike on the hurtling man, but Juba fell through the swirl and buried his blade in the man's gut before tackling him to the ground.

The centurion screamed and slashed, but Juba ignored the pain of his side—surely all his wounds had reopened now—as he reared his blade back and jabbed it blindly into the man's chest.

The man coughed and then went limp.

Moving as quickly as he could, Juba rolled himself off enough to reach for Selene's satchel. He flung it open, but it was empty. The Palladium wasn't there.

Looking back to call for Pantera, Juba saw another Roman, a rough-looking centurion this time, running around the corner of the burning house with his gladius ready in his grip.

Three steps, Juba thought, his mind absently measuring the distance between them. He'd never get his sword around in time. And even if he did, a one-armed man on the ground had little chance against such a foe.

The Roman made it two steps before he gasped loudly and pitched forward onto the stones just feet from Juba. There was an arrow in his back. Its feathers seemed to be twitching as they pointed heavenward.

The Roman wasn't finished, though. He heaved himself up into his elbows, and Juba began trying to pull his blade from the dead man beneath him. It was stuck, and as the Roman looked up, he sneered at Juba with a look of powerful hatred.

Then Pantera rose up out of the dark behind him like a ghost. He planted his feet on either side of the man's back, nocked another arrow, then drove it down into the back of the man's skull like a spike.

Dear gods, Juba thought.

Pantera was fluid in motion. He stepped back over the man, his bow returning to his back even as he ran back to the doorway. Flames were roiling up the wooden face, but Pantera ignored them. With a cry, he launched his body into the burning wood and crashed through it into the smoke and flame beyond.

Juba worked his blade free, then dragged himself into a kind of crouched position. It wasn't much, he knew, but he might be able to slow any other Romans who might appear.

The open door had fed fresh air to the flames, and they had

already climbed the outside of the windows and were jumping to nearby structures. Neighbors were running out from their homes, and though he could not hear what they were saying over the sound of the roaring, cracking flames, he was certain that people were shouting for water. He was certain, too, that the house was near to collapse.

At last Pantera reappeared. He was dragging an unconscious woman out into the street. Coughing, he pulled her over to Juba, who saw that it was Lapis, the wife of Thrasyllus. Even as Pantera let her go, Juba leaned over to listen at her chest. She was breathing.

The light from the fire blinked out, and Juba looked up to see that a massive man had momentarily filled the fiery door-way. He lurched out into the night, and as the blazing light re-turned Juba saw that he was heavily scarred, like a patchwork man—and that Lucius Vorenus was limping out at his back.

Behind them, the roof at last gave way, kicking glowing embers and bits of flame up into the sky.

"Selene!" Juba shouted. He tried to get up, his mind swirl-ing with panic and pain, but Abdes Pantera held him down by the shoulder.

"She's not here!" the archer shouted.

Juba looked up in confusion. "Where?"

But Pantera didn't answer him. Vorenus and the big man were coming up, but the Roman archer was ignoring them, too. He was staring back at the Roman who lay facedown in the street with two of his arrows rooted in his back and head. "I think I'm out of the legion for sure now," he said.

Juba followed his gaze and saw that as the townsfolk swarmed past them with buckets of water, there were three Nabataeans kneeling beside the riddled corpse. Two of them were clearly town guards. The other was an old woman. She looked up and locked eyes with the archer.

"It's you," she said.

"Dorothea," Pantera replied. "I—"

"Not a word," she snapped. She wearily stood, helped by one of the two men. She whispered something in his ear, and he nodded. Then, using a walking stick, she hobbled over the blood to stand before them. Her eyes took them all in—the two other dead Romans, the unconscious woman, Vorenus and the other man, his own free-bleeding wounds—before she blinked and leaned forward on the stick. "For once, I don't think I want to know," she said. "Just run. We'll burn the bodies, but the reach of Rome is long."

"Dorothea—" Vorenus started to say.

The old woman turned to Vorenus, and her gaze was full of pity. "Your girl," she said, "someone said they saw the Romans taking her through the streets."

"Where?" Pantera asked. The desperation in his voice was palpable.

The fire was spreading quickly around them. A wind had arisen from the south. It rushed up against the inferno and pushed the flames ever higher. They wouldn't be able to stay long. Behind the old woman, the town guards had picked up the first of the dead Romans. One holding his feet and one holding his arms, they swung him into the hungry heat of the fire.

Dozens of men were storming up the road on horseback, weapons drawn as if they were looking for a fight. One of them pointed with a sword in the direction of the Roman encampment beyond the fires. "The legion is attacking!"

The people of Petra froze at the shout. They turned and stared, and as if in response, there was a new din over the roar of the fires. Clashing metal. Marching feet. And terrified screams.

Dorothea shook herself into motion, straightening her back

and pointing with her walking stick back into the heart of the city. "Let it burn, children! Pull back to the colonnade!"

People screamed, dropping buckets, and churning into a panic. Vorenus reached out for the old woman's arm. "Where'd they take Miriam?"

Dorothea turned back around, her face full of fury and vengeance. But she met the Roman's eyes and nodded quickly, then shouted back at some of the horsemen. "Horses are no good in the city, and these men need them. Off! Now!"

The younger men of Petra seemed to know better than to argue, and several began to hurriedly dismount. The panicked citizens were a rush of fire-lit terror coursing around them.

"Where?" Vorenus pleaded.

Dorothea looked back to him, and her walking stick shot forward to point toward the black hulk of the mountain above the city. "There," she said.

They all turned to look. The world had been still only moments before, but now they faced into a terrible wind. Upon the summit, lights flashed. Yellow. Green. Violet. Red.

Beneath their feet, the ground suddenly shook like a dying beast. Dorothea started to fall, but Vorenus caught her. Buildings rattled. The stones quaked. But none of them looked away. They saw orange light. And where the sky had been cloudless they saw thick bands of black that were suddenly *there*, swirling around the summit. Lightning flashed within them, like veins pumping with serpentine life, and torrents of rain slashed down upon the mountain.

Something flashed in pale blue, and in that same moment a shaft of the purest indigo light pulsed down from the heavens like a spear sent down by a defiant god. It struck the Mount of Moses, and from on high came new sounds of screaming.

26

The Second Gate

Standing beside Tiberius at the northern edge of the lowered courtyard atop the Mount of Moses—flanked by two of the legionnaires who weren't standing beside a Shard—Thrasyllus and Didymus could only stare as Antiphilus walked to the litter that he'd directed to be placed upon the altar of sacrifice. He knelt beside her, and the girl stirred as if in a feverish dream, but did not awaken.

While he did so, the demon Acme floated to the legionnaire who stood beside the Seal of Solomon, opposite the altar across the courtyard. She ran her fingers along the man's cheek and she spoke soft words. He smiled, and then her hand slipped to the back of his neck and his face froze like the puppet he now was.

Tiberius was fretting with his hands, rubbing at them in nervous anticipation, like a child awaiting a great gift. He was whispering things to himself, but so quietly that Thrasyllus could not hear.

Antiphilus nodded to Acme, and then they began. Antiphilus placed his hands on the Shard of Life upon the girl's chest, and the puppet in Acme's grip reached out and took hold of the Shard of Aether. The demons spoke something—a thread of song in a language Thrasyllus did not know—and he saw a ghostly, shimmering line of energy crawl out from the Seal of Solomon. Like a living thing, visible as the thinnest yellow fog, it wriggled out from the Shard and made its way across the paved stones—stretching out to the other side, searching its way up the steps—until at last it found the Shard upon the Aegis of Zeus. It straightened and stiffened until it was a throbbing line of power along the ground between the two Shards.

In the very moment it did so, green light welled up from the Shard in the breastplate of Alexander the Great. It threaded along the line that had formed, shifting its yellow light into a verdant green. Halfway between the Shards, the powers seemed to come to balance. The yellow and green sparked and rose into a ball of light in the air there, directly above the ornately tiled rectangle of stone that sat amid the paved courtyard.

Antiphilus nodded, smiling, and Acme let go of the man in her grip. The Roman remained as he was, and she drifted across the stones to the slab on which sat the Palladium. The man there couldn't look away from her perfect form, her perfect grace. Then he was looking at nothing, and he reached out to engage the Shard of Air. Sudden wind swept across the summit, spinning in a funneling rush that picked up dirt and debris and lifted it away into space.

Thrasyllus had to shield his eyes, but when he managed to peer through the gale he saw that a violet light now traced the ground between the Palladium of Troy and the point where the lights all met. The atmosphere was crackling with static.

"She's using the men as conduits," Didymus whispered. "Using their lives to activate the Shards."

"What's he doing?" Thrasyllus asked, looking to where Antiphilus knelt beside the girl.

"He seems to be gathering it all, focusing and controlling it."

"To do what?"

Didymus sighed. "I don't know."

Acme moved now to the slab that stood directly in front of the two scholars and the man who thought they were doing his bidding. The legionnaire beside the Shard there started to object, and she nodded in understanding before her hand shot out—quicker than thought—and had hold of his being. Now smiling for the benefit of the men still to come, he reached down to what remained of the Lance of Olyndicus and activated the Shard of Fire. Fierce heat rolled across the courtyard as red light now extended out to join the others.

Already Acme was moving again, this time to the Ark of the Covenant. The man there, entranced by the power of what he was witnessing, needed no charm before she took her grip and he placed his hands on the Shard mounted between the angels upon its top.

The earth beneath them trembled. Thrasyllus felt a wave of power pass beneath him, radiating out from the Ark, and then something broke in the mountain. The astrologer collapsed into Didymus, and together they fell to the ground, still staring at what was happening. Paving stones were shattering like glass sheets, and a crack snapped open across the side of the courtyard, right across the front of the altar. Another crack split the rock nearly at their feet, crossing the summit from side to side.

The demons were making a keening noise like they were in pain, but then an orange light was there, extending out from the Ark to join with the others in the air between them.

Antiphilus was panting, and the girl on the litter had now opened her eyes. She was staring up into the night sky, and her face was frozen in a soundless scream of horror.

The man Acme left behind was trembling but still standing. She was moving faster now, and she passed to the Roman beside the Shard from the Trident of Poseidon. Above the mountain the storm appeared in a flash, thick and angry. Many of the lamps had collapsed to the ground in the quake—their burning oil spread in hellish pools about the earth—and flashes of lightning now helped to illumine the summit as a blue line joined the others.

The rain was sheeting into his eyes, but Thrasyllus hardly dared to blink. The colors were swirling where they impacted each other above the tiled rectangle. He heard the girl and the men attached to the Shards suddenly scream as one, as if their souls were being ripped from their bodies, and the wind shifted inward, as if that point of dancing light above the summit was taking in a deep breath. Tiberius staggered forward a step, covering his ears and screaming in fear of the terrible din.

The astrologer suddenly felt a horrible and unnatural yawning sensation in his stomach, and something about it made him look up. Through the shrieking clouds of wind and dust and rain that sparked and swirled above the mountain, he found he could see a perfect circle of clear, still sky. And through that eye into the heavens it appeared that the stars themselves were no longer fixed. They were dancing.

"Didymus," he started to say, but then that circle above filled with a pulse of blinding indigo light that fell down from the chaos far above.

The impact tumbled Thrasyllus backward into the earth. His head hit the stones, and the world spun in a ringing blackness.

Bit by bit his senses returned. The sound of Didymus telling him to wake up. The hazy flashes of color that slowly resolved themselves into the beams of the power of the Shards upon the ground. And then he was back, and as his fellow scholar helped him to his feet he saw what had been done.

Whatever had split the sky, whatever primordial power had been awakened, it had left in its wake an indigo monolith standing in the middle of the courtyard, perfectly smooth, perfectly still. The beams of the Shards were still linked to it, still feeding it from below. Their colors were twisting around its edge like snakes cursed to chase each other around its frame forever. The storm was gone. The wind was gone. The stars no longer danced.

"My gods," Didymus whispered.

Thrasyllus could only nod.

Antiphilus, his eyes tight in concentration—he's holding all the powers in check, the astrologer abruptly realized—sang something to Acme, and she was floating outward onto the courtyard. She moved around the glowing thing, taking care to step over the lines of power on the ground, until she was facing it from the same side as Tiberius and the scholars. She sang back to her companion.

The son of Caesar seemed at last to gain control of himself. He came forward, striding like a man of authority. "What is this?" he demanded.

Antiphilus ignored him, but Acme turned. She was smiling. And she was looking at Tiberius with a look that Thrasyllus could not quite place. "A gate," she said.

Tiberius gaped. "Gate? You promised me power. Power over all men. You aren't meant to open a gate!"

Acme's smile was wider now. Her teeth were very white. And there was a sharpness to them that Thrasyllus had never seen before. "Who are you to tell us what we were meant to do, *human*?"

Abruptly, the astrologer recognized how she was looking at Tiberius. Not as the son of Caesar. Not as a man at all. Like a wolf might look upon a startled rabbit, she was looking at him as if he were food. And she was hungry.

Tiberius, who'd been seething like a petulant child, stuttered his complaint to a fearful halt, and he took a step backward.

"But it is true that we said we would find power," Acme said, her voice sounding a song once again. "Power over all men. We said we would get it and we will. As promised. Power over all."

"Over all?" Tiberius said in a small voice.

"Oh not for you," she said, laughing lightly. "Why, when we have the Book I think yours may be one of the first names we erase."

"The Book?" Tiberius asked. "What Book?"

Acme was ignoring Tiberius now, singing to Antiphilus, who was nodding and singing back.

Tiberius had taken another step backward. He was looking around at his men, frozen to the Shards in their grips. They were dying, all of them, their lives drained to open the gate.

At the astrologer's side, Didymus suddenly gasped as if he'd been struck. "Oh gods," he said.

Thrasyllus reached over to him. "What?"

"The Book of Life and Death," Didymus said. He was staring, wild-eyed, at the indigo thing before them. "It's a gate. Oh gods . . . It's really a gate."

Thrasyllus blinked. But before he could say anything more there was shouting and the clash of metal from the other side of the summit. Men were yelling. He looked, and he saw a horse pounding into the light. A young man upon its back had a bow drawn. He loosed, and a high whistle sang through the air. One of the men guarding the scholars fell backward—an arrow in his chest—and Acme was shrieking for the Romans to stop them. The horse reared up at the sound of her scream, and the archer slid down from its back onto the ground not far from the Ark of the Covenant. Four legionnaires on that side of the courtyard answered the demon's command and rushed the intruder, who was already putting his bow to his back and pulling a gladius to meet them. Behind the young man, Thrasyllus saw Juba getting down from the horse, too. One half of his body was bloodied and useless, but he had a short sword in the other and he limped forward into the fray with determination and tears upon his face.

Thrasyllus took a hesitant step forward, but a heavy hand grabbed him by the shoulder and he felt cold and sharp metal at his throat. "Stay," one of the guards said.

It was four legionnaires against one young archer and a wounded Juba. Thrasyllus felt a surge of despair, but then one of the legionnaires, preparing to swing at the Numidian, stepped on the throbbing orange beam of power that extended from the Ark to the gate. He screamed in unnatural agony, spouting blood as his body seemed to crush in upon itself. Thrasyllus wanted to throw up, but he also wanted to smile. Three against two was at least better odds.

"Vorenus!" Didymus suddenly shouted.

And there he was, on foot, running into the light on the opposite side of the courtyard from where Juba and the archer were fighting the three legionnaires. A legionnaire still guarded that side, and Vorenus took him at a run, their swords sparking as they met. Then from out of the shadows behind the old Roman came Lapis, running. "Stargazer!" she shouted.

Thrasyllus struggled at the sight of her, felt the guard's blade biting into his skin. "Said to stay," the man said.

Between them, Tiberius was drawing his own blade. He jumped over the pulsing beam of Air upon the ground to intercept her.

Lapis didn't notice or didn't care. She ran with her eyes fixed on Thrasyllus, and as Tiberius swung at her with a killing blow she didn't flinch. Only when the blade of Vorenus turned it aside did she even blink. But she didn't stop running. And Thrasyllus could see she had a small dagger in her hands.

"Kill her!" his guard barked from behind him, and the man's companion nodded and turned in her direction. He took two steps, his gladius drawn and ready to strike.

Didymus fell upon the man's back, scrambling at his sword arm and holding it in check just enough for Lapis to rush by.

Thrasyllus felt the blade at his neck pull away, moving out and away to meet Lapis with its shining point.

He had always been a coward. At times in his life he thought he always would be. But not now. Not for her.

He reached up and caught hold of the man's wrist, fighting to turn it away from the center of her onrushing chest. The man was stronger, though. It wavered but did not move. In desperation, the astrologer jumped backward, his head crashing into the man's face and staggering him back a step. That did it.

Then Lapis was there. She pounced upon them as they fell. Thrasyllus looked up into her face, and he saw that she was screaming as her little blade came down again and again into the Roman. Her eyes were far away, and Thrasyllus did not know what faces she saw in her mind.

"Lapis!" he cried, reaching up to shake her. For a moment she startled and raised the blade as if she meant to kill him, too, but then their eyes met and she started to cry. Thrasyllus pulled himself up to grab her and hold her in the chaos, and he saw that Didymus was weeping, too. The librarian was kneeling, and the other legionnaire was dead at his feet.

Didymus was looking at his own bloodied hands. "Not again," he was saying. "Not again."

Tiberius and Vorenus were fighting upon the lowered courtyard, dancing between beams of power. Vorenus was a good fighter, but he was growing tired. And Tiberius fought with the fury of a man possessed. Vorenus already had several wounds. It was only a matter of time.

Thrasyllus looked to the other side. The young archer was fighting valiantly, trying to make his way to the altar where Antiphilus still knelt beside the girl on the litter. The demon's eyes were closed in concentration, and he was singing a song that Acme matched as she swayed before the indigo gate.

Juba, struggling to fight beside the archer, stumbled on the quake-cracked stone. Thrasyllus watched as he lost his balance and began to fall over into the pulsing green line of power upon the ground.

In that moment, Acme, singing, stepped into the gate and was gone.

27

A LEAP OF FAITH

Lucius Vorenus was a step slower than Tiberius. Strike by strike, he knew he was losing ground.

He was surprised, in fact, that they had made it this far. After the shaft of strange indigo light had descended onto the summit, the earth had ceased to quake, the rain had ceased to pour, and the winds had ceased to howl. But that still left plenty of obstacles. He had doubted that the horses Dorothea had given them would make it up the mountain, for instance, especially when pushed at speed by their desperate riders. He had doubted they'd make it through the first line of guards even if they did.

Luck had taken care of the horses, who jolted and clattered and heaved but somehow didn't fall. And Titus Pullo had taken care of the initial men at the processional gate, wading into them like he was a far younger man, laughing as he swung his blade.

That had only left the rest of the Romans. And the demons. And the son of Caesar. And the Shards. And whatever it was that had been wrought by bringing them together.

In their younger years he and Pullo had argued about whether the gods were real. Vorenus had believed, but Pullo never had until the big man had nearly died in Alexandria. They'd been told that the Shards were signs of the death of God, but they'd then heard Caesarion argue that something of God was left. And now, it seemed, God—or at least a part of God's powers—had been summoned to Petra.

Yes, Vorenus had thought as he'd run onto the summit, it would be surprising if any of them survived this.

Already they had lost so much. Selene was gone. The wonderful little girl, the one who'd grown into such a powerful woman. Pullo had told them all when they rode past the shattered courtyard of the tomb where they'd once kept the Ark of the Covenant. She had died to save Miriam. Like Caesarion before her. Dead to save them all.

Pullo had cried to tell it, and Vorenus had not dared to look through his own tears to see Juba's reaction. There simply was no time for such things now. Either he would allow his pain to feed his will to live and fight on, or he would allow it to swallow him and he would perish. In this moment there was little else to be done. Afterward they could grieve.

If anyone survived.

Vorenus hadn't known what to expect upon the summit, but he was still surprised at what he saw. The Ark, the Palladium, and most of the other Shards of Heaven sat on waist-high slabs of stone around what once had been a beautifully paved courtyard. Light was falling from each of the Shards like liquid power that ran forward across the ground in taut, glowing ropes, pulsing and strong, to join at a central point. Where they met there stood a tall, thin rectangular block the color of pure indigo.

What it meant, what it was, he had no idea. But it was the work of demons, of Tiberius, and it had to be stopped. As Pullo had occupied the men at the gate in the wall, Pantera and Juba had made their assault to the left. Vorenus and Lapis had gone to the right.

There was a Roman beside each of the Shards, Vorenus saw. They were transfixed, staring at the glowing thing amid them.

Their skin was pale, their eyes sunken as if they were being drained of their spirits from the inside.

But past them he had seen the scholars, and his old friend Didymus had shouted out to him.

He thought about killing the men holding the Shards, but he didn't know what that would do. So he'd fought his way toward the scholars. Didymus had saved Lapis when she was about to be killed by Tiberius, after all. And if anyone could tell him what to do now, it would be the librarian. It wasn't much, but it was something.

Tiberius was fighting in a blind but powerful rage, and it was all Vorenus could do to get his blade up for every blow. Even so, the younger man struck with such ferocity that several times even a parry had ended with cut flesh. His left thigh. His right shoulder. Just enough to slow him even further. Just enough to make it inevitable.

There was a popping sound from behind him, a low yawn in the air. Then he heard Thrasyllus shouting off to his left. "A leap of faith!" he cried out. "Didymus! The leap!"

Vorenus blocked another blow, staggered backward, and chanced a look at the scholars. Didymus was kneeling beside a body, and with bloodied hands he pointed at the strange monolith in the middle of the tumult. "Go! The gate! The Book! Stop her!"

Tiberius was coming again. This time, instead of reaching forward to block his strike, Vorenus pulled back. As Tiberius brought his blade slashing forward, Vorenus didn't clash against it. Instead he let it glance off his own, just enough to keep it at bay but not enough to break the other man's momentum. Then, as Tiberius strained to maintain balance, Vorenus lunged forward and brought the fist of his free hand into the back of his skull.

Tiberius clattered forward to the ground, bouncing across

the red line of power that extended out from Shard of Fire. The
son of Caesar screamed, but Vorenus saw him no more. He was
already turning to the strange object that Didymus had called
a gate. In the corner of his eye, he saw that Juba had fallen down
across the green beam of power on the ground. His body was
seizing, his eyes transfixed and unblinking at the heavens.
Behind him, Pantera was fighting three, losing ground even
faster than Vorenus, being pushed out of sight beyond the indigo monolith. What had become of Pullo back at the wall, he
didn't know.

Having faith in his old friend, and not knowing what else to
do, Vorenus took two bounding steps toward the glowing gate
and dove into it.

. . .

All times became one time.

All moments became one moment.

He was frozen in space above the stones of the Mount of
Moses as days rose and fell, as years spun around him, backward
and forward. He was a phantom, a foreign whisper in a haze of
the blurring shadows of faces living and dead and yet to come.

And he was beyond it all, too, in a place where the world
washed away to a point of white light in a rolling wave of darkness, where the darkness then shrank back as the sun rose to cast
its light upon a white shoreline and a green country that stretched
out to the distant horizon beyond it.

Here and not here.

Now and not now.

Vorenus lived. And Vorenus died.

Countless lives and countless deaths.

Endless silence and endless breaths.

Vorenus died. And Vorenus lived.

And then all things merged into one, and he stood in a
running river bright as crystal, on rocks from the beginning of

time. Above and away stretched the expanse of a black dome filled with stars like white diamonds, held high by long columns of gold and silver, emerald and jade, sapphire and beryl, jasper and ruby.

Shapes drifted in the darkness above, and he knew them not.

Ahead, on a rise beside the river, flanked by a crystal book stand, sat a broken throne.

Vorenus moved toward it, and his hair drifted with the motion, weightless, as if there were waters above the waters and he strode through them. He moved through the waters, and the waters moved through him, and as he did so it seemed like the world flipped on a horizontal axis, as if up became down and when he at first thought he was stepping deeper into the river he was actually stepping out of it.

It was a heartbeat. It was a lifetime.

Then he was there. And he saw that the throne before him was shattered, missing pieces, and that the book stand was bare and empty.

You are not to be here, came a voice that was both deep and rich, calming even as it commanded.

Vorenus turned, looked back to where he'd come. The gate he'd passed through was there, an indigo portal above the shimmering glass of the waters. A man who was not a man was floating down to stand between him and the river, silently descending on white wings that stretched out and in with patient ease. He was half again as tall as Pullo, and his thick and strong body was wrapped in plates of golden armor etched with glowing lines of silver. As his booted feet came to rest on the ground his wings swept once more and folded back behind him. A mighty helm had hidden his face, but it, too, folded away from sight, and he stared down at Vorenus with eyes of gilt flame, his jet-black hair wafting from his shoulders in the invisible depths that surrounded them.

He was, Vorenus thought, beyond the wings, the model of a man. Not the fearful symmetry of the demons back on the Mount of Moses, but the exalted embodiment of what a man should be. Powerful and perfect. Exalted and extraordinary. He was, in a word, beautiful.

"You're an angel," Vorenus whispered, reaching back through distant conversations to find the word that befit the being.

I am Michael, it replied.

The angel's mouth moved, but if it made sounds Vorenus could not truly hear them. The voice and the words instead seemed to well up in his mind as if he'd thought them himself. They didn't match the movement of the angel's jaw.

You are not to be here, Michael repeated.

"I know," Vorenus said. He took a step backward out of instinct, and the angel's armor glowed, as if its power were moving to the surface.

You are not to approach the throne, Michael said.

Vorenus froze, uncertain. Then he carefully brought his step forward again, back to its original place. The glow of the angel's armor diminished slightly, but it still seemed full of power.

You are not to be here, Michael said again.

"I didn't mean to come here. The gate—"

You are mortal.

Foot by foot a massive blade folded out from the angel's fist in an action that seemed both mechanical and impossibly organic. Extended, the edge of it began to hum with a heat that shivered the air around it.

This time the angel did not speak. Towering and terrible, it simply slid forward with effortless speed and powerful might—and its great blade swung down upon Vorenus.

Out of instinct, Vorenus raised his gladius, which was still wet from the waters through which he'd passed. It met the blade of Michael, and there was an explosion of pale blue light between them.

Vorenus crumpled to his knees from the blow, but his gladius did not break. The angel drew back its weapon. Impossibly, Vorenus still existed.

You are not mortal, Michael said. The angel's head cocked sideways as if it had never considered such a possibility before. Then it turned to look back to where Vorenus had come from. The waters were there, bright and smooth as crystal, and the indigo gate.

"I am," Vorenus said.

You are not.

"No, I shouldn't be here. But I followed someone. A demon—"

The angel's head whipped back around to look in the other direction, past Vorenus. It opened its mouth to make a soundless scream. The blade in its hand folded inward with smooth precision. Then, in steps so long they seemed to be leaps, it strode past Vorenus to stand before the throne. It looked at the crystal stand.

It is gone, Michael said.

"What's gone?"

The Book of Life and Death. The angel's arm swept across the empty book stand.

"What Book?"

The angel stared at him, his eyes pitiless in his perfectly symmetrical face. *The Book of the fates of the living and dead. You did not take it.*

Vorenus felt like his heart should be racing, but when he thought about it he didn't know if his heart beat at all. "I didn't. The demon—"

It was one of the Fallen.

"Acme," Vorenus volunteered, remembering her evil touch. "The demon's name was Acme. I came here to stop her."

You failed, the angel said. Michael's gaze moved between the gate, the stand, and the great dome of lights above. It almost seemed to be reading something. *The Fallen is gone.*

Vorenus turned, thinking he should run back to the gate, back to the world he'd left behind. "I have to go after her while there's time. My friends—"

Time holds no sway here. You will return when you left.

Vorenus didn't understand how that could be possible. How he could he return at the same moment he left? What about the time that he had spent here?

The angel was staring back at the gate. Its face was impassive, but just as the being's voice had welled up from within him, Vorenus *felt* that he was frowning.

"The Book," Vorenus said. "What can she do with it?"

Inscribed in the Book are the fates of souls, the angel said, as if that was all the answer that was required.

Vorenus was no scholar. He didn't know this place, this being. He didn't know what questions to ask. Wishing Didymus had been the one to be here, he thought through all that he knew of writing, trying to understand. "Can they change the Book?"

The Fallen can erase the names.

"Erase the names?" Vorenus turned his attention back to the crystal stands and what the angel had said. "Would that erase their souls?"

The Fallen is gone, Michael repeated. *The Laws have been broken.*

"Laws?"

But the angel wasn't looking at Vorenus, and it did not answer him. It instead looked up as two more angels descended in glory, their elegant wings sweeping in windless perfection. They landed, and Vorenus stood between them, looking up as they spoke over his head.

One had hair of silver, and appeared to be clad in white robes. *Raphael,* the first angel said, *the Book has been taken. The barrier has been pierced.*

The one called Raphael nodded, and its face appeared to be grave and troubled. *The Laws have been broken,* he said.

The third angel was armored, but whereas Michael was clad in metal plate and exuded power, he was instead clad in a hardened leather cuirass that Vorenus found familiarly Roman. *A Fallen,* said the third angel, *come to the throne.*

Vorenus looked to the throne before them. It was a shattered ruin. This was the throne of God? The Shards were supposed to be pieces of the throne. Wasn't that what Didymus had once told them? Was that why the gate had brought him to this place?

The Laws must be restored, said Michael.

Only Father can restore, said Raphael. *Gabriel knows we are only to maintain.*

We can do little else, agreed the one that Vorenus assumed must be Gabriel.

"Is God dead?" Vorenus asked.

The faces of the three angels turned to him.

He does not know, Raphael said.

He cannot understand, said Gabriel.

Michael stared at Vorenus, as if he was studying him. *God is here,* he finally intoned.

"Here?" Vorenus looked around. They were alone.

God is here, repeated Michael, and his hand rose to point an armored finger at the center of Vorenus' chest.

The Laws have been broken, Raphael repeated, seeming to ignore Vorenus once more. *They must be restored.*

We must maintain, Gabriel said.

Vorenus was looking from Raphael to Gabriel, confused, before he suddenly realized that Michael was still staring at him. *There must be another way,* the angel said.

The two other angels turned to face him, but Michael had turned away to face the broken throne. *Our Father unmade himself for these beings. It is against this that the Fallen fought. It is for this reason they have broken the barrier and have taken the Book. They will unmake the unworthy ones, and so they will unmake our Father.*

Vorenus swallowed hard. He indeed felt unworthy, but he was still determined to try to do what was right. And what did it mean to unmake the unworthy ones? Were those humans?

But God is here, Michael said. *He lives still. He remains in them. One of them can restore the Laws.*

"What Laws?" Vorenus asked.

They have not the strength, Gabriel said.

They have not the knowledge, Raphael said.

"Can I do what needs to be done?"

You have heart, Michael said, *but you lack the strength. You lack the knowledge. The Fallen pierced the boundary. Only one of the Blessed can restore it.*

Vorenus felt hopelessly lost. The Fallen were clearly those angels who'd fought and lost in their war against the divine will and become demons—and the Blessed were no doubt those who'd been loyal to the decree of God, like the three great beings before him. But what was the boundary? What were the Laws?

Still, despite his uncertainty about so much of what was happening, Vorenus was a logical man. It was one of the few things that separated him from his beloved but emotional Pullo. "You need an angel's power in a human life," he said.

God and man and angel, Michael said.

One must go, Gabriel said.

Raphael nodded. *Be born. Live. Die. Repair.*

I will go, Michael said. *I, alone.*

"What are you saying?" Vorenus asked.

But Michael did not answer. The angel was striding past him. Upon the waters of the river he walked, until he stood beyond them, beside the indigo gate. He reached out, and he touched it.

I can go, he said. *A vessel is here.*

You must go, Raphael said.

We must maintain, Gabriel said, and to Vorenus it sounded like a warning.

"I don't understand!" Vorenus shouted.

Raphael turned to him slowly. *You do not belong here.*

"I came to protect the Book," Vorenus said.

You failed, Gabriel said. *But you will return.*

"Return?"

You do not belong here.

"To the Mount of Moses?"

Gabriel nodded. *Yes.*

"I cannot defeat the demons alone."

You must, said Michael. His hand had not left the gate, and he did not turn. *I will come, and you will protect me.*

"Me protect you?"

I will not be what I am. A swollen belly. A child. Pain and suffering. I can see it in time now, but I will not know it soon.

"You'll be a child?"

A soul. With the power of God to repair what has been broken.

You will not remember us, Raphael said. To Vorenus, the angel's voice sounded sorrowful.

You will remind me, Michael replied.

It is the only way, Gabriel said. *The Laws have been broken. They must be repaired.*

"What of the Book?" Vorenus asked. That was what he'd come here to get, what the fate of his world depended upon.

Recover it, Michael said.

Preserve it, said Raphael.

Protect it, Gabriel implored.

There is no other way, Raphael said. *The key of the throne must not be used again.*

The gate must be shut, Michael agreed.

The Shards, Vorenus thought. The gate somehow had to be shut, and there'd be no coming back this way.

The Laws, Gabriel said, nodding sagely.

Vorenus nodded, too, hoping he would remember enough of this to have Didymus explain it all to him someday—if any of them survived at all. But it was simple enough for now. Close the gate somehow. Recover the Book. Preserve and protect.

And survive.

Somehow. Always and ever. Survive.

Vorenus strode through the throne room of God as if he knew exactly what was to come. He moved into the waters of the river, and the waters of the river moved through him. The realms of God turned over upon themselves, and then he was standing before the gate, beside the great angel.

"So I will return the moment I left," Vorenus said.

Michael nodded. *And I with you.*

"Close the gate," Vorenus said. "Save the Book."

And save me, Michael said.

"How will I find you?" Vorenus asked, but already the angel was passing through to the other side.

So Vorenus, feeling like he knew everything and nothing all at once, passed through behind him.

·   ·   ·

As if he'd never left, Lucius Vorenus passed through the indigo gate and stumbled out onto the courtyard of light and storm. For a heartbeat he stood in the tumult, disoriented and blinded. Then he saw that the demon Acme was floating across the courtyard toward Antiphilus. Juba had fallen there, and she was about to step over him. Closer still, Pantera was bleeding, screaming, desperately fighting off the three Romans arrayed against him.

Vorenus, his gladius already in hand, made a decision. His mind was a swirl of images and voices and questions, but he shoved it all aside. He had to close the gate.

He burst forward—faster than he'd ever moved, freer than he'd ever felt before—and his blade was pinching through the back of one of the Roman legionnaires attacking Pantera. "Shoot one with a Shard!" he shouted to the archer.

Pantera saw and understood. Even as another of the men lunged at him, the archer dropped his blade and spun to his knees, pulling off his bow and nocking an arrow in the same smooth motion. He aimed for the first one he saw: the man holding what remained of the Trident of Poseidon.

Before the legionnaire behind him could run him through, Vorenus slashed across the man's wrists, then struck the third man across the face, sending him screaming into the line of fire across the ground.

Acme floated on, but in that moment Pantera released the string. The bow snapped taut, and the arrow flew and hit its mark. In a silent death, the man let go of the Water Shard and fell backward, neatly pinned.

The demon Acme shrieked, and Pantera and Vorenus both turned to the west. Antiphilus was still huddled over Miriam, but the intensity upon his pale face showed that his concentration was close to breaking. Acme was nearly standing just on the other side of the supine Juba, and she was turning to face the two of them.

Vorenus saw the Book in her right arm. A simple thing in a

leather cover. No jewels. No sign of its enormous power. It was no different than any of the thousands of codices amid the scrolls in the Great Library of Alexandria.

The demon's eyes burned with intense fire, and the nails of her left hand looked long and suddenly, impossibly sharp. She crouched as if she meant to leap upon them, a feral smile on her face. Vorenus imagined she was envisioning their dismemberment.

Pantera still had his bow in hand, and before she could pounce he nocked another arrow and let it fly.

The shot sailed wide of her, and for a single instant Vorenus saw the glee upon her face, the look of victory.

But then the arrow buried itself in the chest of Antiphilus, and the demon let go of Miriam.

The Shards in the hands of the Romans around the courtyard fell from their grips. The Ark splintered and broke apart, its black stone tumbling from the stone slab to the ground. The Shards trembled where they fell, twitching as if shaken by invisible hands, and inching closer and closer to the indigo gate along the lines of power that connected them. Miriam groaned.

Then, one by one, the Shards began to slide toward the gate, as if they were falling into it. Earth, Air, and Fire . . . each dancing and spinning across the ground. And when each hit the gate, they smashed into each other like a shining star.

The Water Shard was sliding, too, and without thinking Vorenus dove across the ground and grabbed it. Not far away, he saw Tiberius diving to do the same for the Seal of Solomon, the Shard bouncing around his fingers as if it did not want to be held.

Pantera shouted, and Vorenus—holding down the Water Shard as if it were a live thing—looked back to see the archer drop his precious bow and run toward Miriam and the Aegis of Zeus. Whatever power was drawing the Shards to the gate, it had pulled the girl down from the sacrificial altar. She'd fallen hard, then slid quickly, crashing through the legs of Acme and toppling the demon. Miriam had slid on, and only the still-transfixed body of Juba seemed to be holding her back from crashing into the gate. Pantera dove to help stop her, even as Acme was starting to rise back up to her feet. And behind her, the demon Antiphilus was staggering to his feet, too, his hands gripping the shaft of the arrow protruding from his body.

Between them all, the gate, as if it was taking a deep breath, seemed to draw itself inward upon the Shards that had collapsed together there.

Vorenus, from across the courtyard, saw Antiphilus tug the arrow free and for a moment look up in fierce exultation. Then the demon saw what was happening to the gate. And Vorenus, for the first time, saw fear in his eyes.

The green light that had been emanating from the Aegis, passing through Juba, suddenly blinked out.

Beneath Pantera's protective form, Miriam screamed in raw agony.

And Juba the Numidian, beside her, cried out in a hoarse voice: "Selene!"

Then the gate, with a flash of light and a crack of violent thunder, exploded outward. In the moment before the force of its expanding concussion slammed him back into the step of the lowered courtyard, Vorenus saw that the explosion smashed Acme against the altar of sacrifice. And Antiphilus, who'd been standing atop it, was struck off the edge of the mountain as surely as if he'd been swept away by the hand of God.

The demon disappeared, screaming into the night.

28

DEATH AND LIFE

PETRA, 4 BCE

Juba was falling. His foot had caught on one of the many shattered stones in the lowered courtyard, and now he was going down and the man he'd been fighting was already leaping over him, pressing the attack on the beleaguered Pantera—who even as he already fought two legionnaires was far more dangerous than the one-armed Juba ever could be.

As he fell, he saw the green line of light rising to meet him, and he rolled instinctively. When he struck the ground—when he struck that beam of pulsing power—he was looking up at the crescent moon in a sky of stars.

The power surged into him, a jolting shock through his body, a feeling as if he'd been pulled from the soothing warmth of a hot springs and thrown headlong into a drift of alpine snow. He opened his mouth to scream, but the sounds of his throat— like the sounds of the battle around him—were gone.

His body shook, his veins filled to bursting with the energy that was streaming down from the Aegis of Zeus toward the indigo block that stood between the Shards. It flowed into him, down through his veins, out into his wounds, and then it passed on—a continuous pump of the pure distillation of Life.

. . .

Juba, he heard Selene say.

He was staring up at the moon, and for a moment he thought he could see her face upon the sky—but then he felt and knew that the voice came from within. *Selene? God, Selene, they told me you were—*

My Juba, the voice said, *we have too little time and so much to say.*

You're gone. Juba broke inside to say it, as if it took his admission to make her death real.

Gone, she said, and her voice was filled with sorrow.

Am I dead, too? He felt a kind of hope at the possibility, and he immediately felt guilty for it.

You remain, my love. You've much still to do.

Then how—?

I'm still a memory here. What was left of me in the Shard. Now to be left in you.

I don't want to lose you.

You won't, my love. Her voice ran through him, like a tender caress upon his skin. *I'll live on in you. Two halves made whole.*

I don't think I can.

You must. You will be whole and strong and free.

Juba's body shook. His torn and broken left side felt as if it was in flames. But Juba pushed it away to focus on the whisper in his mind. *What will I tell Ptolemy?*

That his mother loves him still.

You make it sound so simple.

Love is.

Something struck his body, but he didn't know or care what it was. *What will I do now?*

Fight. Live. Go home. Raise our son.

Ptolemy. Juba saw the boy's face in his mind, and saw her face in his. A memory. A reminder. *Will we see each other again?*

When the sun sets on this shore, it rises on another. We all sail west, my love, and I believe we will see each other there.

Her voice was softer, as if she was slipping away like sand through his fingers. *Please don't go, Selene. Please.*

I must. And I never will. Be strong, my husband.

I love you.

And I you, she whispered back.

• • •

The power that had been surging through him shut off like a doused flame, and breath returned to Juba's lungs.

A woman was screaming. Close at hand.

"Selene!" he cried out, and then the whole world seemed to be fire and lightning.

Juba was lifted from the ground and violently shoved forward in a kind of tumbling heap with other arms and legs and bodies. The earth rolled around him. He bounced off the ground, then hit something hard and stuck.

The wave of power passed, and Juba gasped breaths into his lungs, his head spinning. He was on his side, back against stone, and instinctively he reached out with his arms to right himself.

He was up against the altar of sacrifice. The strange lights that had been crisscrossing the summit had all disappeared. Only a couple of oil lamps still sputtered light out upon the lowered courtyard. The others had all been toppled over or snuffed. The strange monolith that had stood in the middle of it all was gone. Where it had stood, sitting inert and lifeless, was a large black lump of glassy stone.

Pantera was at his feet, huddled over Miriam. The archer had already pulled the breastplate from her body. It sat abandoned at his side, a gaping hole where the Shard once had been. The girl was awake, but she appeared to be in shock, staring down at her chest with wild eyes. Her clothing was partly burned away there. Embedded just below the point that her collarbones met, the faintest of white lights gleaming within its black depths, was the Shard of Life.

She was no longer screaming, but her fingers were scrabbling at the foreign thing with probing panic. "Pantera," she gasped. "Pantera."

The archer was simply staring. His hands were frozen above her as if he had no idea what to do.

Me neither, Juba thought, reaching up with his left hand to feel at his throbbing head.

His left hand.

Juba pulled his hand away and looked at it like it, too, was a foreign thing.

Two halves made whole, Selene had said. And so it was. "Selene," he whispered.

"I saw her hit," came a silky voice from behind him. "I knew it would grieve you, Father."

Acme came down the steps beside him, her footfalls light and methodical, as if she had no care in the world. She had a book in her hand, a leather-bound volume, and she stood upon the bottom step like a triumphant queen.

He pulled his eyes from the perfect curves of her, searching the ground for a weapon. There was nothing. Nothing at all. Even Pantera was unarmed. "I told you not to call me that," he said.

"Oh," she said, her lips extending into the slightest pout. "But I don't think you meant it. You brought us here. And now that she's gone—"

"You can rot in hell."

Acme's dark eyes blinked. The smile that spread across her face was no longer seductive. It was knowing and dangerous. "But you see I *have,* Father. We all have. Rotted in hell, banished for believing in the superiority of the superior."

"For believing you're better than us."

"Because we are," she said.

They were indeed perfect to the eye. But Juba knew in his heart what they lacked. It was what he and Selene had shared. The power that even now burned within him. "You're broken."

"Broken?" Her voice lilted at the absurdity of the notion. "We are perfect."

Juba shook his head, more sure with every breath, with every pang of the memory of his loss. "You don't have love."

"Love?" She said the word like it was an alien thing.

Juba nodded. That was the difference, in the end. They were angels once, he recalled from his books. That made the demons immortals. And perhaps it was because they were immortals, because they lacked death, lacked loss, that they couldn't understand what it was to truly love. "Yes," he said.

She blinked, and for a moment Juba felt like he saw doubt tick at the corners of her knowing smile. "We are perfect," she repeated. The nails of her long fingers clicked together.

"No," Juba said. He tightened the muscles of his left leg, which had been useless so shortly before. It was, as Selene promised, whole again. He felt like he could stand, he could jump, he could *run*. He also felt more certain than ever. "You lack love," he said. "And without that, I think, you don't have a soul."

Whatever doubts Acme might have had, they melted away. Her grin creased even more sharply. "A soul?" she said. She patted the cover of the book in her arms. "You'll not have your own soon. None of you will."

"Love wins," Juba said. He didn't know how, but he knew it was true.

"Not tonight," the demon said, and her long fingers began to fold into the pages of the book, as if she intended to open it. "I think I'll start with your love," she said.

Juba saw movement to his left, as Lapis rose up out of the dark.

He saw her arm swing. "You bitch," she cried out, and the blade she threw buried itself hilt-deep in the demon's shoulder.

The demon shrieked, and as she recoiled from the strike, she dropped the book in her hands.

Juba dove over and caught it as the demon staggered backward, then he rolled away onto the courtyard as she caught her balance and swiped at him with her clawed hand.

She missed, and he hit the stone and got to his feet. He stumbled backward, clutching the book, and Lucius Vorenus was calling to him from behind, begging him to run.

Acme had been struck off balance, but she was rising up in control now. She pulled the blade out of herself, and she smiled over at Juba. "A little knife won't stop me, Father."

Pantera abruptly rose up to stand between them. "Go," he said over his shoulder. "Run!"

Acme laughed. "You're an unarmed *boy*," she said.

Juba turned, saw that Vorenus was waving him onward, away from the demon. On the ground, not far away from the lump of cold stone, Didymus was on the back of Tiberius. "Go!" the old man shouted.

Acme cackled in glee, and Pantera cried out in pain, but Juba was already running. Clinging to the book, still not knowing what it was, he followed Vorenus out into the dark.

29

A Good Day to Die

It was disappointing in its way. Long ago, Titus Pullo had joined the legion. And in time he'd been not just a legionnaire, but a commander of legionnaires. He knew what they ought to be capable of doing. He'd trained them.

So when he'd rushed into battle with the men guarding the processional gate—four against one in order to free the others to disrupt whatever was happening on the summit—he had assumed that his death was unavoidable.

His life in that moment amounted to a temporary delay, gladly given that the cause might succeed—whatever the odds.

It was, as he had so often told Vorenus before battles, a good day to die.

But now he stood—an old and broken man—over the corpses of four younger men. His leg dripped with blood equal to the rivulets beading on his blade, but he was alive. Unquestionably and somewhat disappointingly alive.

Standards in the Roman army, he was certain, had fallen far since the days of the one true Caesar.

He had been aided by the bewildering lights, the explosive crashes, and the terrifying screams from higher up on the mountain—distractions, he knew, were a focused fighter's best friend—but despite his concern for what was happening upon the summit, he was too tired to run when the killing of the guard was finished.

A steady lope was the best he could do.

He had not gone far when shapes approached, running toward him. It was only two men, and though he did not recognize them both, he would have known the gait of Lucius Vorenus in a snowstorm. His old friend, a man he loved as dear as life itself, was unmistakable.

"Vorenus!" he called out.

"Pullo! By the gods, you're alive!"

"So far," Pullo replied. The man running beside his friend was a dark-skinned man. Juba the Numidian, Pullo knew. The man who'd once tried to hamstring him, who'd left him a limping and broken man.

Pullo felt his blood start to rise, but he pushed it back down. Didymus said that the man had not been himself. Vorenus had said the same.

And if Pullo could not trust in his friends, what was left in this world?

A man had to trust in his friends, have faith in his love. Pullo believed that.

Vorenus and Juba did not stop running, so Pullo turned to join them, pushing his broken body beyond its thresholds of pain to keep up as they passed the corpses of the men he killed and moved through the open processional gate in the wall that cordoned off the summit.

Behind them, there was an inhuman shriek.

"The demon," Vorenus said. "I think she's coming."

Pullo's lungs burned, and his muscles ached, but his old friend seemed tireless as a new-blooded young man. He didn't pant in the high air. He didn't twitch as his old legs fell on the rocks and the impacts shivered up through his old joints. He ran as if he were jogging, as if he could double the pace and leave the other men far behind.

"And the Romans," Pullo heaved, "will already be halfway through the city." He had to take three more long strides down the steps before them until he had breath again. "I'm sorry, Vorenus. I don't know what to do."

Vorenus nodded in the moonlight, an effortless gesture. "The horses," he said.

There were horses at the base of the stairs that led to the summit. Clambering down to them, Pullo was tempted to close his eyes against the pain of his broken body—but he knew better than to tempt fate on an ancient stone staircase.

At the foot of the stairs, the three men found their horses. Vorenus was the first one mounted. "Which way?" he asked, looking between the path down to the east—past the tomb where the Ark had been kept, the closest path to their home— and the path to the west—which rose up past the twin obelisks on the ridgeline before descending down to the wadi that led from the Siq down the colonnaded avenue past the great god-block of the temple of Dushara toward the west wadi or the main gate of the city.

Pullo painfully heaved himself up and into the saddle of the largest steed he could find. "Romans are to the west," he panted.

"East, then," Vorenus said, and before Pullo was even settled in the saddle his old friend was pulling his horse around to the rise up to the obelisks and the trail to the Siq beyond them.

· · ·

The Romans were indeed coming. Pullo heard their trumpets all the way down the trail, and between his heaving breaths he'd tried to point out to Vorenus how their enemies were closing in. They were pouring over the mountain behind them, and they were charging through the fires in the city ahead.

Lucius Vorenus—who suddenly seemed half his age—only nodded and drove them on and on.

They reached the Siq without incident, but while they'd not encountered the enemy, Pullo knew it was only a matter of time. A fight was inevitable.

"Where now?" Pullo asked. He pointed southeast, up the Siq. It was a narrow path, and it led away from Petra, away from the Romans. "That way?"

"Exactly what they'll expect," Vorenus said, frowning in the light of the crescent moon. "We can't outrun them."

Juba was looking the other direction, back into the city. He was holding something, Pullo realized. A book. He was holding it to his chest as if it was the most precious thing he knew. The Numidian nodded his head toward the colonnade somewhere in the darkness ahead. There was the sound of battle there. "I have another way," he said, and he pulled the book from his chest to toss it to Vorenus. "I need the Shard," he said. "I saw you take it."

Vorenus caught the book. Then, after a moment's pause of reflection, he threw the Water Shard to Juba. "Lead on," he said.

Juba took a firm hand on the reins of his horse, and then he kicked it to the north and west—toward the colonnade and the center of Petra.

The city was filled with the smoke of the burning fires, and the shapes and sounds of war melted in and out of that thick and choking fog. Dorothea had said the Nabataeans would make their stand along the colonnaded street that split Petra in two, and now the three men were riding hard down that road between them. Like men running on the vanishing land between two colliding waves, they pushed to stay ahead of the worst of the fighting that was collapsing around them. The columns that lined the street swept to either side.

In the lead, Juba surged his horse to the left as a line of armed Nabataeans charged out from the smoke between columns to their right. Arrows thrummed in response, rippling through the churning fog.

Juba pulled back to the center of the road. The fighting appeared and disappeared. Phantasms of men in combat.

Pullo looked back. He could see that at least a half-dozen Romans were falling in behind them. "There's no time!" he shouted. "The city gate will be blocked!"

"That's not where we're going!" Juba shot back. The Numidian pulled close beside Pullo, and he tossed his reins to the massive man. Pullo caught them, confused, but pulled them tight with his own, ensuring that Juba's steed kept pace with the hooves of his own horse.

The Numidian had pulled the Water Shard into his hands. "Into the wadi!" he shouted. And then he was focusing on the black stone.

Around them, wisps of a new fog arose and coalesced and knotted. Strand by strand, they built into something bigger and stronger.

A storm was beginning to rise once more over Petra.

This time, though, it did not arise upon the mountain above the city. It formed up over the slopes of the mountains on its north side. Cloud threaded into cloud, wrestling in the smoke-filled sky, and lightning broke in jagged scars across the suddenly starless heavens.

"You're doing this?" Vorenus called out.

Juba nodded, looking up for a moment at what was coming into being. "I'm trying," he said over the pounding of the horses. "But it's weak!"

"Weak?" Pullo asked.

"The Shard," Juba replied. "It's dying."

Pullo nodded, though he had no idea what it would mean for a Shard to die and how that could be so.

Juba had closed his eyes again, gripping the Shard. His brow was tensed with concentration, and Pullo felt a sudden chill in the air.

Then, behind the cold, came the rain.

It hit them like a descending wall—a furious deluge that was gray and hard.

Almost immediately, the street was flooding. The horses were kicking through water. If there were sounds of battle still, Pullo could not hear them.

Juba took back his reins from Pullo, still keeping one hand on the Shard. Then he led them on. The horses were straining. And the rains were falling around them as if a great window to the waters above the sky had been thrown open.

The mighty block of the temple of Dushara arose in a hazy shape to their left, then they were darting to the right—hurtling down a ramp of stone to the muddy cart path that turned and dove into the tighter canyon walls of the west wadi.

The torrent of rain was pushing countless little falls of water off the rocky hillsides, and the once-dry riverbed was rising fast.

Pullo glanced over his shoulder and saw that the Romans had fallen back, but they were still coming. Eight of them, he thought, just at the edge of his vision.

Pullo was certain he'd trodden all of the paths around Petra over the years. He knew where they were headed, and he was sure Vorenus knew it, too: Juba was leading them to the thin little path that was scratched out of the canyon side, leading north to Bayda. It was a gamble, but it was a good one.

The path twisted and turned down the wadi, passing ter-raced vineyards. Pullo was counting them in the moonlight, and he was already slowing his horse when he saw Juba pulling up on his reins just short of the looming darkness where the canyon floor suddenly dropped out in a kind of massive step.

Vorenus had pulled up short, too, and he immediately tried to cross the roaring, rising water of what was now a river in the middle of the canyon. The horse shied and reared in the rain, refusing to go in.

"Damnit!" Vorenus shouted, dismounting.

Pullo and Juba got down, too, trying to lead the horses by the reins. None would budge.

The river was coming so hard that Pullo wasn't sure if he could cross it himself. But if it was lower—"Stop the river!" he shouted to Juba. "Just a moment!"

The Numidian was squeezing the stone in his hand, as if some final drop of its magic might be had. "I can't!"

The horses were wild with panic. Pullo looked back, expecting to see the Romans bearing down upon them. Instead, he saw a thrashing wall of water. And above it, a fast-clearing sky as if a veil was being lifted.

"Turn it!" Vorenus shouted. He was holding the Book to his chest.

Juba had stopped squeezing the Shard. It now seemed nothing more than a simple rock in his hand. "It's dead," he said. His head rose toward the coming flood and the newly visible moon. "I'm sorry," he said, tears in his eyes. "She's gone."

The unnatural wave slammed into them. And just as they were ripped from their feet—just before the wave sent them hurtling out into the void beyond the wadi cliff—Titus Pullo grabbed the two men into his mighty arms and pulled them as close as he could.

Then he tried, as he fell, to watch the stars coming out from behind the clouds.

One by one by—

30

Midnight on the Mount of God

Miriam had awoken in pain, in shock, and in confusion. Something had happened to her. Something had violated her. She was alive. But something was truly and deeply *wrong*.

She'd found the Shard in her chest. Warm and throbbing and alive. She'd felt her miraculously healed belly. Warm and throbbing and alive.

Wrong. Wrong.

And then, through her haze of revulsion and terror, she'd at last blinked up to see Abdes Pantera—her love—struck across the face by the demon that Selene and Lapis had called Acme.

The blow sent him sprawling sideways across the broken pavement stones that lined the ground. There were bodies there—dead Roman legionnaires—and Pantera fell over them. His head struck rock. The demon laughed, high and cruel. "Run, Father!" she sang into the dark. "I'm coming!"

The sight of Pantera falling cut through everything else Miriam had suffered. She winced, slid herself up onto her elbows.

Acme wasn't far away. The demon's back was turned as she leered over the fallen archer. The nails upon her hand were wet. "First you," she whispered, and her song sounded no longer sweet but thirsty.

"Stay away from him," Miriam said, and with every word

there was a new strength, a new power, pushing out into her limbs. Life. More than was possible, more than any human vessel should hold. It was surging in her, muscles twitching in readiness.

On the ground beside her was a breastplate. The middle of it seemed to have been burned out, leaving a gaping hole as wide as her hand. She reached out and picked it up. The breastplate seemed light as air in her grip.

Acme paused, still looking down at Pantera. "Little girl, is that you?"

"Leave him alone." The voice was hers. The urge was hers. But the words seemed to slide into her from a second mind. She rose to her feet. Ready. Resolute. Unflinching. "Never again will you touch him, *Fallen*."

The demon's laugh was soft and mocking as she turned around to face her, but when she saw Miriam, the laugh choked off in what could only be shock. "It cannot be."

Miriam found herself smiling. She felt taller, older, wiser. "You belong to the shadow," she said.

"Cannot be," the demon whispered.

Miriam took a single step forward, her fingers tensing on the broken metal plate in her hand. "It is."

The demon started to step backward, then seemed to catch herself. "Just a girl," she said, but her voice was unsteady.

"Come and see, Fallen."

Acme hissed, teeth baring, and she flew forward.

With a calm focus—something beyond instinct informing her actions—Miriam flipped the breastplate up into the air between them, her right hand gripping the other side as if she intended to use the hollowed armor as a small shield.

The demon was reaching out, long-fingered hands clutching for her throat and face, and Miriam bent forward and down, catching Acme's extended right hand in the hole of the breastplate. Her muscles flexed, twisting, and she snapped the demon's wrist in two.

Acme shrieked as she fell away behind her, staggering to keep her balance as she pulled the shattered limb back to her body. The movement pulled the breastplate from Miriam's grip, and it clattered to the ground.

Miriam glanced over at Pantera, saw with relief that he was moving. Then she came around to face the demon again, entirely unarmed now, and she saw that Acme had somehow stumbled across a sword on the ground. She'd swept it up in her left hand and held it forth. The blade was beautiful, Miriam saw. The sword of a Caesar. The point that flashed at her was steady and sure.

"I'll take these odds," Acme said, grinning.

"I wouldn't," Lapis said, and she drove a blade into the demon's back.

The demon shrieked, but she staggered forward away from the strike, rushing at Miriam.

"Sword!" Pantera shouted.

She glanced back, saw that Pantera had retrieved a gladius from one of the dead men. He was kneeling, one hand to a bleeding wound on his head, but their eyes met. He threw the sword up into the air.

Miriam spun, dancing beneath the midnight moon, her arm reaching out into the darkness to catch the weapon.

When she came back around, the demon was there. Miriam's blade met the side of hers and glanced it off target. Acme's thrust plunged across Miriam's shoulder, gashing her to the bone, but Miriam's point ran true. It caught the demon just below the breastbone, and Acme's momentum ran it through her to the hilt.

The demon coughed, eyes wide.

With strength she didn't know she had, Miriam shoved Acme

back off her, twisting the blade as she pulled it free. For a moment they faced each other, the girl and the teetering, gasping demon. Miriam looked down at her shoulder, saw it knitting itself back together. Then she looked up, took a deep breath, and with one fierce swipe of her blade took the head off the demon.

For a moment there was silence upon the summit. It was the High Place of Sacrifice, she saw. But it had changed. *She* had changed.

She was Miriam. And she was not Miriam. What had happened?

Miriam felt her breathing, steady and sure, and she tried to take solace in that.

Looking beyond the corpse of the demon, she saw that Lapis was running toward something, and Miriam looked over to her right. Two men were there, desperately trying to hold down a third.

Miriam strode to them—passing by a lifeless lump of obsidianlike stone in the middle of the broken courtyard—and she saw that the third man was a Roman. There was a ring on the ground, with the same kind of blacker-than-black stone that was embedded in her chest.

"Help them!" Lapis cried out.

And so Miriam swung down with the butt of the bloodied sword in her hand, striking the Roman on the back of the skull and knocking him out.

Lapis fell upon one of the two men, embracing him in relief. "Thrasyllus," she gasped. "Gods, we're alive. We're alive."

The other, an older man with silvery hair, rolled off the unconscious man with a panting sigh. He looked up at Miriam. "I'm Didymus." He saw the Shard in her chest, and his eyes widened—not in fear or even surprise, but in curiosity. "And you . . . are interesting," he said.

"You're the librarian," Miriam said.

Didymus nodded.

Miriam used the sword in her hand to point at the man she'd knocked out. "And him?"

"Ah," the librarian said. "That would be Tiberius, adopted son of Augustus Caesar and heir of the Roman Empire."

"Oh," she said.

Pantera came stumbling up behind her. "Miriam, are you all right?"

She turned, fighting back tears as she embraced him. Whatever had happened, her love was still hers. "I'm fine," she said, knowing as he gripped her tight that her love was still true even if her words couldn't face what had happened right now. There'd be time. Time enough for tears and whatever else was to come.

The sound of horns and battle and alarm came up from the city below. They all stood and looked down at Petra. Part of the city was in flames, and from the haze of smoke they heard the sound of battle.

"Miriam," Didymus said. "We can't stay long. The Romans will come."

Pantera nodded against the side of her cheek. "He's right."

Miriam swallowed hard. She turned back to Didymus. "Vorenus says you always have answers."

The older man smiled gratefully. "I've always tried."

"I have to know what's happened. Why are we here? Where are my uncles? The Shards—the rest of the Shards—where are they?"

Didymus took a deep breath and then filled in what he could as quickly as he could. The others helped. How Selene had put the Aegis upon her and died. How the Romans had come back and taken them all. How they'd brought the Shards here, used Life and Aether to control the men whose lives were used to bring forth the energies of the Shards. He told how the gate to heaven had been opened and how Acme had come back with a Book that Juba and Vorenus had taken.

When he told her how some of the Shards had fused when the gate was broken, Miriam walked over to touch them and found the lump was indeed dead. Earth, Air, and Fire were no more. The Ark was gone forever. She didn't know whether she should be relieved or dismayed.

Finally Didymus looked over to the ring on the ground. "That's the Seal of Solomon, the Shard of Aether. It's what allowed them to disappear in one place and reappear in another. Vorenus took what remains of the Trident. Which leaves, I assume, Life," he concluded, nodding at the stone in her chest.

"Can you explain this to me?"

"I'd hoped you would tell me," he said. "But I promise you I'll do all I can to help us find out together."

Thunder cracked in the distance, and they all turned to see that a terrible storm had broken in the night sky above the northern edge of the city. It was sudden and powerful and utterly unnatural.

"The Trident," Didymus whispered.

Pantera ran over to the body of Acme and came back with the beautiful sword that Miriam now knew to belong to the son of Caesar. He shrugged. "I'd never afford one otherwise," he said. Then he nodded toward the raging storm. "Let's go."

"Go?" Miriam asked.

Didymus had knelt, and he was holding up the Seal of Solomon, his fingers holding it delicately so as not to touch its dark stone. "See it in your mind and it'll take you there," he said. He stood, carefully handing it to her and then placing one hand upon her shoulder. "It'll take us, too."

Pantera took her other shoulder, and the three of them looked to Lapis and Thrasyllus, who were holding each other close. "Ready?" Miriam asked, hoping she'd really be able to use the Shard.

Lapis looked to Thrasyllus. He smiled. "We'll stay," he said.

"Someone will need to distract Tiberius from his headache when he wakes up."

"But the Romans might kill you," Pantera said.

Thrasyllus looked up at the sky for a moment. "The stars say otherwise." He smiled at Didymus. "Call it a leap of faith."

Didymus came forward and shook his hand. "Be safe, my friend."

"I'm sure we'll see each other again," Thrasyllus said. "And in the meantime, I'll keep Rome off the trail—wherever it takes you." He looked down at the unconscious man. "Anyway, I think I can do a lot of good in his service. I was weak before. I was scared. But you know, I think he's really the weak one. I see that now, and I think I can use that to help people. I think I can save lives."

"Do that," Didymus said.

Miriam nodded at Lapis in thanks, but already her attention was turning back out at the storm. It was dropping down upon itself at the edge of the mountains, collapsing into the west wadi where she'd first seen Abdes Pantera, the Roman archer from Sidon.

She pictured the spot. The terrace. The vineyard. The place where she'd stood to take her aim.

Didymus was once more at one shoulder. Pantera squeezed her reassuringly at the other.

She closed her eyes.

She grabbed the Shard.

. . .

They found them at the bottom of the west wadi, below the now-dry waterfall that had washed them and their pursuers down into oblivion. The Romans were all dead, all swept farther down the canyon by the receding flood.

Miraculously, Vorenus and Juba were alive. They were kneeling on the wet earth. Pullo was between them.

Juba looked up at the flash of their arrival. He stood, coming toward them. His face was grave. He shook his head.

Miriam shoved past him, crying out, and she fell to her knees at his side. "Pullo?"

The big man who'd thrown her into the air and caught her as a babe—who'd helped her learn to crawl, learn to talk, learn to run and dance and sing—almost seemed to be resting in the cushion of the earth. Except there were rocks there, too. He'd fallen directly on them.

"It's his back," she heard Juba whisper to the others as they came. "It's broken."

Miriam reached for his hand. When she folded her own around it, he didn't grip her back. But he turned toward her, his eyes still bright. He smiled, though there was blood at the corner of his mouth.

"Miriam?" His powerful voice, which had far more often rumbled in laughter than it had boomed in anger and authority, was a whisper now. "Is that you?"

"It's me," Miriam said. She squeezed his hand, hoping for a response. "I'm here. So is Didymus. We're all here."

He nodded, and the light of the crescent moon fell across the shadows of the beautiful scars of the face she loved. "Selene," he whispered. "It was her. She said I had more to do."

"You saved us," Vorenus said. He had hold of his old friend's other hand. He was holding it to his chest, to his heart.

Pullo smiled. "Always am."

"Always will," Vorenus said, but the reality cracked his voice.

"Am done, my friend. Is my time."

"No," Miriam said. "We're going to get you out of here."

"I'm glad," Pullo said, his eyes passing over to Miriam and back to Vorenus again. "Glad I got a second chance at love."

Vorenus squeezed his hand tighter and bowed his head to hide his tears.

"We love you, Pullo," Miriam said.

"More than I could ask for," Pullo said. He coughed blood. "I think you were always right about God and all that, Vorenus. Always were the brains."

"Nothing without you," Vorenus said.

"Will need to be," Pullo whispered back. His voice was growing fainter.

"Stay with us," Miriam implored. She was squeezing his hand desperately, hoping for a sign of response. "You're my father," she said, choking on the words but letting them come. "I never say it, but I always think it. You and Vorenus. You're not uncles. You're my two fathers. Please, Pullo—"

"So strong," Pullo whispered. He was looking past them, up at the moon. "Isn't she strong, Vorenus?"

Vorenus was weeping openly now. "Stronger than you or me. We raised her that way."

Pullo made the slightest of nods. "We did."

"So much I want to say, I—"

"I know," Pullo whispered. "Me, too."

"Stay," Miriam said.

"You should see it, Vorenus. White shores . . ."

"Stay!" Miriam shouted. She put his hand to the Shard on her chest. She pressed it there, closing her eyes, but nothing happened. "No," she gasped. "No! Father! No!"

"Miri—" Pullo whispered.

Miriam scraped at the edges of the Shard, weeping, screaming.

Pullo's hand fell away.

Miriam tugged at her flesh as if she might pull the object free. As if she might undo what had been done. The cuts from her nails flashed in and out of being.

"Miriam," Vorenus said. And his steady hand came up and enveloped hers and held her still. "Miriam, he's gone."

She looked down. The big man's eyes were closed as if he was sleeping, but his mighty chest neither rose nor fell. "He can't—"

Vorenus leaned forward and through his tears kissed the big man on the forehead. "Bastard always promised me I'd go first," he said.

"It's not true," Miriam said. "It's not. The Shard. If I can—"

Vorenus reached over Pullo's body and pulled her close to him in an embrace. They held each other, shaking.

And then there were hands on her shoulders. "I'm sorry," Pantera whispered.

Vorenus squeezed her again, long and steady and true, and then he gently lifted her up into Pantera's waiting embrace.

For a moment her sorrow flashed to hot rage and Miriam slammed her fists into her lover's chest. Pantera let her strike, taking the blows until the fury turned back into sobs. Then he held her tight and shared her grief.

"We can't just leave him here," Juba said. His voice was quiet, almost reverent.

Miriam looked back through her tears. Vorenus was still kneeling beside his dead friend, still gripping his once-strong hand. "We won't," her other father said. He looked up at her, his face full of both sorrow and hope. "The tomb," he whispered. "Can you take us there? All of us?"

EPILOGUE

A Book of Life and Death

PETRA, 4 BCE

The battle was over. The Romans had been turned back, but the city was still in tumult. There were cries of horror and of divine wrath: a fire, an earthquake, strange storms, men dead upon the high mount.

In all the chaos, the tomb in which the Ark of the Covenant had long been hidden was forgotten. No one guarded its shattered courtyard, and no one noticed the pale blue light that for a moment flashed into existence there.

Nor did anyone notice when a single torch was kindled and by its light five figures lifted the enormous form of another and carried him to his final home.

They laid Pullo upon the funerary shelf where the Ark had once sat. It seemed fitting, Vorenus said, and no one disagreed.

Didymus had charcoal and some scraps of parchment from his time with the dead Simon's rebel army, and so he wrote a note that they placed beside Pullo. It was written, at the suggestion of both Miriam and Vorenus, to a woman named Dorothea. It told her to honor Pullo. That he'd once been a great legionnaire, a good father, and the most noble friend. It also told her where Pullo and Vorenus had hidden a cache of coins in their house. It would take some digging through the ashes to get to it, but Vorenus was certain that it would be enough to

secure both a proper sarcophagus and the commissioning of a
third statue for the front of the tomb. That middle niche was
still empty, after all.

When it was done, they stood around in a kind of stunned
silence. Didymus saw that Vorenus had placed the Book upon
another of the shelves in the chamber, and so he walked to it.
He saw how unexpectedly plain it was. Just a simple, leather-
bound book. And yet it held everything. It was the Book of Life
and Death, the fate of the world. It was the Book of Thoth,
the Babylonian Tablets of Destiny. How could that be so? What
was truly written on its pages? In what language was it inscribed?

Didymus took a few steps toward it.

"You know," Vorenus said from behind him. "Caesarion
once told Pullo and me what he would do with the Book of
Thoth if we ever found it."

Didymus stopped, suddenly aware of how his arm had already been lifting toward the Book. "What's that?" he asked.

"He said he'd destroy it. 'We're not meant to know the
mind of the gods,' he said."

"Always the best of us," Didymus said. He let his arm come
back down to his side. "The torch, then?"

"No," Vorenus said. "I don't think we really can destroy it.
Preserve it. Protect it. That's what they said."

"They?"

"The angels," Vorenus said, and then he laughed for a few
seconds, almost as if he was trying to convince himself to feel
mirth again. "I guess I have a lot to explain."

"We all do, I suppose," Didymus said. He turned away from
the Book. Juba stood in a corner, staring at scorched marks
upon the wall, lost in thought. Closer, Miriam and Pantera were
embracing. They were in love, and the boy was trying to bring
her mind to better things by saying that what she'd done on
the mount was amazing, and that he hoped he never made her

angry. Miriam smiled, and she leaned into his chest in appreciation of both his efforts and his love, but Pantera didn't see the worry on her brow. Nor did he see the way her hand fell to her belly and held it, as if fearful of what it contained. Didymus didn't understand all these signs, but he understood enough.

"I'm sorry," he heard Miriam saying. "For all this. For whatever it is."

Pantera smiled back, holding her in reassurance. "We'll find out together. Whatever happens, we can face it together."

"We'll find answers," Didymus said to them all.

They looked in his direction. Miriam and Pantera, Vorenus, and even Juba.

"Where?" Vorenus asked.

"Qum'ran," Didymus replied. "A village I've heard about, a community of scholars in the desert. It could be a place to start."

"I must go home," Juba said. "We have a son."

Vorenus walked to him, embraced him. "I understand. We'll get you away from here. Get you on the road home."

Juba nodded, looking at the ground.

"For now, we all need to go," Vorenus said. His voice was cracking, but he was holding back the emotion to get them to safety.

Didymus nodded his head in agreement, and then he motioned for Vorenus to take the Book, for he trusted no one else with the task. "Let's go," he said. His heart was heavy, but there was work to be done. He was certain they all felt the same. "All journeys start with a single step. So let's start with getting out of here."

· · ·

A pale light flashed upon the Mount of Aaron, far to the west of Petra. Then five people stood alone upon its quiet summit. They looked out across the distant city where such horrors had been. There were lights moving upon the Mount of Moses, and they hoped that the friends who'd stayed behind would be well.

As the hours passed they stood or sat or paced. They cried together or alone.

Without words, they came together when the sun began to break over the far horizon.

It was a new day. A new beginning.

No one spoke, but they had agreed to hold hands. One life to another.

And then, in a flash, they were gone.

.   .   .

THE END

GLOSSARY OF CHARACTERS

Abdes Pantera. Tiberius Julius Abdes Pantera is the name of a Roman archer from Sidon whose tombstone was accidentally discovered during the construction of a railroad in Bingerbrück, Germany, in 1859.

Alexander Helios. Son of Mark Antony and Cleopatra VII, twin brother of Cleopatra Selene, he was likely born in the year 40 BCE. He disappears from reliable historical records after the fall of Alexandria in 30 BCE.

Alexander the Great. Alexander III, born in Macedon in 356 BCE, succeeded his father as king in 336. In his youth he led a number of Greek city-states to revolt against what had been a Macedonian-led alliance, and Alexander quickly set in motion a series of campaigns that led him as far north as the Danube and solidified his position as ruler of a united Greek state. Alexander subsequently moved his armies east against the Persian Empire, then the largest and most powerful state in the known world. He led his men to conquer Asia Minor and Syria, routing the Persian armies and defeating city after city. In 332 he entered Egypt, where he was declared to be the son of Ammon, an Egyptian deity. For reasons unknown, he faced off with the armies of the Kush but refused to fight them. Instead of continuing his campaign south into Africa, he moved north and founded the famed city of Alexandria, which subsequently became the capital of Egypt. Returning east, he captured Babylon and put an end to the Persian Empire before entering central Asia and defeating several states. Alexander then journeyed toward India, where his armies, though successful, finally balked at fighting farther from their Greek homes. Throughout his long career, he is said never to have lost a battle, and though severely wounded on several occasions, he was still reportedly vigorously strong. Nevertheless, he died under uncertain circumstances shortly after returning to Babylon in 323 BCE. After his death, he was placed in a golden sarcophagus, which made its way to Alexandria, and his world-spanning empire soon broke into rival states. Pharaoh Ptolemy IX Lathyros melted down his golden sarcophagus around 81 BCE when he was short of money (an act for which the angry citizens of Alexandria soon killed him). Alexander's miraculously preserved body was at that time transferred to a crystal sarcophagus, which remained on display in the city until its disappearance around 400 CE.

Apion. An Alexandrian scholar who wrote a commentary on Homer, he would later become famous for writing an anti-Jewish tract that was replied to by Josephus in his *Against Apion.*

Caesarion. Caesarion, whose full name was Ptolemy XV Philopator Philometor Caesar, was born to Cleopatra VII in 47 BCE. According to Plutarch, he was rumored to have been executed by Octavian after the fall of Alexandria in 30 BCE, though his exact fate is strikingly unknown. While later Roman writers questioned his paternity, there is little reason to question the claim made by Cleopatra that he was the son of Julius Caesar.

Cleopatra Selene. Daughter of Mark Antony and Cleopatra VII, twin sister of Alexander Helios, she was likely born in the year 40 BCE. After the fall of Alexandria in 30 BCE she was placed under the guardianship of Octavia, the sister of Octavian, before being married to Juba II sometime between 25 and 20 BCE. The date of her death is uncertain.

Cleopatra VII. The last pharaoh of the Ptolemaic dynasty, Cleopatra VII ruled Egypt from 51 BCE until her suicide at the age of thirty-nine after the fall of Alexandria in 30 BCE. As pharaoh she had an affair with Julius Caesar, to whom she bore his only known son, Caesarion. After Caesar's assassination in 44 BCE, Cleopatra took the side of Mark Antony in the civil war against Octavian and eventually bore him three children: Ptolemy Philadelphus and the twins Cleopatra Selene and Alexander Helios.

Corocotta. According to Cassius Dio, Corocotta was the leader of a guerrilla campaign against the Romans in Cantabria who personally accepted from Caesar the award that had been established for his capture. Little more is known about him.

Didymus Chalcenterus. Born around 63 BCE, he wrote an astounding number of books in his lifetime on a wide variety of subjects, though he is now primarily known as an editor and grammarian of Homer. One of the chief librarians of the Great Library in Alexandria, his name Chalcenterus means "bronze guts," supposedly a statement about his indefatigability as a scholar.

Dorothea. Unknown to history.

Isidora. Unknown to history.

Juba II. Probably born in 48 BCE, he was left an orphan by the suicide of his father, the king of Numidia, in 46. Adopted by Julius Caesar, the man who'd caused his father's death, Juba was raised as a Roman citizen and ultimately joined his adopted stepbrother Octavian in the war against Mark Antony and Cleopatra. He was restored to the throne of Numidia after the fall of Alexandria in 30 BCE, and around the year

25 BCE he was married to Cleopatra Selene. Some time later he was given the throne of Mauretania. Juba was a lifelong scholar who wrote several books before he died in 23 CE.

Julius Caesar. Born in 100 BCE to a noble Roman family of comparatively little significance, Julius Caesar achieved a position of unparalleled power within the Roman state and thereby laid the stage for the end of the Republic under his adopted son Octavian. A well-regarded orator and savvy politician, Caesar rose to prominence first as a military leader in the field, whose reputation won him election, in 63 BCE, as the religious leader of the Roman Republic. Returning to the military sphere in subsequent years, his extraordinary abilities were proved in successful campaigns in Hispania, Gaul, and Britain. His power and popular appeal eventually led to the Great Roman Civil War when he crossed the Rubicon with an armed legion in 49. Victorious in the civil war, Caesar voyaged to Alexandria, where a civil war had broken out between Cleopatra VII and her brother-husband Ptolemy XIII. Caesar supported Cleopatra, defeating Ptolemy and making her sole pharaoh of Egypt, and she, in turn, became Caesar's lover, bearing him his only known biological son: Caesarion. Returning to Rome, Caesar took solitary control of the state as a popularly supported dictator, effectively ending the Roman Republic. From this position of authority he instituted significant reforms to the Roman calendar, the workings of its government, and the architecture of its capital. Caesar was assassinated in 44 by a group of at least sixty Roman senators, who reportedly stabbed him 23 times before he died. His popularity among the common people at the time of his death was so great that two years after the assassination he was officially deified. Though his murder had been intended to restore the Roman Republic to order, it served only to set off another series of civil wars. These conflicts culminated in the struggle between his adopted son Octavian, to whom Caesar had bequeathed the whole of his state and his powerful name, and his popular former general, Mark Antony, who had taken residence in Alexandria with Caesar's former lover, Cleopatra VII.

Laenas. Unknown to history.

Lucius Vorenus. Along with Titus Pullo, Vorenus is mentioned only once in the existing record: in Julius Caesar's *Commentary on the Gallic Wars*, where their inspiring actions in battle are reported. His birth and death dates are unknown.

Mark Antony. A Roman politician, he was Julius Caesar's good friend and perhaps his finest general. In the years following Caesar's assassination, Antony struggled with Octavian for control of the Roman Republic, though an uneasy peace was reached in 41 BCE when Antony married Octavian's sister. The following year he had an affair with Cleopatra VII, resulting in the births of the twins Cleopatra Selene and Alexander Helios, and soon he was making his home with her in Alexandria, where she gave birth to another son, Ptolemy Philadelphus, in 36 BCE. Open war broke out between Antony and Octavian in 32, with their two great armies facing off at the Battle of Actium one year later. Defeated, Antony returned with Cleopatra to Alexandria, where he committed suicide after the fall of the city.

Octavian. Born in 63 BCE, he was adopted by his great-uncle Julius Caesar just prior to his assassination in 44. Though he originally joined forces with Mark Antony to rule the Republic, their ambitions would not allow the peace to last, and the war between them tore the Roman world in two. His eventual defeat of Antony made him sole ruler of Rome, giving him the power to remake the Republic into the Roman Empire. Known most popularly as Augustus Caesar, the name

he adopted in 27 BCE, he is rightly regarded along with his
adopted father as one of the most influential men in history.

Ptolemy Philadelphus. Born in 36 BCE, he was the youngest son
of Mark Antony and Cleopatra VII. He disappears from
the record after the fall of Alexandria in 30, his fate unknown.

Quintus. Unknown to history.

Syllaeus. One of the chief ministers to King Obodas II of
Nabataea, Syllaeus volunteered to guide Egyptian prefect
Aelius Gallus and his Roman legions to the spice-rich lands
of Arabia Felix. He instead led them to death and despair in
the desert, returning to Petra a hero. In 9 BCE Obodas died,
and Syllaeus was soon accused of his murder. King Aretas
IV put him in chains and sent him to Rome, where he was
declared guilty and flung headfirst to his death from the
Tarpeian Rock.

Syphax. Unknown to history, though it is reasonably certain in
the records that an unnamed slave aided in the suicides of
Juba I and Marcus Petreius.

Thrasyllus. An Egyptian scholar, Thrasyllus of Mendes became
famous as the personal astrologer of Tiberius Caesar. A
trusted servant and friend to the emperor, it is said that he
saved the lives of many in Rome by promising Tiberius a longer life than he ultimately led.

Tiberius. Born in 42 BCE, Tiberius Claudius Nero became the
stepson to Octavian, the future Augustus Caesar, when his
mother was forced to divorce his father and marry the
powerful adopted son of Julius Caesar. In time he became a
strong field general, and he rose quickly through the ranks to
the position of heir apparent to Augustus Caesar. He was
unhappy, however, and for unknown reasons he retired to
Rhodes in 6 BCE, only returning to Rome in AD 2—after
much begging from Caesar. When Augustus died in 14,

Tiberius was declared his sole heir and would rule—a reportedly depressed and dark figure—as Caesar until his own death in 37.

Titus Pullo. Along with Lucius Vorenus, Pullo is mentioned only once in the existing record: in Julius Caesar's *Commentary on the Gallic Wars*, where their inspiring actions in battle are reported. His birth and death dates are unknown.